THE COMPLETE SHORT STORIES OF MIKE CAREY

THE COMPLETE SHORT STORIES OF MIKE CAREY

DIP

This collection was first published in hardcover in 2019
by PS Publishing. This paperback edition is published in July 2019
by Drugstore Indian Press, an imprint of PS Publishing Ltd
by arrangement with the author.
All rights reserved by the author.

2 4 6 8 10 9 7 5 3 1

ISBN
978-1-78636-406-7

Cover and book design by Pedro Marques.
Text set in Sabon. Titles set in A Love of Thunder.

Printed in England by the T.J. International
on Vancouver Cream Bookwove 80 gsm stock.

PS Publishing Ltd / Grosvenor House
1 New Road / Hornsea, HU18 1PG / England
editor@pspublishing.co.uk
WWW.PSPUBLISHING.CO.UK.

CONTENTS

IPHIGENIA IN AULIS

The short that became *The Girl With All the Gifts*. Written for *An Apple For the Creature*.

THE SONS OF TAMMANY

A story featuring Poe's detective, Auguste Dupin. Written for *Beyond Rue Morgue*.

WE'LL ALWAYS HAVE PARIS

A zombie story set in a Paris that has sort of become zombified itself. Written for *Dark Cities*.

SECOND WIND

A Felix Castor short, although Castor himself doesn't appear in it. It's about Nicky Heath, the zombie character from the Castor novels. Sort of an origin story. Written for *The New Dead*.

MY LIFE IN POLITICS

A ghost story set in a small town in the UK in the modern era. Written for *Phantoms*.

THE TALE OF SALT-CARRIER VA

A fantasy short about slavery. Written as back-end material for *Highest House*.

THE NON-EVENT

A superhero heist story. Written for *Masked*.

IN THAT QUIET EARTH

A story set in the world of *Night Of the Living Dead*. Written for an anthology of similar stories called *Nights Of the Living Dead*.

TAKE TWO

A micro-short set in the Garden of Eden. Unpublished.

FACE

A superhero heist story. Written for *Masked*.

REFLECTIONS ON THE CRITICAL PROCESS

A daft slasher story, written a long time ago but revised since for *Psycho-Mania*.

"Iphigenia in Aulis" feels like a good place to start this collection, for two reasons. It marked a very significant change in my career as a writer, and I can pretty much carbon date the actual writing of it. ¶ Early in 2011, Charlaine Harris and Toni L. P. Kelner had invited me to submit a short piece for a planned anthology of horror, supernatural, and dark fantasy stories. The theme was to be school days and school experiences. I said I'd be really happy to write a story for the book, but then half the year rolled by without me finding the time to sit down and write. I was writing for Marvel Comics at that time, working on one of the X-Men books, and comics writing—with its attendant short deadlines—dominated my life. ¶ But in September I took four days off to attend the Raptus comic convention in Norway. The day I left London I felt the first tickling of an idea, and by the time I landed in Bergen it was very solid and clear in my head. Or at least the protagonist, Melanie, was clear. The plot was a lot sketchier, but the story built itself around her with minimum conscious planning. ¶ I wrote "Iphigenia in Aulis" over the four days I was in Norway, from the eighth to the eleventh of September, and sent it in to Charlaine and Toni a week later. They liked it and accepted it for the anthology, *An Apple For the Creature*. ¶ In due course it became the novel, *The Girl with All the Gifts*, and then a movie. In all its forms it was really well received, and in 2017 I won the UK Screenwriters' Award for Most Promising Newcomer for the screenplay. I was fifty-eight years old at the time, so "newcomer" was stretching it a bit, but I'll take it. ¶ More importantly, I had tried out a lot of new things in the story and it felt like most of them had worked. In one way and another, the three novels that followed *The Girl with All the Gifts* were all shaped by what I did here.

IPHIGENIA IN AULIS

Her name is Melanie. It means "the black girl", from an ancient Greek word, but her skin is mostly very fair so she thinks maybe it's not such a good name for her. Miss Justineau assigns names from a big list: new children get the top name on the boy's list or the top name on the girl's list, and that, Miss Justineau says, is that.

Melanie is ten years old, and she has skin like a princess in a fairy tale: skin as white as snow. So she knows that when she grows up she'll be beautiful, with princes falling over themselves to climb her tower and rescue her.

Assuming, of course, that she has a tower.

In the meantime, she has the cell, the corridor, the classroom, and the shower room.

The cell is small and square. It has a bed, a chair, and a table in it. On the walls there are pictures: in Melanie's cell, a picture of a field of flowers and a picture of a woman dancing. Sometimes they move the children around, so Melanie knows that there are different pictures in each cell. She used to have a horse in a meadow and a big mountain with snow on the top, which she liked better.

The corridor has twenty doors on the left-hand side and eighteen doors on the right-hand side (because the cupboards don't really count): also it has a door at either end. The door at the classroom end is red. It leads to the classroom (duh!). The door at the other end is bare grey steel on this side, but once when Melanie was being taken back to her cell she peeped through the door, which had accidentally been left open, and saw that on the other side it had lots of bolts and locks and a box with numbers on it. She wasn't supposed to see, and Sergeant said, "Little bitch has got way too many eyes on her," but she saw, and she remembers.

She listens too, and from overheard conversations she has a sense of this place in relation to other places she hasn't ever seen. This place is the block. Outside the block is the base. Outside the base is the Eastern Stretch, or the Dispute Stretch. It's all good as far as Kansas, and then it gets real bad, real quick. East of Kansas, there's monsters everywhere and they'll follow you for a hundred miles if they smell you, and then they'll eat you. Melanie is glad that she lives in the block, where she's safe.

Through the grey steel door, each morning, the teachers come. They walk down the corridor together, past Melanie's door, bringing with them the strong, bitter, chemical smell that they always have on them: it's not a nice smell, but it's exciting because it means the start of another day's lessons.

At the sound of the bolts sliding and the teachers' footsteps, Melanie runs to the door of her cell and stands on tiptoe to peep through the little mesh-screen window in the door and see the teachers when they go by. She calls out good morning to them, but they're not supposed to answer and usually they don't. Sometimes, though, Miss Justineau will look around and smile at her—a tense, quick smile that's gone almost before she can see it—or Miss Mailer will give her a tiny wave with just the fingers of her hand.

All but one of the teachers go through the thirteenth door on the left, where a stairway leads down to another corridor and (Melanie guesses) lots more doors and rooms.

The one who doesn't go through the thirteenth door unlocks the classroom and opens up, and that one will be Melanie's teacher and Melanie's friends' teacher for the day.

Then Sergeant comes, and the men and women who do what Sergeant says. They've got the chemical smell too, and it's even stronger on them than it is on the teachers. Their job is to take the children to the classroom, and after that they go away again. There's a procedure that they follow, which takes a long time. Melanie thinks it must be the same for all the children, but of course she doesn't know that for sure because it always happens inside the cells and the only cell that Melanie sees the inside of is her own.

To start with, Sergeant bangs on all the doors and shouts at the children to get ready. Melanie sits down in the wheelchair at the foot of her bed, like she's been taught to do. She puts her hands on the arms of the chair and her feet on the footrests. She closes her eyes and waits. She counts while she waits. The highest she's ever had to count is 4,526: the lowest is 4,301.

When the key turns in the door, she stops counting and opens her eyes. Sergeant comes in with his gun and points it at her. Then two of Sergeant's people come in and tighten and buckle the straps of the chair around Melanie's wrists and ankles. There's also a strap for her neck: they tighten that one last of all, when her hands and feet are fastened up all the way, and they always do it from behind. The strap is designed so they never have to put their hands in front of Melanie's face. Melanie sometimes says, "I won't bite." She says it as a joke, but Sergeant's people never laugh. Sergeant did once, the first time she said it, but it was a nasty laugh. And then he said, "Like we'd ever give you the fucking chance, sugar plum."

When Melanie is all strapped into the chair, and she can't move her hands or her feet or her head, they wheel her into the classroom and put her at her desk. The teacher might be talking to some of the other children, or writing something on the blackboard, but she—unless it's Mr Galloway, who's the only he—will usually stop and say, "Good morning, Melanie." That way the children who sit way up at the front of the class will know that Melanie has come into the room and they can say good morning too. They can't see her, of course, because they're all in their own chairs with their neck-straps fastened up, so they can't turn their heads around that far.

This procedure—the wheeling in, and the teacher saying good morning, and then the chorus of greetings from the other kids—happens seven more times, because there are seven children who come into the classroom after Melanie. One of them is Anne, who used to be Melanie's best friend in the class and maybe still is except that the last time they moved the kids around (Sergeant calls it "shuffling the deck") they ended up sitting a long way apart and it's hard to be best friends with someone you can't talk to. Another is Steven, who Melanie doesn't like because he calls her Melon-Brain or M-M-M-Melanie to remind her that she used to stammer sometimes in class.

When all the children are in the classroom, the lessons start. Every day has sums and spelling, but there doesn't seem to be a plan for the rest of the lessons. Some teachers like to read aloud from books. Others make the children learn facts and dates, which is something that Melanie is very good at. She knows the names of all the states in the United States, and all their capitals, and their state birds and flowers, and the total population of each state, and what they mostly manufacture or grow there. She also knows the presidents in order and the years that they were in office, and she's working on European capitals. She doesn't find it hard to remember this stuff: she does it to keep from being bored, because being bored is worse than almost anything.

Melanie learned the stuff about the states from Mr Galloway's lessons, but she's not sure if she's got all the details right because one day, when he was acting kind of funny and his voice was all slippery and fuzzy, Mr Galloway said something that worried Melanie. She was asking him whether it was the whole state of New York that used to be called New Amsterdam, or just the city, and he said who cares. "None of this stuff matters any more, Melanie. I just gave it to you because all the textbooks we've got are twenty years old."

Melanie persists, because New Amsterdam was way back in the seventeenth century, so she doesn't think twenty years should matter all that much. She says, "But when the Dutch colonists—"

"Jesus!" Mr Galloway cuts her off. "It's irrelevant. It's ancient history! The Hungries tore up the map. There's nothing East of Kansas anymore. Not a damn thing."

So it's possible, even quite likely, that some of Melanie's lists need to be updated in some respects.

The children have classes on Monday, Tuesday, Wednesday, Thursday, and Friday. On Saturday, the children stay locked in their rooms all day and music plays over the PA system. Nobody comes, not even Sergeant, and the music is too loud to talk over. Melanie had the idea long ago of making up a language that used signs instead of words, so the children could talk to each other through their little mesh windows, and she went ahead and made the language up—or some of it anyway—but when she asked Miss Mailer if she could teach it to the class, Miss Mailer told her no, really loud and sharp. She made Melanie promise not to mention her sign language to any of the other teachers, and especially not to Sergeant. "He's paranoid enough already," she said. "If he thinks you're talking behind his back, he'll lose what's left of his mind."

So Melanie never got to teach the other children how to talk in sign language.

Saturdays are long and dull, and hard to get through. Melanie tells herself aloud some of the stories that the children have been told in class. It's okay to say them out loud because the music hides her voice. Otherwise Sergeant would come in and tell her to stop.

Melanie knows that Sergeant is still there on Saturdays, because one Saturday when Ronnie hit her hand against the mesh window of her cell until it bled and got all mashed up, Sergeant came in. He brought two of his people, and all three of them were dressed in the big suits, and they went into Ronnie's cell and Melanie guessed from the sounds that they were trying to tie Ronnie into her chair. She also guessed from the sounds that Ronnie was struggling and making it hard for them, because she kept shouting and saying "Let me alone! Let me alone!" Then there was a banging sound that went on and on and Sergeant shouted, "Shut up shut up shut up shut up shut up!" and then other people were shouting too, and someone said, "Christ Jesus, don't—" and then it all went quiet again.

Melanie couldn't tell what happened after that. The people who work for Sergeant went around and locked all the little doors over the mesh windows, so the children couldn't see out. They stayed locked all day. The next Monday, Ronnie wasn't in the class anymore, and nobody seemed to know what had happened to her. Melanie likes to think that Ronnie went through the thirteenth door on the left into another class, so she might come back one day when Sergeant shuffles the deck again. But what Melanie really believes, when she can't stop herself from thinking about it, is that Sergeant took Ronnie away to punish her, and he won't let her see any of the other children ever again.

Sundays are like Saturdays except for the shower. At the start of the day the children are put in their chairs as though it's a regular school day, but instead of being taken to the classroom, they're taken to the shower room, which is the last door on the right, just before the bare steel door.

In the shower room, which is white-tiled and empty, the children sit and wait until everybody has been wheeled in. Then the doors are closed and sealed, which means the room is completely dark because there aren't any lights in there. Pipes behind the walls start to make a sound like someone trying not to laugh, and a chemical spray falls from the ceiling.

It's the same chemical that's on the teachers and Sergeant and Sergeant's people, or at least it smells the same, but it's a lot stronger. It stings a little, at first. Then it stings a lot. It leaves Melanie's eyes puffy, reddened, and half-blind. But it evaporates quickly from clothes and skin, so after half an hour more of sitting in the still, dark room, there's nothing left of it but the smell, and then finally the smell fades too, or at least they get used to it so it's not so bad anymore, and they just wait in silence for the door to be unlocked and Sergeant's people to come and get them. This is how the children are washed, and for that reason, if for no other, Sunday is probably the worst day of the week.

The best day of the week is whichever day Miss Mailer teaches. It isn't always the same day, and some weeks she doesn't come at all. Melanie guesses that there are more than five classes of children, and that the teachers' time is divided arbitrarily between them. Certainly there's no pattern that she can discern, and she's really good at that stuff.

When Miss Mailer teaches, the day is full of amazing things. Sometimes she'll read poems aloud, or bring her flute and play it, or show the children pictures out of a book and tell them stories about the people in the pictures. That was how Melanie got to find out about Agamemnon and the Trojan War, because one of the paintings showed Agamemnon's wife, Clytemnestra, looking really mad and scary. "Why is she so mad?" Anne asked Miss Mailer.

"Because Agamemnon killed their daughter," Miss Mailer said. "The Greek fleet was stuck in harbour on the island of Aulis. So Agamemnon put his daughter on an altar, and he killed her so that the goddess Artemis would give the Greek fleet fair winds and help them to get to the war on time."

The kids in the class were mostly both scared and delighted with this, like it was a ghost story or something, but Melanie was troubled by it. How could killing a little girl change the way the winds blew? "You're right, Melanie, it couldn't," Miss Mailer said. "But the Ancient Greeks had a lot of gods, and all kinds of weird ideas about what would make the gods happy. So Agamemnon gave Iphigenia's death to the goddess as a present, and his wife decided he had to pay for that."

Melanie, who already knew by this time that her own name was Greek, decided she was on Clytemnestra's side. Maybe it was important to get to the war on time, but you shouldn't kill kids to do it. You should just row harder, or put more sails up. Or maybe you should go in a boat that had an outboard motor.

The only problem with the days when Miss Mailer teaches is that the time goes by too quickly. Every second is so precious to Melanie that she doesn't even blink: she just sits there wide-eyed, drinking in everything that Miss Mailer says, and memorising it so that she can play it back to herself later, in her cell. And whenever she can manage it, she asks Miss Mailer questions, because what she likes most to hear, and to remember, is Miss Mailer's voice saying her name, Melanie, in that way that makes her feel like the most important person in the world.

One day, Sergeant comes into the classroom on a Miss Mailer day. Melanie doesn't know he's there until he speaks, because he's standing right at the back of the class. When Miss Mailer says, " . . . and this time, Pooh and Piglet counted three sets of footprints in the snow", Sergeant's voice breaks in with "What the fuck is this?"

Miss Mailer stops, and looks round. "I'm reading the children a story, Sergeant Robertson," she says.

"I can see that," Sergeant's voice says. "I thought the idea was to educate them, not give them a cabaret."

"Stories can educate just as much as facts can," Miss Mailer says.

"Like how, exactly?" Sergeant asks, nastily.

"They teach us how to live, and how to think."

"Oh yeah, plenty of world-class ideas in *Winnie the Pooh*." Sergeant is using sarcasm. Melanie knows how sarcasm works: you say the opposite of what you really mean. "Seriously, Gwen, you're wasting your time. You want to tell them stories, tell them about Jack the Ripper and John Wayne Gacy."

"They're children," Miss Mailer points out.

"No, they're not," Sergeant says, very loudly. "And that, that right there, that's why you don't want to read them *Winnie the Pooh*. You do that, you start thinking of them as real kids. And then you slip up. And maybe you untie one of them because she needs a cuddle or something. And I don't need to tell you what happens after that."

Sergeant comes out to the front of the class then, and he does something really horrible. He rolls up his sleeve, all the way to the elbow, and he holds his bare forearm in front of Kenny's face: right in front of Kenny, just an inch or so away from him. Nothing happens at first, but then Sergeant spits on his hand and rubs at his forearm, like he's wiping something away.

"Don't," says Miss Mailer. "Don't do that to him." But Sergeant doesn't answer her or look at her.

Melanie sits two rows behind Kenny, and two rows over, so she can see the whole thing. Kenny goes real stiff, and he whimpers, and then his mouth gapes wide and he starts to snap at Sergeant's arm, which of course he can't reach. And drool starts to drip down from the corner of his mouth, but not much of it because nobody ever gives the children anything to drink, so it's thick, kind of half-solid, and it hangs there on the end of Kenny's chin, wobbling, while Kenny grunts and snaps at Sergeant's arm, and makes kind of moaning, whimpering sounds.

"You see?" Sergeant says, and he turns to look at Miss Mailer's face to make sure she gets his point. And then he blinks, all surprised, and maybe he wishes he hadn't, because Miss Mailer is looking at him like Clytemnestra looked in the painting, and Sergeant lets his arm fall to his side and shrugs like none of this was ever important to him anyway.

"Not everyone who looks human is human," he says.

"No," Miss Mailer agrees. "I'm with you on that one."

Kenny's head sags a little sideways, which is as far as it can move because of the strap, and he makes a clicking sound in his throat.

"It's all right, Kenny," Miss Mailer says. "It will pass soon. Let's go on with the story. Would you like that? Would you like to hear what happened to Pooh and Piglet? Sergeant Robertson, if you'll excuse us? Please?"

Sergeant looks at her, and shakes his head real hard. "You don't want to get attached to them," he says. "There's no cure. So once they hit eighteen . . . "

But Miss Mailer starts to read again, like he's not even there, and in the end he leaves. Or maybe he's still standing at the back of the classroom, not speaking, but Melanie doesn't think so because after a while Miss Mailer gets up and shuts the door, and Melanie thinks that she'd only do that right then if Sergeant was on the other side of it.

Melanie barely sleeps at all, that night. She keeps thinking about what Sergeant said, that the children aren't real children, and about how Miss Mailer looked at him when he was being so nasty to Kenny.

And she thinks about Kenny snarling and snapping at Sergeant's arm like a dog. She wonders why he did it, and she thinks maybe she knows the answer because when Sergeant wiped his arm with spit and waved it under Kenny's nose, it was as though under the bitter chemical smell Sergeant had a different smell altogether. And even though the smell was very faint where Melanie was, it made her head swim and her jaw muscles start to work by themselves. She can't even figure out what it was she was feeling, because it's not like anything that ever happened to her before or anything she heard of in a story, but it was like there was something she was supposed to do and it was so urgent, so important, that her body was trying to take over her mind and do it without her.

But along with these scary thoughts, she also thinks: Sergeant has a name, the same way the teachers do. The same way the children do. Sergeant has been more like the goddess Artemis to Melanie up until now: now she knows that he's just like everyone else, even if he is scary. The enormity of that change, more than anything else, is what keeps her awake until the doors unlock in the morning and the teachers come.

In a way, Melanie's feelings about Miss Mailer have changed too. Or rather, they haven't changed at all, but they've become stronger and stronger. There can't be anyone better or kinder or lovelier than Miss Mailer anywhere in the world: Melanie wishes she was a Greek warrior with a sword and a shield, so she could fight for Miss Mailer and save her from heffalumps and woozles. She knows that heffalumps and woozles are in *Winnie the Pooh*, not the *Iliad*, but she likes the words, and she likes the idea of saving Miss Mailer so much that it becomes her favourite thought. She thinks it whenever she's not thinking anything else. It makes even Sundays bearable.

One day, Miss Mailer talks to them about death. It's because most of the men in the Light Brigade have just died, in a poem that Miss Mailer is reading to the class. The children want to know what it means to die, and what it's like. Miss Mailer says it's like all the lights going out, and everything going real quiet, the way it does at night—but forever. No morning. The lights never come back on again.

"That sounds terrible," says Lizzie, in a voice like she's about to cry. It sounds terrible to Melanie too: like sitting in the shower room on Sunday with the chemical smell in the air, and then even the smell goes away and there's nothing at all forever and ever.

Miss Mailer can see that she's upset them, and she tries to make it okay again by talking about it more. "But maybe it's not like that at all," she says. "Nobody really knows, because when you're dead you can't come back to talk about it. And anyway, it would be different for you than it would be for most people because you're . . . "

And then she stops herself, with the next word sort of frozen halfway out of her lips.

"We're what?" Melanie asks.

"You're children," Miss Mailer says, after a few seconds. "You can't even really imagine what death might be like, because for children it seems like everything has to go on forever."

There's a silence while they think about that. It's true, Melanie decides. She can't remember a time when her life was any different than this, and she can't imagine any other way that people could live. But there's something that doesn't make sense to her in the whole equation, and so she has to ask the question.

"*Whose* children are we, Miss Mailer?"

In stories, she knows, children have a mother and a father, like Iphigenia had Clytemnestra and Agamemnon. Sometimes they have teachers too, but not always, and they never seem to have Sergeants. So this is a question that gets to the very roots of the world, and Melanie asks it with some trepidation.

Miss Mailer thinks about it for a long time, until Melanie is pretty sure that she won't answer. Then she says, "Your mom is dead, Melanie. She died before . . . she died when you were very little. Probably your daddy's dead too, although there isn't really any way of knowing. So the army is looking after you now."

"Is that just Melanie," John asks, "or is it all of us?"

Miss Mailer nods slowly. "All of you."

"We're in an orphanage," Anne guesses. The class heard the story of Oliver Twist, once.

"No. You're on an army base."

"Is that what happens to kids whose mom and dad die?" This is Steven now.

"Sometimes."

Melanie is thinking hard, and putting it together, inside her head, like a puzzle. "How old was I," she asks, "when my mom died?" Because she must have been very young, if she can't remember her mother at all.

"It's not easy to explain," Miss Mailer says, and they can see from her face that she's really, really unhappy.

"Was I a baby?" Melanie asks.

"A very tiny baby, Melanie."

"How tiny?"

"Tiny enough to fall into a hole between two laws."

It comes out quick and low and almost hard. Miss Mailer changes the subject then, and the children are happy to let her do it, because nobody is very enthusiastic about death by this point. But Melanie wants to know one more thing, and she wants it badly enough that she even takes the chance of upsetting Miss Mailer some more. It's because of her name being Greek, and what the Greeks sometimes used to do to their kids, at least in the ancient times, when they were fighting a war against Troy. At the end of the lesson, she waits until Miss Mailer is close to her and she asks her question really quietly.

"Miss Mailer, were our moms and dads going to sacrifice us to the goddess Artemis? Is that why we're here?"

Miss Mailer looks down at her, and for the longest time she doesn't answer. Then something completely unexpected and absolutely wonderful happens. Miss Mailer reaches down and *she strokes Melanie's hair*. She strokes Melanie's hair with her hand, like it was just the most natural and normal thing in the world. And lights are dancing behind Melanie's eyes, and she can't get her breath, and she can't speak or hear or think about anything because apart from Sergeant's people, maybe two or three times and always by accident, nobody has ever touched her before and this is Miss Mailer touching her and it's almost too nice to be in the world at all.

"Oh, Melanie," Miss Mailer says. Her voice is only just higher than a whisper.

Melanie doesn't say anything. She never wants Miss Mailer's hand to move. She thinks if she could die now, with Miss Mailer's hand on her hair, and nothing changed ever again, then it would be all right to be dead.

"I . . . I can't explain it to you," Miss Mailer says, sounding really, really unhappy. "There are too many other things I'd have to explain too, to make sense of it. And . . . And I'm not strong enough. I'm just not strong enough."

But she tries anyway, and Melanie understands some of it. Just before the Hungries came, Miss Mailer says, the government passed an amendment to the Constitution of the United States of America. It was because of something called the Christian Right, and it meant that you were a person even before you were born, and the law had to protect you from the very moment that you popped up inside your mom's tummy like a seed.

Melanie is full of questions already, but she doesn't ask them because it will only be a minute or two before Sergeant's people come for her, and she knows from Miss Mailer's voice that this is a big, important secret. So then

the Hungries came, Miss Mailer said—or rather, people started turning into Hungries. And everything fell to
pieces real fast.

It was a virus, Miss Mailer says. A virus that killed
you, but then brought you partway back to life. Not
enough of you to talk, but enough of you to stand up and
move around and even run. You turned into a monster
that just wanted to bite other people and make them into
Hungries too. That was how the virus propagated itself,
Miss Mailer said.

So the virus spread and all the governments fell and
it looked like the Hungries were going to eat everyone or
make everyone like they were, and that would be the end
of the story and the end of everything. But the real people
didn't give up. They moved the government to Los Angeles, with the desert all around them and the ocean at their
back, and they cleared the Hungries out of the whole state
of California with flamethrowers and daisy cutter bombs
and nerve gas and big moving fences that were on trucks
controlled by radio signals. Melanie has no idea what
these things are, but she nods as if she does and imagines
a big war like Greeks fighting Trojans.

And every once in a while, the real people would find
a bunch of Hungries who'd fallen down because of the
nerve gas and couldn't get up again, or who were stuck
in a hole or locked in a room or something. And maybe
one of them might have been about to be a mom, before
she got turned into a Hungry. There was a baby already
inside her.

The real people were allowed to kill the Hungries
because there was a law—Emergency Ordnance 9—
that said they could. Anyone could kill a Hungry and it
wouldn't be murder because they weren't people anymore.

But the real people weren't allowed to kill the unborn
babies, because of the amendment to the Constitution:
inside their moms, the babies all had rights. And maybe

the babies would have something else, called higher cognitive functions, that their moms didn't have anymore, because viruses don't always work the same on unborn babies.

So there was a big argument about what was going to happen to the babies, and nobody could decide. Inside the cleared zone, in California, there were so many different groups of people with so many different ideas, it looked like it might all fall apart and the real people would kill each other and finish what the Hungries had started. They couldn't risk doing anything that might make one group of people get mad with the other groups of people.

So they made a compromise. The babies were cut out of their mommies. If they survived, and they did have those function things, then they'd be raised, and educated, and looked after, and protected, until one of two things happened: either someone came up with a cure, or the children reached the age of eighteen.

If there was a cure, then the children would be cured. If there wasn't . . .

"Here endeth the lesson," says Sergeant.

He comes into Melanie's line of sight, right behind Miss Mailer, and Miss Mailer snatches her hand away from Melanie's hair. She ducks her head so Melanie can't see her face.

"She goes back now," Sergeant says.

"Right." Miss Mailer's voice is very small.

"And you go on a charge."

"Right."

"And maybe you lose your job. Because every rule we got, you just broke."

Miss Mailer brings her head up again. Her eyes are wet with tears. "Fuck you, Eddie," she says.

She walks out of Melanie's line of sight, very quickly. Melanie wants to call her back, wants to say something to make her stay: *I love you, Miss Mailer. I'll be a warrior*

for you, and save you. But she can't say anything, and
then Sergeant's people come. Sergeant's there too. "Look
at you," he says to Melanie. "Fucking face all screwed up
like a tragedy mask. Like you've got fucking feelings."

But nothing that Sergeant says and nothing that Sergeant does can take away the memory of that touch.

When she's wheeled into her cell, and Sergeant stands
by with his gun as the straps are unfastened one by one,
Melanie looks him in the eye. "You won't get fair winds,
whatever you do," she tells him. "No matter how many
children you kill, the goddess Artemis won't help you."

Sergeant stares at her, and something happens in his
face. It's like he's surprised, and then he's scared, and then
he's angry. Sergeant's people can see it too, and one of
them takes a step towards him, with her hand halfway up
like she's going to touch his arm.

"Sergeant Robertson!" she says.

He pulls back from her, and then he makes a gesture
with the gun. "We're done here," he says.

"She's still strapped in," says the other one of Sergeant's
people.

"Too bad," says Sergeant. He throws the door open
and waits for them to move, looking at one of them and
then the other until they give up and leave Melanie where
she is and go out through the door.

"Fair winds, kid," Sergeant says.

So Melanie has to spend the night in her chair, still
strapped up tight, apart from her head and her left arm.
And it's way too uncomfortable to sleep, even if she leans
her head sideways, because a big pipe runs down the wall
right there and she can't get into a position that doesn't
hurt her.

But then, because of the pipe, something else happens. Melanie starts to hear voices, and they seem to be
coming right out of the wall. Only they're not: they're
coming down the pipe, somehow, from another part of

the building. Melanie recognises Sergeant's voice, but not any of the others.

"Fence went down in Michigan," Sergeant says. "Twenty mile stretch, Clayton said. Hungries are pushing west, and probably south too. How long you think it'll be before they cut us off?"

"Clayton's full of shit," a second voice says, but with an anxious edge. "You think they'd have left us here, if that was gonna happen? They'd have evacuated the base."

"Fuck if they would!" This is Sergeant again. "They care more about these little plague rats than they do about us. If they'd done it right, we wouldn't even need to be here. All they had to do was put every last one of the little bastards in a barn and throw one fucking daisy cutter in there. No more worries."

It gets real quiet for a while after that, like no one can think of anything to say. "I thought they found a cure," a third voice says, but he's shouted down by a lot of voices all at the same time:

"That's bullshit."

"Dream on, man!"

"Onliest cure for them fuckin' skull-faces is in this here clip, and I got enough for all."

"They did, though," the third voice persists. "They isolated the virus. At that lab in Houston. And then they built something that'll kill it. Something that'll fit in a hypo. They call it a *phage*."

"Hey, you, skull-face." Sergeant is putting on a funny voice. "I got a cure for you, so why'n't you come on over here and roll up your sleeve? That's right. And all you other cannibal motherfuckers, you form an orderly line there."

There's a lot of laughter, and a lot of stuff that Melanie can't hear clearly. The third voice doesn't speak again.

"I heard they broke through from Mexico and took Los Angeles." Another new voice. "We ain't got no government now. It's just the last few units out in the field, and some camps like this one that kept a perimeter up. That's why there's no messages anymore. No one out there to send them."

Then the second voice comes in again with "Hell, Dawlish. Brass keep their comms to theirselves, like always. There's messages. Just ain't any for you, is all."

"They're all dead," Sergeant says. "They're all dead except us. And what are we? We're the fucking nurse-maids of the damned. Drink up, guys. Might as well be drunk as sober, when it comes." Then he laughs, and it's the same laugh as when he said, "Like we'd ever give you the chance." A laugh that hates itself and probably every-thing else too. Melanie leans her head as far to the other side as it will go, so she can't hear the voices anymore.

Eddie, she tells herself. Just Eddie Robertson talking. That's all.

The night is very, very long. Melanie tells herself sto-ries, and sends messages from her right hand to her left hand, then back again, using her sign language, but it's still long. When Sergeant comes in the morning, with his people, she can't move: she's got such bad cramps in her neck and her shoulders and her arms, it feels like there's iron bars inside her.

Sergeant looks at her like he's forgotten up until then what happened last night. He looks at his people, but they're looking somewhere else. They don't say anything as they tie up Melanie's neck and arm again.

Sergeant does. He says, "How about them fair winds, kid?" But he doesn't say it like he's angry, or even like he wants to be mean. He says it and then he looks away, unhappy, sick almost. To Melanie, it seems like he says it because he has to say it: as though being Sergeant means you've got to say things like that all the time, whether that's really what you're thinking or not. She files that thought next to his name.

One day, Miss Mailer gives Melanie a book. She does it by sliding the book between Melanie's back and the back of the wheelchair, and tucking it down there out of sight. Melanie isn't even sure at first that that's what just happened, but when she looks at Miss Mailer and opens her mouth to ask her, Miss Mailer touches a finger to her closed lips. So Melanie doesn't say anything.

Once they're back in their cells, and untied, the children aren't supposed to stand up and get out of their chairs until Sergeant's people have left and the door is closed and locked. That night, Melanie makes sure not to move a muscle until she hears the bolt slide home.

Then she reaches behind her and finds the book, its angular shape digging into her back a little. She pulls it out and looks at it.

Homer. *The Iliad and The Odyssey*.

Melanie makes a strangled sound. She can't help it, even though it might bring Sergeant back into the cell to tell her to shut up. A book! A book of her own! And *this* book! She runs her hands over the cover, riffles the pages, turns the book in her hands, over and over. She smells the book.

That turns out to be a mistake, because the book smells of Miss Mailer. On top, strongest, the chemical smell from her fingers, as bitter and horrible as always. But underneath, a little, and on the inside pages a lot, the warm and human smell of Miss Mailer herself.

What Melanie feels right then is what Kenny felt, when Sergeant wiped the chemicals off his arm and put it right up close to Kenny's face. But she only just caught the edge of it that time, and she didn't really understand it.

Something opens inside her, like a mouth opening wider and wider and wider and screaming all the time—not from fear, but from need. Melanie thinks she has a word for it now, although it still isn't anything she's felt before. Sometimes in stories that she's heard, people eat

and drink, which is something that the children don't ever
do. The people in the stories need to eat, and then when
they do eat they feel themselves fill up with something,
and it gives them a satisfaction that nothing else can give.
She remembers a line from a song that Miss Justineau sang
to the children once: *You're my bread, when I'm hungry,*

So this is hunger, and it hurts like a needle, like a
knife, like a Trojan spear in Melanie's heart or maybe
lower down in her stomach. Her jaws start to churn of
their own accord: wetness comes into her mouth. Her
head feels light, and the room sort of goes away and then
comes back without moving.

The feeling goes on for a long time, until finally Melanie gets used to the smell the way the children in the
shower on Sunday get used to the smell of the chemicals.
It doesn't go away exactly, but it doesn't torment her
in quite the same way: it becomes kind of invisible just
because it doesn't change. The hunger gets less and less,
and when it's gone, all gone, Melanie is still there.

The book is still there too: Melanie reads it until day-
break, and even when she stumbles over the words or has
to guess what they mean, she's in another world.

It's a long time after that before Miss Mailer comes
again. On Monday there's a new teacher, except he isn't
a teacher at all: he's one of Sergeant's people. He says his
name is John, which is stupid, because the teachers are all
Miss or Misses or Mister something, so the children call
him Mr John, and after the first few times he gives up cor-
recting them.

Mr John doesn't look like he wants to be there, in the
classroom. He's only used to strapping the children into the
chairs one by one, or freeing them again one by one, with
Sergeant's gun on them all the time and everything quick
and easy. He looks like being in a room with all the children
at the same time is like lying on an altar, at Aulis, with the
priest of Artemis holding a knife to his throat.

At last, Anne asks Mr John the question that everybody wants to ask him: where the real teachers are. "There's a lockdown," Mr John says. He doesn't seem to mind that the children have spotted him for a fake. "There's movement West of the fence. They confirmed it by satellite. Lots of Hungries, coming this way, so nobody's allowed to move around inside the compound or go out into the open in case they get our scent. We're just staying wherever we happened to be when the alarm went off. So you've got me to put up with, and we'll just have to do the best we can."

Actually, Mr John isn't a bad teacher at all, once he stops being scared of the children. He knows a lot of songs, and he writes up the words on the blackboard: the children sing the songs, first all at once and then in two-part and three-part harmonies. There are lots of words the children don't know, especially in 'Too Drunk to Fuck,' but when the children ask what the words mean, Mr John says he'll take the Fifth on that one. That means he might get himself into trouble if he gives the right answer, so he's allowed not to: Melanie knows this from when Miss Justineau told them about the Bill of Rights.

So it's not a bad day, at all, even if they don't have a real teacher. But for a whole lot of days after that, nobody comes and the children are alone. It's not possible for Melanie to count how many days: there's nothing to count. The lights stay on the whole time, the music plays really loud, and the big steel door stays shut.

Then a day comes when the music goes off. And in the sudden, shocking silence the bare steel door slams open again, so loud that the sound feels like it's shoving its way through your ear right inside your head. The children jump up and run to their doors to see who's coming, and it's Sergeant—just Sergeant, with one of his people, and no teachers at all.

"Let's do this," Sergeant says.

The man who's with him looks at all the doors, then at Sergeant. "Seriously?" he says.

"We got our orders," Sergeant says. "What we gonna do, tell them we lost the key? Start with this bunch, then do B to D. Sorenson can start at the other end."

Sergeant unlocks the first door after the shower-room door, which is Mikey's door. Sergeant and the other man go inside, and Sergeant's voice, booming hollowly in the silence, says, "Up and at 'em, you little fucker."

Melanie sits in her chair and waits. Then she stands up and waits at the door with her face to the mesh. Then she walks up and down, hugging her own arms. She's confused and excited and very, very scared. Something new is happening. She senses it: something completely outside of her experience. When she looks out through the mesh window, she can see that Sergeant isn't closing the doors behind him, as he goes from cell to cell, and he's not wheeling the children into the classroom.

Finally her door is unlocked. She steps back from it as it opens, and Sergeant and the other man step inside. Sergeant points the gun at Melanie.

"You forget your manners?" he asks her. "Sit down, kid."

Something happens to Melanie. It's like all her different, mixed-up feelings are crashing into each other, inside her head, and turning into a new feeling. She sits down, but she sits down on her bed, not in her chair.

Sergeant stares at her like he can't believe what he's seeing. "You don't want to piss me off today," he warns Melanie. "Not today."

"I want to know what's happening, Sergeant," Melanie says. "Why were we left on our own? Why didn't the teachers come? What's happening?"

"Sit down in the chair," the other man says.

"Do it," Sergeant tells her.

But Melanie stays where she is, on the bed, and she

doesn't shift her gaze from Sergeant's eyes. "Is there going to be class today?" she asks him.

"Sit in the goddamn chair," Sergeant orders her. "Sit in the chair or I swear I will fucking dismantle you." His voice is shaking, just a little, and she can see from the way his face changes suddenly that he knows she heard the shake. "Fucking . . . fine!" he explodes, and he advances on the chair and kicks it with his boot, really hard, so it flies up into the air and hits the wall of the narrow cell. It bounces off at a wild angle, hits the other wall, and crashes down on its back. Sergeant kicks it again, and then a third time. The frame is all twisted from where it hit the wall, and one of the wheels comes right off when Sergeant kicks it.

The other man just watches, without saying a word, while Sergeant gets his breath back and comes down from his scary rage. When he does, he looks at Melanie and shrugs. "Well, I guess you can just stay where you are, then," he says.

The two of them go out, and the door is locked again. They take the other kids away, one by one—not to the classroom, but out through the other door, the bare steel door, which until now has marked the furthest limit of their world.

Nobody comes, after that, and nothing happens. It feels like a long time, but Melanie's mind is racing so fast that even a few minutes would feel like a long time. It's longer than a few minutes, though. It feels like most of a day.

The air gets colder. It's not something that Melanie thinks about normally, because heat and cold don't translate into comfort or discomfort for her: she notices now because with no music playing and nobody to talk to, there's nothing else to notice. Maybe it's night. That's it. It must be night outside. Melanie knows from stories that it gets colder at night as well as darker.

She remembers her book, and gets it out. She reads about Hector and Achilles and Priam and Hecuba and Odysseus and Menelaus and Agamemnon and Helen.

There are footsteps from the corridor outside. Is it Sergeant? Has he come back to dismantle her? To take her to the altar and give her to the goddess Artemis?

Someone unlocks Melanie's door and pushes it open.

Miss Mailer stands in the doorway. "It's okay," she says. "It's okay, Sweetheart. I'm here."

Melanie surges to her feet, her heart almost bursting with happiness and relief. She's going to run to Miss Mailer. She's going to hug her and be hugged by her and be touching her not just with her hair but with her hands and her face and her whole body. Then she freezes where she is. Her jaw muscles stiffen, and a moan comes out of her mouth.

Miss Mailer is alarmed. "Melanie?" She takes a step forward.

"Don't!" Melanie screams. "Please, Miss Mailer! Don't! Don't touch me!"

Miss Mailer stops moving, but she's so close! So close! Melanie whimpers. Her whole mind is exploding. She drops to her knees, then falls full-length on the floor. The smell, the wonderful, terrible smell, fills all the room and all her mind and all her thoughts, and all she wants to do is . . .

"Go away!" she moans. "Go away go away go away!"

Miss Mailer doesn't move.

"Fuck off, or I will dismantle you!" Melanie wails. She's desperate. Her mouth is filled with thick saliva like mud from a mudslide. She's dangling on the end of the thinnest, thinnest piece of string. She's going to fall and there's only one direction to fall in.

"Oh God!" Miss Mailer blurts. She gets it at last. She rummages in her bag, which Melanie didn't even notice until now. She takes something out—a tiny bottle with yellow liquid in it—and starts to spray it on her skin, on her clothes, in the air. The bottle says Dior. It's not the usual chemical: it's something that smells sweet and funny. Miss Mailer doesn't stop until she's emptied the bottle.

"Does that help?" she asks, with a catch in her voice. "Oh baby, I'm so sorry. I didn't even think . . . "

It does help, a little. And Melanie has had practice at pushing the hunger down: she has to do it a little bit every time she picks up her book. This is a million times harder, but after a while she can think again and move again and even sit up.

"It's safe now," she says timidly, groggily. And she remembers her own words, spoken as a joke so many times before she ever guessed what they might actually mean. "I won't bite."

Miss Mailer bends down and sweeps Melanie up, choking out her name, and there they are crying into each other's tears, and even though the hunger is bending Melanie's spine like Achilles bending his bow, she wouldn't exchange this moment for all the other moments of her life.

"They're attacking the fence," Miss Mailer says, her voice muffled by Melanie's hair. "But it's not Hungries, it's looters. Bandits. People just like me and the other teachers, but renegades who never went into the Western cordon. We've got to get out before they break through. We're being evacuated, Melanie—to Texas."

"Why?" is all Melanie can think of to say.

"Because that's where the cure is!" sobs Miss Mailer. "They'll make you okay again, and you'll have a real mom and dad, and a real life, and all this fucking madness will just be a memory!"

"No," Melanie whimpers.

"Yes, baby! Yes!" Miss Mailer is hugging her tight, and Melanie is trying to find the words to explain that she doesn't want a mom or a dad, she wants to stay here in

the block with Miss Mailer and have lessons with her forever, but right then is when Sergeant walks into the cell.

Three of his people are behind him. His face is pale,
and his eyes are open too wide.

"We got to go," he says. "Right now. Last two chop-
pers are loaded up and ready. I'm real sorry, Gwen, but
this is the last call."

"I'm not going without her," Miss Mailer says, and
she hugs Melanie so tight it almost hurts.

"Yeah," Sergeant says. "You are. She can't come on
the transport without restraints, and we don't got any
restraints that we can use. You come on now."

He reaches out his hand as if he's going to help Miss
Mailer to her feet. Miss Mailer doesn't take the hand.

"Come on, now," Sergeant says again, on a rising
pitch.

"I'm not leaving her," Miss Mailer says again.

"She's got no—"

Miss Mailer's voice rises over Sergeant's voice, shouts
him into silence. "She doesn't have any restraints because
you kicked her chair into scrap metal. And now you're
going to leave her here, to the mercy of those animals, and
say it was out of your hands. Well damn you, Eddie!" She
can hardly get the words out: she sounds like there's no
breath left in her body. "Damn . . . fuck . . . rot what's left
of your miserable fucking heart!"

"I've got to go by the rules," Sergeant pleads. His
voice is weak, lost.

"Really?" Miss Mailer shouts at him. "The rules? And
when you've ripped her heart out and fed it to your limp-
dick fucking rules, you think that will bring Chloe back,
or Sarah? Or bring you one moment's peace? There's a
cure, you bastard! They can cure her! They can give her
a normal life! You want to say she stays here and rots in
the dark instead because you threw a man-tantrum and
busted up her fucking *chair*?"

There's a silence that seems like it's never going to end. Maybe it never would, if there was only Sergeant and Miss Mailer and Melanie in the room. But one of Sergeant's people breaks it at last. "Sarge, we're already two minutes past the—"

"Shut up," Sergeant tells him. And then to Miss Mailer he says, "You carry her. You hold her, every second of the way. And you're responsible for her. If she bites anyone, I'm throwing you both off the transport."

Miss Mailer stands up with Melanie cradled in her arms, and they run. They go out through the steel door. There are stairs on the other side of it that go up and up, a long way. Miss Mailer is holding her tight, but she rocks and bounces all the same, pressed up against Miss Mailer's heart. Miss Mailer's heart bumps, rhythmically, as if something is alive inside it and touching Melanie's cheek through her skin.

At the top of the stairs, there's another door. They come out into sudden cold and blinding light. The quality of the sound changes, the echoes dying suddenly. Air moves against Melanie's bare arm. Distant voices bray, almost drowned out by a mighty, droning, flickering roar.

The lights are moving, swinging around. Where they touch, details leap out of the darkness as though they've just been painted there. Men are running, stopping, running again, firing guns like Sergeant's gun into the wild, jangling dark.

"Go!" Sergeant shouts.

Sergeant's men run, and Miss Mailer runs. Sergeant runs behind them, his gun in his hand. "Don't waste rounds," Sergeant calls out to his people. "Pick your target." He fires his gun, and his people fire too, and the guns make a sound so loud it runs all the way out into the dark and then comes back again, but Melanie can't see what it is they're firing at or if they hit it. She's got other stuff to worry about anyway.

This close up, the smelly stuff that Miss Mailer sprayed on herself isn't strong enough to hide the Miss Mailer smell underneath. The hunger is rising again inside Melanie, filling her up all the way to the top, taking her over: Miss Mailer's arm is right there beside her head, and she's thinking *Please don't please don't please don't,* but who is she pleading with? There's no one. No one but her.

A shape looms in the darkness: a thing as big as a room, that sits on the ground but rocks from side to side and spits dirt in their faces with its deep, dry breath and drones to itself like a giant trying to sing. It has a door in its side: some of the children sit there, inside the thing, in their chairs, tied in with straps and webbing so it looks like a big spider has caught them. Some of Sergeant's people are there too, shouting words that Melanie can't hear. One of them slaps the side of the big thing: it lifts into the air, all at once, and then it's gone.

Sergeant's arm clamps down on Miss Mailer's shoulder and he turns her around, bodily. "There!" he shouts. "That way!" And they're running again, but now it's just Sergeant and Miss Mailer. Melanie doesn't know where Sergeant's people have gone.

There's another one of the big rocking things, a long way away: *A helicopter,* Melanie thinks, the word coming to her from a lesson she doesn't even remember. And that means they're outside, under the sky, not in a big room like she thought at first. But even the astonishment is dulled by the gnawing, insistent hunger. Her jaws are drawing back, straining open like the hinges of a door. Her own thoughts are coming to her from a long way away, like someone shouting at her through a tiny mesh window: *Oh please don't please don't!*

Miss Mailer is running toward the helicopter and Sergeant is right behind. They're close to it now, but one of the big swinging lights turns and shows them some men running towards them on a shallow angle. The men don't have guns like Sergeant does, but they have sticks and knives and one of them is waving a spear.

Sergeant fires, and nothing seems to happen. He fires again, and the man with the spear falls. Then they're at the helicopter and Miss Mailer is pulled inside by a woman who seems startled and scared to see Melanie there.

"What the fuck?" she says.

"Sergeant Robertson's orders!" Miss Mailer yells.

Some more of the children are here. Melanie sees Anne and Kenny and Lizzie, in a single flash of one of the swinging lights. But now there's a shout and Sergeant is fighting with somebody, right there at the door where they just climbed in. The men with the knives and the sticks have got there too.

Sergeant gets off one more shot, and all of a sudden one of the men doesn't have a head anymore. He falls down out of sight. Another man knocks the gun out of Sergeant's hand, but Sergeant takes his knife from him somehow and sticks it into the man's stomach.

The woman inside the copter slaps the ceiling and points up—for the pilot, Melanie realises. He's sitting in his cockpit, fighting to keep the copter more or less level and more or less still, as though the ground is bucking under him and trying to throw him off. But it's not the ground; it's the weight of the men swarming on board.

"Shit!" the woman moans.

Miss Mailer hides Melanie's eyes with her hand, but Melanie pushes the hand away. She knows what she has to do now. It's not even a hard choice, because the incredible, irresistible human flesh smell is helping her, pushing her in the direction she has to go.

She stops pleading with the hunger to leave her alone: it's not listening anyway. She says to it, instead, like Sergeant said to his people, *Pick your target.*

And then she jumps clear out of Miss Mailer's arms, her legs propelling her like one of Sergeant's bullets.

She lands on the chest of one of the men, and he's staring into her face with frozen horror as she leans in and bites his throat out. His blood tastes utterly wonderful: he is her bread when she's hungry, but there's no time to enjoy it. Melanie scales his shoulders as he falls and jumps onto the man behind, folding her legs around his neck and leaning down to bite and claw at his face.

Miss Mailer screams Melanie's name. It's barely audible over the sound of the helicopter blades, which is louder now, and the screams of the third man as Melanie jumps across to him and her teeth close on his arm. He beats at her, but her jaws are so strong he can't shake her loose, and then Sergeant hits him really hard in the face and he falls down. Melanie lets go of his arm, spits out the piece of it that's in her mouth.

The copter lifts off. Melanie looks up at it, hoping for one last sight of Miss Mailer's face, but it just disappears into the dark and there's nothing left of it but the sound.

Other men are coming. Lots of them.

Sergeant picks up his gun from the ground where it fell, checks it. He seems to be satisfied.

The light swings all the way round until it's full in their faces.

Sergeant looks at Melanie, and she looks back at him.

"Day just gets better and better, don't it?" Sergeant says. It's sarcasm, but Melanie nods, meaning it, because it's a day of wishes coming true. Miss Mailer's arms around her, and now this.

"You ready, kid?" Sergeant asks.

"Yes, Sergeant," Melanie says. Of course she's ready.

"Then let's give these bastards something to feel sad about."

The men bulk large in the dark, but they're too late. The goddess Artemis is appeased. The ships are gone on the fair wind.

"Iphigenia in Aulis" didn't happen in a vacuum. In fact it happened at a time when everything in my life, including my writing, was in a state of flux. ¶ The Castor novels, written between 2005 and 2009, had enjoyed a very modest success. My publisher had faith in me but wanted me to try a different approach, ideally something more mainstream, in the hope of attracting a wider audience to my other work. ¶ I tried. I wrote (under a pseudonym) two conspiracy thrillers that had no fantasy, horror, or sci-fi tropes in them at all. This was in the days when Dan Brown was topping the fiction charts. My efforts dropped into the overcrammed conspiracy thriller market without raising a ripple. ¶ Okay, said my then editor, let's try a body-swap thriller. And I almost did. The reason I didn't was because I had been working on another project and it had come to seem far more important to me than the prospect of writing a mainstream bestseller. This other project was a collaboration—in the end, two collaborations—with my wife, Linda, and our daughter Louise. It was a really enjoyable process, and I for one was delighted with the results (I think Lin and Lou were too, but I don't want to speak for them). ¶ We were writing in a style that owed a lot to *The Thousand and One Nights*, with nested stories, long digressions, and a large cast who took centre-stage by turns. When I wrote "Iphigenia in Aulis," I was carrying some of those ideas forward into a very different arena, and to my great satisfaction they still worked. I've really never looked back. ¶ The following story was one of the digressions in the first of our two co-written novels, *The City of Silk and Steel*. Zuleika is an assassin, and a very good one. For very complicated reasons she ends up in a sultan's harem, where, having been tasked with killing him, she goes to great lengths to keep him alive. ¶ This is her origin story—the story of how and why the legendary Imad-Basur, the black-apparelled teacher, took on his first and last female student, and what she had to do to earn her place at his school for assassins.

THE WOMAN named Zuleika was born in the city of Ibu Kim, and lived there until her fifteenth year. Ibu Kim lies to the South of Bessa, exactly as far as Perdondaris lies to its North; and if Perdondaris, with its palaces of marble and its roofs painted with gold, may be taken for Heaven, and Bessa for the ruck of common Earth, then Ibu Kim can surely stand for Hell.

Ibu Kim was a city of brigands, jackals, and cutthroats: a kleptocracy, a failed state, a gangsters' paradise, and a rigged town. With few and insignificant farmlands, it relied on trade for its prosperity, but even its artisans were shiftless ne'er-do-wells, happier to steal than to make, happier to fence than to steal. Whatever required the least effort was holiest gospel in Ibu Kim.

Within the streets of that town, the crime of rape did not exist. To despoil the wife or daughter of a wealthy citizen was, to be sure, asking for trouble, because wealthy citizens are chary of all their possessions, but it wasn't illegal. A poor woman, without friends, had to stay off the streets at night or else fall victim to the first man she passed who had a mind to cope her. Nor could she call out for assistance, in such extremity: the city watch would either ignore her cries or, if it was a slow night, stroll up and wait their turn.

Zuleika, as I have said, survived to the age of fourteen in this horse-deficient cesspit. She was sharp of mind and fleet of foot, and she took no heedless risks, but nonetheless, in that time, she had many narrow escapes.

Her father, Kishnothophur, known (to the few who needed to refer to him at all) as Kish, was an innkeeper, at the sign of the Blue Wheel, and in his own small way a whoremonger too. The profits he made from the twelve women in his employ were much greater than the profits he made from renting rooms, but in Ibu Kim, by a fine irony, for a woman to sell her sexual services was considered a crime—whereas for a man to take them by force was part of the ordinary rough-and-tumble of life. So the Blue Wheel was officially an inn, and a regular bribe of shiny silver coins prevented the city watch from inquiring into anything else that went on there.

Kish had taken a young wife and fathered one child on her before she died of a quartan fever brought on by drinking bad water (the wells of Ibu Kim were used by footpads as a convenient place to dump bodies, and so were almost always unsafe to drink from). Thereafter, the girl fell from his thoughts: Zuleika was raised by whores, and much loved and doted on by them. They protected her from the myriad dangers of that highly dangerous place, which meant, among other things, that they kept her both out of her father's sight and out from under the feet of the clients.

Some of the whores came and then went, without fuss or notice: some, for reasons Zuleika was too young to appreciate, had more staying power. If the child had a favourite, it was Ehara, a woman of statuesque frame and generous nature. Ehara looked less like a prostitute than like a public building, but still inspired strong loyalty from her clientele. Zuleika's duties at this time were many: buying food at the weekly market, drawing water, sweeping the floor of the inn, washing the wine cups and jars at the end

of the evening and the bed linen twice a month, anointing
the walls with white lime when they were soiled, and taking the weekly bung of ten silver dinars to the sergeant of
the guard. Whenever she was not engaged in these pursuits,
Zuleika would sit with the older woman and help her with
her toilet—combing out her long hair, painting her toenails,
or otherwise beautifying her various extremities.

Only on the nights when the moon was absent from
the sky was Zuleika barred from Ehara's company. It was
then that the inn received a clandestine but much valued
visitor: Vurdik the Bald, the bandit chieftain of the Yashi-
fia. Vurdik was a legend in Ibu Kim: his men harried the
caravans of every neighbouring city from sunrise to sunset,
and though his industry was much admired, he was still a
proscribed criminal with a price (which varied according to
the season and the vagaries of government) upon his head.

But in the Blue Wheel, Vurdik was a paying customer.
He went by a different pseudonym each month, lived lavishly, and was rewarded with every luxury the house had to
offer. One of those luxuries was exclusive access, whenever
he stayed, to Ehara's body.

It happened once that after a visit of this nature from
the bandit chief, Ehara was unable to work for three days
because of a beating he gave her when he was in his cups.
Zuleika tended to her friend's injuries through those
days. Her father decided not to summon a doctor, both
because of the expense and because of the awkward questions that might be asked about the identity of Ehara's
assailant.

Still a child, untutored in the world's ways, Zuleika was
moved to rage and tears at how Ehara had been hurt—and
then to horror at Ehara's own reaction. "Oh, Vurdik isn't
so bad, my love," the older woman told the girl, through
thickened lips. "I could do without the beatings, but the
beatings are nothing compared to what he'd do to me if
I ever tried to leave. And with a man who's just a thug, if

you're quick, you can always dodge the worst of it. It's the clever ones you want to watch. They've got worse ways to hurt you, and you don't always see them coming."

I mention this anecdote because of its wisdom and wide applicability—and because it stayed in Zuleika's mind and ultimately formed the foundation of a more advanced social theory. Different people menaced you in different ways, it seemed, and you needed to have a suitable answer for all of them. It was a long-term project for Zuleika, but it started on that day.

Meanwhile other things were going on in the young girl's life, and some of them presented with a lot more urgency. She was coming into her change, now, and men were starting to notice her. One of these men was her father, who she caught watching her on a number of occasions with a thoughtful expression. She knew Kish well enough to discount the possibility that he wanted to bed her himself: he was fastidiously uninterested in sex, except as a commercial proposition. He did, however, know what virginity was worth, and how best to package and retail it.

Another man who showed a definite interest was the saddler (if he had a name, he kept it to himself) who lived and worked directly opposite the Blue Wheel, in the Courtyard of the Trades. This gentleman watched Zuleika stumble-step towards puberty, and he conceived a lust for her. In Ibu Kim, a woman's first bleeding is taken to be a gentle reminder from the Increate that she should by now have been married or sold. The saddler saw this moment coming, from a considerable distance, and (as it were) decided to stake a prior claim.

On Zuleika's fourteenth birthday, he made Kish a gift of a silver-inlaid saddle, with a brushed silver saddle horn, and complimented him on his daughter's great beauty. "She'll make someone a fine wife," he hinted, over a jar of wine (the cheap stuff) which Kish had cracked open for the occasion.

Kish agreed that Zuleika promised well.

"A woman is like a camel," the saddler opined. "If a man cares for her, she will carry him in comfort through the longest journey."

Kish allowed that this was so. Further, he argued, it was so even of a camel that another man has already ridden.

The saddler looked up from his drink, and a complicated discourse of raised and lowered eyebrows ensued.

"The two cases are not comparable," the saddler said. "A camel that's already been broken in becomes more valuable as a result. A woman, substantially less."

"But if it were a choice," Kish mused, "between an unbroken wife and no dowry at all, and a broken wife with silver in her train, a man's very reasonable expectations might be tempered by a certain judicious pragmatism."

"Broken once?" the saddler asked bluntly. "Or broken many times?"

"Once," said Kish.

"And how much silver?"

"Twenty pieces."

"Ah."

"At least twenty."

"Ah, well."

"Possibly thirty."

"Ah, well now."

Zuleika witnessed all this camel-trading in solemn silence, even when the saddler smiled and winked at her—as though his blunt bargaining for her body were some sort of compliment or tribute to her beauty. He was a huge man, as big and shapeless as a pile of flour sacks, and radiated a stench of sweat so strong and searing that even in the open air it made the eyes of those passing by blur with sudden tears. The dyes he used to turn raw leather into finished saddles had stayed on his skin in places, giving it a hectic, par-boiled appearance.

Zuleika did not love him. This is not a matter of size or smell or dappled pigment: it is a mystery, as all must agree. She could not give to him the part of her soul that was relevant to the matter. As to her body, she knew she could trust the two men to come to a mutually agreeable arrangement.

In the end, it was decided that Zuleika should stay in her father's house until she was fifteen. At that time, she would be inducted into the profession of prostitute and then cashiered out of it again in the same night: she would entertain a single client, chosen and vetted by Kish himself, and on the very next day she would be married to the saddler. "Whoever lies with her, he must be clean!" the saddler insisted, many times. But of course he would be clean: he would, after all, be rich, and the one presupposes the other.

So Zuleika had a year to wait before she was given over to this unwelcome destiny: a bare year, and she had no plan. There were few options, in that city and at that time, for a girl who wished to be more than a beast of burden. In Bessa, it was said, women could sell goods at market, run inns and brothels, work in stable yards and mills. Bessa was a three days' journey for a camel, nine or ten if you had to rely on your own feet.

In the spring of that fifteenth year, Zuleika packed a few clothes into a bag, stashed the bag under her bed where it would be ready to hand, and waited for a night of thick cloud.

It duly came. Zuleika stole down the stairs in her bare feet, carrying her sandals in one hand, the rest of her meagre possessions in the other.

Her father was waiting for her in the yard. He dragged her back inside the house by her hair and beat her black and blue.

In spite of his stolid demeanour, Kish was no fool. He had noticed the resolve growing in his daughter and had decided that the best way to head it off would be to allow it

to grow to fruition and then to come down hard. He didn't
see this as cruelty: only as good husbandry, of the same
order as beating a dog to teach it not to foul the floor.

Ehara wept for the girl, and washed her bruises with
wine vinegar. Zuleika didn't weep for herself. She thought
about her mistake, and promised herself that she would
never misclassify a man again: you couldn't base good
decisions on bad taxonomy.

But she was still a child, and she still saw the world—
or parts of it, at least—in ways that were romantic and
simplified. There was a boy four years older than her,
Sasim, into whose orbit she fell, slowly and thrillingly, in
the weeks after she recovered from the beating.

She met the boy for the first time when she was walking to market with a basket in each hand and a sack tied
to her back for vegetables. She met him again, the next
time she carried the weekly bribe to Rhuk, the sergeant
of the guard—and then a third time, when she went to
the well for water. Eventually, it occurred to her that the
tall, dark-eyed lad who loitered at the corner of the street
close to the inn yard and greeted her so civilly when she
passed was not there by chance. She began to slow down
when she passed him, and exchange a few words: remarks
about the weather; jokes about how many bags and bas-
kets one girl could carry; finally, with a prickle of forbid-
den pleasure, given names.

Their courtship was an astonishing thing to Zuleika:
she had already come to associate men with danger, and
now here was one whose company, whose voice, whose
gaze, brought dizzying pleasure. She was cautious: she
had learned that much, at least. But when he told her that
he loved her, and offered himself as the solution to all her
problems, she did not know how to resist. They could run
away together. He could protect her from her enemies,
take her out of their reach, marry her so that her father's
claim on her lapsed.

Zuleika didn't see the contradictions or the logical lacunas in these promises: she just accepted them, as a starving man might accept a turd if you painted it to look like a loaf. She told Sasim which room, in the three-storied edifice of the Blue Wheel, was her own, and she pointed out to him the cracks in the stonework by which an agile climber might reach her tiny window. She told him the window would be unlocked. She put herself in his hands.

He came to her that night, and they made love in reverent silence. The creaking of the bedframes in the rooms of the whores provided more than enough camouflage, so Zuleika could have abandoned herself to loud and indiscreet yells with no real risk, but her father's room was close, and she was fearful. Also, the whole thing was over so quickly that they seemed to move directly from the anticipation to the aftermath.

"When will we leave?" Zuleika asked Sasim, as they lay in each other's arms.

The question seemed to throw him. "When will we what?"

"When will we leave, Sasim? When will you take me away, and marry me?"

The boy was silent for a few heartbeats.

"It's not a good idea to rush into something like that," he told Zuleika at last. "I'll have to make arrangements first. Find a house for us to live in, and explain to my father. And clothes. You'll need clothes."

"I've got clothes."

"I mean decent clothes. Suitable for a wife. What you wear makes you look like a whore."

Zuleika felt a shiver of presentiment. Her best friends were whores, and she saw no shame in what they did: in her opinion, formed by the daily experience of life in a brothel, only the men who first used whores and then spoke the word with such vehemence were to be despised.

But how do you say that to a lover, with the blood of your own virginity drying on your thigh?

Zuleika knew she had taken an irrevocable step. She had given away for free something which figured very largely in her father's short-term profit forecasts, and the storm that was sure to rise when he found out was not one she wished to weather. She had to make good her escape before that happened, and Sasim was her only hope. She kissed him and embraced him and welcomed him into her a second time. Then, with many protestations of love, he exited via the window.

He came to her often in the weeks that followed, climbing in through the open window with unconscious grace, sliding into her bed and into her body as smoothly as an otter slides into a river. Their ardour was undiminished, their lovemaking hectic and joyous, but the small talk afterwards began to take an alarming turn. Was it true, Sasim asked, that Zuleika's father had a fortune salted away? Where did he keep it? Did the door of the inn open with a key alone, or was it secured from the inside by deadbolts or chains?

Zuleika actually knew the answers to all these questions: they were, respectively, a moderate fortune, under a loose stone in the kitchen floor which was too heavy for her to lift, and two deadbolts and a bar. But unnerved by Sasim's predatory fascination, she feigned ignorance. Sasim shifted tack. Perhaps, he said, Zuleika could make him a map of the inn's interior, showing the location of her father's room and of any storerooms she knew about. Perhaps, also, she could ask among the whores: Kish was certainly sampling his own wares, after all, and he might in the throes of drink or passion have let something slip.

Zuleika listened to these musings with a heavy heart. When the dark of the moon came next, bringing with it Vurdik the Bald and Ehara's regularly scheduled ordeal, she acknowledged what in her heart she already knew; that men were for the most part unfit for any good purpose, and that the hopes she had harboured from Sasim were reeds already broken. Worse, she knew that if the two of them carried on rutting like rabbits in the springtime, the odds would sooner or later go against her. If she got pregnant, she was truly dead.

From now on, she decided gloomily, she would bolt her window shutters and take a different route to market.

At this point, two things happened: the order in which they happened is hard to determine, since one of the two happened only in Zuleika's mind. The universe of mind and the universe of matter rattle along reasonably well together most of the time, like two horses bound in the same yoke, but you can't easily jump from one horse to the other: and even if you could, you couldn't do it with a ruler in your pocket.

Zuleika realised that she had to save herself by her own efforts.

And a deus ex machina popped up right inside her guard.

The deus ex machina was, embarrassingly enough, another man—as though Zuleika didn't already have a superfluity of those in her life. But this was no suitor, potential or actual: he came to stay at the inn of the Blue Wheel, a paying guest, and Zuleika, who was waiting tables when he walked into the room, knew from the sudden silence that this was a man of some importance.

She would not have known as much from the man's build or bearing, or anything else about him. He was of unremarkable height, had a bland and forgettable face which looked as though it had been sanded smooth, and wore a drab tan djellaba that had known better decades.

But her father's deference to the man was very marked. He was offered wine without ordering it, and the wine was the good stuff from one of the jars with a black line painted around its base. When he asked for a room, he was given the sky chamber, which faced the East on the inn's top floor and was the best and largest room the Blue Wheel could boast of.

Plucking up her courage, Zuleika asked one of the other patrons who the stranger was.

The man looked at her in surprise, as though she'd asked what day of the week it was, or the name of the city in which she lived.

"That's Imad-Basur."

The name was enough, without any qualification or description. Imad-Basur, the Caliph of Assassins, the black-apparelled teacher, was known everywhere, and commanded through fear a level of respect as great as any real caliph had ever enjoyed. Indeed, he numbered caliphs among his victims. He was feared by the rich and powerful, but also extensively employed by them, his immunity from harassment guaranteed both by the secrets he held and by the vast resources of the shadowy organisation he commanded. Nobody knew how many assassins had studied under him, or where they went once they graduated from his tutelage: nobody wanted to find out in a way that involved knives, poison, or strangling cords.

Zuleika's mind, when she heard that name, went into overdrive. Obviously, Imad-Basur had come to Ibu Kim to kill someone: and it must be a prestigious commission, or else he would have sent an underling. The Increate had dropped a priceless opportunity in her lap, and despite the dangers involved it would be madness for her to ignore it.

When everyone in the inn had retired for the night— even the whores clocked off at last when the moon rose— Zuleika knocked on the door of the sky chamber, and the stranger's voice, from the other side of the door, bade her enter.

She walked in, carrying a tray on which was a jug of wine and a bowl of candied fruit. "Compliments of the house," she said.

Imad-Basur was sitting in the window seat reading from a slender scroll. He appraised the girl for a few moments with a cool, neutral eye before finally pointing to a table beside the bed. "Thank you," he said. "Set it down there."

Zuleika did: then she stood back and waited, arms at her sides, trembling slightly.

Imad-Basur stared at the small pile of coins that the girl had put down next to the tray, and then at the girl herself.

"What's this?" he asked her, a slight edge of irritation or perhaps of warning in his voice.

"I'd like to hire you!" Zuleika blurted. That was all she could manage to get out.

The assassin king stood. His movements were slow and measured, as though in everything he did he was enacting a pre-existing ritual. He walked across the room, picked up the coins, and counted them. He weighed them in his hand. Meagre as they were, they represented the sum total of what Zuleika had been able to squirrel away over the past year.

"Seventeen coppers," Imad-Basur said, his voice like a knife in a sheath. He stared at the girl again. "You think a man's life is to be bought with such an amount?"

"Two men," Zuleika said. "I need two men killed."

There was a moment of strained silence, but then Imad-Basur laughed—a near-silent heave of chuckles that shook his frame, and went on and on until Zuleika almost screamed. This wasn't an answer! This wasn't anything!

"Two men," Imad-Basur agreed. "Of course. So long as the intended targets live close together, cut rates can usually be arranged. Who are they, if I may be permitted to ask?"

"My father," Zuleika said, relieved that they were getting down to specifics now. "He's the innkeeper here. And the saddler who lives across the yard."

"And what have they done to deserve death?" Imad-Basur pursued.

"My father wants to whore me out, and the saddler wants to marry me."

"Contradictory goals," said the assassin.

"No. They've sealed the bargain already."

Imad-Basur crossed to the girl, took her hand, and pressed the coins into it. "Go to bed, child," he said. "This will be our secret. I think it might go hard with you if your father found out you had spoken to me in this wise. But he won't. Go to bed. Sleep. Tomorrow is another day."

Zuleika stayed where she was. This was a blow, but she was not ready to admit defeat.

"So you won't take the commission?" she asked the assassin.

Imad-Basur chuckled again, his face no longer blank and bland but creased with amusement. "No. I won't take the commission."

"But you train assassins too, don't you?"

"I've trained many."

"Then would this money be enough to buy a lesson?"

The smile slowly left Imad-Basur's face: he looked at the young girl with a sort of puzzlement. "No," he said. "But even if it were, I didn't come here to teach. And the first lesson wouldn't help you. Nor the second."

"Then give me the third lesson," Zuleika suggested.

Imad-Basur slowly shook his head. "No."

Zuleika opened her mouth to speak again, but the assassin king raised his hand in a forbidding gesture. "No more words," he said. "I have to meditate, and then I have to work—and after that, I intend to sleep. There's nothing I can do for you tonight."

Defeated, patronised, shamed, Zuleika strove to keep at least a little of her dignity. She nodded, bowed, and turned to the door.

When her hand was on the latch, Imad-Basur called out to her. "Wait."

Zuleika waited, her gaze still on the floor.

"Kill them yourself," Imad-Basur said. "Both of them. In different ways."

"And then?" Zuleika asked, her heart in her mouth.

"Then come to me, at my school in the mountains north of Perdondaris, and tell me how you achieved it. If the story pleases me . . . "

"Yes?"

"Then I may teach you some of the rudiments of the craft, although being a girl, you couldn't formally enrol with me as a student."

Zuleika looked up, and met the assassin's gaze one last time. "Thank you," she said.

"You're welcome."

The footing of their relationship seemed to have changed, in a way that defied definition. Zuleika struggled with various formulas of farewell.

"I pray the Increate smiles on your business here," she said at last.

Imad-Basur bowed to her. "And on yours," he said gravely.

Retiring to her room, Zuleika immediately set her mind to the task before her. She spared not a moment of compassion or doubt for her father: her years of unpaid servitude quit any debt she owed him for her birth, and his cold-blooded bartering over her body, as though it housed no soul, sealed his fate. For the saddler, she had some slight qualm, but it passed when she remembered his leering wink. To the lowest hell with him, and the dog that had sired him: this was about survival.

It was about a lot of other things too, though, and the more Zuleika looked at the problem, the more intractable it seemed. She believed she could cut a throat, if she were brought to it, but to carry out two murders by two different methods was a problem of a different order. She knew, of course, why Imad-Basur had made that stipulation: it would be proof that she could approach the task of killing with the proper professional detachment. Anyone could kill in hot blood, without reasoned thought. But reasoned thought was what the assassin king insisted on.

Reason told Zuleika that she was unlikely to succeed in two assaults against men much bigger and stronger than she was.

So she lengthened the odds, and went for four.

She began with Sasim. The next night, for the first time in a week, she left the shutter of her window unbolted. She thought it might take more than that, but it was like putting out a bowl of jam to attract honey bees: Sasim hauled himself over her sill a little after midnight and stood looking down at her with a mixture of wariness and arrogance.

Zuleika beckoned him to her, and gave him what he'd come for. Then, when they lay spent in each other's arms, she told him about the saddler across the yard. "He wants to marry me, and he was boasting that I wouldn't need a dowry because he has so much wealth already. Sasim, he showed me a bag bigger than his belly—too heavy for me to lift, although a strong man like you could lift it. He said it was full of gold!"

Sasim was very excited at this news, and begged Zuleika to tell him where in the saddler's house the bag was hidden. "He didn't let me see where he took it from," she told him. "But I thought I'd go to him and ask to see the bag again—and this time, I'll spy on him when he goes to fetch it. And I'll make absolutely sure it's full of gold. Would that be a good thing to do?"

"An excellent thing!" Sasim assured her, and he embraced her warmly. Got you, you avaricious little rodent, Zuleika thought—but she was overwhelmed by a sense of loss and longing when she thought of how she'd loved him and believed in him. Of the four, his death was the saddest for her to contemplate.

All that remained now was to wait. On the day before the moon's dark, Zuleika's father gave her the weekly bribe for sergeant Rhuk. She put the purse in her pocket and went to see not the sergeant but the saddler. He was hard at work in his shop, tanning hides in a vat as big around as a millwheel. He was astonished to see her, and even more astonished when she confessed to him, shyly and with many comely blushes, that she could not wait until the year was out. She had to be with him.

The saddler was both flattered and delighted—but saw the downside of this suggestion at once. "What about your father, though?" he grunted. "He'll be furious if you lose your maidenhead, and there'll be no dowry."

Zuleika reminded him that a woman and a man, if they are so minded, can disport themselves in many ways that offer no harm to a hymen. The saddler's mind filled at once with incandescent, carnal visions.

Zuleika said that she would slip away—alas, not that night, because she had too much work to do at the Blue Wheel; but the next night, for certain. She told him to leave his door unlocked at midnight, and to expect her soon after—and before she left, she made him show her how to find her way, in the dark, from the door to his bed. The saddler was minded to put the bed to good use right there and then, but Zuleika slipped out of his grasp. "I'm still a maiden," she reminded him, demurely but firmly. "I'd blush to take off my dress and stand naked in a full light. Put a candle by the street door tomorrow night, beloved, but make sure there's no lamp in your chamber!" Then she took to her heels.

From the saddler Zuleika went again to Sasim, who she found loitering in one of his usual haunts. She put on a sad and chagrined face, and let him see that she was cast down. When he asked her what ailed her, she shook her head and blinked away imaginary tears.

"I've been a fool, Sasim," she said. "I went back to the saddler, and I told him I didn't believe his boasting. And he went to his workshop and reached into the biggest of the three vats there. That's where the bag was. But it wasn't full of gold."

She waited out Sasim's reaction, the sudden draining of hope from his face. Then she took his hand and pressed five of her father's ten dinars into it. "It was only silver," she said.

Sasim's face was a marvel to behold: he stared at the dinars with incredulous joy. "A bag full of silver!" he exclaimed, his voice trembling. "You did well, Zuleika. You did very well. It's not gold, but still . . . A whole bag full of silver! A man could live like a king!"

Sasim's delight abated a little when Zuleika told him that the layout of the saddler's house was very complicated. But when she offered to come along on the raid herself, and lead him to the right place, his doubts vanished and he embraced her with as much fervour as he ever had in her narrow bed.

"But tomorrow night is best," she told him. "It will be dark of the moon, and we won't be seen."

It took a little more persuasion—Sasim's impatience was hard to curb—but finally he accepted Zuleika's argument as good sense and agreed to wait a day. "Bring a knife," she told him as they parted. "If the saddler wakes, we'll have to kill him." Sasim assured her that he would come armed and ready.

Now, at last, Zuleika went to the guard station for her weekly encounter with Rhuk. Normally this was brief and straightforward: she handed over the silver, he counted it, gave her a curt nod, and she left.

This time, she handed over an empty purse. Rhuk held it upside down and shook it, as though the missing dinars might somehow have lodged in its lining. "What's this?" he growled.

"My father has decided he can get better protection from the watch post by the Eastern Gate," Zuleika said. "He won't pay you anymore."

Rhuk gave her a look of glum ferocity. "Is he mad?" he asked her. "I know damn well he runs a gaggle of whores in that flea-pit. I can have him in chains before sunup if he tries to cheat me!"

Zuleika shrugged. "For whoremongering, he'd get a fine of five dinars. He thinks that's preferable to paying you ten a week."

Rhuk sighed, stood, and reached for his sword belt, which spent far more time hanging on a nail next to the door than it ever did around his waist. It clearly pained him to have to go to such wearisome lengths to administer justice.

"If you kill the cow," Zuleika said quickly, "you can't milk it afterwards. I know a way you could turn this to much better advantage, and profit both of us."

Rhuk sat down again, with an even bigger sigh. "I'm listening," he said.

Zuleika spoke with the captain for some several minutes, and left him well pleased with the intelligence she had provided. Returning to the inn, she went to Ehara— her final port of call—and asked her for a favour: she even told her a little about what she was planning, but omitted some salient details. Ehara was worried for the young girl, but agreed to fall in with her scheme for the sake of the friendship that had long existed between them. "But you need to watch yourself, my sweetness," she warned her. "If this goes bad on you, you'll have nowhere to run."

If it goes bad, Zuleika thought, I won't live to see another morning. It was all or nothing, and she felt that she could accept either of those extreme outcomes. It was the broad spectrum in between that terrified her.

That night she couldn't get to sleep at all. She thought of all the ways in which she could fail: of how flimsy her plan was, in the end, and how much it depended on her understanding of these men whose downfall she plotted. What if she was wrong about one or more of them? What if her system of classification still had some bumps and holes in it?

But she was in the hands of the Increate now: it was already much too late for doubts or second thoughts. She endured the night, and the day that followed, with all the stoicism a fourteen-year-old can muster. The sun rose and fell again: the moon absented herself. The night was a quilt as thick as wool.

Sasim was the first link in the chain, and Zuleika knew him, at least, very well indeed. So much so, that when he arrived at the back door of the inn a little after midnight, and confessed to her that he had forgotten to bring a knife, she handed him, without a word, a seven-inch carver from her father's kitchen on which she had put an edge that could have parted a flea's leg hairs. She also had a wooden mallet with iron bands wrapped around the head to weight it—a weapon her father kept stowed behind the bar for use on rowdy drunks. This she retained herself.

They went together to the saddler's house. Sasim was ready to pick the lock, but Zuleika tried the latch and the door opened at once. "Look," she said. "The fool has left his door unlocked!" She stood aside deferentially to let Sasim enter first, as was only right and proper, then once inside she led the way, not to the saddler's workshop but to his bedroom. The door stood ajar: again, Zuleika opened it wide, and stood aside meekly to let Sasim precede her.

He stepped inside, and found himself in pitch darkness. He stumbled on a sandal that was lying on the floor, and the saddler, lying awake in an erotic fever, sat bolt upright at the sound.

"Most fragrant of blossoms!" he cried. "Come to me!"

Sasim, when that huge bulk rose up before him in the dark, was almost petrified with fear. But he had a knife in his hand, and instinct took over. He ran at the saddler and stabbed him through the heart. The saddler fell back onto the bed, with a sound like a broken bellows.

Sasim had never killed a man before, and in the aftermath of the act he was rooted, for a moment, to the spot. In that moment Zuleika struck, hitting him a stunning blow on the head with the iron-chased mallet. Sasim collapsed in a heap on the blood-slicked floor.

Zuleika ran to the saddler's workshop and threw the five dinars she still had (the remainder of Rhuk's diverted bribe) down on the floor beside the big vat. This detained her for only a second, but she could already hear Sasim stumbling and cursing behind her: she had only dazed him with the blow, not knocked him unconscious. She threw the window bolt and slipped out into the night.

Sasim had a shrewd suspicion that he had been betrayed, but he was still thoroughly focused on the prospect of the bag of silver in the saddler's shop. Lighting the lamp with trembling fingers, he found the largest vat demonstrably empty, but a scatter of silver dinars lying on the ground beside it.

These few coins told a clear story. Zuleika had been there before him, and had stolen the bag of silver!

Enraged beyond reason at this duplicity, Sasim found his way back to the door, staggered across the courtyard and rounded the façade of the inn until he stood below Zuleika's room. The shutters were ajar, and a lamp burned within. So the little double-crosser thought she was safe, did she? She was going to find out how wrong she was!

Sasim had made this climb a score of times. Woozy though he was from the knock on the head, he made it again now, scaling the rough stones with the kitchen carver clenched in his teeth like a bandit in an old story.

He slammed the shutters wide and jumped over the threshold, transferring the knife to his hand so he could bellow out the words that boiled in his chest. "I'm going to slice you thinner than paper, you filthy little traitor!"

Vurdik the Bald did not enjoy being interrupted in the act of love: and it was considered prudent in the circles in which he moved to keep a sword or a dagger ready to hand, even in the quietest moments. He was already rolling off Ehara's voluptuous body and reaching for the blade he'd left under the bed before Sasim had taken three steps into the room.

On the fourth step, as Sasim was slowing down in the realisation that he was not addressing Zuleika after all, the bandit's scimitar came up and knocked the carver from his hand with a ringing clash of steel.

There was no fifth step. The bandit's blade swept across Sasim's throat on the repass, and so keen was its edge that it all but decapitated him. The boy sank to his knees, his mouth opening and closing on voiceless protests and reproaches, and then fell face forward on the floor.

"Why did he call me a traitor?" Vurdik wondered, belatedly. "I don't even know him."

Down below, in the inn's kitchen, abandoned at this hour, Zuleika lit a lamp and waved it three times out of the window—left to right, right to left, left to right. Watching for her signal, Sergeant Rhuk ordered his men to move from hiding and surround the inn. The door of the Blue Wheel was knocked down with a wooden ram, and watch officers poured into the building.

In vain, Kishnothophur the innkeeper protested and remonstrated, pleading both that he was innocent and that he was up to date with his bribes. Rhuk ordered a search of the inn's many rooms, and although it yielded no whores (the whores having been warned by Zuleika to leave quietly on the midnight hour, except for Ehara who Zuleika swore to the officers was her own dear mother), it did produce one bandit chieftain, just as Rhuk had been promised. Vurdik injured three officers before he was subdued, but finally a thrown club laid him low. He was arrested for multiple thefts and murders, and Kish for harbouring a known desperado.

The double execution was held on a market day, and

was therefore very well attended. Seeing his daughter in the crowd, Kish cursed her with sobs for her treacherous heart and her whore's lies. Zuleika took out an apple and ate it slowly, in his sight, until the trapdoor fell open and the last breath caught in his throat.

The stone under the kitchen floor that was too heavy for Zuleika to lift offered no problem to a dozen determined women. Ehara counted Kish's hoard carefully, in full sight of the other whores, and then divided it into twelve equal portions. She wanted to give Zuleika a share too, the more so because Zuleika had given her the Blue Wheel to own in perpetuity. But sergeant Rhuk had been as good as his word, and passed on to the girl a full quarter of the reward he won for the capture of Vurdik: Zuleika already had all the money she needed, and a little over.

The time had come to part. Ehara asked Zuleika, not for the first time, to stay with her and be her daughter. Zuleika embraced the older woman fervently, and thanked her for all her many acts of kindness, but she had no intention of staying in Ibu Kim. Through many tears on both sides, she promised to return and visit often.

The next morning, on a fine camel bought with her share of the reward money, she left the city alone and took the direction of distant Perdondaris. Many things can befall a woman alone in the deep desert: Zuleika feared none of them so much as she feared dying in the city where she had been born.

Imad-Basur was surprised to see her, but listened with rapt attention to her story. He admitted, when it was done, that Zuleika had certainly succeeded in the challenge he had set her. Two men hanged, and two others dead by the blade: it was a tally that few of his students could claim for a single night's work.

"Will you teach me?" Zuleika asked him, bluntly.

The caliph of assassins thought long before replying. To train up a woman in the arts of death! Such a thing

defied all convention, all propriety. But clearly this was a
most unconventional woman—and Imad-Basur had never
thought propriety worth a fart.

"I will teach you," he told her. "And I believe you will
make me proud."

Like "Iphigenia in Aulis," this story came out of an invitation. Paul Kane, my good friend from many a Fantasycon, was one of the editors on a planned collection of stories featuring Edgar Allan Poe's detective Auguste Dupin. I agreed to contribute, but I was mindful of the fact that the Dupin canon is a fairly tiny thing. He appears in only three short stories. Sherlock Holmes, by contrast, was the lead character in more than 50 short stories and four full-length novels. ¶ I started looking for an entry point that was non-obvious, and one of the mental exercises I used was the tried-and-true one of finding out what else was going on at the time. I discovered that there was a fairly substantial overlap between Dupin's (wholly theoretical) lifespan and the heyday of the corrupt Tammany Hall organization in New York. I also found that the construction of the Brooklyn Bridge took place in that same time window. ¶ Two other ingredients got thrown into the melting pot. One was an article I read about caisson fever, which was what doctors used to call decompression sickness (aka the bends) before they discovered that it arose from the behaviour of dissolved gases in the human bloodstream. The second was *Doomed By Cartoon*, an awesome book by John Adler and Draper Hill about the work of cartoonist Thomas Nast. ¶ A negative review of this story said that my Auguste Dupin is more like a bad-tempered Hercule Poirot. I plead guilty to this. I didn't get Dupin's voice and character exactly right. In my own defence, I was more interested in the fascinating and sinister history of that time and in weaving real facts into a preposterous but hopefully plausible mystery.

THE SONS OF TAMANNY

MY NAME is Thomas Nast. I'm sixty-two years old, and to be honest I don't expect to be able to hold up my hand after another year's seasonal turnings and returnings to say I'm sixty-three. I'm dying, at long last. And death dissolves all the bonds of obligation except the ones I owe to God. That being the case, I feel like I'm free at last to talk about the events of August 1870, which formerly I had held back from doing on account of they implicate a whole lot of people in a whole lot of queasy doings, and I couldn't really back up what I was saying with anything you might count as actual proof.

But when a man's staring straight down the barrel of his *Nunc Dimittis,* and the writing's not just on the wall but on the face that stares back at him out of the mirror, he stops fretting about the legal niceties and starts to think about setting the record straight. Which is what I aim to do.

In 1870, I was residing in New York City and working as an artist and cartoonist on that excellent periodical, the *Harper's Weekly,* under the editorship of George William Curtis. I counted Curtis as a friend as well as an employer. But when he called me into his office on the morning of August 13th of that year, he was wearing the boss hat rather than the friend one.

Curtis gave me a civil nod and gestured me into one of the two visitor chairs. Already ensconced in the other chair was a man of a somewhat striking appearance. Although, having said that, I'm going to show myself a weak sister by admitting that I can't really say what it was about this gentleman that was so singular.

He was a good deal older than I was, and he'd seen enough summers to get a slightly weather-beaten look around his cheeks and jowls. He was kind of short and dumpy in his build, which was neither here nor there, but he had one of those half-hearted little moustaches that looks like it's about to give up and crawl back inside, and to be honest that was sort of a point against him in my book. If a man's going to go for moustaches, he should go all-in for one, say I, and Devil take the hairiest. He was toying with a cane that had a carved ivory handle in the shape of a lion's head—an effete sort of a gewgaw for a man to be playing with. And he had a suit with a waistcoat, and the waistcoat had a pattern to it. In my experience, that doesn't speak to a man's moral seriousness.

I guess, thinking about it, it was the eyes that were the selling point. They were a dark enough brown to count for black, and they had a sort of an augur-bit quality to them. It was the most startling thing. Like when this gentleman looked at you, looking wasn't really the half of it, and maybe you needed a whole other verb.

"Tommy, this here's Mr Dupin," Curtis said. "Visiting from Paris. Not the Texas one, the t'other one, over in France."

"Well, it's good to meet you, Mr Dupin," I said, taking the collateral of the eyes against the rest of the stuff that was on offer. Curtis pronounced the name "du*pan*", which I estimate is French for "out of the pan", as in the thing you bail out from before you end up in the fire. Which wasn't a bad name at all for this particular customer, as things transpired.

"Only he ain't a Mister," Curtis added, scrupulous as you'd expect a good editor to be. "He's a *chevalier*."

"What does that mean?" I asked.

"Means he's got a horse stashed somewhere, as I understand it."

"Good job," I said. "With that waistcoat, he may need to access it in a hurry."

"Monsieur," the little man said in a waspish voice, "I speak excellent English, and I thank you for the compliment. I can, if you wish, give you the address of my tailor."

"Oh, that won't be necessary," I told him. "I think one of those things in the world at any one time answers the purpose pretty well."

The Frenchman surprised me by laughing at that—and it was a big, loud horselaugh too, not the little snigger you'd expect would come from underneath that lamentable moustache. "Perhaps you are right," he said. "One at a time. Yes."

And then Curtis got to the point, which was that Mr Du Frying Pan wanted to see something of New York while he was here. What's more, he carried letters of introduction from a job lot of people who were (as you might say) the human equivalent of big guns on big limbers, and could blast Curtis and me and Mr Harper and the subs' desk and Uncle Tom Cobley and all into the Hudson if we didn't show their friend Dupin a good time.

"So I thought perhaps he could come with you today when you go to sketch the bridge," Curtis wound up.

I knew that was where he was aiming at, so I took it in my stride. "I think that's a swell idea," I said. "Sure. Mr Dupin, come and see my city. She's something to see. George, you want to come along?"

"Oh no," Curtis said hurriedly. "I'm tied up every which way here, and I won't see daylight this side of Tuesday. You guys go and have a good time. Lunch is on Mr

Harper, so long as you don't get into a second bottle. And you can take a cab to get down there." He waited a decent length of time—maybe a slow count of five—before adding, "Trolley car will bring you back."

"And what is it you do, way over there in Paris, Mr Dupin?" I asked, as we toiled down the stairs. The Equitable Life Building, which they'd just finished building over on Broadway, had its very own hydraulic elevator, but every time I mentioned that to Curtis he walked the other way.

"What do I do?" Dupin repeated doubtfully.

"Yeah. What's your motive and your métier? What's the singular thing that you pursue?"

"Ah." The little man's face lit up with understanding, but then it closed down again as he took that question over the threshold of his ruminations and worried it some. "The truth," he said at last. "The truth is what I pursue."

"Really? There any profit to be had in that?"

He gave out with that belly laugh again. "No. Not usually."

We waited for a cab on the corner of Forty-First Street right next to Pearson's cigar store. Mr Du Griddle Tray kept taking sideways glances at the cigar store Indian as though he might be looking to pick a fight. "That there is Tamanend, of the Lenape Nation," I told him. "He's widely known in these parts, despite having turned up his toes back in sixteen-ought-eight."

The Frenchman's answer surprised me. "Yes," he said. "Of course. Because of the Society of St Tammany, to which many members of New York's current civic administration belong."

I gave him a nod, and probably my face showed him that I was impressed. "One up to you, Dupin. That's the connection, all right. The Great Wigwam, they call it—the Tammany Hall, down on Fourteenth Street. And it's got its share of famous patrons, like you say. Our illustrious mayor,

Oakey Hall. Judge George Barnard, who doles out wisdom to the city benches. Hank Smith, who's the president of the Police Commission. Oh, there's a whole ring of them."

I didn't mention the grand sachem, William "Boss" Tweed, in the same way that you don't speak of the Devil—in case you turn around and find him breathing over your shoulder.

"Political corruption," Dupin mused. "It is a scourge."

And yes, it is. But this was my city we were lambasting, and I don't care to see my city, good-time girl though she may be, roughly handled by a stranger. So I changed the subject and talked about the bridge instead. And not long after that, we managed to hail a cab.

In deference to Du Sausage Cutter's hind parts I picked out a Duncan Sherman, which had a sprung undercarriage and a horse with something of an imperturbable nature. Truth to tell, we could have made better time walking— but you've got to push the boat out when you've got a guest to entertain, and besides it was setting in to rain a little. On a rainy day, Fifth Avenue is a lot more fun to ride down than to walk down.

As we rode, I carried on waxing lyrical about the bridge. "Over yonder," I said, pointing, "to the east of us, those buildings you see are not a part of the fair city of New York. They belong to our neighbour polity, Brooklyn, which like New York is a thriving metropolis, home to close on a half a million people. It's got just as many warehouses and factories and refineries as we do, and we'd like nothing better than to increase the ties of mutual amity and profit between the two cities. Only trouble is, there's sixteen hundred feet of water lying between them. It would need a bridge longer than any in the world to cross that gap."

"That would seem to be an insuperable problem," said Dupin, who knew what was required of a straight man.

"Well, sir, you'd think so. But Mr John Augustus Roebling, of Ohio, drew up a plan for a suspension bridge whose spans would be supported by steel wires redoubled inside flexible housings. He died before he could start in to build the thing, but his son, Washington Roebling, took over. Then Washington got sick from the caisson disease, and deputed his wife, Emily, to see the project to completion. Now the Brooklyn tower's mostly up and they're laying the foundations for the New York side. Hell of a thing to see, I'll tell you. When it's done, it will bestride the East River like a colossus."

"Remarkable," Dupin observed, dryly.

"Yes, sir, it is."

"And yet, dogged by ill fortune and tragedy."

I shrugged that off. I was a younger man, then, and more easily impressed by big dreams and big ideas. The misfortunes of the Roebling family didn't seem like such a big almighty deal to me. "Well, the salient fact is that this will be the biggest suspension bridge in the whole damn world. Biggest one right now is in Kentucky, and Roeblings built that too. America is a place where anything's possible, Mr Dupin."

The Frenchman nodded solemnly. "Yes," he agreed. "I believe that is so. That is one reason why I wished to see it."

I was opening my mouth, about to parrot some more facts and figures about steel wires and three-way overlapping joists, when I realised that I'd lost my audience. Mr Dupin was staring ahead down the street towards the Centre Street Pier, or rather just before it, which was where they'd erected the scaffolding for the tower on the New York side of the river.

"It seems," Mr Dupin said, "that we have chosen a busy day."

And in truth there was a crowd milling in the street beside the pier, the like of which I hadn't seen since the draft riots. They didn't seem to be up to any mischief, but there was a lot of shouting and shoving of the kind that normally signals something unusual has happened, and—undeterred by that past tense—people are jostling to line up in its wake. A few city police were trying to keep some kind of order, along with a crew or two from the new paid fire service, which had replaced the volunteer brigades a few years back. They were having a lively time of it.

I paid off the cab and we pushed our way through the crowd, my press badge making little difference to the citizens but winning me a little headway with the cops and the firemen. Finally we got through the police line and into the building yard. In front of us was the massive, complicated apparatus known as a caisson—the chief aid and comfort of bridge builders everywhere, and (sadly) the scourge and terror of their workers. It only showed six or seven feet above the ground, but it extended a great long way beneath us.

Normally, this building site was such a humming pit of industry that you had to duck and weave as you walked along, leading with your elbows like a forward in the Princeton University Football game. Today, though plenty of workers were around, nobody was actually working. Most of the men were sitting around looking unhappy or sullen. The rain was coming down steadily now, turning the earth to mud, but it seemed like nobody cared about the cold or the wet. Some had their heads in their hands. The winch that lowered food and coffee to the men down in the caisson was standing idle, and the old Italian man who ran it was slumped against the scaffolding, his arms draped over it, like a prize fighter who's barely made it to his corner. He looked to have been crying.

I collared a foreman who was bustling past, red-faced and urgent, and compelled him to stop. "See here, brother," I told him, "we're from the *Harper's Weekly* and we'd like to know what's going on here."

The yegg tried to pass us off with some mumble about asking the shift manager, but Dupin spoke up then, and either his gimlet eyes or his weird accent took the wind out of the foreman's sails. "What is your name?" he demanded.

"O'Reilly," the man mumbled truculently.

"Your given name, as well as your family name," Dupin snapped, for all the world as though he had some kind of right to ask. "Come, come."

"John. John O'Reilly."

"*C'est ça*. Tell us what has happened, John. Be brief and precise, if you please."

The foreman didn't seem to know what to make of this strange little guy in the fancy clothes. But on the principle that most people he met were going to turn out to be more important than he was, he coughed it up. "We got twenty men dead. The whole night shift. I went away to sign in the morning crew, and when I got back they was all . . . " He faltered into silence and pointed down into the caisson, as if the period of his sentence might be found down there.

"Twenty men?" Dupin echoed, and O'Reilly nodded. "Twenty men is a full complement, then? A full workforce?"

"It depends what's going on," O'Reilly said. "There's less men on at night, on account of we just light the lanterns up in one half of the caisson. There's a fire hazard, see?"

"No," Dupin said forcefully.

"What?"

"No, I do not see. Show me."

"Listen here, I got to . . . "

"Show me."

If the situation hadn't been so tragic, I might have laughed at the spectacle of this queer little foreigner taking charge so decisively. Dupin followed the foreman and I followed Dupin, my materials case clutched in my hand like a doctor's Gladstone bag—only there wasn't going to be any good I could do down there, I thought as we skirted round the wheezing steam pump. Not unless you count bearing witness.

The caisson was eighty feet long, sixty wide, and forty deep. The last ten feet or so were under the bedrock of the East River, so the air had a hellish dampness to it. We went down through several successive chambers, each sealed off by greased tarpaulins laid out in overlapping sheets. You had to lift a corner of the tarpaulin each time, like turning the page of a massive book, to expose the trapdoor and carry on down to the next level. Below us, candle flames flickered fitfully like someone was keeping vigil down there. The bellows of the steam pump kept up a consumptive breathing from up over our heads, and from below us that sound was compounded by the muttered conversations you mostly get around the bedsides of dying men.

The floor of the caisson was one half packed earth and one half new-laid stone. There weren't any dying men there, only hale ones and dead ones. The dead ones were laid out in rows, like men sleeping in a dormitory. The living ones stood over them, candles in their hands, looking impotent and terrified as behoves men who are in the presence of such a disaster.

The shift manager, a clerkish-looking man of middle age named Sittingbourne, introduced himself to us, and we returned the favour. I was vague about exactly who Dupin was, but emphasised our association with the *Harper's Weekly*. That put a woeful look on Sittingbourne's face, as well it might. This was the sort of thing he would probably have wanted to keep out of the papers until he'd talked to his bosses about what shape his future might likely take.

"See here," he said, "don't you go talking to none of my people without me being in on the conversation. Is that understood?"

"You got any people left for me to talk to?" I countered—and he deflated like a punctured soufflé.

"It was an accident," he said. "A terrible accident. I don't see how anyone could have foreseen this, or done anything to guard against it."

"Perhaps not," Dupin said acerbically. "But perhaps—yes. That is what we must ascertain. I wish to see the bodies."

This came as a surprise to all of us, but principally to Mr Sittingbourne, who thought he was dealing with newspapermen and now wondered if he was maybe dealing with something even scarier than that. A state commissioner, maybe.

"The . . . The bodies?" he temporised.

Dupin brushed past him, taking his candle out of the man's hand in an *en passant* move that made me wonder if he'd ever done any sword fencing. He squatted down beside the nearest body and brought the candle up close to its face.

I winced, but I didn't look away. I'm a sketch artist, and looking away isn't in my religion. The dead man's face was lividly pale, his lips blue rather than a healthy red. His face was twisted in a desperate travail, the eyes bulging half out of his head. All in all, it looked like death when it finally came for him might have been something of a relief.

"Poor bastard," I muttered.

"*Oui, le pauvre gosse,*" Dupin said. He moved the candle from face to face. "They all seem to have died in the same way. Or at least, they all display the same symptoms."

"It's known that working in the caissons is dangerous," Sittingbourne said. He was hovering at my elbow, nervously wringing his hands. "There's a condition . . . "

"Caisson sickness," I said.

"Caisson sickness, to be sure. And we've had our fair

share of it. But nothing like this. Nothing on this scale. I honestly . . . I don't know what to say. I really don't."

He was talking to Dupin's back. Dupin was still examining the bodies, his mouth puckered into a grimace. "The light is inadequate," he commented.

Sittingbourne looked around, startled. "Get your candles over here!" he called out to the other men. They clustered round us, looking like they were about to burst into a Christmas carol.

Dupin stood. "Who turned out the lanterns?"

"I don't know," Sittingbourne confessed.

"Then find out."

The Frenchman swept past us and headed back for the ladder, but he couldn't climb up because there was a whole posse coming down. It was hard to tell in the sepulchral light of the candles, but they looked to be in uniform. Once they touched down, I was able to identify them as New York City cops—the Eastside variety called spudpickers elsewhere in the City because they're bog Irish and Tammany men to a fault.

The two in the vanguard were sergeant Driscoll and his lackey, Flood. Driscoll looked as saintly as a christening cloth, and Flood looked like a nasty stain that somehow got smeared onto it, but I knew for a fact they were as bad as each other and a good deal worse than most.

"What are we having here?" Driscoll asked mildly. "Mr Nast, is it? You must have sneaked past us all quiet like, when we were quelling the angry mob."

"I'm sorry, sergeant," I lied emolliently. "I didn't realise you were restricting access. But I'm here as a representative of the press."

"A guy who draws funny pictures!" Flood sneered.

"My associate makes a cogent argument," Driscoll said. "You can't be painting pictures in the dark, Mr Nast, so I'll thank you to bugger off out of this." To the room at large, he added, "These workings are hazardous, and they're not being properly maintained. I'm closing them down, herewith. You can apply at City Hall for a new license, subsequent to a complete overhaul of the safety procedures and a thorough inspection at the contractor's expense."

"But . . . " Sittingbourne protested. "Please, sergeant. If I can consult Mrs Roebling, I'm . . . I'm sure we can—"

"I'm sure you can't," Driscoll told him, deadpan. "Not unless you want go around Boss Tweed."

That shut Sittingbourne up, *instanter*. You could go around William Tweed, of course. Topographically speaking, I mean. He was a mighty obstacle, but you could do it. The trouble was, you'd need to be properly provisioned for a journey like that, and your troubles would set in as soon as you were out of sight of the high road, as it were. I knew men who'd tried it. I even knew where some of them were buried.

"Might I inquire why this is being done?" The voice was Dupin's, the tone was sharp, and nobody was more surprised to hear it than I was. Well, maybe I was runner-up. Driscoll's face was a picture. He made a show of peering around on his own eye level for a little while before he looked down and found Dupin a foot or so below.

"Who the hell are you?" he demanded.

"Le Chevalier Auguste Dupin, at your service. I repeat, why is this being done?"

Driscoll didn't seem inclined to dignify that question with an answer, so Flood obliged us instead. "He already told you, you moron. These workings ain't safe. Twenty men died here."

"Twenty men died here," Dupin agreed. "But not because of the presence or absence of adequate building standards."

"And you'd know?"

"Yes. I would know. They were murdered."

Flood's face went through a series of discrete states,

like a slide show. Astonishment, then a sort of ghastly dismay, then anger. "You fuck!" he spluttered. He balled his hand into a fist and drew it back.

Driscoll caught it in mid-air and held onto it. He moved as quick as a snake, and he didn't seem to be exerting any particular effort to hold the constable immobile. "I think you should get your friend home, Mr Nast," he said mildly. "Otherwise, I'll have to arrest him for breach of the peace."

"Breach of the peace?" The Frenchman glanced at me with an interrogatory expression.

"Means you're stirring up a riot," I translated. "Come on, Mr Dupin, we're leaving."

"Yeah, you better," Flood spat. The sergeant gave him his hand back and he glared at us, rubbing his wrist, as I hauled Dupin over to the ladder.

"I have further questions for the gentleman in charge," Dupin protested.

"They'll have to keep," I muttered. "Trust me, these two will break your head as soon as look at you."

"They are agents and representatives of the law."

"Nope, of the city. Not the same thing at all."

I steered him ahead of me halfway up the ladder, but then he stopped—which meant I had to stop too, since the only way up was through him. "Monsieur!" he called down to Sittingbourne. "Hola, Monsieur! Who put out the lanterns?"

Sergeant Driscoll slipped his nightstick out of his belt and tapped it meaningfully against his palm.

Sittingbourne made a helpless gesture. Dupin tutted and carried on up. But he'd got the bit fairly between his teeth now, and he certainly didn't seem interested in leaving. He went over to the steam pump and started to walk around and around it, inspecting it from all angles. It looked a little beaten-up here and there—especially around the protuberant valve assemblies to which the hoses were attached. A pump like this was like a heart in a human body, working mightily without cease. It was an amazing thing in its own right, that allowed even more amazing things to be done.

"You know how a caisson works?" I asked Dupin.

"Yes," he said. "I believe so. It is a hyperbaric environment, no?"

"It's a what?"

"It utilises air at higher than atmospheric pressure to create a dry working space below sea level. Or in this case, river level. Air is pumped in by artificial means to maintain the pressure, which may be two or three times greater than that in the ambient air outside the caisson."

"Well, yeah," I said. "That's more or less how it's done."

Actually, Dupin seemed to understand the process better than I did. He was starting to fiddle with the controls on the steam pump now, and the foreman came running over hell for leather.

"Say hey, now," he yelped. "You don't want to be messing with this. This is delicate equipment. And that outlet connection there is loose!"

Dupin gave him a withering glare. "Nonsense!" he snapped. "This is a Jacquard-Sevigny pump, made from a single moulding. You could take a hammer to it—and indeed, it looks as though someone has—but still it would not break."

O'Reilly faltered a little, but only for a moment. "It's private property," he said. "You keep your hands off it, or I'll sic the police on you, see?"

I felt like we'd had more than enough of that already, so I took Dupin by the arm with a view to getting him moving again, but he slipped out of my grip and went after O'Reilly like a terrier after a rat. "You found the bodies?" he demanded.

O'Reilly backed away. "Yeah, I did," he said. "So?"

"So. How did you find them? Tell me."

"I just . . . well, I went away, and I come back, and they was dead. I don't know how. I don't know anything about it."

"When was this?"

"It was eight o'clock. On the turn of the shift."

"Did you disturb the bodies?" The foreman was still moving backwards and Dupin was still following, almost stepping on his toes.

"No! I never touched them!"

"And yet they were arranged in rows. Was that how they died?"

"No. Yes. I moved them, obviously. But that was afterwards."

"And the lanterns?"

The foreman was looking a little bit desperate now. "The what?"

"The lanterns. Did you extinguish them?"

"No. They was already out."

Dupin stopped dead, and turned to me. "*Bien*," he said. "We are finished here."

That was news to me, since I was the one who was meant to be showing him the sights. But I guess we'd gone off that agenda a while before. "Okay," I said. "You want to go see the Equitable Life Building? It's got a hydraulic elevator, made by Elisha Otis, and you can ride all the way up to the . . . "

"I want to see the lady you mentioned, Monsieur Nast," Dupin interrupted forcefully. I was a little mystified at this, and I must have looked it. "Madame Roebling, I think the name was? The lady who builds this bridge."

I tried to explain to him that we couldn't just walk in on the Roeblings, but Dupin wasn't having any of that. There's a thing called a New York minute, and inside of one of those we were pulling up at the door of the Roebling house in Midtown in another cab that Curtis was going to get all sore about paying for. And Dupin was explaining to some sour old curmudgeon in a spiffy black and silver livery that he was the godson of Colonel Maximilian Roebling-Lefevre of the Légion d'Honneur, and on that basis would be delighted to pay his respects to the lady of the house.

The curmudgeon went away and came back with a different face on. Mrs Roebling would be delighted to see us in the morning room.

She didn't look all that delighted, though. It was like walking in on a funeral, which I guess in one sense we were. Mrs Roebling looked as pale as death, and though she rallied enough to greet us, she couldn't find a whole lot to say.

"You'll have to forgive me, gentlemen," she said. "I . . . I've just had some very bad news. Twenty workers on one of our construction projects have died in the most tragic of circumstances. It appears that our working practices may be to blame. The caisson sickness has incapacitated a number of our masons and navigators, and laid my husband low. And now—now it seems it's taken a score of men at a single stroke!"

She started in to crying at this, which was a distressing thing to see. I made the usual *there, there* noises, but Dupin surprised me—surprised both of us—by laughing. Not the belly laugh, this time, but a little snort like a steam kettle saying it's ready. Mrs Roebling gave him a startled look.

"Pray, sir," she said, affronted, "what can you find in these awful facts to amuse you?"

Dupin made a dismissive gesture. "The facts, Madame," he said, "the facts are not amusing at all. What is amusing is the refusal of all parties concerned to acknowledge them. You feel responsible for the deaths of these men?"

Mrs Roebling blanched at the blunt question. "Why yes," she said. "To some extent, I do."

"Then calm yourself. You are not responsible at all, and I will prove it. But tell me, how was the news brought to you?"

"By a runner," Mrs Roebling said. "Sent by the foreman, Mr O'Reilly, shortly after eight o'clock."

"And then?"

"And then, hard on his heels, an attorney came from the mayor's office to tell me that my building permits had been revoked. We now owe the city a great deal of money. We must pay for a full inspection, which will be expensive and onerous. There will be a fine, besides, for so serious a breach of safety regulations. And of course, compensation for the families of the dead men must also be found. I fear this may sink our project completely."

Dupin glanced at me. "The mayor's office?" he queried. Evidently I'd been appointed his personal perambulatory encyclopaedia.

"Two Fifty-Three Broadway," I said. "Don't tell me you want to go see the mayor, Dupin. It's a long haul back the way we came, and a long haul west, and I let the cab go."

Dupin didn't seem to be listening. He'd turned his attention back to Mrs Roebling again. "At what time, precisely, did these runners arrive?"

Mrs Roebling couldn't say—not precisely—but the butler (the gent in all the black and silver) was called and he knew the times to a nicety. See, that's what I mean about clothes and moral seriousness. The runner from the works had arrived at 8:27, and the clerk from City Hall at 8:33.

Dupin absorbed this news in solemn silence, then turned to me again. There was a kind of a gleam in his eye. "I do not, Monsieur Nast, wish to see the mayor. But I think perhaps I would like to see the commissioner of police."

Mrs Roebling gasped. "Do you honestly believe, sir, that a crime has been committed?" she demanded, her face clouded with bewilderment.

"I believe, in fact," Dupin said, "that several crimes have been committed. But I will not speak of things I cannot prove. For this morning's events, I can speak with absolute certainty. Those men were murdered, and the culprit is already known to you." He turned to the lady again. "Madame," he said. "I request you to remain here, and to ignore for the moment any communications from the mayor's office or from city officials of whatever provenance. I will tell what I know, and we will see what we will see. But I assure you, you will pay for no inspections nor levies. The compensation, yes, since the men are dead and you would not wish to leave their families destitute. But that will be the limit of your exposure."

We left the lady in a pretty confused state—and to be honest, I was more than a little consternated myself. Otherwise, I think I would have put up more of a resistance. But Dupin had the hang of summoning cabs now, and that was a terrible power to put in a Frenchman's hands. He waved his cane like an orchestra conductor, and a two-horse rig rolled to a halt right in front of us. He was jumping up onto the running board even while I was explaining that this was a fool's errand. I had no choice but to jump up after him.

"You can't just walk into the police commissioner's office and make wild assertions, Dupin," I told him, in something of a panic. "Especially not in this city. It just won't wash."

"*Pourquoi ça, Monsieur Nast?*" Dupin snorted. "Why will it not wash?" He wasn't even looking at me. He'd taken out a fancy silver pocket watch and was consulting it with a look of deep deliberation.

Where to begin? "Well, for starters, you're not even armed."

"But yes. I am armed with the truth."

"Oh, jumping Jehoshaphat!"

I carried on remonstrating with him, because I kind of

felt like it was incumbent on me to be the voice of reason. But there wasn't any way of shifting him. I just got sucked along in his wake, and before I knew it we were walking up the steps of the police headquarters building.

Two officers standing up on the top step like bouncers at the door of a bar room looked us up and down and asked our business. Dupin was looking at his watch again, so I handled the introductions myself—with something of a sinking feeling in my stomach. I said we were from the *Harper's Weekly* and we'd love to talk to Commissioner Smith and maybe sketch his portrait for the papers.

One of the cops led us inside, leaving the other one to take care of the business of looking tough and surly by himself for a while. We got some curious glances from the flatfoots sitting in the bullpen, and the officers in their little working cupboards. Dupin looked neither left nor right, but when we finally approached the commissioner's door he put on a turn of speed and got there first.

"See here," our tutelary spirit said. "I got to announce you, is what."

"I am the chevalier Auguste Dupin," the Frenchman declaimed, with fine contempt, "and I will announce myself."

The door was already ajar. Dupin threw it wide with a thrust of his cane and walked inside. I followed him, into a fug of smoke chopped into lines of solid white and solid black by the sunlight filtering through the window blinds. It looked like the men in that room had put the sun in jail, almost. Had thrown it behind bars. A fanciful notion, obviously, but they were the men to do it, if such a thing could be done.

There were six of them, but I only saw four of them out of the gate. Police Commissioner Hank Smith, whose office this was, his doughy face overshadowed by a massive brow like the ledge over a cave. James Kelso, his superintendent, who looked like a cardinal of the church of Rome, thinning hair swept back and thin lips pursed.

Mayor Oakey Hall, with his pendulous, bifurcated moustache like the mandibles of a huge spider.

They were sitting around a big table, off to one side of Smith's desk. At the head of the table sat not Smith but Smith's boss and the boss of everyone else here.

William Magear Tweed rose slowly from his chair as we entered the room. He towered above us. The man was architectural in his build—well over six feet in height, three hundred pounds or more in *avoir dupois*. But he looked a whole lot bigger and a whole lot heavier than that. His tiny round eyes might have looked weak on another man. In his face, the eyes being the windows of the soul, they looked like pinholes pricked into a black inferno.

"Well, now," he said. His voice was a deep basso rumble like a trolley car going by. "It's Mr Nast, and his friend with the dapper clothes and the funny accent. You going to introduce us?"

"Actually, Mr Tweed," I said, "we just came here to sketch the commissioner's portrait. But since he's busy, we'll come back another time."

"Wouldn't hear of it," Tweed said. "Pull up a chair for Mr Nast, and . . . I don't know, what do you say to a high stool for the little guy?"

He was talking to the two remaining men, who stepped out of the smoke and shadow then. Sergeant Driscoll closed the door. Constable Flood kicked two chairs in our general direction, his face suffused with a nasty grin as with a bruise.

That sinking feeling I was talking about sunk about another twelve storeys, quicker than any hydraulic elevator yet invented.

"Sit down, you yeggs," Flood sneered. I slumped down in one of the chairs, but Dupin didn't even acknowledge the loaded courtesy.

"You are Boss Tweed?" he demanded. "I have heard of you."

"Most people have," Tweed allowed. "As a humble servant of the city of New York, I hope. So you gents came here to paint a pretty picture?"

I opened my mouth to answer, but Dupin was in there a sight too fast for me. "No."

"No?"

"Not at all. We are here to report an act of mass murder."

Something like a soundless shockwave went through the room. The two cops and the three seated officials braced themselves against it, seemed to tremble slightly as it passed. Not Tweed. He just raised his eyebrows up a little and let it go by him.

"Mass murder," he ruminated. "I thought you ran a tighter ship than that, Hank. Any mass murderers you know of that you didn't put on payroll yet?"

The police commissioner gave a sickly grin. "Very droll, Bill," he muttered. "Very droll. You better watch what you say, Mr Nast. Perjury's still a crime in this state."

"Although it's also somewhat of an industry," Tweed added. Everyone except Smith laughed at that, even the two cops.

Now I hadn't said a thing to the purpose, let alone under oath, so the perjury shot went wide. But then it wasn't a writ I was afraid of here. I took Dupin by the shoulder, hoping we could still steer a way out of these choppy waters, but he didn't budge an inch. And it probably wouldn't have mattered if he had, because Driscoll and Flood had taken up station at the door. Driscoll had his hand resting on the holster at his belt and Flood had his nightstick out, casually resting it athwart his shoulder. There wasn't any way out except forward.

"The murders I speak of," Dupin said, "were committed at eight o'clock this morning at the site of the bridge that is being constructed close to the Centre Street Pier. The principal agent and perpetrator is most likely the foreman at that site, a gentleman named O'Reilly, but I believe he had confederates whose names he might be made to divulge under questioning."

"Oh, you believe that?" Tweed asked politely.

"Yes."

"Those weren't murders," Jimmy Kelso said, all windy self-importance. "We already looked into that. Those men was killed by the caisson disease."

"That," said Dupin, "is an absurd conclusion. Every single observation that can be made says otherwise."

"And what observations are those?" Tweed asked. He was looking highly amused, which I didn't like at all.

Dupin seemed pretty happy too, and I realised he'd been building up to this. He struck a stance. "To begin with," he said, "caisson sickness is a malady with a slow onset and a slow progression. The idea that it might afflict a score of people all at the same time, and kill them at a stroke, is absurd."

"Horse puckey!" Kelso said with force. "Nobody even knows how the caisson disease even works, so nobody can say what it can and can't do."

Dupin's lip turned at the corner as he stared at the superintendent. "There is already a body of literature relating to hyperbaric environments," he said.

Kelso blinked. "There's a what?"

"There are essays, monsieur, and monographs, and longer studies, about the conditions in which these unfortunate men worked. The caisson sickness seems to be a side effect of those conditions—conditions which, though they may be imperfectly understood, are extremely well documented. I have myself visited le professeur Fontaine's hyperbaric chamber at the Sorbonne and studied its operation. Air from the outside world is excluded by welded seals and tight-fitting doors. Breathable air, under higher than atmospheric pressure, is injected into the caisson by means of a Jacquard-Sevigny steam-driven pumping apparatus. The same machine draws away exhaled air and expels it outside the caisson, so that the level of oxygen—that indispensable gas identified by Monsieur Lavoisier, another of my countrymen—remains constant."

"You talk beautifully," Boss Tweed said, every bit as easy as before. "But not to the purpose. Who cares how the pump works?"

"I do, monsieur," Dupin said. "I care very much. When I examined the bodies in the caisson, I found that they all had livid skin and blue lips."

"So?"

"*Alors.* If they had died from caisson sickness, their skin would be bright red. An urticuric rash, as from the touch of nettles, would have been visible on their faces and necks. This in itself was enough to arouse my suspicions. What confirmed them was the fact that the lamps in the caisson, essential to the continuing work there, had all been extinguished.

"And that, monsieur, could mean only one thing. A wind or breeze, in that space where air was so carefully rationed, was impossible. The only thing that could have put out those flames was the absence of the oxygen on which they fed. The lights died for the same reason that the men died. They had no oxygen to consume, and without it, had not the wherewithal to continue in existence."

Something like a frown passed across Tweed's big, heavy-featured face, but he rallied pretty quickly and managed a pained smile. "You're saying someone stole the air?"

"*Bien sûr que non.* Not the air. Only the oxygen from the air."

"And how does a man go about stealing that, exactly?"

"A man," Dupin said with grim emphasis, "attaches the outlet hose on the steam pump back into the inlet valve, creating in effect a closed system. A *boucle*. A loop. The men's exhaled air, depleted of the vital oxygen, is fed back to them, again and again, until they suffocate. Which does not take long at all."

There was a deathly silence in the room. The men at the table looked to Tweed, as if they weren't willing to venture an opinion on this subject until the boss had spoken. I kept quiet too, but for a different reason. I was thinking of those men's last moments, and my mind was reeling. I couldn't imagine a worse way to die—and I couldn't imagine the mind that could have cooked up something like that. At the same time, I was starting to put things together the way Dupin had, running along after his thought processes the way a dog runs after a fire tender.

"The marks on the pump," I said. "That outlet valve did look all beaten up. As though . . . "

"As though someone had levered it off, with a wrench or a crowbar," Dupin finished. "And then replaced it again, after it had served its purpose. Yes, I believe that to be the case."

"But whatever you believe," Boss Tweed said, with the calm of complete indifference, "you can't prove who did it."

"Ah, but I think I can," said Dupin, sealing our fate. "The runner who came from City Hall to announce that the workings were unsafe and had to close arrived at thirty-three minutes past the hour. Let us assume that a message was sent from the worksite as soon as the deaths were discovered, and that the mayor"—he gave Oakey Hall a perfunctory bow— "delivered his decision immediately. The two journeys, cross-town and then north to Mrs Roebling's house, require a minimum of fifty minutes to complete. It can therefore be established by a very simple calculation that the messenger sent from City Hall must have been dispatched before any notification could have arrived from the site."

Hall blanched as Boss Tweed shot him a cold, disapproving glance. "That true?" he demanded.

"I thought we wanted to shut them down fast," the mayor protested, with something of a whine in his voice. "I didn't think anyone was going to be standing on the street with a damn stopwatch."

"No," Tweed agreed. "You didn't think. You never do, Oakey. Maybe it's time I replaced you with someone who does." He gave a hitch of his shoulders, which was evidently a sign to Driscoll and Flood. Driscoll put his gun in my back, and Flood grabbed a hold of Dupin.

"But . . . But why?" I demanded. Given the extremity of the situation, talking back to the Boss didn't feel like quite as fearful a prospect as it would normally have been. "Why would you do something like this?"

Tweed seemed surprised to be asked. He shrugged his massive shoulders. "The usual reason," he said. "Come on, Nast. You're a newsman, not a babe in arms. The New York to Brooklyn bridge is the biggest building project this city has ever seen. All we wanted was a decent kickback. The old man was dragging his feet, so we arranged a little accident for him. We started leaning on the son, and he was just about to roll when he got sick. That left us with the lady, who's the toughest nut of the lot. Or maybe just the stupidest. She didn't seem to understand that when we said we could help her with her licenses and her on-site security, we were asking for a bribe. She just said thank you and goodnight. So we thought we'd move things along a little."

"By killing twenty men?" I asked, my throat dry.

Those tiny black eyes blinked slowly, the way a cat's eyes do. "Well, you know what they say about omelettes. If you're serious about making them, you can't afford to get sentimental about eggs."

"You murdering bastard," I said. "Some of those eggs had wives and kids."

"They'll break too," the Boss replied laconically. "Sooner or later makes no difference. It's not like eggs are built to last." He gave Driscoll a meaningful look. "Get rid of them," he said. "Somewhere real quiet. Say a few words over the bodies, then take the evening off."

That was the end of the interview. Driscoll and Flood hauled us out of there, and took us via the back door of the building to a paddy wagon. They pushed us inside and locked the door. We could hear Flood hitching up the horses, with a lot of cursing, while Driscoll berated him for his clumsiness.

It was a long, uncomfortable ride, all the way uptown to the northern tip of Manhattan Island. The swampy ground around the Palisades was slowly being reclaimed, and the city was obviously going to head out that way in its own good time, but back then it was a wilderness. The few tracks there were petered out quickly, leaving you adrift in an endless expanse of couch grass and stunted trees.

"I'm real sorry, Mr Dupin," I muttered.

"About what?" Dupin demanded.

"All this. Dying in a ditch is a poor sort of a way for your day of sightseeing to end. And I'm the native guide here. I should have headed this off before you got too far into it. Mind you," I added, "I didn't know you were going to be accusing Boss Tweed himself of multiple counts of homicide."

"*Je vous en prie,*" Dupin demurred, and since I had no clue what that meant the conversation ended there.

The paddy wagon slowed to a halt. We heard Driscoll and Flood jump down from the driver's seat, and a second later the doors were hauled open. Driscoll had a pistol levelled at us, and Flood had some kind of a sap—shorter than his nightstick but just as lethal looking.

"Last stop, my buckos," the constable said cheerfully.

We climbed down out of the wagon into a desolate landscape. We were only a few miles outside the city limits, but there wasn't a building in sight. The sun was touching the horizon, and there was a sharp wind getting up, making the leafless trees lean over like they were hunching down against the cold.

Sergeant Driscoll chucked me on the chin with the barrel of the pistol, as though to coax a smile out of me.

"Any last words, Mr Nast?" he asked, mildly. "A prayer, perhaps? Or a confession? We're not in any hurry."

It was a thoughtful offer in the circumstances, but I couldn't think of anything either reverential or splenetic that was worth detaining him with. I'd sort of resigned myself to death, now, and I just wanted to get the unpleasant business over with. I shook my head.

Dupin seemed even more detached. He wandered over to a flowering bush and prodded it with his cane. Flood stood over him, sap in hand, guarding him until it was his turn to be dispatched.

"Right then," Driscoll said. "May the Good Lord have mercy. I can speak for my shooting, so your only worry's what happens afterwards."

He took aim at my forehead, and I braced myself for the world to come.

At that point, constable Flood gave a sudden, constricted gasp and sank to his knees. Driscoll turned, astonished.

"What's the matter with you, you idiot?" he demanded.

Flood opened his mouth, but nothing came out of it except a thin trickle of blood. He pitched forward onto his face.

Dupin swished the sword that had appeared from nowhere in his hand. "Direct your thoughts, monsieur," he suggested, "to what happens afterwards."

Driscoll was as fast as a snake, a trait I believe I've remarked on earlier in this narrative. He swung the pistol round in the blink of an eye, but Dupin's arm dipped and rose and intersected the other man's at some significant point in its arc. The gun went flying away through the air and Driscoll started back with a cry, nursing his hand.

The sword flashed again and the sergeant's legs buckled under him. A spurt of crimson from his severed throat splashed my sleeve as he fell. I stared at it stupidly, only decoding its meaning when Dupin slid the slender blade back into its housing in his cane. "*Voilà*," he said.

"You . . . You had . . . " I stammered. "You were . . . "

"Armed," Dupin agreed. "The truth is all very well, but sometimes one needs a little more. Come, Monsieur Nast. We have a carriage and horses, but not much daylight left. It would be a good idea, I think, to get back to the city before night is fully upon us."

In fact, he left me at the edge of town. He purposed to hire a boat or a berth at the tiny harbour on Spuyten Duyvil Creek, rather than risk buying a ticket home anywhere in New York City itself. He had a shrewd suspicion that Boss Tweed might be looking for him, once he realised that his two spudpicker assassins had misfired. The haulage men at Spuyten Duyvil would take him on up the coast to Bridgeport or Westhaven, and he could continue on his travels from there.

"My survival, Monsieur Nast," the Frenchman assured me, "will be the earnest guarantor of yours. Tweed and his associates will want you dead, but they will not dare to move against you so long as I am free and able to speak of what I know. I cannot, of course, prove that he was involved in these murders, but I can embarrass and clog the machine of which he is a part. And I will do so, if he defies me."

We shook hands and parted company. Dupin rode away northwards and I hiked down to Morningside. There, I was able to prevail on a fisherman to give me a lift on the back of his cart when he took his day's catch down to Peck Slip, and I was home only an hour or so after sunset.

Dupin, I learned later, had put pen to paper before he embarked from Spuyten Duyvil. Whatever it was he wrote to Tweed, the Tammany machine rescinded its writs and remands against the Roebling family and their great construction project and withdrew any and all accusations of unsafe working practises. A warrant was issued for the arrest of the foreman, O'Reilly, on twenty counts of murder, but his room in a seedy boarding house at Red Hook was found to have been emptied of all moveable items. Verbal descriptions were issued, along with a promise of reward, but O'Reilly never turned up again, and I doubt he will now—not until the last trump brings the dead up out of their graves.

Dupin wrote to me too, enclosing a letter for Mrs Emily Roebling but also a few lines for my own edification. *Your Mr Tweed*, he wrote, *trades very strongly on the appearance of invulnerability. If you wish to harm him, you must first encourage the perception that he is susceptible to harm. I mention this, my dear friend, because your own trade of cartooning seems to me to be very admirably suited to this purpose. You asked me a question when we first met: What is your motive and your métier? What is the singular thing that you pursue? I ask you now to consider this very question yourself. I believe that your answer will be the same as mine—that you are a servant of truth. And you will know to what I am referring when I say she arms her servants well.*

Well, I chewed that over a while, and I saw clear enough that he was right. So I took up my sword (it was shaped somewhat like a Woodson & Penwick number 1 black sable paintbrush) and I went to war.

FOOTNOTE: From 1870 to 1873, Thomas Nast's editorial cartoons mercilessly lampooned the corrupt activities of the Tammany Ring, and its formidable front man, William "Boss" Tweed. *Harper's Weekly* rallied behind him, and one by one the other New York newspapers joined the crusade. In 1873, Tweed was arrested on multiple charges of fraud and racketeering. He died in prison five years later, having been convicted on all counts.

I'd already written my Auguste Dupin story, "The Sons of Tammany", when I was invited to write a story for an anthology of urban horror. So I abandoned my first thought, of using New York as a setting, because I didn't want the story to feel like a retread. I settled on Paris instead. My wife Lin and I were just back from a holiday there, and its beautiful streets were still vividly in my mind. But over the weeks that I mulled over the story I was in Central London almost every day, meeting with TV producers to talk about the series that ultimately never happened (which I think makes up about three-quarters of a screenwriter's life). ¶ Something weird happened. I'd start imagining a Parisian setting, and London or New York would creep in somehow. Or I'd transpose an idea from one city to another to see how it played in the different milieu. I got progressively lost, inside my own head, and once in real life (because Covent Garden isn't Les Halles). ¶ Getting lost can be strangely pleasurable. In *The Man Who Was Thursday*, G. K. Chesterton has one of his characters complain about the dreary reliability of the railway system. "Why do all the clerks and navvies in the railway trains look so sad and tired, so very sad and tired? I will tell you. It is because they know that the train is going right. It is because they know that whatever place they have taken a ticket for, that place they will reach. It is because after they have passed Sloane Square they know that the next station must be Victoria, and nothing but Victoria. Oh, their wild rapture! Oh, their eyes like stars and their souls again in Eden, if the next station were unaccountably Baker Street!" ¶ I decided to write a story about a city where the next station could be Baker Street, Times Square, L'Étoile, or Krasnogorsk. It turned out to be a zombie story, but there's only the one zombie and you might miss it at first even though it's a seriously big bastard.

WE'LL ALWAYS HAVE PARIS

I WILL take the trouble to set this out for you, because I feel it's important that you understand. I must ask you to listen and to refrain from asking questions while I speak. I believe the most pertinent issues between us will be very clearly explained in the course of my story. If at the end of it you still find yourself puzzled, unclear as to why you are about to die, then in that respect and that respect alone you will have good reason to reproach me.

In the 14th arrondissement of the city, close to the Brooklyn Bridge and the Alhambra, there is—or used to be; it is hard to be categorical—a patisserie whose terrace looks out directly onto the Seine. It had been my custom ever since I found the place to have a breakfast croissant there, watching the lazily ambling waters of the river while the particulars of the cases on which I was currently working flowed through my brain with a similar lack of haste or direction. This ritual had afforded me many valuable insights, and I had come to rely on it more and more in these recent times of turbulence and irreplaceable loss.

So naturally, this was where the latest body had been found.

I was summoned to the Rue Asselin at 6:00 a.m. on a morning in October—this last October, which was neither mild nor merciful. You remember it, yes? The chill of

winter was already in the air despite the warming smell
of baking Viennoiseries carried on the westerly wind. The
cafés had not opened at that hour, but they were already
preparing for the early morning onslaught.

The corpse was lying at the edge of the pavement, one
arm stretched out into the road. He looked as though he
had met his demise in the act of hailing a cab. He was formally dressed in a black tuxedo whose satin edgings had
lost their lustre forever, stained as they were with their late
owner's cerebral matter. His skull was not only smashed,
it was also seriously truncated. Monsieur Crâne, very evidently, had struck again.

The Irishman, Sergeant Riordan, was there before me
and was scraping at the dead man's fingernails, where presumably something of value was to be found. An assailant's
blood and tissue, perhaps, or the rare earth of some specific
and identifiable quarter of the city. I don't care much for
Riordan's irreverent manner but I admire his stubborn per-
fectionism and his dedication to duty. When the dead rose
and became the undead he fought indefatigably in the city's
defence. It was said that he had put a bullet in the head of
his own wife when she clawed her way out of the body bag
and tried to eat their only child. Afterwards he had carried
her corpse three miles to lay her down in the mass grave in
the Jardin du Luxembourg along with all the other *zombis*.
Respect must be paid to such a man.

A young woman, her hair wet as if she had just stepped
out of the shower, was standing beside him. She was taking
photographs of the crime scene. Not of the body, but of the
buildings round about. Curious, I thought. She was curious
herself. Her pale blue eyes and ash blonde hair, the extreme
pallor of her skin seemed to belong to another place and time.
She might have been one of the city's marble statues come
to life. Or she might have been one of the *zombi* revenants,
but there were no revenants now. We had won that war, at a
cost—to each and all of us—almost too high to reckon.

I took up a station immediately behind Riordan, leaning against the wall of an adjacent building. I was resigned
to a long wait. The Irish detective's methods are exhaus-
tive, and exhausting. "So," I said to pass the time, "do
you have any ideas as to the cause of death?"

The woman—apparently Riordan's partner or assist-
ant—looked around as I spoke, her gaze taking me in
from toe to crown. Her stare allowed the possibility that
I might be, or become, interesting. It explicitly did not go
any further than that.

"You're a very funny man, Inspector Philemon,"
Riordan murmured. "It's a struggle to restrain my merri-
ment with you making such jocular observations."

The woman walked across to the edge of the pavement and took a series of photographs of a small dog that
had wandered up to join us. It stared into her lens with
a long-suffering patience, as though it was used to such
impertinences. "Is the dog a suspect?" I asked Riordan.

He looked around at the woman, at the animal, and
gave a little snort that conveyed no information at all.

The woman took my picture next. The magnificent
frontage of the Hotel Belle Époque provided a very pho-
togenic backdrop, but I doubt it did anything to offset the
shadows under my eyes or the rumpled, lived-in state of
my clothes.

Riordan straightened. He was looking similarly lived-
in, to be honest. Both of us had been on this case more
or less continuously since it had first broken more than a
month before, and we were far from the only ones. The
body of a young woman, a streetwalker, had been found
lying in the middle of the Champs Elysées. In swerving
around her, the cars had made hundreds of concentric ruts
in the autumn mud, roughly circular but tapered at either
end: a *yoni* mark, as though in deference to her profession.

The top of her head had been removed. There was
nothing above the bridge of her nose. The resulting damage,

however, had none of the neatness of an incision. It had not been done with a scalpel or a bone saw. It was more in the nature of a crush injury, as though someone had pounded the woman's head repeatedly with a hammer until the resulting mass of pulped flesh and bone fragments could be scraped away. What was left of the skull and the head bore the typical signs of crushing: the bone fragmented along parallel lines of stress, and pulled free of the muscles in the same vertical plane. Striated trauma artefacts extended all the way down into the shoulders and upper back.

Monsieur Crâne had left his calling card. He was to do so again a further twelve times in the following weeks. Today's corpse brought the overall total up to fourteen, and still we were no closer to an arrest, or even to establishing a suspect.

We were still recovering, of course, from the great war between the living and the dead. Perhaps on some level we could not help but see the victims as potential enemies. Certainly we carried our scars from that war, every one of us. We were the walking wounded, emotionally and psychologically depleted. The world we lived and moved in seemed drained of colour. It was as though that high tide of death had left us beached and we were only waiting for another wave to carry us away.

There were, of course, more prosaic problems with the investigation. Logistical ones. The victims were bafflingly diverse. The first, a prostitute who must have been attacked in the course of her nightly work—an occupational hazard, one might have thought. But the second body to appear was a Japanese commodities broker well known on Wall Street, and the third was a respectable lady who ran a cantina on Juarez Hill. Back to the gutter for victim number four, a homeless drunk. And so, and so, and so. Perhaps there was no scalpel involved, but Monsieur Crâne's needle pricked the fabric of society at every level and pulled it into a tight, unlovely gather.

I took these musings to the establishment I mentioned earlier, the Café Moche on Fifth and Taylor, just off Unterdenlinden, and stirred them into lethargic activity with a double espresso. I ordered a croissant too, but left it untouched. I considered lacing the coffee with brandy, a great specific both against the weather and against unpleasant thoughts, but it was still very early in the day. I usually endured my stations of the cross without anaesthetic until the middle of the afternoon. Otherwise I would have been drunk all the time. To make a continuing investment in what was left of my life and work required me, occasionally, to be sober.

But the waiter, Sam, must have seen the temptation cross my mind. "You want a slug of something hard in that, Phil?" he shouted from the bar.

I shook my head. "Not unless you have the Koh-I-Noor diamond ready to hand."

He laughed—a loud and raucous sound. "Still on order. I'll let you know."

"I'll take a brandy, though, if you're offering," said the young woman from the crime scene. She slid into the seat opposite me and shot me a cold smile. "Lutetia. Lutetia Lumière. In case you're wondering, you're very pleased to meet me."

I looked around for Riordan. He was not on the premises.

"You seem to have misplaced your partner, Madame detective," I observed. "Should I telephone the precinct and ask them to conduct a search?"

The woman—Lumière? A good name for a photographer, I supposed—ignored the question. She pushed some photos across the table at me. I pushed them back, which caused her to twist her very expressive lips into a warning frown. "I need you to look at these," she said. "They're part of my inquiry."

"But not of mine," I pointed out mildly. "The Sûreté and the Garda are not collaborating on this case.

I'm sure Sergeant Riordan would be quite homicidally distressed to know you were canvassing the details of his investigation with an officer of a rival organisation."

Lumière grinned. "Sergeant Riordan can keep his investigation. I'm talking about mine. And I don't work for the Garda."

"Then why . . . ?" I began, but she stopped me with a raised finger. She was still smiling, but something hard and sharp glinted beneath it like broken glass in a flower-bed. "Hey. Excuse me. I said I don't work for the Garda. I also don't work for the Sûreté or the Policezni or the Aktionsstyrke or the Kogu-Keisatsu. I'm strictly freelance, inspector. Which is why I'm sitting here talking to you now, under the possibly mistaken impression that you actually give a shit about all these dead people we keep tripping over. If I'm wrong, I'll just move right along."

It was an impressive speech, though it was slightly undercut by the arrival at that precise moment of her brandy, delivered by Sam with a wink and a smirk. I knew very well what had put that leer on his face. We had fought together, the two of us, and killed together those who were already unarguably dead. He was misinterpreting this meeting as a romantic liaison and he was pleased on my behalf. He was an optimist, and looked out continually for signs of a thaw in my perpetual winter. And I continually disappointed him.

Lumière thanked him for the brandy, then turned the searchlight of her attention back to me. "Okay," she said, "Let's start at the beginning. What do we have?"

I raised an eyebrow. "Assuming, for the sake of argument, that there is a composite entity that could reasonably be called *we*, what *we* have is fourteen bodies killed at various places around the city in a one-month period. Nothing to tie the suspects together, and nothing for that matter to link the murders themselves apart from the manner of death, which in all cases is severe crush injury to the head."

Lumière shook her head sternly. "Sloppy, sloppy, sloppy," she said. "Three times over, for the three things you left out. If we're going to work together, I'm going to need you to be a little more forensic."

I considered what might be added to my summary. The alternative would have been to get up and walk away, which I wasn't inclined to do since I had been there first. "All the killings were at night," I offered. "At least, the bodies were found in the morning in the vast majority of cases."

"Good. What else?"

"The crush injuries aren't the only consistency in the evidence. In all cases the crime scene was surprisingly clean. There was blood and cerebral tissue to be found, and some bone fragments, but far less than one would expect from such an extreme physical trauma. Oh, and some of the bodies also bear lacerations to their lower legs and ankles, as though they had been bitten, *ante mortem*, by a large animal."

"And that's two. Finally?"

I shrugged irritably, taking another sip of my coffee. "I don't know. You tell me."

"Accelerating pace, inspector. The intervals between the killings have been getting shorter. These last two were on successive nights."

This was true. I had shied away from saying it because I was trying not to think about it. It meant that tonight would almost certainly yield a new horror which I would have to face come tomorrow morning. I had had enough of such sights. Possibly I had had too much. On a day like this it was hard to shake the feeling that I was nearing some psychological terminus at a reckless and irrevocable velocity.

"So that is what *we* have," I summed up, with brittle emphasis. "What we don't have is anything in the way of witness testimony, any fingerprints or physical clues left at any of the scenes, or any clinical evidence that might help to identify a suspect. Therefore, after one month and fourteen bodies, *we* are still very much where we were at the outset. Which is to say, desultorily masturbating while the world goes to Hell."

I would not have used such a crude analogy if the woman had not insulted my professionalism. But Lumière didn't seem shocked or taken aback. She drained half of her brandy in one gulp, rolling it around her mouth before she swallowed. "When I masturbate, inspector," she said, "it's never desultory. Look out of the window."

I took a glance. The fog had settled in thickly, conclusively deciding the uneven struggle between afternoon and evening. "It's foul," I agreed.

"Not my point," said Lumière. "Now look at your plate."

I glanced down at my uneaten croissant and said, "Perhaps I was not so hungry as—"

The sentence remained unfinished as the pale woman lashed out, as quick as a snake. I was suddenly lying on the floor of the café with my own blood welling up thick and cloying in my mouth.

She stood over me, holding the stem of her broken brandy glass. Her face was calm and perhaps a little solicitous. "I'm sorry about that," she said. "But the liquor will sterilise the cut. And if it needs a stitch or two, I've got a kit right here in my pocket. Get up, inspector."

I did so, but I drew my Chamelot-Delvigne as I rose, and by the time I was on my feet again I had it pointed at her face. The café's other patrons had mostly remained seated, but were watching us warily. A debacle like this one could turn serious very quickly. Sam was watching too. He had picked up the stout shillelagh he kept behind the bar, but seeing that I had the situation in hand he made no move to deploy it.

"You're under arrest," I told Lumière coldly. "For assaulting a police officer."

She seemed unperturbed. "Tell me again about your croissant," she invited me.

"What?" I demanded. "What in the world are you . . . ?"

Once again I faltered into silence, although this time not because of an incised wound. It had been morning when I came into the café. That was why I had ordered a croissant. Now it was evening. The day had passed in the space between two breaths.

"Merde alors!" I exclaimed.

Lumière laughed. "I know, right? It gets easier to see through the bullshit, trust me, but the first time you pretty much have to be in severe pain. I got my hand slammed in a revolving door. Blessing in disguise, although I fucked and blinded like a longshoreman at the time. All these things are tied together, inspector. I can show you how. Are you up for this?"

I hesitated, but only for a heartbeat—and mostly because her idiom had left me a little confused. "Up for, *c'est quoi?*"

"Ready. Motivated. Inclined to pursue a specific course of action."

"Yes," I assured her. "I am very much up for this."

She took me first back to the site of the latest murder. There was no fog now. We had opened the door of the café to find the street cold, clear, and lamplit. "I tried three times with that Irishman," she told me as we walked through the frigid dusk. "Smacked him in the mouth, bit him, and stabbed his hand with a letter opener. He couldn't see it. So I thought I'd try you. Glad I did."

"You weren't tempted to work alone?" I asked her. "If you're still walking around loose after doing all those things to Mr Riordan you must be a woman of formidable talents."

"Thank you, Inspector Philemon. But this is much too big for me to handle on my own. Probably too big for the both of us together but hey, misery loves company."

My own misery did not. I almost said as much, but she slowed and stopped. We had come to the exact corner, the place where the dead man had been lying when I first arrived on the scene that morning (or an hour ago, for both of those statements seemed correct). There was no body to be seen now. The liveried doorman in front of the hotel stood with his hands clasped at his back, his fastidious sneer making any crime here seem not just impossible but *déclassé*.

"You said earlier," Lumière reminded me, "that there was no physical evidence left at the crime scenes. I think there is, but people are missing it for the same reason they miss all this messed-up time-shifting."

I looked around, but at first could see nothing.

"Try chewing your lip," Lumière suggested. "The torn bit. Stick your tongue in the wound to make it smart."

I felt no inclination to do that, and it wasn't necessary. Just grimacing so that the wound cracked open again was enough. I winced in pain, and at the same moment saw what I had failed to see before.

"The hotel!" I said, pointing. "I think . . . I'm almost sure . . . "

Wordlessly the pale woman handed me one of the photos she had tried to show me in the café. It was a photo of me that morning, standing exactly where I was standing now. To my left, a brass sign announced with many Romanesque flourishes that this was the Hotel Belle Époque.

Now it stated in stiffly serifed copperplate that it was the Waldorf Astoria.

"That . . . That isn't possible!" I whispered.

"And eighty-minute days are?" Lumière's tone was sardonic, even flippant, but there was tension in her face. She held out the rest of the photos for me to take.

I leafed through them with shaking hands. I easily recognised the common theme. Each of them showed one of the scenes where a body had been found. Each of them ignored the body and concentrated on the physical landmarks in its vicinity. A street sign, an awning, in one case the elegant neo-classical façade of the Bundesbank.

Looking at them made my head ache. I sensed in each case that a substitution had been made similar to that which I had just witnessed. Tverskaya Street had once been the Boulevard St Germain. The Hafiz Mustafa was formerly the Patisserie LaRochelle.

"What is happening?" I demanded. "What does all this mean?"

"I have no idea," Lumière said sourly. "All I know is that the murders are accompanied by these inexplicable phenomena. These transformations. And that most people walk right past them without even slowing down. They're completely unaware that anything has changed."

A memory struck me, coming out of nowhere. "This morning," I said. "Your hair was soaking, though the weather was dry."

Lumière nodded approvingly. "Very good, inspector," she said. "You're getting the hang of this. A block away, it was raining. I walked through it to get to the crime scene. The weather changes, as well as the buildings and the time of day. And as my last exhibit, suppose I were to ask you the name of this city? The one in which you've been living for—I would suppose—the last several years."

"I was born here," I told her. "Right here in . . . "

I had to struggle to finish the sentence. The word just wouldn't come. I twisted my lips to form the opening consonant, fought to push the breath out of my throat.

"Almost there," Lumière encouraged. Or did she mock me?

"Paris!" I yelled like a lost soul. "I was born in Paris!"

Lumière clutched my shoulders, her eyes shining. I was wrong, there was no mockery here. "Oh, nicely done!" she said. "Excellent! This was Paris once. But it takes an exceptional man to remember that. I knew as soon as I heard your voice, inspector, that you wouldn't let me down!"

I took no comfort from these words. Indeed it is hard to describe the anguish and rage I felt right then. I thought I was inured to sorrow, that it had become my element, but this new pain cut through the dullness of my despair like a scalpel. Paris was my home, my second mother, and she had been taken from me in the way a sneak-thief takes your wallet, *en passant*, leaving you none the wiser. I almost wept. I almost screamed.

Lumière put a hand on my shoulder. "Bear up," she told me, with gruff compassion. "There's work to be done."

I shook my head, meaning both that I would survive the blow and that I did not believe her. "What work?" I asked her, when I trusted myself to speak. "What can anyone do against this?"

"You're a cop investigating a murder. So I humbly suggest that you investigate. I've given you pretty much everything I've got. Now it's your turn. Maybe you can see something I haven't. Something that will let us come at this from another angle."

I was about to say that I had nothing. It would have been true only an hour before. But I realised, with a startling suddenness, that it was no longer true. Lumière's photographs had given me a fresh perspective on things I had thought I already knew. A kind of parallax. And from this novel position, novel vistas were abruptly visible.

"We must go to the precinct house," I told Lumière. "I need to access my files."

We rode on a trolley car whose route, according to the sign painted on its side, ran along Van Ness and Market Street. Upon reading those words, alien geography stirred obliquely in my mind. We got out at the Boulevard Raspail, however, and it looked—praise God!—the same as always. We walked past the statue of Napoleon, eclipsed now by the huge memorial to the dead and undead of our recent war. Grieving citizens had heaped the steps leading up to the memorial (two men facing each other over an open coffin) with bundles of cut flowers or in some cases bare branches.

I stopped to pay my respects. I did this nightly, seeming to leave behind each time a larger piece of my soul.

"Did you fight, inspector?" Lumière asked me.

I shrugged the question away. "Of course. Everyone fought who could. I would have given my life to keep the city from succumbing to that plague."

Lumière nodded and asked no more.

It was late. Or rather it seemed late. When we arrived at the precinct house there was no clerk on duty at the desk. We rode up in the rickety elevator, whose creaks have always seemed to me to be the complaints of an unhappy poltergeist. Normally I find that reflection amusing: just then it filled with foreboding those few hollows in my mind that were not already too full to take any more.

"So this is where you work," Lumière said, walking beside me down the rows of empty desks. "It's charming."

"It's an office," I replied brusquely, in no mood for badinage. "A place of work. It's not required to be charming. Only functional."

When we reached my desk I took off my jacket and the shoulder holster beneath it, hanging both on the back of my chair.

I pushed armloads of open files off my desk onto the floor. Each of them represented a stranger's life and some measurable part of my own, but right then they were unwelcome distractions. I unfolded the map on which I had plotted the current epidemic of murders, as a doctor might plot the spread of some actual epidemic. I added both today's and yesterday's to the tally, and then stood back to study the map at a distance.

"Is there something I should be seeing?" Lumière asked me.

"There is a pattern," I said. "There was already the suggestion of one, but with these two latest atrocities it stands out much more clearly."

Lumière leaned over the map, glaring at it in deep concentration. "There's no pattern," she said. "The placing of the bodies seems almost random. The Marais. Bloomsbury. Greenwich Village . . . "

My pride was a little restored at this proof that I saw some things more clearly than she did. "It's not random at all. We can join all the crime scenes with a single line, thus." I did it as she watched. "They are all, as you see, on the circumference of what one might loosely describe as a circle. Not a single body has been found within that circle. I am taking it for granted, of course, that the bodies are found some distance from where the victims were actually killed."

"Hence the lack of physical evidence."

"Exactly. So. The place where all these poor souls met their end must be somewhere within our circle," my hand hovered over the map, "and probably close to its centre. The murderer may well have thought that he was placing the bodies at random. Certainly he chose a random direction in which to walk after each killing. But he walked for more or less the same length of time, the same distance— so keen to keep his location secret that he was impelled always to stay on a straight line that led away from it."

I took a ruler from the desk drawer. "It might be possible, therefore," I said, "to use those same lines to track him backwards to his source. If we were to connect the dots through the centre, rather than around the periphery, we might be able to discern the centre of this atrocious web. The place where the spider sits."

"Do it!" Lumière urged me.

It was a rough and ready form of divination, at best. I took the northernmost and southernmost points and drew a line between them. Then I did the same for their nearest neighbours, and so on, going clockwise around the edge of the circle. Fourteen murders produced seven straight lines. There was no common centre, but it was close. Very close. All seven lines passed through the Rue Garancière, most of them within a hundred yards or so of the point where it is crossed by the Palatine. Something about that location pricked my memory in a way that was far from pleasant.

Lumière was staring at my face. "What?" she demanded.

I tapped the map. "There was a murder at exactly this point," I murmured. "Or at least, a possible murder. The body was never found. Only blood. A great deal of it. The man who called us said that there had been a body. That of a woman. But she was gone by the time we arrived. He said he had recognised her as one Sylvia Astor, a student of literature at the Sorbonne. I arrested and held him for a time, thinking that he might have killed and abducted the woman himself, but he knew no more than he had told us. And Sylvia Astor was not seen again."

Lumière's fixed stare still interrogated me. I shrugged, for I had nothing more to add. "This was before Monsieur Crâne began his reign of terror, of course. That has somewhat monopolised our attention since."

"How long before?"

"Five, perhaps six days." I held up my hand, for she seemed about to break in. "Yes, Lumière, I know. The timing is perfect for Mademoiselle Astor to have been the first victim. And the place of her death, if indeed she was killed, was here. Here at the confluence of these lines, at the very centre of the web."

"The Church of St Sulpice."

I nodded. "There is a stairwell at the side of the building, leading up from the crypt. The blood was pooled on the steps. If the woman had been attacked down there and then had tried—wounded, bleeding—to find her way back up to the street, that would match what I saw."

Lumière's face was cold and hard. Once again, she reminded me of a statue. "Is that enough evidence to call in a manhunt?" she demanded.

"More than enough," I assured her. "I will put it on my superintendent's desk as soon as he arrives tomorrow."

"I don't want to wait that long."

"No?" I confess I was not surprised. I felt the same

impatience myself. "What should we do then? I suppose I could call on him at his home, and ask him to swear out a warrant tonight."

"Or we could go there ourselves, right now, and make the arrest ourselves."

I pondered this invitation for several moments. It held some appeal. Clearly, however, I must not go to St Sulpice without leaving some record of my discovery. I found a scrap of paper and quickly scribbled down a message, a letter to Superintendent Faber explaining the discoveries we had made and what we now proposed to do. I took it to his desk, found an envelope and addressed it to him.

Lumière was at my shoulder the whole time, full of urgency. "Let's go, Philemon. You know there's going to be another murder tonight."

I hesitated, uncertain of where the letter would be the most likely to be seen. Finally, Lumière snatched it from my hand and tucked it under the arm of the winged Victory statue of which the superintendent is so inordinately proud.

"I said let's go," she repeated. Her voice had a grating edge to it and her eyes were dark. There was something personal at stake for her in this, clearly. Well, so there was for me also. I was desperate to see the face of the killer who was murdering not just my city's inhabitants but—however insane it sounded—my city herself.

The trolley car or the Métro would have taken us to St Sulpice, but Lumière set off at a brisk walk, almost a run. It seemed the urgency of our business and the agitation of her spirits would not allow her to wait. I fell in beside her.

"When we get there," I told her, "you should wait out on the street. It's unwise for both of us to go inside." She made no answer to this, but only speeded up her stride.

It was now well past midnight, if such terms retained any of their meaning. The streets were all but empty. Here a demimondaine staggered home from some sordid tryst, tottering on dysfunctionally high heels. There a homeless drunk sorted through the rubbish behind a trattoria in hope of finding either a late supper or an early breakfast. Nobody accosted us, or even seemed to see us.

The church's frontage, that breath-taking arcade with its towers and doubled array of columns, was completely dark. It had been closed by order of the city some years earlier, after a fire had all but destroyed it. It looked most unwelcoming. If a building could be said to have an aspect, the aspect of this one was solitary and introspective.

I approached the main doors. Above our heads, in faded black paint, was the legend that had been added to the façade in the days following the revolution. *Le Peuple Francais Reconnoit L'Etre Suprême et L'Immortalité de L'Âme.* It is good to be explicit about such things. A thick chain had been threaded through the handles of the doors and secured with a heavy padlock. There was no getting in that way.

"The crypt," I said, "is to the . . . " Lumière did not wait on my words, or my pointing finger. She led the way around the building to the north side, where a flight of marble steps led down into profound darkness. By the time I reached the top of the steps she was already at the bottom, invisible to me. Her voice floated back up to me. "There's a door!"

I followed, taking the steps with care. Even so I almost tripped and fell when I reached the bottom, the sudden levelling of the terrain deceiving and unbalancing me. I groped around until I felt the outline of the door Lumière had described. It stood open. From beyond it came a whiff of immemorial dust and damp.

Had I searched the crypt on the day when Sylvia Astor's body was found? I could no longer remember. Too many other bodies had intervened.

"Over here," Lumière's voice said from the pitch dark.

"I can't see you," I told her.

"Follow the sound of my voice."

I drew my service revolver and advanced. One step, a second, then a third. My skin was prickling, wanting to recoil from a touch it had not yet felt. There might be a murderer in this room with us. Monsieur Crâne, with his inexorable hammer and his burning madness.

"To the left," said Lumière.

I turned and moved in the direction of her voice.

I had gone perhaps two steps further when something bit down on my leg just above the ankle, all the way to the bone. The shock was almost as terrible as the pain. I screamed aloud, and fell to the stone floor, clutching at my injured leg. A band of thick metal had closed on it. Or rather two half-bands, for there were hinges or brackets at either end.

As I wrestled in vain with the trap, an electric torch clicked on a few feet away from me. Its beam was pointed directly at me so I could see almost nothing beyond it: only the vague outline of a shape that had to be Lumière.

"Sorry about that," she said.

I took aim with my revolver and fired it repeatedly. The forlorn click of the hammer striking an empty chamber sounded with each stroke of my finger on the trigger.

"Emptied it," Lumière said. "Back at the precinct. While you were writing this." She set the torch down, and an envelope right beside it. The envelope bore Superintendent Faber's name, in my own hand.

She sat down facing me, almost close enough to touch. But the leg-trap, I saw by her torch's light, was secured by a chain that was embedded somehow in the floor of this wide, low-ceilinged room. My freedom of movement was not very great.

"I hate to lie," Lumière said. "Especially to a man like you. A native. It goes against the grain. And since there's no need for it now, let me tell you that my name, when I was alive, was Sylvia Astor."

I must have groaned or cried out at this. Certainly I felt a movement of despair. We had fought so hard, so bitterly, to scour our city of the *zombis*, and now they were back.

"It's not as you think," Lumière assured me quickly. "Let me explain. You deserve that, at least."

What she told me was simple enough, and terrible enough. The undead had indeed been defeated, and eradicated. But their infected bodies had been laid in mass graves hastily dug in the city's many parks. The gardens of the Luxembourg Palace, the Champ de Mars, the woods of Boulogne.

The infection had continued to spread, unseen. It sank into the soil.

"The city got sick," Lumière said. "With the *zombi* sickness. It forgot what it was. It thought it was other cities of which it had heard or dreamed. Fantastic places with names like New York. London. Lima. Dublin. Some of the undead had been tourists. Perhaps the city could not tell their memories from its own.

"And it hungered, with the *zombi* hunger. It ate me first, after I committed suicide on the steps of this church. It drank from me and clutched me to its heart. I became its servant. Willingly. My memories of my old life were gone. I was reborn in that moment, a part of something very old, very strong and very beautiful."

Lutetia, I thought. The Roman name for Paris. And my city has always been called the City of Light, which is what *lumière* means.

"I procure the bodies, for the city to eat," the pale woman went on. "But I'm very careful. I have to get to know them first. Only native Parisians will do. Only those who can remember the city as it used to be. That way, when it assimilates your cerebral tissue it takes your memories too and is able to claim back some portions of itself." She smiled sadly. "I showed you the photos out of sequence, inspector. I hope this will console you. The changes . . . they're going the other way. Paris is remembering. With each death, each feeding, as she eats the brains of her *citoyens*, she heals. Recovers some of her lost memories."

"But the hotel," I objected. It was hard to think through the pain, but I wanted very much to understand. "The Belle Époque. It changed into a building from New York."

"Well that was me cheating," Lumière said. She actually blushed, which produced a strange effect on those bleached-bone cheeks. "The building didn't change at all. I just took down the old plaque and put up a new one. I paid the doorman ten francs to look the other way. I needed you to believe me, and to believe me you had to see with your own eyes. Or think you had seen."

She reached into the darkness beyond the torch's beam and retrieved, from somewhere, a sturdy hammer whose head was foul with blood and brains. "I use this," she said. "Mostly it's enough. The leg trap is for those who are biggest and most dangerous. To hold them still while I strike.

"I smash the skulls and pulp the brains. The brains are the part that matters, of course, and a semi-liquefied state seems to be best from the point of view of absorption. I scrape them up, take them away in a bucket or a picnic hamper and sow them in the parks and gardens where the *zombis* were buried. Apply the medicine to the site of the infection, as it were. *Je sème à tout vent*, like a good daughter of the Republic."

She paused, and regarded me. After a long moment she reached out to touch the back of my hand. "I really am sorry," she said softly. "You're wrong when you say that everyone fought against the *zombis*. A lot of people just ran and hid. I hate to take someone like you, who did his duty and never asked for thanks. But your memories are very vivid. You still speak French, which almost nobody else does. You eat croissants. You have a hip flask which I would bet good money is full of cognac. You're just too tasty, Inspector Philemon."

"That is not an accusation I've ever had to defend myself against," I answered her. Lumière laughed, but her face was sad.

"It's all right," I told her. And it was almost true, although I was afraid that having my brains bashed in would hurt. "Do what you have to do, Lutetia. I like the sound of being part of . . . what was it you said?"

"Something old and strong and beautiful. But I don't know if it will be the same for you, Philemon. The city drank my life-blood. Absorbed me. But it didn't devour me." She tapped her temple. "There's still a brain in here."

I considered this fine distinction, fascinated.

"Then let it absorb me too," I suggested at last. "And I'll help you find new subjects. The two of us together will be able to accomplish twice as much."

Lumière seemed taken aback. "You'd do that? As a policeman, you're pledged to protect and serve."

"To protect and serve the city. That was both the letter of my oath and its spirit."

Silence again. Lumière bowed her head and knelt in complete stillness for what felt like a very long time.

Then she looked up, and abruptly smiled. "She says yes," she told me. "We're going to be partners."

She gathered me into her arms, which were as hard and cold as funerary monuments. Something woke inside me, and opened. I did not recognise it at first, because it had been so long since I experienced it.

It was joy.

So now, you see, I have given you—in telling you my story—the most circumstantial explanation of your fate. You say you are not French, but your accent is good and your grasp of idiom very convincing. You certainly have very recent and very vivid memories of the city.

I look forward to sharing them.

My first five novels were all part of a single series and featured the same protagonist: Felix Castor, an exorcist for hire in an alternate version of London where the dead have begun to rise. Castor is the narrator too, and although he uses a very British idiom the inspiration for his voice came in the first place from Raymond Chandler. Castor is very much in the mould of a Chandleresque private detective, morally compromised but fundamentally decent, haunted by his own bad choices and by a desire to do the right thing in a world that always seems to pull in the opposite direction. ¶ One of the pleasures of writing the series was building up the supporting cast: the succubus Juliet; Rafi Ditko, who thanks to Castor is a horse for the demon Asmodeus; fellow exorcists like Gil McClennan and Trudie Pax; and the reclusive zombie, Nicky Heath. ¶ I loved writing Nicky, even though in many ways he's a terrifically unlikeable character. A conspiracy theorist, a misanthrope, and a world-class pain in the arse, he lives in an abandoned cinema that he's fitted with his own version of climate control in the form of industrial freezers. But it's hard not to love a lover, at least a little bit, and Nicky's passions (for movies, red wine, and early jazz) are heartfelt and obsessive. He's also really smart, and Castor uses him mostly as a paid researcher when he needs esoteric information fast. ¶ This is sort of an origin story for Nicky. It doesn't feature Castor at all, apart from one very off-hand reference.

HERE'S MY problem with dead people: they fall apart.

Okay, I grant you, the transition to being a stiff is a shock to the system. You wake up one morning, and you feel like shit: death warmed up, as they say, or rather death cooling rapidly towards background ambient. You feel for a pulse: not verifiably present. But is that because it's not there, or because you're a klutz and you can't take a pulse?

You can't feel a heartbeat either. That's ominous, because you're so fucking scared by this time that your heart should be racing, not parked at the kerb with the hand-brake on.

You draw a ragged, stressy breath . . . and it just stays there. Nowhere to go. Your body isn't metabolising oxygen anymore, and your formerly autonomic functions are all unplugged from the board. The pressure doesn't build. You could keep that breath pent up behind your teeth for a minute, an hour, a day and a half, and you're never going to feel the slightest need to let it out again.

The sign on the door just flipped, from OPEN to CLOSED. This is it. Grammatically, you can never start a sentence with "I am" again. It's was-not-was, all the way.

But that's no reason to let up, is what I'm saying. Too many people use death as an excuse, and I'm sick of hearing it. The world's still out there, people. It's not going away. The rules of the game didn't change because you croaked, and like they say, if you don't get back in the saddle you're gonna end up trampled and covered in horseshit. Your choice.

I used to be a stockbroker, which is probably what killed me. Or rather, being a great broker is what killed me—having the kind of obsessive edge that took me to the top of the NASDAQ while most of my respected peers were still flossing their teeth and picking out a tie that matched their hand-stitched braces.

It's a tough gig, don't mistake me. When you're playing a bunch of DAX-listed stormtroopers off against a third-party boiler room, taking a trim on buy and sell at the same time and cutting your T+3s so tight there's no skin left on your fingertips, it's a bit like riding a log flume must be. Hundreds of millions of euros are rolling under you, behind you, and you know damn well if you lose the flow and try to stop it before it's ready, you'll go down and never see daylight.

So yeah, there's a certain level of stress that you live with. I won't say "thrive on", because that's macho bullshit: the adrenalin surge is pleasant for about a half an hour, tops: after that your body starts shaking itself to pieces and you're swallowing heartburn. A day in the dealing room is a day in the slaughterhouse: you come out of it with other people's blood and sweetmeats spattered on your shirt, and that's if you've done okay. If you fucked up, it's your own.

I had my first heart attack when I was twenty-six. I usually tell the story so it happened on my actual birthday, but in fact it was the day after. I'd been out all night, flying high on wings of coke and frozen Stolichnaya, then I showered, popped a few dexies, and went back to work. The two guys I was with, they did the same thing, more or less, but they flaked out in the course of the morning—

sneaked off to the room with the folding beds that the management lays on for quitters, to keep the crash at bay with a snatched half-hour of sleep. I kept right on going, because I was on one of those flux-market rolls where nobody knows what's happening and you can squeeze the shit from one exchange to another to ride lag on a price you already know is falling. Too good to miss.

But like in a bad movie, I start to get a reverb on my hearing. Well, okay, what the fuck? I don't need to hear properly to see the numbers scrolling up the screen. I'm low-pointing, I'm settling, I'm re-staking dead buys, I'm making those Tokyo asswipes breathe my farts and think it's good fresh air.

And then I'm on the ground, with a couple of invisible sumo wrestlers sitting on my chest. Tokyo's revenge, I think, as I black out.

Three days at the Portland Clinic on caviar and tenectaplase. Back in the saddle, clip clop, clip clop. Because the guys who stop never start again, and that's the gospel truth. I've seen it enough times to know that it's a natural law.

The second attack caught me by surprise, because this time I wasn't even working: I was with a woman—using "with" to denote the act of coitus. Normally I'm pretty good at sex: I can reach a plateau and stay there for as long as I like until my partner of choice is ready to join me for the final pull towards the summit. On this particular occasion, however, the lady had to struggle out from underneath my inert body and call the emergency services. I'd been wearing her panties as a party hat, and I still was when I woke up—not at the Portland but at the Royal Free. Fucking paramedics. They ripped off my diamond cufflinks too, but how the hell do you prove it? When you're unconscious, people can take all the liberties they like.

So that was two, and the doctors said I should expect strike three to come over the plate pretty damn soon if I didn't change up and get myself some Zen-like calm. I didn't waste any time on that prescription: I am what I am, and I play to my strengths.

So I looked death square in his poker face, I saw what he was holding, and I implemented plan B.

Look, this isn't just me talking big, okay? I don't need to impress a z-list shmuck like you, and in any case it's basic. Basic stuff. Anyone with any sense can take the temperature and pack for the weather they know is rolling in.

The dead started coming back a few years ago now, around the turn of the new millennium. Actually it probably started a whole lot earlier than that, but that was when the trickle turned into a flood. Some of them come back in the spirit, some in the body. An acquaintance of mine who makes what he humorously calls a living as an exorcist says it's all the same thing: zombies are people whose ghosts cling to their own dead flesh out of fear or stubbornness or sheer habit, and learn by trial and error how to get things moving again. You hear crazier stories too—human ghosts ram-raiding animal bodies and doing a little forcible redecorating. Formative causation, they call it, or some other bullshit periphrasis: you look like what you think you should look like, at least most of the time. But the animal soul is still in there with you, and when you're at your weakest it will try and slip out from under. That, the so-called experts tell us, is what werewolves are.

Ghost, zombie, or loup-garou: those were the options I was looking at, assuming I didn't just go gentle into that goodnight like some passive-aggressive moron. So I planned accordingly, in between strike two and strike three. I had a shed-load of money put by already—salted away against a retirement I clearly wasn't going to live to enjoy. Now I put some of that cash to work, although first of all I set up a Celtic knot of offshore-registered shelf companies to handle my assets: dead men can't legally own jack-shit, but corporations are immortal. I bought a lot of real estate, because the property bubble had finally burst, around about then, and you could pick up some really sweet deals. Partly I was just diversifying my holdings, but I was also looking for a place where I could set up post mortem. What I needed was a pied-à-terre that was both huge and invisible—standing on its own grounds, because nosey neighbours would be the last thing I needed.

I settled on a disused cinema in Walthamstow: the Gaumont. It was going for a song, despite having a Cecil Masey façade and most of the interior fixtures and fittings still intact. Nineteen-thirties vintage, and it had never been either burned out or turned into a bingo hall. It had been a porno theatre briefly, but I wasn't too worried about sticky carpets. In fact, I wasn't worried about the auditorium at all. I stripped out the projection booth and fitted it with a bespoke arrangement of air conditioning and freezer units. Temperature and humidity control were going to be key.

Somewhere around then was where my personal extinction event happened. RIP, Nicholas Heath: no flowers or known grasses, by request. But I'd been expecting it. It was, you know, a bump in the road. Nothing more. I'd already decided which kind of dead man I was going to be, and I'd made sure that the funeral parlour would hold off on the burial for at least a week, to give the other shoe a chance to drop.

To be honest with you, I don't like to talk about that part of it. Some people say they see tunnels, blinding white lights, heavenly messengers or moving stairways. I didn't see anything. But I did have the sense of not being completely in control, and that fucking scared me. I mean, for all I knew it could be a lottery. Maybe you didn't get to choose which way the ball would bounce. I might find myself looking like Casper the friendly fuckwit, or Lassie, or in some other stupid, inconsequential, unworkable shape. Or nothing. Nothing at all. Not all the dead come back, even now.

But I did: and I came back as me. I sat up on the morgue slab, signed myself out, collected my effects and hit the road. Forget about statutory notice, or packing up any of the stuff from my apartment. Dead men aren't covered by contract: my job was gone, my casa was someone else's casa, and the landlord had probably already changed the locks. I headed straight for the Gaumont, bolted the doors and got on with the job.

It was good timing, in a way: I'd finally got the air conditioning units working properly at two degrees Celsius, and I had the place all set up to move into. Which was just as well, because it was the last moving I did for a while: the fucking rigor mortis hits you right after you sit up and look around, and for the next twenty-four hours it's all you can do to roll your eyes to the heavens.

So I'm lying there, in the dark, because I didn't get a chance to turn the lights on before my muscles seized up, and I'm running through the list in my mind.

Rancidification.

Black putrefaction.

Butyric fermentation.

Dry decay.

These, collectively, were the joys now in store for me. And every second I wasted meant more hassle later, so as soon as the rigor passed, I spat on my hands—figuratively speaking—and started taking the appropriate measures.

Rancidification, the first stage, is far and away the most dangerous. That's when all the fluids in your body rot and go sour. The smell is fucking indescribable, but that's not what you've got to worry about. The souring releases huge quantities of gas, which builds up in your body cavity wherever there's a void for it to collect in. If you don't do something about it, the pressure of the gas can do huge damage to your soft tissues—rip you open from the inside out. But if you make incisions to let out the gas, every hole is a problem that has to be managed at the putrefaction stage.

I got a long way with some ordinary plastic tubing, which I shoved into a great many places I'm not keen to talk about. In the end I had to make some actual incisions, but I kept them to a minimum: I was also helped by an amazing substance called Lanobase 18, which is what undertakers use to soak up the fluid leaking from your internal organs and turn it into an inert, almost plasticised slurry.

As far as the putrefaction stage went, I was already ahead of the game just by having a cold, controlled space of my own. No insects to lay their eggs in my mouldering flesh; no air- or ground-borne contaminants. I used that time to start the embalming process; I needed it because by now my stink had matured into something really scary. I kept having to pour cologne onto my tongue to blitz what was left of my airway and nasal passages, because even though I wasn't inhaling the smell was still getting through to me somehow.

By the time I hit phase three, I was more than half pickled—and now it started to get easier. What was left of my flesh changed its consistency, over the space of a couple of weeks, into something hard and waxy. Adipocere, they call it. It's kind of unsettling at first, because it doesn't feel like anything even slightly organic, but it has the huge upside that it doesn't smell of anything much. I could live with myself now.

Dry decay mainly affects your bones, through a leeching of organic compounds called diagenesis, so I just let it happen and turned my attention to other things.

Unfortunately, I'd missed a trick or two while all this was going on. I had the projection booth itself and the adjacent generator room armoured up like the fucking führer-bunker, but I hadn't bothered with all the ground-floor doors and windows. I didn't think I'd need to: the Gaumont had stood empty and undisturbed for so many years—who was going to pay it any attention now?

But the key word there is *undisturbed*. I'd had a whole lot of kit delivered when I was setting up my freezer and air conditioning arrays, and I'd had some guys in to reinforce the upstairs walls and doors. I might as well have put out a fucking welcome mat: I was telling all the neighbourhood deadbeats that the cinema was now inhabited, and that it might contain something worth stealing.

In point of fact, it didn't: everything that was valuable was locked away behind steel bulkhead doors up on the first floor. But that didn't stop a variegated collection of scumbags from breaking in downstairs, smashing the windows and ransacking what was left of the old furniture, looking for something they could purloin, pawn or piss into. Some of them had even moved in, and were now squatting in the auditorium or the storerooms behind it.

First things first. I made some calls, using one of the false names and email addresses I'd set up for my offshore holding company, and hired some guys from a private security firm to come in and clear out the squatters' little rat nest. They threw everything out into the street: then they maintained a presence while I got the builders to come back in and make the place secure.

Steel shutters on the ground-floor windows; steel bulkhead doors over the old wooden doors, attached to I-beams sunk two feet into freeway-mix concrete. I had the work team coat the window sills and door frames with green anti-vandal paint too: the losers could still sleep in the fucking doorway if they wanted to, but I wasn't going to make it comfortable for them, and that was as far as they were going to get. As a dead man walking, I was too vulnerable: I wanted to have the freedom of the building, without worrying about who I might run into. In any case, this was my retirement home now: why the hell should anyone else get the benefit of it? That's not how life works—take it from a dead man.

Relaxing isn't something I do all that well, but now I felt like I could finally slow down and take stock. I'd ridden out the roller coaster of physical decomposition, at least to the point where I could maintain a steady state; I had my place secured and my lines of communication laid down so that I could get what I needed from the outside world without dealing with it directly.

I took a day off. Watched some movies on cable. Opened a bottle of Pauillac and sniffed the wine-breath, since drinking it without any digestive enzymes was an idiot's game.

It was half a day, actually. Half a day off. By the afternoon I was restless, worried about what I might be missing. I fired up the computers—three of them, each registered with a different ISP and apparently logged on in a different time zone—and put some of my money back into play on the New York exchange.

That was a good afternoon, and an even better evening. Stress couldn't touch me now—look Ma, no glands—I couldn't get tired, and I didn't need to take bathroom breaks, so I kept going steadily through a fourteen-hour session, not logging off until the exchange closed.

Then I switched to the Nikkei-Dow and did the same, for another five hours.

Man, I thought, this is . . . you know . . . liberating. Death means never having to wipe your ass again: never getting pulled out of the zone by your body's needs, or by someone else blabbing in your ear like they've got something to say. It means you can keep going forever, if you want to.

Of course, forever is a long time. A long, long, long fucking time.

On day three, the deadbeats broke in again. They'd actually sneaked back while the concrete was still setting, and pushed one of the steel plates up out of line, so they could work it loose later with a crowbar. I could hear them doing the same thing with the door of the projection room—my fucking holy of holies.

Yeah, dream on, you verminous little bastards. That door, and the wall it was set in, was about as porous as a bank vault: not needing to breathe meant not having to cut corners where personal security was concerned. All the same, I couldn't stop thinking about what would have happened if the door had been open—if I'd been down on the ground floor picking up my mail or something. I couldn't take that risk again.

This time I thought it through properly: defence in depth was what I needed, not one big-ass door with one big-ass bolt on it. I had the builders—none of whom ever met me in person, of course—completely redesign the ground floor, replacing all the existing walls with steel bulkheads and at the same time putting in a whole lot of new ones. I took my inspiration from the crusader forts of the late Middle Ages, turning the Gaumont into three separate keeps, one inside the other. Only a single vault door connected the outer keep with the middle one, and the middle keep with the inner one. Other doors were devoid of bolts, locks or handles: they were all independently lockable via a computer-controlled system, and the first thing I did was to slave the whole damn thing to the main server up in the projection booth. I put CCTV cameras in too—dozens of them, set up so there were no dead angles. I could check out any given stretch of corridor, any given room, and make sure it was clear before I opened the doors and cleared myself a route.

What? This sounds like overkill? No, genius, it wasn't. I was thinking things through, that's all. Every fortress can turn into a trap, so every fortress needs a back door. And this particular fortress needed a mail slot too, because for some of the things I was doing online I still needed physical documents, physical certification, actual rather than digital signatures. It's stupid, but it's true: some parts of the world haven't started surfing the electron tide yet, and they only believe in what they can hold in their hands. Hah. Maybe not so stupid, when you think about it.

So now I can swing back into top gear, stop watching my back. And I do. Believe me, I do.

To tell you the truth, I got lost in it. I must have spent a week or more at a time just bouncing from one exchange to another in an endless, breakneck rhythm. You know those velodromes, where the racers ride their bikes almost horizontally on the canted walls? Well, that's what I was like. The only thing that kept me touching the ground at all was my unthinkable velocity. Which is fine, so long as you never slow down.

But I did.

It was subtle at first—subtle enough that I didn't even realise it was happening. I missed a spike here, came in slow on a deal there: not big things, and not connected. I was still coming out ahead, and still in control. It took me a couple of days to realise that I was too much in control: that I was going through the motions without feeling them, and making conscious decisions instead of letting instinct play through me.

I tied down, cashed in, and logged off. Sat there in silence for a while, staring at the screens. A wave of grief swept through me, and I don't care if that sounds stupid: a sense of bereavement. Nicky Heath was dead. I hadn't really got that fact in my head until then.

If you stop, you never start again: my own golden rule. But I didn't feel like I could touch the keyboard right then. I was afraid of screwing up: afraid of hitting some rock I would have seen a mile off back when I had a functioning endocrine system. Look Ma, no glands.

I think I must have been hearing the noises in the walls for a while before that: bangs and scrapes and scuffles, muffled not by distance but by the thickness of the brickwork and the layers of steel plating. But now I let myself listen to them. Jumbled, discontinuous, slightly different each time. It wasn't the freezer unit, or the big electrical generator downstairs. The only things that made noises like that were living things. People. Animals. Members of the big but still exclusive club of entities-with-a-pulse.

I turned on the CCTV monitors and did the rounds of the cameras. She wasn't hard to find, once I started looking: she was in the outer keep, way down on the ground floor, in a blind stretch of corridor between two of my self-locking doors—nowhere near the big steel portal that led through into the middle zone.

It was still a nasty shock, though. Sort of like scratching your balls and coming up with a louse.

From what I could see, she had to be one of the homeless people: probably in her early twenties, but looking a damn sight older, huddled in way too many layers of clothes in a corner made by the angle of wall and door. She had dirty-blonde hair and a sullen, hangdog face. Hard to tell anything else, because she was folded down into herself, knees hugged to her chest and head down. It was probably cold down there, in spite of all the layers.

Where the hell had she come from? She couldn't have been in there since the last invasion, because I wouldn't have missed her and in any case she'd be dead by now. There wasn't anything to eat or drink, and she clearly hadn't brought anything in with her that she couldn't carry in her pockets.

I backtracked with the cameras until I found the smoking pistol: a vent pipe for one of the freezer units that had been run through the outer wall of the building. She'd just hit it with something—a hammer or a stone—again and again until the flimsy metal bent back on itself far enough for her to squeeze through. That had let her into a part of the building that was on the route I used when I went down to collect the mail. She must have scooted through a door or two that was unlocked when I came through, and then got caught in the dead-end stretch of corridor when I made the return journey and locked up again.

She'd tried to get out: those were the sounds I'd heard. She'd hammered and clawed at the door and probably screamed for help, but only faint echoes had come up to the projection room, and I'd been too absorbed in what I was doing to decipher them.

Now she looked to be in a bad way. The monitor only

resolved in black and white, but there were dark patches on her hands which I assumed were probably blood—her fingernails damaged from trying to pull on the edge of the door-jamb—and when she briefly came out of her huddle to grab a gulp of air I saw that her lips were swollen in a way that suggested dehydration.

I got up and paced around the room, trying to think it through. I wasn't capable of panic, but I felt a dull blunt volume of unhappiness expand inside me, like the intestinal gases back in the first stage of decay.

I could just let her die, was the first thought that came to mind.

I could open up the doors to let her back out the way she'd come, but she might be too weak to move. She might die anyway.

If I opened the doors, someone else could get in. Safer just to leave her.

But someone could have seen her climbing inside, and not coming out again. Someone might be looking for her right now, or calling the police, or crawling through that hole with torches and crowbars and . . .

No, nobody else had found the hole. The CCTV cameras didn't show anyone else, either in the room where the vent let out or anywhere else in the outer keep. I should have put more sophisticated alarms in, I thought irrelevantly: movement sensors, or infra-red scanners, or something. I shouldn't have let this happen. Now here I was, already guilty of false imprisonment or some such bullshit, with the police probably searching the goddamn neighbourhood and Christ only knows what kind of trouble to look forward to if she was found here, alive or dead or anywhere in between.

I stopped pacing because I'd come up hard against a wall. I wanted to punch it, but that would have been a really stupid thing to do: no blood flow, so no scabbing, no skin repair. Any wound I opened in my own flesh would stay open unless I sewed it shut.

I stared at the wall for maybe five minutes, galloping through the same rat-runs inside my head. When I'd done it enough times to be sure they always ended up in the same place, I got moving again.

I had no choice. I had to bring the dumb bitch up to good-as-new spec before I cut her loose. I had to make sure there was no harm and no foul, whatever that took.

I found a bucket the builders had left behind, and a washbasin in what had once been a cleaner's cupboard behind the projection booth. I cleaned the bucket out as far as I could, then filled it with cold water. I flicked some switches on the main board, releasing the locks on all but one of the doors between me and the woman—leaving just the door that she was leaning against.

Then I went down, let myself out through the inner and middle keeps and made my way around to her stretch of corridor. She must have heard me coming, because when I turned the last bend I caught the sound of her fists banging on the other side of the door, and her voice, muffled through the thick wood, telling me she was stuck.

I left the bucket of water right in front of the door and went back up to the projection booth. I watched the woman on the CCTV hook-up: she was still hammering and shouting, pushing at the door, thinking or at least hoping that someone could hear her.

I relocked all the other doors before opening just that one. Since she was leaning her weight against it, she just tumbled through when it opened. She saw the bucket, stared at it with big incredulous eyes, and finally cupped her hands and drank from it. She coughed up a storm, and vomited a little too, but she was alive, at least. That was a good start.

Food was more of a problem, because unless a few hardy rats were down in the basement somewhere, there was nothing edible in the entire building. I got around that by going to the Ocado website, whose online order form allows you to specify exactly where you want the food to be dropped off. I specified the mailbox, which was actually a double-doored receptacle like the ones post offices use—big enough to take thick bundles of legal paper, and as it turned out, big enough for a bag of groceries too.

I ordered stuff she could eat cold, to keep things simple: turkey breast; bread rolls; a bag of ready-cut carrot slices; some apples. I added some fun-sized cartons of orange juice, and then on an impulse a bar of Cadbury's Dairy Milk.

This time I had to approach her from the opposite direction, since she'd gone through the door to get to the water bucket, and was now on the other side of it. It didn't matter: from the master board up in the projection booth, I could open up any route I liked, and make absolutely sure of where she was before I moved in, did the drop-off, and retreated again to the booth and the CCTV monitors.

At the sound of the lock clicking, she went scooting back through like one of Pavlov's dogs.

She wolfed the food down like she hadn't seen bread since the Thatcher years. It was a fucking unedifying sight, so I turned off the CCTV and left her to it for a while.

The next time I checked, she was done. The floor was strewn with wrappers, apple cores, a crumpled juice carton. The woman had spotted the camera, and was staring at it as though she expected it to start talking to her. Actually, it could do that if I wanted it to—the cameras came with a speaker as standard. But I didn't have anything I wanted to say to her: I just wanted her to eat, drink, wash, fix herself up, and fuck off out of there.

Wash. Okay. I ordered some more groceries, and added soap and shampoo to the list—not to mention another bucket. The next time I fed her, I left both drinking water and wash water, but she didn't take the hint—maybe because the water was cold. Too bad. I didn't have any way of heating it up, and I wasn't running a fucking guesthouse.

I spent about three days plumping her up. On the second day I left her some plasters and antiseptic for her fingers, which she ignored just like the wash water. On the third day I made a similarly useless gesture with some clean clothes, ordered online in the same way from the Asda superstore at Brentwood.

Okay, so my reluctant houseguest wasn't interested in personal hygiene, even on a theoretical level. I don't know, maybe the dirt acts like insulation out on the street: and maybe after the first month or so your panties get welded to your privates past the point where you can take them off. Maybe not, though, since she had to be managing to piss somehow. Following that thought through, I realised it was probably a good thing that the cameras had such crappy resolution. I could see the corner she was using as a latrine, now that I looked for it, and I sure as hell didn't want to see it any clearer.

Well, the bottom line was that she had to go out looking no worse than when she came in: I wasn't under any obligation to make her look better.

On day four I drew her a map, showing her how to get back to the vent pipe, and left it with the food. Then I threw the lock on the door behind her, and all the other locks leading back to the outer wall and her exit point.

She examined the map as she ate her breakfast, which was croissant and apricot jam. She'd shown a real taste for pastries by this time, and none at all for fresh fruit or cereal.

But after she'd finished, she didn't make a move to step over the threshold. She just wiped her mouth on the napkin provided, dropped it into the water bucket—which always drove me crazy because I had to fish the fucking thing out again—and settled back down against the wall.

What was she playing at? She had to realise I was allowing her to leave.

"Come on!" I shouted at the monitor. "Get out of there. You're free as a bird. Go!"

She settled into her characteristic, head-bowed huddle. Impulsively, I flicked the microphone switch on the

CCTV board. I'd never used it before, so I had no idea if it even worked, but a light flashed on the board and the woman jerked her head up as though she'd just heard something: a click, maybe, or else a little feedback flutter from the speaker.

"Hey," I said. "What do you think you're doing? Time to go, lady."

She blinked twice, her face full of comical wonder. She took her time about answering, though, and when she did it was kind of a non sequitur.

"Who are you?" she demanded.

"The owner," I said, and then, not to be put off, I repeated "Time for you to get out of here."

She shook her head.

I blinked. "What do you mean, no?" I asked, too incredulous even to be pissed off. "This is my place, sweetheart. Not yours. You're not wanted here."

The woman just shrugged. "But I like it here."

The way she said it made me want to go down there and upend the water bucket on her head. She sounded like a little kid asking if she could stay a bit longer at the beach.

"How can you like it?" I demanded, really annoyed now. "It's a fucking corridor. What, you like sleeping on concrete?"

"That's what I was doing outside," she said, calmly enough. "And at least here I don't have homeless guys wanting to charge me a blowjob for a place by the fire."

"Because there is no fire."

"But there is food."

"Food's off," I said bluntly. "That was the last of it."

She put her head between her folded arms again, as a way of telling me the conversation was over.

"I mean it," I said. "Food's off. You stay here, you starve to death."

She didn't answer. Fine, so she wanted to be alone. I turned off the sound and left her to it.

"Dumb bitch," I said to the monitor, even though she couldn't hear me now.

That was going to be the first item in a varied agenda of invective, but I realised suddenly what had just happened: what was still happening. I was angry. I'd managed to get angry, somehow, even though on the face of it I didn't have the necessary equipment anymore.

If I could do anger, then presumably I could do other flashy emotional manoeuvres too. Quickly I fired up my computers and logged onto my US trading board. I didn't surface for five hours, and by that time I was three hundred thousand up on the day.

Saint Nicholas was back, with gifts of ass-kickings for all.

After I closed out on the day, I checked in with the woman. She seemed to be asleep, but she stirred when I clicked the mike back on.

"What's your name, darling?" I asked her.

"Janine," she muttered, looking muzzily to camera.

"I'm Nick."

"Hi, Nick."

"You can stay here tonight," I said. "Tomorrow we'll talk."

But we didn't. Not much anyway. I made a food drop at 6:00 a.m., before she was even awake, then came back upstairs and logged on. I had another good day on the markets, and the day went by in a blur. I did order a folding bed, though, and some blankets and pillows to go on it. I picked a local store that could deliver immediately, had them leave it round by the back door and lugged it in myself after they'd gone. It made my skin prickle just a little to be in the outside air again, even though it wasn't a warm day or anything. Just psychosomatic, I guess.

Over the next few days, I furnished Janine's corridor pretty lavishly. She furnished, it, I should say: all I did was buy the stuff and bring it to the door, then let her choose for herself where to put it. I'd started to leave the mike on by this time so she could tell me what she wanted: a chair and a table, a kettle for making tea, a chemical toilet, even a little portable DVD player and a few movies for her to watch while I was busy on the trading boards.

The weirdest thing of all, though, was that I actually started talking to her while I was dealing. It seemed to help me concentrate, in some way I couldn't quite define. Most of the things she liked to talk about were stupid and irritating: her favourite celebrities; previous seasons of *Big Brother*; her hatred for super-models. I just made "I'm still listening" noises whenever they seemed to be called for, and channelled the aggravation into some world-class short-selling.

It got so that if she actually shut up for a while, I'd throw in a question or two to get her talking again. Questions about herself she didn't like to answer, except to say that she was living on the street because of something that had happened between her and her stepfather back when she turned eighteen. I got the impression that it had been a violent and dramatic kind of something, and that the stepfather had got the worst of the deal.

"He came on to you?" I asked, genuinely—if slightly— curious.

"I suppose. He came into the bathroom when I was showering one morning, and tried to get in with me."

"That's pretty unequivocal," I allowed.

"Pretty what?"

"Clear cut. Hard to misinterpret."

"Yeah, right. So I smacked him in the mouth with the showerhead, really hard, and then I ran out."

"Naked?"

"No, Nick. Not naked."

"Then you were showering in your street clothes?"

A pause. "I didn't run out straight away. He fell down and hit his head. I had time to grab some stuff."

This was in Birmingham, Janine told me, as if I

could possibly have mistaken her accent. She'd taken a bus down to London the same day, hoping to stay with a friend who was studying hairdressing and beauty at Barnet College. But the friend had acquired a boyfriend, and wasn't keen on that arrangement. She passed Janine off to another girl, whose floor she occupied for a while. Not a very long while, though: there was an argument about the rules for the use of the bathroom, and she was out on her ear again before the end of the week.

I was starting to see why Janine wasn't big on washing.

"So what about you, Nick?" she asked me, when we'd been doing this for maybe a week or so. "What do you do for a living?"

"Well," I said, "when you put it like that, Janine, the answer has to be nothing."

"I can hear you typing away up there," she said. "Are you writing a book?"

"Yeah," I lied. "I'm writing a book. But it's not to earn a living."

"How come? You're already rich?"

"I'm already dead," I said.

That remark led to a very long silence. The next time I checked on her, she was asleep.

In the morning, she asked me if she could see me.

"The cameras only work one-way," I pointed out.

"I don't mean on the cameras. I mean, you know, face to face."

"I'll think about it," I lied.

But she wouldn't leave the idea alone: she kept bringing it up last thing at night, when I was logging off and cashing in. I kept being evasive, and she kept going quiet on me, which was fucking annoying. I'd say goodnight, get nothing back: she went to sleep each night surrounded by a miasma of hurt silence.

In the end, I did it by accident. Almost by accident, I should say. When I unlocked the doors one morning so

I could drop off a food delivery, I flicked one switch too many. She was waiting for me as I turned the corner, leaning against the open door with her arms folded in a stubborn, take-no-prisoners kind of pose. The crazy thing is, I sort of knew on some level that I'd done it—that I'd opened the final door and removed that last degree of prophylaxis between us. I just didn't let myself think about it until we were face-to-face and it was too late to back out.

She stared at me for a long time in silence. Then her face wrinkled up in a sort of slo-mo wince. "You look horrible," she said.

"Thanks," I answered inadequately. "You say the sweetest fucking things."

That made her laugh just a little, the sound pulled out of her almost against her will. She took a few steps towards me, then stopped again and sniffed the air cautiously.

"What's that smell?" she wanted to know.

"Which one? I have a complex bouquet."

"It's like . . . antiseptic, or something."

"Formaldehyde, probably. I'm pickled inside and out, Janine. It's why I don't smell of rotten meat."

"You smell of that too."

I bridled at that—like some living guy accused of having bad body odour. "I don't," I said. "I went to a lot of fucking effort to—"

She made a gesture that shut me up—kind of a pantomime of throwing up her hands in surrender, except that she only threw them up about an inch or so. "I'm sorry," she said. "You're right. You don't smell rotten. You just look like you should smell rotten. Your skin is all waxy and sweaty, and I can see stitches in your neck."

My carotid artery was one of the places where I'd inserted a trocar to draw off some of my bodily fluids way back when I was fighting the war on rot. "Don't get me started," I advised her.

So she didn't.

"Show me where you live," she suggested instead.

She stayed upstairs with me for an hour or so, wrapped in three coats against the cold. Then she retired back to her little dead-end corridor home sweet home, and spent the rest of the day watching movies. Musicals, mostly: I think she was plugging herself back into the world of the living to make sure it was still there.

The next day I bought her a couple of hot water bottles, and she was able to stay longer. I didn't mind the bottles, so long as she kept them under the coats so the heat stayed right against her skin. The thermostats were still set at the same level, so the room didn't warm up at all, and she didn't come close enough to me for the heat to be a problem.

I think that was the first day I forgot to lock her in, and after I'd forgotten once, it kind of felt like going back to that state of affairs would be a slap in the face to her—a way of saying that I thought I could trust her, but then decided I didn't, after all.

That thought raised all kinds of other thoughts, because it suggested that I did trust her. There was no reason why I should. Back when I was alive, I'd never felt more for people like her than a kind of queasy contempt, mixed with the unpleasant sensation that usually translates—by some spectacular whitewashing process—as "there but for the grace of God".

But God doesn't have any grace, and I don't have the time or the temperament for helping lame ducks over stiles. If I meet a lame duck, generally speaking, I make duck à l'orange.

So what the fuck was going on here anyway?

At first, I justified it to myself by counting up my market winnings. Janine could make me feel things again, as though my endocrine system was pumping away like it did in the old days—and that gave me a lot of my wonted edge back. But plausible as that explanation was, it was ultimately bullshit. After a week or so,

I was spending more time talking to her than I was in managing my portfolios. A week after that, I wasn't even bothering to log on.

At this point I was even making a loss on the deal, because I kept buying her stuff. It wasn't even stuff she needed to live anymore: it was chocolates and beer and doughnuts and even—I swear to God—a fucking hat.

You're probably thinking that there was some kind of a sexual dynamic going on. Janine certainly thought so. When I presented her with the final little chatchke—the straw that broke the camel's neck, so to speak—she stared at it for a long time without reaching out to take it. She looked unhappy.

"What?" I demanded. "What's the matter? It's just a necklace. See, it's got a J on it, for Janine. Those are diamonds, you realise. Little ones, but still . . . "

She looked me squarely in the eye—no coyness, no pissing around. "Do I have to blow you to sit at the fire?" she asked.

I thought about that. I wasn't insulted: it was a fair question, I assumed, given the way she lived outside on the streets. I also wondered for a split-second if she might be offended if she realised how far I was from being attracted to her. She was dirty, she was as skinny as a stick, and she had bad skin. Back when I had a pulse, I would have sooner fucked a greased oven glove.

"There is no fire," I reminded her.

She nodded slowly. "Okay then," she said, and took the necklace.

But the writing was on the wall, because once I figured out what it wasn't, I couldn't hide anymore from what it was.

That shitty old poem: it's not "lame ducks over stiles". It's lame dogs.

I watched her sleep that night, and I knew. I let myself see it, instead of hiding from it. Fuck, it was nice, you know: watching ghost expressions chase themselves across her face. Hearing her breathe.

The next morning I gave her a roll of notes—maybe twenty grand, maybe a little more—and told her to get lost.

She cried, and she asked me what she'd done to hurt me. I told her she'd figure it out if she thought about it long enough. When she asked about the money, I said it was a one-off payment: she should use it to get the hell away from here, and not talk about me to anyone she knew on the street, or else I'd have all the homeless schmucks in Walthamstow climbing up my drainpipes.

She cried some more, and I knew she didn't buy it. It didn't matter, though: that was all the explanation I was prepared to give her. I walked her down the stairs, through the maze, all the way to the door. I unlocked it for her. She stepped across the threshold, then turned to stare at me.

Neither of us said anything, for the space of three heartbeats. Maybe four: my memory isn't reliable in that respect.

"Imagine if the necklace had been a collar," I said.

She nodded. "I get it," she said.

"And if I fitted a little leash to it. Took you out for walkies."

"I said I get it, Nicky. I don't think it was like that."

But I knew she was wrong. Old ladies have their cushion dogs, their ugly little pugs and Pekes and Chihuahuas: dead guys have homeless women.

"Thanks," Janine said. "For the money. It's more than I ever had in my life."

"You're welcome," I said. "Rent a flat. With a bath, or a shower or something."

She refused to be insulted: she just gave me a slow, sad smile.

"It's not good for you here," she said.

"It's great for me here. Two above freezing. Low humidity. A perfectly controlled environment."

"Stay in the world, Nicky," she murmured, her eyes

still brimming in a really unsettling, organic way.

"Is that the same as the street?" I countered. "I'll pass, thanks."

She made like she was going to hug me, but I raised a hand to ward her off and she got the point: no body heat or radiated thermic energy, by request.

"Bye, then," she said, with a slight tremor in her voice.

"Bye, Janine," I said.

"Is it okay if I write to you?"

"Why not? So long as you make sure there's adequate postage."

She turned and ran, pretty much, across the car park and out of sight around the corner of the building. That was the last I saw of her.

I waited to see if she was going to come back: it seemed quite likely that she might do that—think of one last thing to say, or ask if she could stay one more night or something. I gave her ten minutes, in the end, despite getting that prickly feeling again from having real, unfiltered air flow across my flesh. Finally I shut the front door, did a quick round of the outer circle to make sure I hadn't taken on any more unwanted passengers, then went back upstairs and locked myself in again.

It was really quiet. Quiet as the tomb, like they say, except for the freezer units humming away behind the far wall. I thought about going down and blagging one of her DVDs, but they were all feel-good shit that would make me want to hawk.

I didn't really feel like going online: the vibe was wrong, which meant the best I could hope for was adequate. But finally, around about midnight, I fired up my digital engines of destruction and got back in the hot seat for a few hours of Far-Eastern mayhem. Because, it's still true, you know? Still gospel, in my book.

The guys who stop never start again.

This story is from *The House of War and Witness*, the second of my collaborations with Lin and Lou. As with our first outing, there were lots of stories-within-stories and the digressions were a large part of the point. This time, though, we were trying our hand at a ghost story. And at historical fiction, since our setting was the Europe of the mid-eighteenth century. ¶ The book's protagonist, Drozde, is a camp follower with a small company of soldiers stationed at a disputed border outpost. She finds herself in an old house, Pokoj, which houses hundreds of ghosts. The ghosts, who seem to know Drozde very well even though they've only just met her, insist on telling their stories to her and to each other. This is one of the stories. The setting, in our modern era, is Poland. In Drozde's time it was Silesia. And in the prehistoric time the storyteller is talking about . . . well, she'll tell you herself. ¶ By the way, our original working title for the book was *Many Mansions*, and we still think it was a good one. Every story except this one features the house, Pokoj, in one of the varied forms and functions it took over the centuries. This story is set before the house existed, but in the same location.

THE DEMON IN THE WELL

IT IS HARD to say when my time was in relation to your time. It was a handful of handfuls of handfuls of years ago, and probably some years more. My people lived on this ground, and we called it Khethyu. We called ourselves Khethyu also.

It was very hot and very humid, with warm winds coming all the time from the east. Like living inside the chest of a man who is snoring, or in a bread oven when the bread is rising. It was a blessed place. The earth teemed with life and the possibility of life, so that if a man chewed tree bark and spat on the ground a tree grew in that place. And if a woman squatted to piss, the stream became an oasis and deer came there.

The blessings came from the river goddess, Panafya. She loved the Khethyu as any mother loves her children, and wanted all good things to come to us. We gave her our love and worship in return. We promised never to drop stepping-stones into her body: the proper way to cross a river is to wade or to swim, trusting the goddess not to take you though she always could. And whenever we dipped so much as a foot in her waters, we felt Panafya's caress and knew her love for us.

We had no other gods, but there was one devil who we were compelled to acknowledge. His name was Shin and he lived in the great well that he dug out with his claws in the before times—the well that gave us water even in the dry season. It was Panafya's water, of course. She gave water freely to everyone. But sly Shin never drank his water. He hoarded it at the bottom of his well and counted the drops the way a farmer counts his goats.

So when the dry season came and the only water to be had was from Shin's well, we Khethyu came to borrow it. But we placated the devil with prayers, and we always paid him back in the spring when the river flooded.

We placated him in another way too. Every year, a boy and a girl were chosen to dance for Shin on the great flat stone beside his well—a very difficult and complicated dance. They danced naked, and afterwards they fucked with all of the Khethyu looking on and singing a praise. In this way they dedicated both their skill and the beauty of their bodies to the devil.

But one year, the girl who was chosen for the dance was Arinak, a vain and empty-headed thing. It is no spite or envy in me to say this, because Arinak was me. I had no thought in my head beside the thought that I was cleverer, more beautiful and more admirable than any woman had ever been. I thought the devil was lucky that I'd been chosen to dance for him, and the boy, Dimut, was lucky that he would get to fuck with me. I thought the sun was lucky to shine on me and the earth to bear my feet.

And those were the thoughts that were in my heart when I danced.

It was a glorious day, a wild dance, and a joyful love-making. I had never been so happy. When we were done, Dimut asked me if I would walk under the marriage tree and pick a fruit and eat it with him. I kissed him—because his admiration made me happy—but I told him no. I wanted an older man with more than a single handful of goats to his name. I was sure that plenty of older men would come to court me.

But that was not how things fell out.

The morning after the dance I pushed my friend Venni in play and she fell the wrong way, so that her leg broke. Her furious family demanded half our herd and half our honour stones in compensation, and the elders agreed it. They were right to do so. The leg healed thwart and Venni was crippled.

Then my mother fell ill of a fever that would not abate, until in the end her wits left her and she could no longer talk. Only sit in the fire pit and run her fingers through the warm ashes as though she had lost something there.

Then five of our goats died in five nights, one after another, with no sign of sickness. They just fell to the ground as though someone had hit them with a stone.

So many disasters in so short a time caused people to ask what curse had fallen on my family, and what sin it could have been that had brought the curse down. My father, made furious by such wicked gossip, told them to mind their own affairs. And so they did. A circle cleared around our house, as though there was plague within it.

Dimut was the only one who still called on us, and still greeted us when we walked abroad. What's more, he proposed to me again. He didn't mind, he said, if I was cursed. He'd rather be cursed with me than blessed with some other woman.

I'm ashamed to say this, but I took his kindness badly. It looked like pity to me, and I told him sharply to take his nonsense to someone who had the time to listen to it.

But his words set me thinking. Up until then, I had thought of these troubles as belonging to us all alike—to my mother and my father, my sisters and brother, as well as to me. Only when Dimut said, "if *you* are cursed", meaning me and me alone, did I begin to wonder if this could possibly be true.

And once I had thought that thought, I had to know the answer. I asked my great uncle's wife, Ghuda, what steps I should take to find out a curse, and she told me a very powerful finding spell. I can't tell it to you because it belongs to my people and isn't mine to give, but I can tell you it involved the blood of the moon and the shadow of a cat that had eaten its own kittens.

I bled the moon, and walked the outline of the cat's shadow. I did ten other things besides, and as the thirteenth thing I turned in my own footsteps to see what was behind me. If there was a curse on me, it should have been standing or lying there upon the ground, plain to see. But there was nothing. Nothing at all that I could see.

I laughed with relief.

And then stiffened in horror, because another voice laughed alongside mine.

"Who's there?" I cried.

"Who do you think?" said the other voice. And the cruelty in its tone made me shake like a spider's web in a rainstorm.

"The devil from the well," I said, because somehow I knew that that was who it was.

"Give me my name."

"Shin!"

"Yes. I am Shin, and I will hound and torment you until you go mad and die by your own hand."

"But why?" I wailed. "I danced for you!"

"Ah, but you danced with stupid, skittish and disrespectful thoughts in your mind. The dance is meant to be tribute to me. Yours was mockery."

"I didn't mean it as mockery!"

"All the same," the devil said, "that was how I took it."

I was aghast. I knew now what I'd done, and that all the terrible things that had happened were due to my transgression. I had already blamed myself for Venni's being maimed, and for the loss of my family's wealth and honour, but the dead goats were my fault too. And worst of all, I had visited madness on my mother.

I spent the night on a bare rock over a precipice. I was dazed with guilt. A hundred times I thought to cast myself down into the abyss, I hated myself so much—and Shin encouraged me to do it, telling me that I would never know any peace in this world until I was dead.

But I endured, somehow, and in the morning I went before the elders. I told them what I had discovered—that the demon from the well was persecuting me and all the people I loved. I begged them to allow me to dance before the well again, or failing that to try to appease Shin with some other offering.

They refused outright. As far as they could see, they said, the sin was mine and the punishment was also mine, which was right and good. Since Shin hated me, he would probably not be happy to see me dance again. And if they offered further sacrifice, Shin might come to expect it in future years, which would be a burden to all the people forever. Better to let things run their course.

They told me that I was banished. They told me to expect no help or welcome from the people, then or ever.

I was weeping with grief and rage when I left the elder circle. I almost walked into Dimut, who had been waiting outside for me the whole time. He told me again that he loved me and would be happy to marry me, even with the demon's hatred and the banishment thrown into the bargain.

The boy was clearly mad. But his bravery and his devotion warmed and cheered me. And goddess, I was cold and miserable then! It would have been easy to fall into his arms. But it would have destroyed him. I could feel Shin's breath on my shoulder. If I showed any fondness for Dimut, I would only be teaching the demon where to strike next.

"Don't you have anybody else to bother?" I shouted at him. "Do you have to be crawling around my feet all the time? A dream told you that you loved me, and you believed the dream. Wake up, and see the truth. I won't be yours until the river wets the treetops!"

I left him there and turned my steps towards home. But I heard the demon's steps echoing mine, and my loathing of him rose in me like a flood. I began to run.

I ran into the forest, where the thorns are thickest. They tore my skin to ribbons, but it would not avail me. "I'm still here!" Shin chuckled. "Nothing you can do will shake me loose."

I ran into the desert, where the sun beats like a hammer. I pushed on through the heat of the day, letting it burn my skin red and black, but it would not avail me. "I'm right at your side," Shin gloated. "You're wasting your time."

I ran to the cliff edge where I had sat the night before, and jumped from rock to rock over drops so steep they made the breath stop in my throat, but it would not avail me. "I like it here," Shin sighed. "It's very cosy when it's just the two of us."

I stopped running, then, and sat me down and thought. Was there any place in the world that would be easier for me to bear than him? Any place where I might cast him off? At first I could think of none. But at last a strange inspiration came to me. Blasphemy and disrespect had brought me to this terrible situation. Perhaps they could save me too.

I jumped to my feet and began to run again. I ran to the flood plain, which—this being high summer—was an endless wasteland of cracked mud. I sought a place I knew, and when I found it I stood my ground.

"What did that achieve?" Shin jeered. "It was barely a stroll to me, while you seem to have used up the last of your strength."

It was true that I was exhausted, but I defied him anyway. I spat on the ground at his feet. "You are nothing!" I shouted. "Your power is so weak, a baby could topple you!"

That seemed to anger him. "You little animal!" he growled. "Your mind isn't big enough even to imagine my power! There is nothing like me in the world!"

"Nothing like you," I agreed. "But many things greater than you."

"No! Nothing! Nothing greater!" His voice was right in my ear now, as though he stood at my side and leaned his head forward to disgorge his answer at me.

"Yes there is. There is the goddess!"

"Panafya? That dull-eyed cow! I'd smack her head right off her shoulders if she ever dared to cope me! I'd rip her heart and lungs and lights out if she so much as—"

"If she so much as what?"

The voice that cut across Shin's was so vast and loud it was like a mountain falling on us—and yet so musically beautiful that my arms, which I had raised to cover my ears, remained frozen in the air halfway.

Panafya rose before us, a tower of water with a face that frowned down on the demon and on me from the zenith of the sky.

This was her place. The place where the river flows in autumn and winter and spring. But in high summer there was no water there to show where it ended or began. When I had spat, I had prayed a summoning—water of any kind being a right offering to the river goddess. I had brought her there so that she might hear Shin's blasphemy against her, if he could be coaxed into uttering one.

"Panafya!" the demon gasped. "Great one! I . . . I meant no insult!"

"Then why insult me? Why drag my name through your stenching mouth at all?"

I saw Shin now for the first time, as the goddess's gaze stripped him of all his protections and disguises. He was not as impressive as I had imagined him. He was a good deal taller than a man, but his limbs were gangly and pocked with sores, and the splintered teeth in his grimacing mouth stuck out in all directions like sticks of kindling on a bonfire.

But water, not fire, was his nemesis.

Panafya raised her hand—she had not had a hand until then, but she had one to call on when she wanted it—and brought it down. A great wave kicked us, as hard as a wild horse kicks, and knocked us off our feet.

I heard Shin wailing and begging as he was dragged under.

I saw riverweeds wrap around his arms and legs and throat to still his struggles.

I saw the silt of the river bottom swallow him like a mouth.

Then I saw only sparkling lights and encroaching darkness, because I was drowning.

But strong arms embraced me, and lifted me to the surface, where I gulped and wriggled like a fish on a line. It was Dimut, of course. We rode out the flood tide, he and I, each in turn giving strength to the other when the other seemed ready to give up and slide under. We held each other more tightly than we had in our lovemaking.

When the deluge abated, we lay in each other's arms in the clinging mud, so spent that for a long while we could not even speak. When we could, Dimut asked me again to be his wife, and I said yes. We did not need a marriage tree.

"We'll go away," he said, "and find another people that will take us in. We're young and strong, and we can work. Someone will want us. Or else we'll start our own tribe, somewhere in the hills where there's a lake for the goats to drink from and wood to make a house."

It was a pleasant dream. But I liked the river plain, I loved my family, and I had a better idea.

I went back to Khethyu. To my people. I told them Shin was dead, by my hand. I told them the goddess had risen at my bidding, even in the bone-dry summer, and shown her winter face.

I told them that Dimut and I were to be numbered among the elders now, and that anyone who said no had better be a strong swimmer.

We lived long here. We had thirteen sons and daughters, and ten of them lived. So many were the generations of my children that they called me *Arinak Imat Basya*, thousand-times-blessed Arinak.

But they called me Demonslayer too, and I liked that name better.

This is one of my most recent stories, and it reflects some of my current obsessions. The commission came from Marie O'Regan, who gave me an extremely broad and accommodating brief. It was, and I'm relaying Marie's exact words, "Write me a ghost story." ¶ So I revisited some things I'd been brooding on, including the morally bankrupt way in which refugees and asylum seekers are treated in the UK, and came up with a ghost story that may not even have any ghosts in it. I suppose it's comparable to my zombie story with one largely invisible zombie. Here the score is either zero ghosts or two thousand, depending on how far you rely on Denise's version of what happens in the story. ¶ What the story does have is a monster. It will come as no surprise to anyone who knows me when I say that the monster is a career politician. I think Tom Peverill is the vilest character I've ever created. If anyone is inclined to see him as a caricature, I'd like to point out in passing that as I write this, in July of 2018, the Conservative Party has just appointed as its vice-chair a man—Ben Bradley—who in a recent blog post suggested that the unemployed should get vasectomies to prevent the UK from "drowning in a vast sea of unemployed wasters". How do you caricature that?

MY LIFE IN POLITICS

TONIGHT AFTER supper Mum tried out her speech on me and it was really good. It made me cry. She said Mr Peverill—Tom—was a great man and a great politician, and that his name will shine out like a beacon for all time to show what people can do when they've got vision and moral courage. I clapped when she'd finished, and said, "Encore! Encore!"

Mum didn't like that. "Don't be doing that tomorrow, Denise," she said. "You'll make an exhibition of yourself. Oh my God, I think my nerves will go."

Mum has trouble with her nerves. I think maybe I do too, although we get different medicine so it's not the exact same thing. It's just sometimes I get anxious if people want me to do something and I don't know what it is, and then I get confused and I don't always follow.

That's how Dad says it. "Try to follow, Denise," he says, "for Jesus Christ's sake." When we're watching *Days Of Our Lives* or *General Hospital*, and I ask who that one is, or what he meant when he said that, or whether she knows he loves her. And I do try to follow, but sometimes I can't.

It's a big honour that they asked Mum to do the eulogy. Dad thought it should be him because he's been the treasurer of the Constituency Association for seventeen years, but Mum is the chair which is more important.

It was thanks to Mum that I got to work for Tom, before he got to be an MP, when he was just our local candidate. And then after he won and he went to the House of Commons to represent all of Coddistone I carried on working for him but not in the Palace of Westminster. Just here, in the constituency.

It was a good job and I was happy, although not as happy as I was when I worked at Costella's Café. At Costella's Shamin let me take home Cornish pasties that weren't the right shape or got burned, and if I worked on Saturday I got an extra ten pounds that didn't go into the brown envelope but Mr Costella put it in my hand.

"You can't go wrong with ten pounds in your hand, now can you?" he always said. And I used to keep it tight in my hand all the way home, pretending it was magic. And once a boy who was skateboarding on the pavement really fast stopped dead right before he hit me, as if he'd hit a wall I couldn't see, but I don't know if that was the ten pounds or not.

After Tom—Mr Peverill—went to the House of Commons I didn't see him as much, even though I was still working for him. He was writing his bill and then he was getting people to vote on it and it took up most of his time so he didn't come back to Coddistone very much.

Until that last day when he came back to make his speech on the Town Hall steps. I wish that hadn't happened. Any of it. I wish he didn't come. I wish Mum hadn't made him a briefing pack. And I wish she hadn't told me to drop the briefing pack off at his house. Whenever I remember about it, I think my nerves will go.

The only time I saw Tom before I went to work for him was when I was still in school. I was in year eleven and he came to Bishop Laud on prize day. He gave the science prize to Angela Brereton, but before he gave it to her he made a speech about moral courage. He said moral courage was about doing what was right even when everyone was telling you it was wrong. He said if you lived right and followed your own vision, no man or woman could reproach you.

It was a very inspiring speech. I wrote an article about it for the school newspaper and Miss Charles said it could go into my coursework folder. "You need something else besides your weird little fantasy pieces, Denise," she said. "This looks like it will do very nicely."

I got an A for English, in the end—nearly an A star— and I think that article was the reason. It was the best thing I ever wrote. I used FOLLOW YOUR VISION as the headline, and I put a photo of Tom next to it, looking up towards the ceiling and off to the right. It was a photo that mum took for his campaign posters.

English was my only A. I got Cs in art, religious studies, and geography, and the rest were Ds. My Mum went into school to talk to Mr Nuttall. She said I should be allowed to stay on and do A levels because an A that's nearly an A star is outstanding. I'd shown what I could do if I got the chance.

I dream, sometimes, what I could do. Like fly in places that aren't even places, and scoop up the shiny stuff that makes the stars and press it all against me until I'm shiny too. Sometimes I used to write the dreams down, and that was what Miss Charles called my fantasy pieces, but in the dreams it felt real and anyway I only put down the parts I could find the words for. Some of it was just feelings.

Mum got her way, like she usually does. Mr Nuttall said I could do English and Geography A levels and retake my maths. But then I got sick with my appendix and I missed a lot of time. My mum said, "You've just got to apply yourself, Denise, that's all." And she got the school to send homework packages for me every day I was in hospital, but I was very tired and very sore after the operation and I couldn't apply myself all the time even though I really tried to.

Part of that was because I just hated being in the hospital. My room was small and dark, and sometimes when I was there by myself it got smaller and darker. I heard one of the nurses say they were scared to come in there. She said she thought the ward was haunted. It wasn't though. I never saw any ghosts there.

I got Ds in the Christmas exams and they weren't even good Ds. Mr Nuttall suggested I should take the rest of the year off and start the course again in September. "A clean slate," he said. My mum and dad said no, I didn't need a clean slate. I could make up the lost time in the spring. And I promised I would, and I did try to, but for a lot of reasons it didn't happen. So I left at the end of year twelve and got a job at Greggs in the High Street and then at Costella's Café.

My mum didn't like that. She thought working in a café was beneath me, and that I was shaming the family. She talked about it with my dad a lot, late at night when they both thought I was asleep. Some of the talk was about which side of the family I took after and whose fault I was, but some of it was about finding a better job for me to do that wouldn't shame anyone.

Then one day my mum went to a Constituency Association meeting and came back very happy and excited. She said Tom Peverill had got the party's nomination to stand for Coddistone in the next general election. A local man! Mum was especially proud because she went to school with Tom Peverill's wife Violet, who I had to call Auntie Vi when she came to visit, so Tom was almost one of the family. "And that's good news for you, my lass," she said to me. "I had a word with Vi and she had a word with Tom, and what do you think? You're going to work in his office!"

I was sad to leave Costella's. Mr Costella said there would always be a job there for me if I changed my mind. Shamin told me don't look back, just do it. "There's more things in life than taking meat pies out of a sodding oven."

And she hugged me, which was a bit of a surprise but very nice. Mum doesn't do hugs. She says she's never been one to get all touchy-feely and she doesn't trust people who are.

So I went to work at Tom's office, which was in Holland House behind the Co-Op, in the same building as the Constituency Association. In fact it was a room they rented as a storeroom, and everyone's first job was taking all the boxes out of it and putting them out on the landing where they stacked up all the way to the ceiling.

After that, I did stuffing envelopes, and printing out fliers and putting them through doors. There were seven different fliers, depending on which part of town we were going to. They all said Tom Peverill will protect local interests and keep Britain for the British, but then there was a list of other things he would do which was different. If you lived in the centre then it said he would get tough on noise and drunks when the clubs let out. If you lived in the flats by Wilding Park, it said he would repair the footpath and the bridge. I forget the others, but they always said things that were about where you lived. And they always had Tom's face, looking up and to the right, and a Union Jack which is actually a Union Flag unless it's flown at sea.

Some of the people who worked in the office also did what my mum called doorstepping, which was talking to people about what a great man Tom was and what he would do for Coddistone, but they didn't make me do that. I was glad, because I'm not good with people. What I did do, sometimes, was carry extra boxes of fliers out to the doorstepping teams if they ran out, and once I was in a van with loudspeakers on the roof, handing out fliers while my mum said, "Turn out tomorrow and vote! Vote For Peverill! A vote for Peverill is a vote for security!"

Sometimes Tom came into the office, which was always quite exciting. Everyone stopped work to cheer and clap their hands whenever he came into the room, and he would clap his hands too, pointing at us to say that we were the ones who deserved it.

Tom gave speeches and held meetings too, and when he did those things I went with him and did stuff outside the speech or the meeting. Sometimes I took people's coats and gave them tickets with numbers on, and sometimes I gave out fliers to people when they came into the room.

I wasn't usually inside the room when the speech or the meeting happened, but one time I was. That one was a candidates' debate, and Tom won it hands down. Especially the part where the audience got to ask the candidates questions. This was when Africa was getting too hot to live in, and all the boats were coming, and the question from the audience was: what should we do with the boats. Tom said the Royal Navy should blockade the English Channel so no boats could get in. One of the other candidates, I think the green one, said that was inhumane, and Tom said hands up everyone if you would want to have a refugee from Africa living in your house. Only a few hands went up.

"Congratulations on playing to the lowest common denominator," the green lady said.

"You have contempt for your constituents," Tom said. "And that is why you can't represent them in the House of Commons." I don't remember the exact right words, but it was something like that.

And my mum punched the air and whispered, "Yes!"

Then it was election night, which was the most exciting night of my life. My mum and dad had a party for the people from the Constituency Association, and the food was Marks & Spencers. It was really lovely. My dad said at least the Jews were good for something.

Coddistone was one of the last seats to report, so I got to stay up really late. I was eighteen by this time, so really I could go to bed whenever I wanted, but I was living in Mum and Dad's house so mostly I couldn't. At ten o'clock, or half past, Mum would say "Denise" and look at the clock, and that would mean I had to go to bed. Only that night she didn't say it. I don't think she remembered to. She was sitting on the sofa from midnight to two o'clock, hardly saying anything, just watching. We knew the party was going to win, because they were fifteen points ahead in the polls, but Mum desperately wanted Tom to win too. And when the returning officer said, "Thomas Peverill, eighteen thousand seven hundred and six" she screamed. But it was a happy scream, not a scared one. My dad got a bottle of champagne out of the fridge and popped it, and we toasted Tom and the party and the next five years. I had lemonade to toast with, of course, not champagne. "We don't want to set you off, do we?" Dad said.

I wondered as I sipped my lemonade whether we would all go to London and work for Tom there. That would be amazing! We didn't, though. He had a London office, but it had London people in it and we stayed where we were.

Nothing much changed in the office, apart from Tom not coming in there anymore. I still printed fliers and delivered them. Sometimes I got to write them too, although it wasn't really writing. It was cutting and pasting text from the party's website and then dropping in quotes from Tom, taken from our database of his speeches and interviews.

We saw him on the news sometimes. Almost always he was talking about the refugee situation. Most European countries were taking some refugees by then, because Africa had suffered what they called a complete ecological meltdown. At least the bit in the middle had, and all the people there were going north and when they got to the coast they got into boats and sailed across the sea.

Tom said they shouldn't do it, and we shouldn't encourage them to do it. He was drafting a bill that was about not having to let the refugees in when they got here.

It kept him very busy, so he didn't get to come up to the constituency very much at all, and when he did he mostly didn't come into the office. Mum said constituency business was still really important to him; he just had to prioritise right now.

There were people in the association who weren't happy, though. They said Tom was still working for Coddistone and how could he do that if he never came to any Association meetings or even talked to the committee?

That was when Mum had the idea of the briefing packs. Every time we heard that Tom was coming back to Coddistone, someone would go to his house first and drop off a briefing pack, which was all the minutes of all the meetings he'd missed and all the important news from around the constituency. Mum would stay up late typing everything out and then it was usually me or Lucy who took them over.

"It's okay if he's not there," Lucy said to me once. "I wouldn't want to be alone in the house with him, would you?"

"Why not?" I asked her.

She raised both her hands and wiggled her fingers. "You know," she said. "Wandering hands. Wandering everything, Eileen Franklin told me." She winked, and I laughed, but I was only pretending to understand. I knew that Eileen Franklin had gotten expelled from the Association for inappropriate behaviour. I didn't know what wandering everything meant.

Tom's house was really nice. It had three floors and six bedrooms, and the living room was so big it took me twenty-three steps to walk from one end of it to the other. It had a chandelier too, with all these glass leaves hanging down that tinkled when you opened the door or when there was a wind.

There was also a statue in the front next to the driveway of a man with goat legs playing a pipe. I used to pretend the goat-man could talk, and I would ask him on my way into the house to play some music for me. I would say, "Play it, Sam," like Humphrey Bogart in *Casablanca*, and point my finger at the goat-man on my way into the house. And sometimes I would hear the sound of pipes playing when I was inside, but it was just one of my fantasies or maybe the radio in the house next door.

One time Tom came back to the constituency because a ship, the *Wayfarer*, had gone down in the English Channel and it was full of refugees. "The bloody media are all over him," my mum said. "As if it was his fault they piled two thousand people on a ship that could only hold five hundred! He can't get a moment's peace down there."

She gave me a briefing pack to take over to Tom's house, and also a fruit loaf that she had baked for my dad, with a card saying *Best Wishes from all in the Association*. I took them over and left them on the kitchen table the way I usually did. And then I went into the living room and walked from one end of it to the other, listening to the sad sound of the goat-man's pipes.

It was such a big house! And Tom lived in it all on his own, ever since Auntie Vi left him and took the kids away with her (I wasn't allowed to talk about her after that). It seemed sad to me, and a waste, that most of the time that lovely house was empty.

I pretended I was talking to the refugees who drowned when the *Wayfarer* sank. They had two thousand voices, so when they talked it was more like music than it was like ordinary talking. They said it was sad that they had had got so close to a new country and then hadn't made it to shore. "That is sad," I agreed.

And we lost our ship, the refugees said. *We can't find our way into the next world without a ship. We're lost, Denise. And we're so unhappy. But because we're at the bottom of the sea, nobody can hear us crying.*

"You should live here," I said, "in Tom's house.

There's plenty of room. And maybe you can build a new ship, or maybe I can find you one. But in the meantime you should stay here."

Thank you, Denise, the refugees said. *We will.*

The goat-man smiled at me when I left the house, and gave me a nod as though he thought that I had done a good thing. It was just one of my fantasies, of course. The whole thing was.

As it turned out, Tom didn't get that briefing pack. He didn't come back to the constituency after all. He went to a place called Martinique and he stayed there for two weeks. My mum said it was for a fact-finding mission but I don't know what facts he found.

Then Tom's bill got its final reading, with a big debate in the House of Commons. A lot of people talked about the *Wayfarer* ("Bleeding hearts!" my mum said. "Hypocrites and bleeding hearts, the lot of them!"), and Tom said it was a tragedy but it wasn't *our* tragedy. "It was made in Africa," he said, "and it should have stayed there. It was no business of ours to intervene in it. It is sheer vanity to suggest that we can solve the world's problems when we have so many problems of our own."

When the house voted on the bill it passed by thirteen votes. The *Daily Mail*'s front page the next day was just a photo of Tom with the single word VICTORY. Mum photocopied it thousands of times for a flier that we put through every door in Coddistone.

Then Tom got his cabinet seat and we didn't see him at all. Mum was doing the briefing packs regularly now, every week, and mostly it was me who dropped them off. I always got Sam to play for me and I always said hello to the refugees. They were still sad, and they still talked a lot about not having a ship.

You said you would find us one, Denise, they said.

"I said I'd try," I told them. "But I don't know where to look. Please don't be angry with me."

We're not angry. But it's very dangerous to lie to us.

"I'm really sorry," I said. "I'll do my best." And I did look up to see how close the canal came to Coddistone but it was thirty miles. And canal boats can't even go on the ocean, let alone into the next world so I didn't know what I was going to do and I wished I hadn't promised.

I said we didn't see Tom anymore, but of course we did. He was on TV all the time. He was still talking about refugees but also about things like compulsory registration and prison sentences and patriotism and how free speech is a paradox because it comes at a high price. "People talk more about their rights than about their duties," he said, and he said that had to change. The *Daily Mail* had his picture again, this time in Parliament Square with Big Ben behind him, and the headline was "TIME FOR CHANGE".

"He's going to go for it," my mum said, when she saw that headline.

"He'll get it too," my dad said. "And he'll make us proud. By God he will."

They hugged each other, and then they both hugged me, and we did a little dance together in the living room. It was nice. I didn't know what Tom was going to go for, but I was sure that he would make us proud.

That week's briefing pack had a letter my mum wrote. It was supposed to be private and I got all the way to the house without reading it but then I couldn't help myself. *You carry all our hopes and dreams,* it said. *Everyone in the Association and in the whole town is proud of you.* I didn't read any more than that because the refugees came and all the lights in the room got darker.

Where is our ship? they asked.

"It's coming," I said. "I'm sorry. It's coming soon." I almost wet myself. I hadn't done anything since I looked up where the canal went. I got out of the house quickly. I even forgot to thank Sam for playing for me.

I had my twentieth birthday three weeks after that.

My present from Mum and Dad was a coat. It had a wide collar and two rows of buttons and I liked it a lot. I remember it because I was wearing it the next time I went to Tom's house.

I was going to say it was the last time I went to Tom's, but it wasn't. It was only the last time I went inside.

It was a Tuesday, exactly one month after my birthday. I was at the office and I was adding some more of Tom's interviews to the database, when the phone rang and my mum answered it. It was Tom's PA, Lionel Gates. He said Tom was coming to Coddistone that night so he could have a press conference the next day on the town hall steps. "Thank you, Lionel," my mum said. "Can I take it he's going to announce?"

When she put the phone down everyone in the room was watching her. She didn't say a word for a long, long time. Then she said, "That's a yes," and everyone shouted and cheered.

"What's he going to announce, Mum?" I asked her. She just looked at me and shook her head. She said, "In a world of your own half the time, aren't you?"

Eileen told me that Tom was going to run for leader of the party now that Maura Voss was standing down. I remembered then that there had been a thing on the news about Maura Voss, so it was probably that. If Tom won the leadership it meant he would be our next prime minister, because the party didn't lose elections anymore.

Mum got busy making up a briefing pack. It was like her usual briefing packs except that it had a bottle of champagne as well as all the papers and the USB drive. Actually it was different in other ways too. She went online and got all the opinion polls from the last year and made graphs and charts out of them and showed Tom which people liked him for which things. It took ages to do and we all had to stay late helping her find all the figures for the charts. She wanted it to be the best briefing pack ever. I think she wanted Tom to remember her, and the Constituency Association, and how they had always helped him right from the earliest days when he was an MP and before that when he was in the council.

She asked Lucy if she could drop the pack off on her way home. But Lucy wasn't happy about having to stay in the office until after seven o'clock and she said no. "Sorry, Mrs Tanner. I'm going to Rosehead to pick my mum up from her physio, and I'm late already. I'll be driving in the opposite direction."

Mum turned to me. She didn't look happy. "It will have to be you, then," she said. "Put your new coat on. Make yourself presentable, in case he's there already. And if he is, you call him Mr Peverill, not Tom."

"Okay," I said.

"Well what are you waiting for?" Mum said. "Off you go."

It was already dark when I left the office. There was a moon, but there were clouds too and mostly you only saw the edge of the moon behind the cloud. But it came out when I got to Tom's house and the goat-man shone like he was a light bulb.

"Play it, Sam," I whispered as I went past him.

I was going to go in through the kitchen door, the way I usually did, but then I saw there was a light on in the living room. Tom must already have arrived from London, like Mum thought. So I rang the doorbell and after a moment or two the door opened.

Tom looked tired. He was wearing a suit and a tie, but the tie was undone and hanging down. And his hair wasn't combed properly, so it stuck up a bit at the front. He didn't recognise me at first, until I said hello to him. "Oh," he said then, and he seemed to relax. "Denise. Right. What is it?"

I showed him the stack of papers I was holding. "It's from the Constituency Association, Mr Peverill," I said.

"Your briefing pack. My mum spent all afternoon on it."

Tom laughed, and rolled his eyes. "My briefing pack," he repeated. "Of course." Then he saw the champagne bottle, which was wrapped in gold paper with a red ribbon on it. "Is that from the Association too? Shit, you should have led with that. Come on in."

I went inside and he closed the door. "Living room for that lot," he said. "I'll take the bottle."

The living room was the same as it always was, except for a little suitcase with its handle still sticking up that Tom must have brought with him. I put the briefing pack on the biggest of the coffee tables, and as I was doing that I heard the pop of the champagne cork from the kitchen.

A few moments later, Tom came in holding two glasses full of champagne. "The party never stops," he said, and he laughed again. "Here you go."

He held out one of the glasses to me. There were all bubbles in it, and it looked as though some of the bubbles were bursting in the air over the top of the glass. It was really beautiful. "My mum and dad don't let me drink alcohol," I told Tom.

"They're not here, though, are they?" Tom said. He put the glass in my hand and I took a sip before I even thought about it. It was the fizziest thing I had ever tasted, fizzier than Coca Cola when you drop the can but you open it anyway. "It's really nice," I said.

"More where that came from," Tom said. He tilted the glass when I took my next sip, so I drank more than I was going to and got the hiccups a bit.

I could hear goat-man Sam playing his pipes in the garden. It was a sweet, mournful sound.

"Let me top you up," Tom said. And then "Do you want to take that coat off? It looks ridiculous indoors." And then "Let's sit down. Over here. Come on. I won't bite."

I was starting to feel dizzy. I don't think I did sit down, but I was on the sofa somehow. On the arm of it and then half onto the seat, with Tom's hands on my shoulders and Tom's face up close to my ear. "I really feel like I ought to have taken the time to know you better," he said. And then he licked my ear.

It was so gross I yelled out "Ow! Stop!" as though it hurt me. It didn't hurt me, it just surprised me. I dropped my champagne glass so I could put both hands up to push him away. But he wasn't going away, he was putting his arms around me and one of his hands was on my bum. When I tried to move it he grabbed my wrist tight with his other hand. "Just relax," he said. He sounded angry with me and I didn't know why. I wasn't hurting him, he was hurting me.

"I want to go home," I said.

Tom didn't answer. His face was moving up and down against mine. He was trying to make his lips be where mine were so he could kiss me, but I kept turning one way and then the other way so he couldn't.

"I want to go home," I said again, louder.

Goat-man Sam stopped playing. *Is he hurting you?* he asked me.

No, I said. *But I think he's going to. I'm scared, Sam! Can you help me?* I knew he couldn't. It was just one of my fantasies, and I needed help that was real. I knew enough about what happens when a man is with a woman to know what Tom was going to do to me, and I didn't want him to do it.

No, Sam said sadly. *I can't help you. I'm out here in the garden and I can't come into the house.*

All right then, I thought. I'll lie down on the sofa and then when Tom tries to climb on top of me I'll bring my knee up between his legs. But he was sort of slantways on top of me, not properly on top of me, and I couldn't get my leg free.

Well now, the refugees said. *It's about time you woke up to your obligations.* The music of their voices came out of nowhere, from all directions, filling my head.

Please help me, refugees! I said. *Tom is going to rape me.*

You must give us permission, the voices said. *In the old words and the old cadence. Do that, and perhaps we will be able to solve each other's problems.*

I don't know the old words or the other thing you said, I said. Tom's hand was up between my legs and his weight was all on top of me and it really did hurt now.

Just repeat what we say. But say it aloud, so that all may hear. I gift you this ship, to sail in.

"I gift you this ship to sail in!" I yelped.

To your journey's end.

"To your journey's end!"

"Be quiet," Tom said. "For fuck's sake."

No god nor man gainsay you.

The words came out one at a time, because of the hiccups from the champagne and because of Tom moving on top of me to try to get inside me.

"No"

"God"

Tom stiffened, and he shook a little bit.

"Nor"

"Man"

Tom got very still again. He made a sound that was like a sigh.

"Gain"

"Say"

"You!"

Tom slid off the sofa onto the floor. His face was white and when I bent down to listen I couldn't hear him breathing. I don't know how to do that thing where you feel a pulse with your fingers so I didn't do it. Anyway, I could see that he was dead.

Dead, the refugees said. *Yes. He was a bad man. But he will make a fine ship.*

They climbed inside him, and sailed away in him. Not in his body. That stayed where it was, except that it looked even deader now. They sailed away in his soul, which they hollowed out so they could fit in it. It was just one of my fantasies but it felt so real.

I grabbed my coat and my handbag and ran out of there.

Is all well? Goat-man Sam asked me.

It's fine, Sam, I said, as I was running down the driveway. *I'll tell you later.*

The news said Tom had a heart attack. My mum cried and cried, as if she was never going to stop. She asked me how Tom had been when I saw him and I said he seemed fine. "He was really happy. He even gave me a glass of champagne so I could celebrate with him."

I had to say that, because the police would have found the two glasses and they would already know I'd been in the house. But there was no sign that anything bad had happened. Tom just died because his heart stopped working, so nobody thought I could have done anything wrong and really I don't think I did. It wasn't my fault if Tom had wandering hands and wandering everything. It was his.

I go back to the house a lot, but I'm really careful not to be seen and I never go inside. Sam and I just meet in the garden. It's lovely there on summer nights when the moon is full and it's just the two of us, but it can be a bit cold at other times of the year. Sam says we should go somewhere else. He knows a place called Arcadia, where it's summer all the time and the goat men dance and drink sweet wine as well as playing music.

I think I'll go with him. Politics is more Mum's thing than mine.

This is another very short story, although not quite a micro-short. I wrote it initially as a self-contained part of a sci-fi novel that never quite happened, which would have been called *The Salt-Carrier*. Then I reworked it slightly so I could include it as backup material in the French edition of *Highest House*, my most recent collaboration with Peter Gross. It's a story about slavery, which is a major theme in that book. It's also about family and identity, which are the binary stars that most of my writing orbits.   ¶   I was aiming for a mythic or folkloric style here, by which I mean a style that remains deadpan and penny-plain in the face of miracles and atrocities. It's a tricky thing to get right, and I'm not saying I did. I wanted to hit a note that was the exact opposite of the kind of all-overworked-similes-all-the-time approach that some fantasy writers grab a hold of when they do folklore (e.g., "Her desire as she beheld him was as boundless as the ocean when it rears up from its bed to embrace the moon, and his love as he beheld right back at her was as deep as the Tsangpo Canyon in Tibet, considered by many to be the deepest canyon on Earth, ergo it's fair to say it was pretty damn deep.").   ¶   In my opinion, forged by a fair amount of experience, you don't make your audience feel something by telling them what they should be feeling. A dispassionate, stripped-down style at moments of high intensity pays massive dividends. If you want to break your readers' hearts—and sooner or later, if you're a writer, you will want to do that—then leave the violins in their cases and keep a straight face.

THE TALE OF SALT-CARRIER VA

SHE KNEW who she was, and so do we, although we have no inkling now of her parentage or what her name might have been. That is to say, her original name, before she became Va. Before she became the salt-carrier.

She was someone-daughter-of-someone, of Va Keep. Not the tallest or the strongest or the most beautiful, but still a child of that place. She lived in Va's halls, slept in a chamber in one of Va's towers. Or, as it might have been, a stable in its yards. A hut against its wall. A pallet in its cellars. We do not know. What we know is that she lived there.

Then the Teth came, with men of war and horses and fire and great spells, and they levelled Va to the ground. They killed the men of the keep, and they killed the women. The women wore the same armour as the men, fought in the same lines, so who could tell? The children if they fled were mostly ignored, but if they stayed the Teth soldiers killed them too, so as not to have to hear the weeping of children. The weeping of children casts a man down and keeps him from peace with himself.

Lord Tollu of the Teth came upon a man who was twisting a spear into the side of a child, and the sight made him unhappy. "Forbear," he said. The warrior withdrew his spear and stood back. He was startled at the order, whose purport he could not understand, but he was loyal to his lord and so obeyed.

"Do you live still?" Tollu asked the child. She was a girl, of perhaps ten years. Her name, as I told you, is long since lost. It was not the only thing lost that day. She had seen her kin cut down, her lord's head mounted on the end of a pike, her home brought to the ground so that stone did not stand upon stone. She was, at that moment, almost nothing.

But there is immensity, sometimes, in an almost.

"I live," the little girl told the great lord. "It's not so great a wound."

Lord Tollu nodded. "Then walk with me," he said. And he passed on into the keep.

The girl found her feet, somehow. Blood ran freely from the gash in her side but she found her feet and followed the lord. The soldier who had wounded her watched her go with a heart that was somewhat troubled. If she died what he had done was nothing, one of a thousand bloody acts on a bloody day. If she lived—and especially if she lived in Lord Tollu's favour—it might be different.

Tollu walked across the great courtyard. The killing was mostly done now. The men of the Teth were leading out the horses from the stables of the keep, carrying the gold and silver and cloth from the family rooms, heaping up the weapons from the armouries. Already it was obvious that this was a rich prize and all would benefit from it.

The little girl followed Tollu. Blood from her wound ran down her side, down her legs. The courtyard was floored with rushes and the rushes stuck to the bloodied soles of her feet. She stumbled many times and once she almost fell, but she reached out and steadied herself against the flank of a horse that stood patient, waiting to be led away. The horse was white. The girl left a red handprint upon its shoulder.

Lord Tollu reached his own mount, and climbed up into its saddle. He watched the girl coming along behind him, more slowly. He waited until she reached him. All his men waited too, watching. The girl was the last living inhabitant of Va Keep, not counting the animals. They waited to see what the Lord would do with her.

Tollu looked down at her where she stood, swaying a little, beside his great black charger. Perhaps he read an omen in her stare, in her being alive at all when her house and kin were gone. Still, she was only alive because he had intervened. It was most likely that she was no omen at all, but only a child. That was all she looked like.

"What is your name?" he asked her. And his hand was resting on the hilt of his sword as he spoke.

"Va," the girl said.

The answer startled Tollu, and vexed him. "Va is the name of this place," he said. "Va is fallen. Choose another name."

The girl said nothing.

"Choose another name," Tollu commanded her again. And still she did not speak.

The Lord was aware that if he commanded her a third time and received no answer he would have to cut her down. Perhaps, he thought, that would even be for the best. But he had become entwined in her life when he told the warrior to spare her. If he were to go back on that decision now, his earlier mercy might be read as weakness. And in some measure the girl touched his heart, standing there robed in her own blood.

These, or some other thoughts, ran through his mind. He did not ask a third time. He reached down and she took his hand. He lifted her into the saddle behind him, and together they rode from that dead place. Lord Tollu knew that his warriors would set aside for him the share of what they had won that was rightfully his. Perhaps they would count the girl as part of his share, perhaps not. It was common enough to take slaves from among the conquered, but the Teth at that time were not wont to do so. They would take a noble prisoner sometimes, for ransom, but even that was rare. They slew their enemies and took their enemies' cattle. They knew the difference.

Highest House was not yet built. Ik Imil was the strong-hold of the Teth and Lord Tollu's house, and to Ik Imil he returned now that the campaign was over. He gave the girl to the leeches to be healed. He told them who she was, but not the name she had given herself. He just said she was a girl of Va Keep who he had decided should live. He was the Lord, so none of the men spoke against his decision.

His wife and daughters did.

His wife, the Lady Stone, said it was bad luck to bring a wounded child, a child of the enemy, within Ik Imil's walls. The ghost dogs, who follow the scent of blood, might even now be sniffing out her trail. If the Teth's luck changed for the worse they would know that it was their Lord's reckless act that had brought the ghost dogs to them.

His daughters said that bringing the girl into Ik Imil might be read as a reproach to them—as though he were saying that a foreign child had found better favour with him than his own kin.

Tollu told them to be quiet and say no more. And to confound them, for his nature like many men's nature worked by contraries, he gave the child when she was well again the task of carrying salt to his table.

This was a great honour. The hall at Ik Imil was a hun-dred strides across and a dozen families ate there. Lord Tollu sat at the highest table with the fire at his back and his wife and daughters at his side. To carry salt to him, Va had to walk past all the other tables, all the lesser families. She car-ried the salt bowl, which was of beaten brass, and the salt paddle which was of poured silver. She placed these precious things before the Lord, then when he had taken she placed them before his lady, and so on down the ranks of his daugh-ters to Shia Alia, the youngest. Lord Tollu had no sons.

There was great surprise and great remark among the Teth at what their Lord had done, bestowing such a favour on a foreign girl who by rights he should have killed. Those who had kept silent before, about the sparing of her life, complained now at her being raised over slaves with ten or twenty or thirty years of service on their backs.

The soldier who had almost slain her, whose name was Bekt, spoke loudest of all. He said he wondered if his Lord was mad, that he came between a man and his kill without a reason and then set the carrion up in robe and boots to serve him salt.

Lord Tollu came to Bekt in the great hall after meat and mead. He stood before him with his hand on his hilt. "You think me mad?" he asked.

"Only what you did," Bekt said, fearful of Tollu's anger. "Not you."

"And who does mad things but only a madman?" Tollu said.

Bekt saw his death in his Lord's eyes, and did not fight it. He knelt and bared his neck. Tollu took head from shoulders, cleanly, and no man spoke against Va after that. Even the Lady Stone and those lesser ladies who had sprung from her loins kept their counsel. They were not afraid, except of diminishing Tollu in the eyes of his liege-men. Out of love for him, they stayed silent, though they had not changed their minds.

Years went by in this wise. The girl Va grew to womanhood. The Lord Tollu grew old.

Every night the girl Va, and then the woman Va, carried salt to him at his table. Every night she picked up the bowl and the paddle from where it stood in the kitchen and carried it along the corridor that led from the kitchen into the hall. The walls of the corridor were rough stone. Nine paces were all it took to walk it from one end to the other.

Every night the girl Va, and then the woman Va, scraped the edge of the salt paddle against the wall. Not for all nine paces. With the first step she could still be seen from the kitchen. With the last step she could be seen from the hall. But for the remaining seven paces she was visible to nobody.

So she set the paddle to the stone for those seven paces.

Seven paces were not enough for her to test the sharpness of the edge. She could not stop or slow, or lower her other hand which held the bowl. All she could do was to strop the paddle against the stone, one short stroke every night.

"The girl Va is a woman," Lady Stone said to her husband. "It's not meet that a woman serve salt to you. She might have lain with a man, and the sin of it will steal the savour of the salt."

"She has not lain with a man," Lord Tollu said, and he spoke truly. No man of the Teth would lie with her.

"The girl Va is a woman," his daughters said. "You should marry her away to the Luma or the Kashete. Or else make a gift of her."

"I will not marry her away," Lord Tollu said. "Or make a gift of her." And he spoke sense. No man of the Luma or Kashete would take as gift or bride a woman with no kindred.

Time for that girl had stopped when she was spared. Though Tollu had prevented her death, he had not given her life. He knew that now. He should have let her die, or adopted her as his daughter. Either of those things would have been good. But he had held her in between, and now must hold her still.

Years went by in this wise, until one night Va came into the hall, a woman old enough to have daughters and sons of her own. One step she took, then seven steps, then one more. And this night she did not strop the paddle, but instead tested its edge against the skin of her leg. It was sharper than any sword: it laid her flesh open, though she barely pressed at all.

She went on into the hall. She stood before Lord Tollu, and she set down the bowl. But she did not set down the paddle.

At the last moment, the Lady Stone saw the blood trickling down Va's leg and guessed she had a weapon. She rose from her place but she was too slow. The paddle was at Lord Tollu's throat and it had broken the skin there, though she barely pressed at all. The Lord's arms were at his sides. He could not move before Va slew him, nor no man or woman there could come between.

"You killed my kindred," Va said to the Lord.

"In the way of such things," Tollu answered her. He could not nod. Even in speaking he widened the little wound she had made.

"And now I will kill you," Va said.

"In the way of such things," he answered her. "But let me speak first."

"I will let you speak a dozen words," Va told him. "No more."

Tollu said, "I name this girl my daughter. No man or woman harm her."

Then Va drew the paddle across his throat, and Tollu died where he sat.

The warriors in the hall drew their swords and would have slain Va. But the Lady Stone with tears flowing down her cheeks bade them let her be. "My husband was your Lord until he died," she said. "And he gave you a command before he died, which you and I and all of us must obey."

So Va became a woman of the Teth, and when they were done hating her for slaying their Lord they honoured her for her courage and her loyalty to her clan. If she was as loyal to the Teth as she had been to the Va, they said, she would do well enough.

Lord Tollu, as I have said, had no sons. Lady Stone led the Teth for seven years before she died of a fever in the Black winter.

Then Va led them. She led them well for forty turns of the sun, and they grew mighty under her. Their deeds in war were great and bloody. They won lands in the south that were rich in metal, and a mountain fastness in the north where Highest House now stands.

And she is counted in the lineage of Lord Tollu. And so are her children, and the children they bore.

I made my breakthrough as a comic book writer with *Lucifer* (2000–2006), an on-going series set in the same fictional universe as Neil Gaiman's masterpiece *The Sandman*. It was the first of many series and graphic novels I wrote for DC's Vertigo Comics. Over fifteen years I wrote somewhere in excess of two hundred scripts for them, and I was privileged to work with editors of the calibre of Shelly Bond, Alisa Kwitney, Pornsak Pichetshote, and of course Vertigo's founder, Karen Berger. ¶ But from 2004 onwards I also wrote for Marvel Comics, where I got my febrile hands on characters such as the X-Men, the Fantastic Four, Daredevil, and the Vision. I had been massively addicted to superhero stories as a child, and they were my entry point all over again when I went back to reading comics in my late teens. I still love them, although I don't write them anymore (BOOM! Studio's *Suicide Risk* will probably be my last). ¶ So when I got the chance to contribute to the *Masked* anthology, and to invent a superhero continuity of my own, I jumped at it. "The Non-Event" imagines a world in which virtually everybody has superpowers—and the cat-and-mouse game between heroes and villains has become embedded in the fabric of society. It was crazy fun to write, and I occasionally toy with the idea of bringing Lockjaw back for a swan song. ¶ As a footnote, the ridiculous superpower of turning base metal into live frogs turns out to be much more formidable than I thought. My friend Camden Ford, a materials scientist, talked me through some of the awesome and horrendous things you could do with it. Should you ever get bitten by a radioactive tadpole and develop this power, you could do worse than talk to him.

THE NON-EVENT

Pᴛᴀʜ! Pfff! Kah!

Nice to have that gag out of my mouth. Got anything to take the taste away? Water, you say? Well, if it's all you've got, I'll take it. But it's your choice: I'll sing a lot louder and clearer if you give me whisky.

So you want me to talk about Gallo. Sure you do. And you want to hear about how he came to be lying there, with no head on his shoulders, and if I feel any remorse about killing him.

Well, you know, I don't feel much about it one way or the other. The man was an idiot, and worse than that, an idiot who spat when he talked. A pornography addict who liked to talk about his hobby; a man who fell for pyramid selling schemes and wanted all his acquaintances to join the club; a serial drinker of cheap supermarket beer that made him so flatulent birds fell out of the sky wherever he walked.

But nothing in his life became him like the leaving of it. Gallo died classy. I'll give him that. That's why I agreed to come here. I'm making this statement. I'm co-operating with your dumb-fuck investigation, even though I know the conviction is a lead-pipe certainty whether I talk or not.

I'll tell you the whole story about Gallo's death. I just feel like somebody should. The rest—the confession and everything—yeah, you can have that too. Take it and choke on it, you fuckers.

So to start with, it was Pete's idea. Pete Vessell, that is, aka Hyperlink. Not Pete Haig, who is Vessell's brother-in-law. Haig's deal is converting base metal into live frogs, which as you'd imagine is not a power that's in great demand anywhere where sane people gather. Vessell has teleportation powers, and even though they're not as good as the teleportation powers Mass Transit has, say, or even those of Doctor Phase or Little Johnny Blink; they still raise some interesting and suggestive possibilities.

Let me spell it out. Vessell's deal is that he can instantaneously appear anywhere where his name is written down. I know, I know, it's like a bad joke. You blink out of reality and reappear inside a fucking mailbox, right? Great party trick. And then you stay there for a good half hour, because that's how long it takes Vessell to recharge. Before he came up with that Hyperlink name, I suggested Return to Sender and Eponymous Boy. He didn't laugh.

Anyway, Vessell brought me in, because I do the whole talking-to-locks thing. I suggested Naseem Hadid, who goes by Perspective, and George Gruber, the Tin of Rin Tin Skin. Then Naseem brought in Cindy Fellows, aka Guesswork, who I think was her girlfriend at the time. It was a good balance of powers, all things considered. But everything depends on the context, of course. Everything depends on the actual job.

The job in this case was a bank vault: DeJong's, on Aldwych. It's technically Dutch soil, by means of some obscure legal switcheroo, so the filthy rich use it as a left-luggage locker for all the stuff they don't want to pay UK tax on: their Krugerrands and their diamond necklaces, their Fabergé eggs and their bearer bonds. There's a nice concentration of obscene and highly portable wealth, and Vessell—who used to be a banker himself before the endoclasm—had scoped it out pretty well.

We met up in his basement—which he's done up okay, but which still smells of sour milk no matter how many pot pourris he puts down there—to go over the logistics and sniff each other's dog tags. The basement was a necessary part of the equation because it's lined with lead, which means nobody is going to be reading your lips from five miles off using their X-ray vision. Lead is a nostrum that seems to work against a whole range of superpowers, for reasons nobody has ever been able to explain; but Vessell is friends with Timeslide and Granite Phantom too, so he'd managed to get the room time-proofed and phase-sealed. Or at least he said he had. You never know how much is bullshit with him.

He'd made an effort, I'll say that for him. There was wine and beer, and a party plate from Marks and Sparks with little sausage rolls and vol-au-vents on it: everything except massage chairs. Vessell seemed to want to make the planning of the robbery a festive occasion, whereas mostly they tend to be fairly task-centred affairs.

So there was a good atmosphere, as far as that went. But when we ran through the plan, it was obvious it still had a serious flaw. Probably more than one, if the truth is told, but certainly one that kind of jumped up, grabbed you by the collar, and screamed "serious fucking flaw!"

We could get into the building, at night when it was empty. We could break the vault, and get our hands on a good proportion of what was in it. With Naseem on board, we could even stow the goods where they couldn't be found until the heat died down and it was safe to sell them on.

But we didn't have a strong guy. None of us, not even George, had the serious offensive capability that would allow us to walk away after the job through the shit-storm of super-powered cops who would come down on us out of a clear sky, bringing to bear such a ridiculous variety of powers that our feet would not touch the fucking ground. We needed at the very least the Rainbow Bandit or Ultravox, and preferably one or more of the four Apocalypse Boys. Otherwise there was no way we were getting out of that vault in units of more than one molecule across.

I should say here that this stuff hurts me. It hurts me in my heart. I was a career criminal back in the old days, before all this bullshit, when all you needed was a crowbar and a hopeful disposition. These days, you can't even knock over a post office without Doctor Doom, Lex Luthor and the marching band of the radioactive zombie death-ray commandos on your team. And even then, it's ten to one that one of the really big hitters like Saint Seraph or the Epitome will amble along and you'll go to the wall anyway.

It's not the endoclasm that's the problem, you know? It's human nature. The endoclasm gave about one in ten people superhuman powers, but most people are scared shitless when microwaves shoot out of their arses or their chins sprout adamantium bristles or they wake up one morning lying upside down on the ceiling. They fall apart quickly, burn out in some really nasty super-powered suicide, or else repress their abilities so deeply they effectively depower themselves: psychic castration, the experts call it. Two kinds of personality ride the crisis out okay: the deeply criminal, and the deeply moral, or as you might say, the walking ids and the walking superegos. And those law-and-order bastards seem to outnumber us enhanced villains by about a hundred to one.

I don't mean super-villains, you understand: I mean good, old-fashioned burglars, bank-robbers, and stickup merchants who just happen to have picked up powers during the endoclasm. We're not interested in ruling the world, or destroying it, or having a big, pointless punch-up with a bunch of twats in tights. We just ply our trade, when we're allowed to, do the job and then clock off.

So yeah, anyway, we're contemplating the ruin of Vessell's plan, and we're thinking too bad, because it's a nice bank vault full of all kinds of good stuff, and it would be a pleasant thing indeed to get in there and have a rummage around. Then Vessell said, "In case you're wondering about the getaway, I'm thinking we'll use Gallo."

There was a blank silence. It was just amazement at first, but then I went right on through to being angry. Seems I was wrong about why Vessell had brought me in—it wasn't because I'm Lockjaw; it was just because I used to be friends with Gallo.

"Gallo?" Gruber echoed. He's not good with civilian names.

"He means the Non-Event," Naseem said. "And he's out of his bloody mind."

"I agree," I said, getting up. "Thanks for the vol-au-vents, Vessell, but fuck you very much for the rest of it. I'm not galloping into town with Rizzo Gallo on the next horse, that's for friggin' sure. Good luck with that."

Vessell jumped up hastily, making calming downward movements with his hands so he looked like a chicken that was having trouble taking off. "No, listen, Davey," he said. "I'm serious. I've thought it through and it's going to be fine. Really. Just hear me out. If you don't think it will work, then you can walk."

"I can walk now," I pointed out, demonstrating.

"But what do you lose by staying one more minute?" Vessell insisted, stepping into my way. He was sounding kind of whiny now, and I started to remember all over again some of the reasons why I didn't like him. "You listen, you make up your mind, if it doesn't work for you, you're gone. Come on, you owe me that much."

I didn't owe him a thing, truth be told, and we both knew it. He's brought me in on a job or two, sure, and I've always carried my weight. But that's the sort of fruit-less argument where once you get into it you can end up ripping out each other's teeth with pliers. I prefer to keep the moral high ground if I can help it. I shrugged, remained on my feet but stopped heading for the door. Folding my arms, I adopted a "so convince me" stance.

And he did. He convinced me. As he explained his plan, by some fluke or intuition he met all my objections in the order they came to me. By the time he was done, I was thinking—very much to my surprise—that this thing might actually have a chance of working.

"Well I'll talk to Gallo," I said begrudgingly. "No harm in that anyway."

Sure. No harm at all. God likes a good laugh now and again, doesn't he? That's what irony is for.

Gallo was living all on his own in a rat's-ass workman's cottage just outside Luton—the only inhabited building on a condemned row that was short but not sweet. I mean, someone would have had to drop serious money on the place to bring it up to the point where you could describe it as a slum. Right then it was just four walls and—intermittently—a roof.

Gallo didn't mind much. His needs were modest, and he enjoyed his own company. More to the point, he was scared shitless of anybody else's. The Extra-Normal Affairs people were talking back in the day about giving him a pension to stay away from major population centres, but then the Tories got in again and the mood swung. They left Gallo to starve on his own time.

And that gave me my in, as it were. I pointed out to him that this job would set him up for the rest of his life. He could buy a place in the country, a thousand miles from anywhere. Buy a tent and live on top of a mountain in Tibet, or out in the Kalahari, I don't know. Anywhere except the ragged edge of fucking Luton: even a dog deserves better than that.

Gallo shook his head slowly, clearly not liking the idea. "I don't know, Davey," he mumbled, in that sing-song way of his. "I mean I really don't know. I'm doing all right here."

I looked around his living room, staring in turn at the two cracked teacups, the sway-backed Formica table, the ancient portable TV zebra-striped on top with cigarette burns. I didn't need to say anything: Gallo knew what I was thinking.

"But it's all right for me," he said, throwing out his arms in what was either a shrug or a plea. "I don't miss anything very much. And at least . . . out here . . . I can't hurt anyone. That's the most important thing. There's nothing much to upset me, but if I do get upset, then nobody gets hurt." Both times he said the word hurt he lingered on it, almost making it into two syllables. I knew where he was coming from, and I even agreed with him up to a point: there are two kinds of bad jobs, the screw-ups and the slaughterhouses. Worst kind of all is the kind that starts off as the one and slides into the other.

"Okay, Rizzo," I allowed. "So you're doing nobody any harm. But fuck, you're not doing a damn bit of good to anyone either. You're barely living. You've got all that power stored up inside you, enough to bring a whole city to a standstill, and you're living like a cockroach under a brick. You don't think you deserve a little better, maybe? I mean, who dares wins, man. Specifically, who dares wins a ticket out of this shithole into a nicer shithole, with hot water and clean towels, and a well-stocked liquor cabinet."

I mentioned that last point because Gallo used to put it away like a sailor on shore leave, and because despite being pathetically happy to see me, he hadn't offered me one of the three cans of lager staying semi-cool in a red plastic bucket full of water on the floor next to his chair: husbanding his resources, I figured.

Gallo rubbed the bridge of his nose, where he used

to wear big bottle-glass spectacles before he gave up the unequal race against his birth defects. He made a non-committal sound. "I thought you didn't do this stuff any-more," he hedged. "Since . . . you know . . . what hap-pened to Kim."

It was a low blow, in a way: Gallo breaking the estab-lished ground rules to fend me off. I don't talk about my kid, and what happened to her when she lost control of her phasing powers. I'd even trained myself out of think-ing about it. That turned out to be a dumb move, though: one time when I opened the wrong drawer and got hit by a photo of her, aged nine, blowing out her birthday can-dles, it took me a second even to remember who she was. I'd gotten that good at editing out my own memories, my own feelings. I'd cauterised Kim right out of my fucking mind.

"Yeah," I said. "Thanks for bringing that up, Gallo. You're right. I got out of the blagging habit for a while. Then I got back in again. What the hell, you know? It passes the time." By which I meant it's better than sit-ting at home with two bottles of whiskey and seeing how far you make it into the second one before you pass out.

"I don't know," Gallo said again.

"You don't know what?" I demanded, a little testy now.

"Well, I might let you down, is one thing. I'm not . . . you know . . . " He shrugged again. "I can't control it. When it happens, it happens. But I can't *make* it happen."

Part of me wanted to walk away from this, but the other part—the part that had swallowed Vessell's line and was already figuring out how to spend all that money—was bigger and stronger and a whole lot more devious.

"Rizzo," I said, "your powers kick in whenever you get upset or scared or nervous or even just surprised. I think I can guarantee that if you go into that bank next

Tuesday, one or more or possibly all of those things is going to happen. You don't need to do a thing except turn up. And the beauty of it is, even if they nail the rest of us you're in the clear. Nobody will ever be able to prove you had a thing to do with it."

Gallo seemed to like that part. "They won't clock me for the inside man?" he asked, wanting to hear me say it again.

"No reason why they should," I said. "Psi-screening is illegal in the EU, so the only people who can finger you are you and us. We'll be in Jamaica, where extradition is just a bunch of sounds you can limbo to, and you'll get a big fat freshly laundered cheque in the post three days later. Or more likely, the key to a safe deposit box in Switzerland where your share will be waiting for you to claim it whenever you want to."

Gallo's eyes misted up. He was thinking of colonnades of cheap beer, enchanted caverns of porn—his usual low-rent pursuits writ large and glorious. I felt like a shit pulling this number on him, but in my own defence I meant every word. I really didn't have the slightest inkling of how things were going to go.

I had to hang around a while longer, but I didn't really have to work at it anymore: Gallo was talking himself around now, without any help from me. I let him do it, shook his unpleasantly moist hand and hit the road.

Three days to make it happen. Then the rest of my life to lie back at my ease in some place where rain never falls, and tell the story to eager, admiring women with California tans and Garden of Eden wardrobes.

Three days wasn't long enough, as it turned out. As soon as he heard that Gallo was on board, Vessell got retrospectively serious about the reconnaissance. He decided he wanted to know which super-normal security firms

DeJong's had on retainer, as well as the shift rotas at New Scotland Yard. It was good to know who might be coming to the party, and how long it might take them to get there. He wanted to leave as little as possible to chance—a sentiment I could very much get behind.

So we ended up switching the target date from Tuesday to Wednesday, which sounds like nothing much but actually contributed significantly to our downfall. Am I talking too fast for you, flatfoot? I said, "contributed significantly"—the word you wrote there looks like it has at most six letters. I'm not signing a précis, you understand me?

The other change, which made a whole lot of sense in the context of Vessell's master plan, was that we were going to do the job right in the middle of the day, rather than at night. That felt weird, I have to admit. As Lockjaw, I usually prefer to have my conversations with deadlocks, bolts and security systems in the peace and quiet of 2:00 a.m., when you're generally guaranteed a little privacy. This was going to be a different kind of operation, but I felt like I could handle it. We all felt like we could handle it.

Naseem went in at 10:00 a.m. She'd already opened an account the day before, and paid the first quarter's rental on a safe deposit box. She went to the desk now and asked if she could get access to the box and drop off a few items. She held up a little lead-lined case that looked as though it might contain jewellery.

They took her down to the vault, where a superpowered security guard (it was Tom Tiptree—Telltale) scanned her for weapons or suspicious items, finding nothing at all. The little case was full of necklaces and trinkets: maybe a little cheap for this place, but what does a cop know about jewellery? They let her through. Telltale and another guard, the Iron Maiden, went in with her and stood at a discreet distance while she went to her safe deposit box and opened it.

There was nothing inside the safe deposit box except the documents Naseem had left there the day before. One of them was a legal-looking letter signed by one Peter H. Vessell.

There was a blinding flash and a whiff of ozone as Hyperlink—right on cue—zeroed on his name and teleported in. He had a bulky rucksack on his back, and his hands were open in front of him as though he was making an offering: Tin and me were sitting on his right and left palms respectively, having been shrunk by our good friend Perspective an hour before to about half an inch in height. She restored us to normal size in front of the astonished faces of the guards, and I punched Telltale out before he'd even got done saying "What the fuck?" Tin had a harder time of it with Iron Maiden, who quite frankly outclassed him in the smarts department and fought like a gleaming, rust-free ninja. In the end he won on mass, ramping up the density of his metal body until his feet were sinking into the concrete when he moved and his punch was like a slap in the head from a wrecking ball. The Maiden went down with serious dents in her chassis.

We checked our watches. 10:07, which meant we were well within the margin of error. Vessell got to work, hauling out the other safe deposit boxes and piling them up in front of Naseem. She shrank them in batches of a dozen or so, turning each big, heavy steel container into a dinky little thing about the size of a thumbnail. Into her jewel case they went, in clattering handfuls.

Meanwhile I sweet-talked the door to the secondary vault, which Vessell's sources said was full of bullion. My power is a little weird, if the truth is told: a little . . . well, analogue. Soft around the edges. I talk to locks, and they instinctively like and trust me. I can't give them orders, but I can usually persuade them. A little bit of flattery goes a long way, and tone of voice is just as important as what I say.

It took me three minutes to coax the vault door to open. It had a time-lock, so it had a lot of inhibitions about opening up in the middle of the day, so far off the normal schedule. I reassured it that I'd still respect it in the morning, told it all the usual things a lock likes to hear about the quality of its build and the fine balance of its tumblers, and finally there was a slo-mo *click-cluck* sound as it opened up for me.

By this time, Naseem had finished with the deposit boxes. She zapped the bullion bags, of which there were fewer, and piled them in on top until the case was brim-full. Then she miniaturised the contents by another 50 per cent or so and piled in some more. Finally she closed the case, locked it, checked the seal—which had to be per-fect—and gave us the nod.

"Okay," Vessell said tersely. "Ten fifteen. Let's go."

In a perfect world, of course, we could all have gone back the way we'd come, by means of Vessell's Hyperlink powers. But there's that half-hour downtime to factor in, and the near-certainty that we'd be followed all the way to Hell and back by whatever super-goons the bank and the Met put on our tails.

But the plan had allowed for all this.

I chatted up the main door of the vault and it sprung very readily: in my opinion, it had probably been sprung before. We stepped out and headed on up the stairs. There was another guard at the top, but he had a brute force power of some kind and Tin walked right over him just as he was starting to Hulk up.

A clatter from behind us made us all spin round, Tin already pulling back his fist for another juggernaut punch. But it was only Perspective. She'd tripped over a mop and bucket that were just lying there on the stairs, dropping the jewel case, which made a deafening clatter as it bounced back down two or three steps. She retrieved it, gave it a cursory check and hurried back up to join us.

Wednesday. The cleaner was halfway through her shift, and she left that stuff right where she was going to need it again after her break. That was all it took. Funny, huh? How you can be dead and buried and still keep right on walking, not knowing you took the hit.

We walked into the bank proper, where the ultra-rich citizenry were conducting their everyday transactions—taking out another million in small change to see them through the weekend, making a down payment on a Caribbean Island, stuff like that.

"This is a robbery," Vessell commanded. "Nobody move."

A mother with twin girls shrieked and clutched them to her bosom. A fat man gave a strangled sob of terror. An A-list celebrity forgot for a moment that this was real life and stepped out of line to confront us, then caught a warning glance from Tin and stepped right back again.

Of course, there were digital sound pickups all over the room that would respond immediately to the word "robbery": also, despite the stern tone, we weren't doing anything to stop the tellers from punching their panic buttons, so silent alarms were going off all around us. Obligingly, we walked out into the centre of the room, well away from the innocent bystanders. All except for Vessell. He went right up to the nearest line of people, unshipped his rucksack and took a machine rifle out of it. It was, to be honest, the scariest thing I'd ever seen. It looked like Rob Liefeld had drawn it.

By the miracle of super-speed, teleportation, time manipulation and dimension-jumping, we were suddenly surrounded by heroes. We were expecting them, of course, but Altered State, Beast Man, Telstar, Green Glow and Razor Wire, Cy-Bug and the Zen-tity make a pretty impressive entrance. Truth be told, I pissed my pants. Only slightly, but credit where it's due: these guys were ready to kick our arses all the way to Land's End, and they looked like they could do it without even getting an elevated heart rate.

Vessell took them in his stride, though. He just jabbed backwards with the butt of the gun and broke Gallo's elbow with it.

That part wasn't in the plan, and it probably wasn't even necessary. Gallo had been standing in line since 10:10 a.m., waiting for us to come up the stairs and the whole thing to kick off. He'd probably been fighting off panic for much of that time, so the likelihood is that his powers would have manifested as soon as he got a good look at the opposition. But Vessell wasn't leaving anything to chance.

Gallo howled and crashed to his knees, clutching his injured arm. Then the howl modulated into something else: something that wasn't sound or sight or fish or fowl or anything human beings have a name for—an invisible energy that curdled the air and rippled outwards from Gallo (if invisible things can do that) to saturate the room in an instant and permeate on through its walls into the wider world.

For a mile or more on all sides of us, things stopped happening. Car engines misfired. Phone calls got disconnected. Card readers on ATMs became dyslexic. BIC lighters refused to spark. Even the wind died.

But these were just side effects. The full brunt of the Non-Event's terrible power was felt by those of us belonging to the super-normal persuasion. Tin lost two-thirds of his body mass between one moment and the next: he staggered and almost fell as he changed back into flesh, screaming out a breath that was now too big for his altered lungs. The Zen-tity crashed even more painfully into reality, his liminal forms coalescing into one with a sound like a flag cracking in the wind. He groaned and crumpled to the ground in a heap. Green Glow's flames guttered and died; Beast Man shed all his fur in a second and stood before us stark naked, conclusively answering that question about his sexual equipment; Altered State turned from cobalt blue to ordinary flesh tones, made a sound like a hamster being stepped on and fell neatly on top of the Zen-tity.

All of which left Pete Vessell holding the only gun in the room, and facing a clutch of heroes who were suddenly powerless.

This is how it should have gone, then. We should have corralled the impotent fuckers into a corner of the room, backed out through the door where Guesswork was waiting with a van, and vanished into the sunset to the tune of a humorously twanging banjo.

What we'd lost sight of in all this, of course, was Perspective. Gallo's ripple wave went through her too, and while we were all watching the heroes dropping like autumn leaves, she lost control of the contents of the jewel case. Sure, it was lead-lined, and therefore impermeable to Gallo's null-wave, but the lining had broken open in one corner when she dropped it on the stairs: just a tiny crack, but it was enough.

Fifty bags of bullion and close on four hundred steel deposit boxes expanded to full size in a half of a heartbeat. It was like a fountain—except that a fountain doesn't weigh two and a half tons, and it doesn't explode outwards at mach two in big hard sharp-edged pieces.

Naseem caught one of the boxes in the face as it sprang back to full size: it punched her off her feet and she hit the floor hard, her head impacting the tiles with a sickening crack.

The mother with the twins went down under the bullion bags, still trying to shield them with her own body. It was impossible to tell how much weight landed on top of them: they just disappeared from sight in an avalanche of glittering gold.

The fat man got a deposit box slammed into his chest, and fell backwards, pole-axed. The movie star was pulped by a cascade of the damn things, and got a death scene more visually impressive than anything he'd ever managed on-screen.

It was all over in a second, and we were left staring open-mouthed at the carnage. There was an appalled silence that was absolute except for a patter of blood on stone from away to my left: I resolutely didn't turn my head to look. Then the screams and the sobs started up from all around.

"Okay," Vessell said in a strangled voice. "Nobody make a—"

Razor Wire gave a wordless yell and threw himself at Vessell. More by instinct than anything else, Vessell pressed down on the trigger and the gun spat staccato fire. Razor Wire was chopped to pieces in mid-air.

"Nobody move!" Vessell bellowed, more authoritatively. "Nobody fucking move!" He looked around at us wildly, desperately. "Davey, Naseem, Gruber, pick up those bags and drag them out to the car."

None of us made a move: Naseem because she was unconscious on the floor with blood pooling underneath her fractured skull, George and me because we couldn't have made our legs work right then if God himself had leant down out of Heaven and given us the order to quick-march.

"Vessell," George said inanely. "Oh my God, Vessell. Look what happened!" He was staring at Naseem, and I saw tears running down his cheeks.

"The job's not finished yet," Vessell spat. "Let's go, let's go!"

There was a distant wail of sirens.

"I don't think we're going anywhere," I said. A great weight of exhaustion and misery hit me like a bag of bullion to the back of the head. It was the kids: I think it was anyway. On Tuesday they wouldn't have been there, and I wouldn't have seen them get buried. Something inside me wouldn't let go of that image, as much as I wanted to. "I don't think we're going anywhere, Vessell."

"Drop the gun," said Telstar, grimly, "and give yourselves up. One of Zen-tity's other selves has healing powers. You have to let him work."

She had a point, as far as that went. But it was going to take a lot more than throwing our hands in the air and saying "Kamarade!" I held out my hand to Vessell.

"Give me the gun, Pete," I said.

He pointed it at me instead. "The job's not over," he repeated, his eyes wild and his teeth bared in a snarl. "We're walking out of that door, with as many bags as we can—"

Tin slammed a deposit box into the side of Vessell's head, and dropped him. Telstar went for the gun at the same time as I did, but I got to it first and she skidded to a dead stop as I swung it up to cover the heroes.

"Easy," I said. "You just stay back there. There's something I've got to do."

I found Gallo in among the wreckage, half-buried. His breathing was loud and harsh, like a broken bellows. There was blood trickling out of his nose and the side of his mouth.

"Davey," he quavered, his voice weak and ragged. "Did anyone get hurt?"

I nodded solemnly. "A lot of people got hurt, Rizzo. Kids and all. A lot of people. You think you can turn your powers off?"

His face took on a distant look for a moment or two as he concentrated. Then he shook his head. "No," he said. "Too scared. And it hurts too much. I have to be quiet, by myself, to make it stop."

He noticed the gun in my hands for the first time. He stared at it in total mystification for a moment, as though it was a copy of *The Sound of Music* he'd inexplicably found in his porn stash. Then he looked up at me, and we sort of understood each other.

"Oh," Gallo said. "Oh."

"I'm really sorry, Rizzo," I said. "I shouldn't have dragged you into this."

He shook his head wordlessly. I don't know if he was disagreeing, or if he just meant it wasn't worth talking about. I started to explain about Zen-tity and the healing thing, but I think he got the broad idea without needing to know the details.

"I'm scared," he said. "I'm really scared. I don't want to see it coming."

"Close your eyes," I said. He closed his eyes.

"Now count backwards from a hundred."

"A . . . A hundred . . . "

The gun was on full automatic. At that distance, it turned his head and shoulders and upper torso to paste.

That's the meat and potatoes, isn't it? Armed robbery. Assault. Murder. Anything else you want, feel free to add it on: it won't make any difference at this stage.

We worked with the heroes to excavate the survivors from under the bullion bags and deposit boxes. Zen-tity did his miraculous thing, and most of them were okay again: the woman with the twins, the fat man, even Naseem. The movie star stayed dead, though, and so did Gallo: even miracles have limits. And it turned out the guard on the stairs, who Tin had trampled down, was dead too. So there you go. Even if everything had gone according to plan, we'd still have had blood on our hands.

Look at us, eh? The endoclasm turned us into gods, and all we do is play cowboys and fucking Indians. I reckon we deserve what we get. Most of us anyway. I feel a little bit sorry for the likes of Gallo, who don't want to play but get sucked in anyway.

That's all I've got to say. You'd better put the gag back on, now, and lock it tight. Otherwise I'm going to start sweet-talking these manacles, and you'll have a jail-break on your hands.

This is the transcript? Okay, somebody give me a pen. I'm all yours, fuckers.

The last project that filmmaker and writer George Romero signed off on before his death was a collection of short fiction that was either set in the world of *Night Of the Living Dead* or was at least entirely compatible with it. ¶ "In That Quiet Earth," the third and last zombie story in this present volume, was my offering. I decided to honour the spirit of the original movie by making the scope of the story as small and tight as I could. It's really just one man's story, with the zombie apocalypse happening way off in the background. ¶ The title comes from the closing lines of Emily Brontë's *Wuthering Heights*, which has the narrator, Lockwood, visiting the graves of Cathy and Heathcliff. "I lingered round them, under that benign sky: watched the moths fluttering among the heath and harebells, listened to the soft wind breathing through the grass, and wondered how anyone could ever imagine unquiet slumbers for the sleepers in that quiet earth." Despite what you might think, I'm not putting those words to any ironic use here. ¶ By a weird coincidence, about a week after I finished writing the story I was contacted by the Brontë Society and invited to write a short prose piece for an exhibition commemorating the bicentennial of Brontë's birth. I was really delighted to say yes, not least because that beautiful sentence was still rattling around inside my head.

IN THAT QUIET EARTH

LATER, WHEN the risen dead were at high tide and the world as it used to be was scarcely even visible anymore, Richard Cadbury came to see his wife Lorraine's demise as the first domino, which in toppling had brought down everything else. Though that made no logical sense, on an emotional level it was compelling.

In her passing, Lorraine had tilted the world.

Cadbury rolled with it, to the furthermost edge of existence. In the months following his bereavement, he seemed to retreat into a smaller and smaller space, excluding in succession all of the people he knew—friends, family, work colleagues, neighbours—from his interior life. It was not that he ceased to feel affection for them; it was rather the opposite—that he wished to spare them the utter anomie, the lack of meaning and sense and direction that now defined and delineated his life.

These changes in him were profound, but they were hard to see from the outside. Cadbury continued to drive to the lab every day and put in a full day's work. He took a single day off for the funeral and then returned to his bench, politely declining the offer of compassionate leave and the equally well-intentioned, equally misguided offer of counselling. What he felt he could not utter. Even within his own mind it remained entirely unarticulated. There was, simply, a hole where his heart had been. The rest of him was falling into it in a slow motion cascade that would probably last until his death.

In a sense, then, death became his vector. Perhaps that was why—despite his profound isolation—he became aware of the risen dead very quickly. He was unable to remember later on where and when he picked up the first hint. It was most probably through a radio item, but he turned on the TV shortly afterwards and watched the longer and longer segments devoted to the crisis on the TV news.

He made the journey from scepticism to belief quickly and smoothly.

It was easy to be dismissive at first, when all anyone had to go on were the verbal accounts of inarticulate witnesses remastered into media-speak by bored TV anchors who didn't believe or care what they were saying. Easier still with those preposterous fragments of found footage, so ineptly framed and focused they screamed amateurishness and implausibility. The men and women lurching around streets and parks looked as though the night before had instantaneously turned into the morning after. Nothing worse than that. No hint of a new ontology, a turning point in the history of life on Earth.

But when Cadbury opened his door the next morning to go to work he saw the lurchers out in the street. Saw them seeing him, and switching their attention to him. Converging on him, even while he got into his car and drove away. Quite an extraordinary length to go to, for a hoax. Some of them had wounds on their body that looked very convincing.

He didn't get into the lab. The receptionist, Sheila, was on the other side of the double doors, throwing herself repeatedly against their shatterproof glass. Her face was a pulped mess in which bloodied teeth worked constantly, as though she could gnaw her way through the glass to get to him.

In the ninety seconds or so that Cadbury stared at her, irresolute, almost a dozen lurchers appeared around the corner of the building or from the alley behind the storage sheds, all stumbling and staggering towards him. The smell of decay came with them on the light breeze, mild but unmistakeable.

So then he knew. Knew what everybody else knew anyway. Death had become a reversible condition, but something was lost in that brief crossing of the threshold. Something profound, evidently. The returned seemed to be neither blessed nor burdened with sentience. They enjoyed a more rudimentary existence, governed by a single impulse.

What that impulse was, he saw for himself on his journey home. A number of lurchers had trapped a dog and were devouring it messily even as it struggled to get free of them. Cadbury was distressed by the creature's suffering but could see no way of alleviating it. Within a few seconds it was borne down, the teeth of a middle-aged woman fastening in its throat. The woman's handbag still hung from her left shoulder, vestigial and grotesque.

When Cadbury got back home he had to run the short distance from the kerbside to the house, keys at the ready. Even so, the lurchers scattered around his lawn and his driveway almost got to him before he was able to get the door open and get inside. He slammed it shut on clutching fingers, severing two that seemed from their appearance to come from different hands.

The phone was ringing. He hurried across the room and picked it up.

"Hello?" he said.

"Dr. Cadbury? Richard? Is that you?" It was the senior supervisor at the lab, Graham Theaker, but his voice was so high-pitched and his diction so broken that it took Cadbury a moment to identify who was speaking.

"Hello, Theaker," he said. "The most astonishing thing is happening. I wonder if you're aware of it?"

"Aware of it? Dear God, Richard, it's . . . it's the end of the world! It's the apocalypse! The . . . The dead! The dead are coming back to life to devour the living!"

"I know that, Theaker. They've been talking about it on the news. And when I tried to get into the lab half an hour ago I saw what had happened to Sheila."

"Sheila." Theaker sounded close to tears. "She has three children. Sweet Jesus, if she's spread the infection to them . . . "

"Is it an infection?" Cadbury inquired. "I wasn't aware that any explanation had been generally accepted yet."

Theaker didn't seem to have heard him. "But it's not just Sheila, Richard, it's everyone. Almost. Almost everyone. Dr Herod. Lowther. Alan . . . "

"Alan?"

"The intern. He went into Dr. Herod's office to deliver her mail. She bit him in the throat! He was able to get out of the room and lock her inside, but he died soon after from loss of blood. Or he . . . he seemed to die. We called for an ambulance, but nobody came. And then an hour or so later he stirred, and got back up again. Harrison had to strike his head off with a fire axe. It was horrible. Horrible!"

"Yes, no doubt, no doubt," Cadbury agreed. The bulk of his attention was already elsewhere, parsing the meaning of this strange apocalypse. That is, its meaning for himself, and for his dead wife. He tried to offer Theaker some solace, but really he just wanted the call to be over so he could pursue his thoughts to where they seemed to be leading. "You should turn on the TV," he suggested, "or the radio. The government is coordinating local taskforces to deal with the situation. It might be a few days before they get a handle on it, but they're coming. I would imagine that the best way to survive is to remain in complete isolation until they arrive."

"Isolation?" Theaker repeated.

"Absolutely. Stay at the lab. It's more easily defended than your house. Go out once to secure some food and water, if you must, but then barricade yourself in and wait for the all-clear. Use the security shutters, so long as you can fit them without exposing yourself to risk."

"Of course!" Theaker sounded energised now, and even hopeful. "And you'll join me, Richard? If you drive your car right up to the doors—"

"I will be working from home," Cadbury said. "Goodbye, Theaker, and good luck."

He hung up the phone. When it started to ring again he first ignored it and then unplugged it at the wall. He had work to do.

Obtaining a specimen was the first order of business, and it wasn't hard. The lurchers converged on the living without hesitation, and every such encounter left casualties. There was a window of time, some few hours, before these casualties underwent the same metamorphosis as their killers. Cadbury cruised around the neighbourhood until he found a dead man lying at the kerbside. He quickly bound the man's hands with kitchen twine and muzzled him—after a fashion—with wire mesh taken from a garden centre, the loose ends twisted together with pliers.

He drove home with the dead man in the trunk of his car. He didn't open the trunk until the car was in the garage with the rollover door drawn down and locked. By that time, the dead man was no longer dead. He was squirming and writhing in the trunk, trying to break free of his bonds. Cadbury considered trying to remove him and secure him to a workbench, but thought the risk too great. He got out his circular saw instead and removed the man's head directly. There was less mess than he expected, possibly because of post mortem changes to the viscosity of the man's blood. It had not coagulated completely but it had thickened to the consistency of molasses.

Cadbury took the head into his basement, which he had long ago converted into a laboratory both for his own pet projects and for unofficial overtime. He excised the brain and examined its structures on a microscopic level with growing fascination.

They were, for the most part, no longer viable. The brain had already begun to decay, but it seemed that with the quickening back to life that process had been arrested. Even within a head that had been severed from its body, the brain was inexplicably drawing—from the syrupy blood, or the ambient air, or some storehouse as yet unidentified—the nourishment it needed to keep itself alive.

But that word seemed tendentious, in Cadbury's opinion. Like its opposite, dead, it assumed a binary system in which all things that were not in group (a) must be in group (b). But the risen dead were anomalous. They had a tithe, a fraction of what might be called life, rather than the whole complex extravaganza of thought and feeling, selfhood and sentience. The minds of these revenants should have shut down entirely: instead they were open just a crack, like the door of a child's room at night before the child has accustomed himself to the dark.

For his second sample he did not remove the head. He searched for a small and manageable corpse, and found one at last after two hours of driving around. She was a woman of very slight build. She began to stir to life while Cadbury was binding her, which was alarming but fortunately not fatal. He was able to keep her pinioned with one knee on her chest while he tied her arms, and then to wrap the mesh around her mouth from behind. She bit him in the hand despite all his precautions, but he was wearing thick gardening gloves and the bite did not break the skin.

With the woman bound in a chair in his basement he measured the electrical flow through her brain using a device of his own manufacture—an encephalometer. He found that most aspects of brain function were no longer present. Instead of the rich three-dimensional ebb and flow of charge, the endlessly rewoven tapestry of neural connectivity, there was a single cyclical pulse. A powerful stimulus endlessly repeated, like the radio signals sent out by pulsars.

Cadbury remembered the old saw: the fox knows many things, the hedgehog knows one big thing. The risen dead were not cunning. They were not versatile. The panoply of human response had been pared down in them to one impulse, one behaviour. It was a minimal, utilitarian sort of resurrection.

Was it though, in any sense, elective? Could a man enter that state of his own volition, and control his immersion into it?

He thought of Lorraine, awake in the earth, alone. Of his own life, in the free air but still no less entombed. This situation, he felt, was not supportable. He had to go to her. But there was no point in embracing her if she saw no more in him than a warm meal.

Five cadavers later, Cadbury took his research from the universal to the personal. He constructed a machine whose business end was a plastic bucket with layers of padded latex covering most of its open end. He could thrust his head into the bucket and then seal it by means of an adjustable metal collar into which the overlapping pleats of latex were gathered. Oxygen could then be extracted from the air within the bucket by means of a Jessom-Simmonds filter and an electrically operated pump.

The hardest part was the timer. Cadbury needed to be able to calibrate it very finely, but also to adjust it in use without being able to see the numbers on the dial (because his head would be inside the bucket). He taught himself the rudiments of braille and labelled the dial with carefully placed dots of hardened resin.

Over the next two days he subjected himself to 182 near-death experiences. Each was unique, minutely different from the others either in the percentage of oxygen depleted from the air or in the duration of the ensuing suffocation.

His head began to throb after only a dozen of these self-inflicted ordeals, but he did not falter. He made notes, at first in his usual meticulous hand but then in an increasingly messy and uncoordinated scrawl. Orthography was the least of his worries. After the blood vessels in his eyes began to burst it became harder and harder to see what he was writing.

You can't break an omelette, he reminded himself stoically, without breaking a few eggs. He was the egg, in this scenario. He broke himself time after time, and charted the damage with precision. The encephalometer became his map, and his holy writ. He squinted at its endless printouts with his head tilted back almost to the horizontal, the angle that seemed optimal for what was left of his erratic vision.

The dividing line, he finally decided, was three minutes and fifteen seconds at an 8 per cent oxygen saturation. The encephalometer's read-out showed a progressive simplification of neuronal activity from two minutes and forty seconds onwards. He had ventured as far as three minutes and five seconds and come back—but only just.

He had actually felt the change. The replacement of his brain's complex staging of past, present and future, real and counterfactual, felt and believed, with a single bellowing hunger. But he had still been himself. The bellowing was a din through which he could still hear, a splash of hyper-saturated red through which he could see. And think. And be.

Ten more seconds, then, to take him up onto that knife-edge, but not over it.

The lab had a van with a portable generator. Cadbury ventured out and requisitioned it. He saw Theaker watching from one of the upstairs windows. The man did not look well. He waved frantically at Cadbury and tried to get the window open to shout down to him, but by the time he had done so Cadbury was inside the van and driving away. He had nothing to say to Theaker, and no interest in hearing what Theaker had to say to him.

The generator was not at maximum charge, but it would be more than adequate for his purposes. Cadbury loaded the van with his suffocation device, as well as a shovel, a screwdriver, a crowbar, and a double-barrelled shotgun. He hoped he would not have to use either of these last two, but it was as well to be prepared.

He drove to the cemetery. There was a parking area just inside the open gates but he ignored it, taking the van up over the cement verge and in among the graves. It was difficult to navigate here, the way very narrow, but he needed to have the generator close at hand for what came next.

The lurchers were an additional hazard. They were very numerous here, for whatever reason, and they did not move as the van bore down on them. He felt their bodies crunching under the wheels, the van rising and falling as it rode on over them.

He pulled in at last, right beside the familiar headstone. LORRAINE MARGARET CADBURY, it read, followed by two dates and a platitude: SHE IS BUT SLEEPING. He hoped with all his heart that was a lie. That Lorraine was wide awake, and waiting for him.

He opened the door and stepped out. All the lurchers in the vicinity immediately swivelled and headed in his direction. He took out as many as he could. A headshot was required to despatch them, and a headshot could not always be managed. Before the vanguard got close enough to be a threat he got back into the van and decamped to another spot, a hundred yards away.

The lurchers followed, and Cadbury saw off another half dozen as they lumbered towards him. Again he got back into the van before any of them were close enough to be a danger, and again he relocated. He repeated the manoeuvre seven more times before he had finally cleared the area.

He returned to Lorraine's grave and set himself to dig.

This physical labour was the hardest part of the whole procedure. He was unused to using his hands to manipulate anything heavier than a pipette, and the effort told on him. Before long he was panting and sweating, his hands trembling and his shoulders aching from the unaccustomed effort.

Did the lurchers hunt by scent? He did not believe so, but it was an unnerving thought. He might be taken as he toiled in the deepening hole, unable to escape to the van before he was overrun.

But his luck held. By five in the afternoon or so he had completely uncovered the coffin. Moreover he discovered to his intense relief that the screws were largely pristine. If they had rusted he would have been forced to resort to the crowbar, prising the casket open by main strength and damaging it in the process.

As it was, a few minutes sufficed to remove all six screws. Long before he had finished he could hear the faint scrabbling from inside the coffin. He threw open the lid and beheld her, his lost love.

Cadbury was a realist when it came to physical processes, and he was not squeamish. He had prepared himself mentally for what he was about to see. There was therefore no moment of shock or resistance. If anything he was amazed at how recognisable Lorraine still was. Wasted, of course, and decayed, with her face sunken in and more of her hair lying on the white silk behind her head than on her scalp. A grey fungal growth on the left side of her chin made her look, strangely, as though she had decided in death to sport a beard but had trimmed it too recklessly.

Her upper body squirmed as she tried unsuccessfully to raise herself. Nine months dead, her muscles were too atrophied and eaten away to support and animate her frame, meagre and hollowed out though it was. Her eyelids fluttered but could not close over the dry, sunken pits of her eyes.

"Lorraine," he said. "It's me, Richard." He did not know if she could understand him. He presumed not. But he did not wish to intrude on her privacy without announcing himself.

He set the dials. Eight per cent. Three minutes and fifteen seconds. He slid the bucket over his head and pressed the switch. The van's generator chugged and the pump hummed, industriously extracting oxygen from the air circulating around his mouth.

The descent seemed to take much longer than it had the other times. Perhaps, though, that was merely because this time he had an actual destination. His head began to pound around the end of the second minute. His lungs sucked helplessly for sustenance that would not come. A wave of dizziness compelled him to sit down, and then to lie full length on the ground.

The third minute was an eternity; the final fifteen seconds longer still. His last, failed breath was drawn out unfeasibly, his chest taut and quivering, until the muffled ding of the bell announced that his time was up.

He struggled out of the helmet. It took a long time: he could barely remember where the fastenings were, or how they worked. His thoughts passed through his brain like flotsam bobbing on a sluggish tide.

But Cadbury had measured the time and the saturation to a nicety. He had dosed himself with death, as a man might dose himself with penicillin. He was one of the reanimated now, yes, but he was still himself. His descent into death had been a series of progressively longer immersions, all of them under his own control. His resurrection was the same.

Piecemeal.

Fragmented.

Mediated.

He felt the stirrings of the all-consuming hunger that defined the rest of the risen, but it did not overwhelm him.

He could think through it, though it took a vast effort and a vast time. He remembered himself, and his purpose.

Slowly he stood. He advanced to the lip of the grave and lowered himself into it, careful not to step on Lorraine in the narrow, confined space.

He squeezed in beside her, gradually and gently.

As he had hoped, she did not respond to him as food now. He was of the dead, as she was—at least to the point where his proximity did not stir her appetites.

He tried to speak to her, to tell her not to be afraid, but speech was no longer available to him. Though he could form the words, he had no breath to push them out into the world. They lay on his tongue, which vibrated with stillborn syllables.

He lowered the lid of the casket.

He settled himself into as commodious a position as he could find, on his side so that he took up less space and did not press against Lorraine in a way that might be constraining. Her body stirred softly against his. Perhaps she was still trying to raise herself up, but he thought not. The movement had nothing of urgency about it. Rather it seemed that, like him, she was making herself comfortable.

Goodnight, my love, he said. There was no sound, only the flexing of his throat and the rise and fall of his tongue against his palate.

He found her hand, and held it. He closed his eyes.

Eternity passed, on the whole, very pleasantly.

This is another story from *The City of Silk and Steel*. Its protagonist, Anwar Das, wasn't in our original plan for that book. We just made him up along the way, and liked him enough to keep going back to him.   ¶   That's a wonderful thing, when it happens, and I think it's what writers mean when they say, as a humblebrag, that their characters take on a life of their own and rebel against their creator's plans. It's a lot more prosaic than that, in my experience. In the writer's head, characters generally start out as place-holders. You have a sense of who they are and where they're going, but until you voice them and expend imaginative energy on them you don't really know them. Sometimes, by the time that process is finished, you're left with something that takes you a little by surprise. That was what happened to me with Gaudium in *Lucifer* and Mr Bun/Pauly Bruckner in *The Unwritten*, and it happened again with Anwar Das. He was just the least disreputable and the least stupid of a gang of brigands that our female protagonists encounter. Pleading for his life, he assures the women—particularly Zuleika, who wants to cut his throat on the spot—that he can be of use to their enterprise. And when they finally have a city to call their own, he makes good on his promise.   ¶   It's a playful story about politics. As such it's an oddity for me. Normally when I get close to anything political I become dark and doom-laden.

THE GOLD OF ANWAR DAS

"You know why I asked you to come, Anwar Das?"

"If I may speak my heart, Lady Gursoon, I think it's because the City of Women finds it expedient to have a man for its ambassador—and you don't know that many men who you actually trust."

"Do you think you could take on this role for us?"

"Of course. My previous job involved a great deal of diplomacy and protocol."

"You were a camel thief."

"Yes. The diplomacy and protocol arose more in the fencing of the camels afterwards. But tell me, lady. What does Bessa need most at this point in its trajectory? Wealth? Influence? Accurate intelligence as to its rivals' doings?"

"Stability, Anwar Das. We need something that will ensure we can survive, and thrive, in a future that is uncertain and likely to be stormy."

"And now I have my brief. Thank you, lady."

"Thank you, Anwar Das. When can you start?"

"I was on payroll, wise and beauteous one, from the moment when I bowed to you."

Arriving in Heqa'a on the back of a camel whose name was Muzra, the Whirlwind, Anwar Das of Bessa took up residence in the Imtil. From there, he sent gifts of wine and dates to the esteemed and noble house of Omran Injustari. He did not, at this time, present himself at that house, but announced his willingness to do so at a time that might be mutually convenient.

Only silence in reply, but Anwar Das was not discouraged. He obtained privy access to Injustari's sister, the celestially beautiful Siyah Sireyah. Extremely privy access: they made love for the best part of an afternoon, in a great variety of positions, and afterwards lay in each other's arms, spent and sweaty and highly satisfied with the day's labours.

"You are a strange man," Siyah Sireyah murmured.

"Am I?" Anwar Das affected dismay. "I thought I was a comparatively well formed one."

"Oh, as to that," the lady murmured, "I have no complaints. But it's strange that the City of Women should send us such a—what's the word?—such a *virile* ambassador."

Anwar Das frowned judiciously. "Bessa, lady, is far more than that sobriquet suggests," he told her. "A city whose populace were entirely female would be doomed to last only a generation, unless women, like bees, could find the secret of reproducing their kind without the intervention of the male sex. Until that happens, we men will always be at your side, ready at need to play our part in the propagation of the species."

"Such selfless devotion!" said Siyah Sireyah, caressing Das's manhood with warm affection. "This generosity of spirit must be rewarded!"

She rewarded it in a way that Das found impossible to argue with, and another hour or so passed without either of them looking at the glass or troubling to turn it. Then, regretfully, the lady began to dress. In a foreign city, she explained, her brother was always anxious for her safety. She had told him that she was abroad to visit friends, but he would look for her return before sunset.

"Lady, I have gifts for you," Anwar Das said. "Unless

you think that gifts would profane the near-mystical communion we've just enjoyed."

"Not at all," Siyah Sireyah said enthusiastically.
"Next to the near-mystical communion we've just enjoyed,
I enjoy presents best of all. Wheel them out!"

Anwar Das did so, and the lady's eyes became wide as
she saw the beautiful things the Bessan envoy had brought
her. Peerless silks, delicate brocades, silver necklaces, and
bracelets inset with coloured glass beads most cunningly
wrought. Her breath caught, for a moment, in her throat.

"So lovely!" she sighed. "So lovely!"

"Their loveliness will be consummated when you
wear them," Anwar Das said, kissing the lady's neck. And
they took their leave of each other with many protestations of love.

The next day, Anwar Das sent gifts of pears and
spiced meats to the esteemed and noble house of Omran
Injustari, along with another discreetly worded suggestion
that at some point, a meeting might be arranged to their
mutual advantage. Silence again.

A lesser man might have been deterred. Anwar Das
merely shrugged and went out on the town. In Heqa'a
there is a house, the House Several, where musical per-
formances are sometimes staged, and there he went. To
the strains of buzuq, mijwiz, and tanbura, he made the
acquaintance of the lady Afaf Nusain. It became an inti-
mate acquaintance shortly afterwards, in one of the upper
rooms of the House Several.

Kissing the lady's thighs and belly, after the imme-
diate fires of passion had somewhat abated, Anwar Das
asked her if she would be insulted to accept a gift from
him. "Besides the gifts already proffered?" Afaf Nusain
sighed contentedly.

"Of a different order," Anwar Das answered her.

"I should not be insulted, Ambassador. Not in the
slightest."

Anwar Das gave her jewels and patterned cloths of great beauty, which she received with enormous pleasure. He begged her, when she wore them, to think of him, and she vouchsafed to do so—promising, besides, to spare him more than a passing thought when she took them off.

On his third day in Heqa'a, Anwar Das sent gifts of apricots and almonds to the esteemed and noble house of Omran Injustari, indicating in the accompanying letter that he wished to bend that gentleman's ear at some point before they both died of old age.

He expected no reply, and so was not disappointed.

That night he visited another noble house and met the wife and daughters of the Ibiri princeling, Namuz, in that royal gentleman's absence. There was no amorous play, but plenty of stories, in which—as in the act of love—Anwar Das was adept. The women were thrilled at his narrative skills, and the evening passed agreeably for all. Before leaving, Anwar Das presented all three of them with gifts of jewels and dresses of exquisite design, and they thanked him effusively. They asked if there were any way that they could show their gratitude, and he gave them the same answer he'd given the lady Afaf Nusain—if they thought of him kindly, from time to time, he would be well rewarded.

On the fourth day, Anwar Das rested. That evening, Prince Namuz was hosting a party to which all the nobility of Heqa'a were invited, and Das, as envoy plenipotentiary of the city of Bessa, was naturally invited too.

In the course of the evening, he found occasion to sidle up close to the esteemed and noble Omran Injustari, and introduce himself.

"Oh," Injustari said gruffly. "You're the one that's been bombarding me with fruit, aren't you? Well listen here, Ansul Bas, or whatever you call yourself. I don't need whatever it is you're selling, and throwing dates and apricots over my garden wall isn't going to change that.

I've got profitable partnerships with every city West of Baram-Saal, and I'm not about to shake that tree while I'm standing under it, you understand me?"

Anwar Das confirmed that he did indeed understand, and turned the conversation to other things. As they spoke—about the shocking state of the city walls, and the best oasis to use between Stesh and Ibu Kim, and the chance of Abdul Mu'izz writing a decent poem one of these days—Injustari's attention kept wandering to the women who passed on every hand, dressed in uncommon splendour. Anwar Das noticed the frown that appeared on the great merchant's face, and could not forebear to smile.

Omran Injustari saw that smile, and slowly, its import dawned on him. "Yours," he said.

Anwar Das shrugged. "That depends on how you define these things," he replied.

"Bessan silk."

"No."

"Bessan silver."

"No."

"What, then?"

Anwar Das took a sip of wine, drawing out the moment. "Bessan weavers," he said at last. "Bessan silversmiths. Bessan carders and dyers and artists and glassblowers. We produce no raw materials, Excellency. We have no mines, and few farms. But we have the finest artisans in the region."

Injustari was silent, but many thoughts visibly pursued each other across his face.

"You're wondering," Anwar Das interpreted, "whether you can keep this secret, at least until you lock your current customers into longer-term agreements. Excellency, you cannot. Many of these ladies have husbands and fathers who are merchants in their own right, or who sell contracts on behalf of the Heqa'a principate. Each of them will by now have had a conversation which began with the words

'My dear, where did you get that?' The secret is not in your keeping, nor—any longer—in mine."

Injustari made a gesture—opening his fingers as though releasing some matter that, while annoying, was so insubstantial that it could be trusted to float away on the slightest breeze. "My contacts here are long established," he said. "They know me, and they're happy to trade with me."

Anwar Das nodded as if to say, *Of course, of course, and I have a bridge in a city not yet built which you might be interested in purchasing.*

"You offer me no threat," Injustari insisted.

Anwar Das threw out his hands. "I don't mean to," he said. "I'm only trying to find a market for these goods, which I'm sure you'll agree are superb. If, in so doing, I steal your client base away from you and leave you and your family in the most abject and unrelieved poverty, that will be regrettable and entirely unintended."

They stood side by side for some minutes, Anwar Das respecting the other man's profound inner struggle.

"How much do you want?" Injustari growled at last.

"For a five-year contract," Anwar Das said, "during which period Bessan goods will reach Heqa'a, Diwani and Perdondaris entirely via your trade caravans—for this, ten thousand in gold per year, rising to thirteen by annual increments, plus one half of all profits over twice the cost of manufacture, the books to be opened to your clerks whenever necessary and a review of these terms to be carried out twice per year or at any time during the life of the contract, should either party realise profits which the other considers excessive."

Omran Injustari blinked.

"But," he said at last.

"Yes, Excellency?"

"But those terms are entirely reasonable! What's the catch?"

"Ah," said Anwar Das. "The catch. I'm glad you asked."

From Heqa'a, the uncomplaining Muzra took Anwar Das at astonishing speed to Perdondaris, the white city of the north. Into the great metropolis, he fell as a single drop of water falls into Ocean, and is lost. But unlike that drop of water, he had letters of introduction from the esteemed and noble Omran Injustari, whose trade caravans wove in and out of Perdondaris's marbled streets every day of the year. And therefore, unlike that drop of water, he was admitted to a private audience with the Caliph.

It never rains in Perdondaris in any case, by the way, so it was a fatuous metaphor to start with.

The Caliph, the most Serene and Exalted Kephiz Bin Ezvahoun, was not surprised to see Anwar Das. He'd been tracking the Bessan ambassador's progress across the blessed hinterlands for a year and a half, wondering how and when he would finally thread the maze that led to Perdondaris's throne room. Now that Das had at last arrived, the Serene and Exalted felt moved to congratulate him.

"You had a bugger of a job," he said, "if you'll pardon my Turkish. The bureaucracy here has my official calendar sewn up five years in advance. In Perdondaris, spontaneity means only filling in seven forms before saying good morning instead of the usual eleven."

"Your Highness's jest is all the more amusing for being the literal bastard truth," Anwar Das said, performing a graceful and protracted *salaam*. "But is it your wish, this fine morning, to throw all that camel dung out of the window and be truly spontaneous?"

"Get yourself into a position you can sustain without a cramp," the Serene and Exalted invited him, "and give it your best shot."

Anwar Das settled into a more comfortable cross-legged posture and got to the point. "Perdondaris is like an elephant, highness," he said. "It is great, and it is mighty, and everyone is impressed when they see it—but their choices, at the end of the day come down to two. They can ride on it, or they can stay well out from under its feet."

"A fair summary," the Caliph agreed.

"Some of your nearest neighbours, sadly, have been denied access to either of those options," Anwar Das pointed out.

"You mean Bessa?" the Serene and Exalted asked, slightly thrown. "Bessa is far enough away from us, I think, that she need not fear us."

"Your pardon, Excellency. I didn't mean Bessa, I meant Sussurut."

The Caliph's eyebrows rose. "Susurrut? That's much closer, certainly. You know there are factions within Perdondaris that view Susurrut as an unruly suburb."

Anwar Das knew this very well, but pursed his lips as though the folly of such a view pained him deeply. "Excellency," he said, "we're both men of the world and we're neither of us fools. You know as well as I that Perdondaris has conquered Susurrut three times in living memory, but never held it for longer than five years at a stretch. The irregular exercise of your subjects' wilder aspirations costs both cities dearly."

The Caliph stood up. "We will continue this talk," he said, "in the gardens."

As they walked among the plenty of nature, sustained most unnaturally in this dry and thirsty place, the Caliph admitted Anwar Das's point—which was a lot easier than admitting it in the throne room, in the hearing of two dozen attendants and twice two dozen spies. "The cost to both cities of these futile skirmishes is indeed very high, Anwar Das. But it's a lot higher for the Akond of Susurrut than it is for me," he mused. "And in many ways, I prefer the war party here to be weakened and attenuated by the war draft and the war levy. I always make sure they pay more than their share."

The Serene and Exalted stopped on a terrace overlooking the sunset. Anwar Das stopped with him. That symbol of ending and endlessness made them both sombre.

"A man's life is like a wave that breaks on a beach," Anwar Das observed. "The water that was the wave rolls back down the strand to join the water of Ocean, and it has no knowledge of itself, any longer, as a separate thing. In the same way, a man's body joins the elements again and there is nothing left to show that he stood and thought and moved. Except for men like you, Excellency, whose lives touch the lives of others in myriad ways, and who may be remembered for their deeds long after their bodies are dust."

"You negotiate with philosophy," the Caliph said, "because your bag is empty."

"My bag is empty," Anwar Das countered, "because I would not insult so great a king with anything so paltry as a bribe. I would bribe you with history, serene and exalted one. I would bribe you with the words that will be spoken when you can no longer hear them."

"What words?" Kephiz Bin Ezvahoun asked.

"He took the fragile flower of peace and tied its stem to a stout stake, so that it grew stronger and stronger. Before him, Perdondaris and Susurrut exhausted themselves with war. Now they clasp each other in amity, and each is richer than it was before. The alliance between the two can never be broken, and neither need fear any enemy, for if any man rises against the one, the other will strike him down like the hammer of high heaven."

The Caliph laughed long and hard, but the glance he turned on Anwar Das was curious. "You have a fine line in camel dung yourself," he said.

"Your Excellency is too kind," Anwar Das said, bowing low.

"And if I said yes—ticking off the warmongers mightily—Bessa would be the broker of the peace?"

"A truly neutral party would be needed for such a delicate job. I would be honoured to act as mediator, and to lay out the terms of a suitable treaty for your own and the Akond of Susurrut's approval."

The Caliph grinned. "You want a crowbar," he summarised.

"Of the finest manufacture, tipped and filigreed with silver."

"What did you do before you were a politician?" Kephiz Bin Ezvahoun asked. "Were you by any chance a camel thief?"

For a moment, Anwar Das was discountenanced. "It was far south of here," he began. "I never stole from Perdondaris, Excellency, or from any of its . . . "

The Caliph roared with delighted laughter. "It was a joke, man! But you're telling me it's true? Oh, that's too wonderful!" He wiped tears from his eyes. "A thief! A bandit! Bessa appoints a bandit as her ambassador! But of course she does, because her soldiers are odalisques and her citizenry are sultans! Wonderful! By the Increate, truly wonderful!"

Recovering his composure a little, Anwar Das suggested that they might run up a rough draft for a possible treaty right there and then.

The Caliph shook his head vigorously. "Oh, the details I leave to you. Only make sure that they include the abandonment of the forts on the Yildriziah, and the re-opening of the Pass Paved with Iron. I need to have a few fig-leaves to flaunt in front of my fanatics." He was chuckling again by this point. "I meet so few camel thieves! If they're all like you, I'm surprised we have any camels left at all!"

They went back into the throne room, where spiced wine was brought. They talked for some turns of the glass about the many ways in which stealing camels and governing cities were not so dissimilar as might be thought, until at last Anwar Das took his leave, with effusive thanks for the Serene and Exalted's great generosity.

Thence to Susurrut, where Anwar Das arrived in the middle of the night. This being Susurrut, night or day made little difference: everything is for sale in that place so long as a man knows where to apply, and Anwar Das had old acquaintances there. Among them was Bethi, the former servant maid who had now become the most stalwart of his spies. She welcomed him with honeyed fruits, and with the sweeter gift of her embrace.

"How many times did you have to put out in Heqa'a?" she asked him teasingly, after they had pleasured each other.

"I am a loyal and uncomplaining servant of the Bessan polity," Anwar Das told her, his face grave.

Bethi marvelled. "That many times! Your poor manhood!"

Bethi's reasons for being in Susurrut included the clearing of the ground for a meeting between Anwar Das and Rudh Silmon, the merchant prince and so-called Keeper of the Fields of Gold. She had scattered bribes so judiciously and sweet-talked all interested parties with such address that Anwar Das was ushered, before noon of the next day, into the presence of the man himself.

Silmon was inspecting samples, as he did most mornings, sitting in a dark room with the windows barred and sniffing judiciously at dozens of dark-coloured powders arrayed in the recesses of a long tray built for that purpose alone.

"Anwar Das," Silmon said. *Sniff, sniff!* "The Bessan ambassador." *Sniff!* "Come with a shopping list, no doubt."

"The Keeper is as clear-sighted as he is morally irreproachable," Anwar Das said, civilly, and he handed Silmon a scroll

Silmon undid the ribbon, and the scroll fell open: it fell all the way to the floor, and had not completely unwound when it got there.

Silmon read the list, his lips moving as he silently recited its contents. Before he had got more than five lines into it, he set it down and stared at Anwar Das.

"Are you mad?" he asked him.

"I believe not," Anwar Das answered.

Silmon threw the scroll back across the table to his guest, in irritation or perhaps disgust. "You are wasting my time," he said, "and your own. I will sell you spices and scents in any quantity, assuming you have sufficient gold to pay my admittedly outrageous prices. But the items on this list I will not sell for a king's ransom."

"I have no such fortune," Anwar Das said, opening his hands to show his empty palms.

The Keeper glared at them. "Then you are an idiot, sir!"

"But I have this." Anwar Das drew something slender and elongated from his belt. Silmon gasped and drew back, for a moment fearing an assassination attempt. Susurrut had enemies who would be only too happy to kill him, if they could do so without being found out.

But what Anwar Das handed him was only another scroll, broader but much shorter than the first. The Keeper stared at the seal, which was the seal of the most Serene and Exalted Kephiz Bin Ezvahoun, Caliph of Perdondaris.

"What is this?" he asked stupidly, his resources of speech and intellect briefly abandoning him. Perdondaris's whimsical pleasure and displeasure were the diastole and systole of life in Susurrut: Silmon could not regard that seal with equanimity.

"Read it," suggested Anwar Das, "and see."

Silmon broke the seal and scanned the letter. Anwar Das stood silently and patiently by while the older man went through the requisite stages of awe, disbelief and violent perturbation.

"Peace?" he said at last in a strangled gasp. "Peace with Perdondaris?"

"Well, a treaty with Perdondaris," Anwar Das corrected him scrupulously. "A treaty which guarantees peace for a period of . . . Pardon me, I have misremembered the precise details."

"Ten years!" the Keeper ejaculated.

"Ten years. You are right. And the review to be carried out in the ninth year, by men of wisdom and goodwill from both cities, with a guarantee that if there have been no skirmishes or debacles in that time, a second period of not less than a further decade will be agreed. Susurrut must abandon the forts on the Yildriziah, and keep the Pass Paved with Iron open to all travellers and caravans of any provenance whatsoever. These are the only stipulations."

At this point, Anwar Das's greatest ally was time. Settling back in his chair, he took a pipe and tobacco from his pack, prepared a toke and lit up, while Rudh Silmon read and re-read the entire screed from its initial fanfares to its closing pompousities. Das had written it himself, so he knew these flourishes were good and needed to be savoured. Moreover, he was aware that Silmon was weighing in his mind all the implications of a peace treaty with Perdondaris, and that this weighing was likely to be a complex and protracted process.

When he had almost finished his pipe, the older man set down the scroll and fixed him with a stare. "I'm no politician," he said, stating the obvious. "These matters are not for me to decide."

"No," Anwar Das agreed. "In this place, and at this time, they are for *me* to decide. I have won the ear of the Caliph Kephiz Bin Ezvahoun, and I don't mean in a game of hazard. For the time being—who knows how long it will last?—I have his permission to broker a peace on his behalf.

"But let us be clear, Rudh Silmon. These matters do have a direct bearing on your business. Peace with your great neighbour means an opening of trade routes kept closed for whole generations. Only imagine how far you could expand your empire, and how great the house of Silmon could become!"

Silmon was imagining precisely this: Anwar Das's words merely played, like the fingers of a skilled musician, across the already tautened strings of his thoughts.

Still, the Keeper rebelled against the price that was being demanded of him. "But what you're asking in return would threaten both the city and my enterprises!" he protested.

Anwar Das met this objection with a smiling countenance. "Only if Bessa entered into direct competition with you," he said. "A second treaty could easily be drawn up, not between Bessa and Susurrut but between Bessa's merchants and yourself. A treaty not of peace but of trade and commercial strategy. If the cities of the plain were imagined as one enormous confection, concocted of fruit and sugar and covered in glazed pastry, we could agree which slices went to you and which to Bessa."

Rudh Silmon examined this comparison, and found it both potent and suggestive. "That might be done," he agreed. "But once I give you what you ask for, you'd be bound by nothing but your word."

And there they were, at last, at the point which they had always been destined to reach. This time what Anwar Das took from his sash was indeed a knife, but in the numinous strangeness of that moment, Rudh Silmon did not quail from it. "We would be bound only by our word," Das agreed. "Excellency, let me show you what the word of Bessa means." He laid his right hand down upon the table, palm down, and poised the knife above it.

"I swear," Anwar Das said, "on my rank and eminence as Bessa's ambassador to Susurrut, that at your request I will cut any finger from this hand—including the forefinger, though it would be with some sadness because I play the buzuq in a small way and it's a lot harder to strum with that particular finger missing."

The Keeper looked from the hand to the knife, and thence to Anwar Das's face. He saw only calm, cold resolution there, and he did not doubt that the ambassador meant every word he said. "I am as serious in this," Das told him, "as I am in everything I've said to you. In the past, diplomats have been famed for their lies and equivocations. The diplomats of Bessa are as truthful as priests, and there are no priests in Bessa because the Increate has not decided yet what to make of us. You may believe everything I say, Rudh Silmon. My words follow my heart, and my deeds follow my words. I, who lived for years as a thief and a murderer, swear this to you in solemn sooth."

Silmon blinked.

"The . . . The forefinger then," he said.

Anwar Das's hand came down, and he began to carve.

"No! No!" Silmon cried, hastily. "I require no amputations, and the inlay on that table is of cedar and mahogany! I believe you, Anwar Das. I trust your word."

"I am heartily glad of it," Anwar Das said. The knife had already broken the flesh at the base of his finger, and a single drop of blood welled there like a ruby. "Then perhaps we might turn to the items on my list."

When he left Susurrut, Anwar Das rode at the head of a caravan of forty camels. They bore in their saddlebags many tens of thousands of seeds and seedpods, from which could be grown crops of cassia and cinnamon, marjoram and cumin, fennel, nutmeg and cardamom, and a dozen spices besides. Rudh Silmon had not stinted, and indeed had added in—after a visible struggle with himself—an additional panier of unimpressive red-brown seeds which he forebore to name. "Give them," he had told Anwar Das, "to your Sultana. Tell her it is a gift from the house of Silmon."

But since Bessa had no Sultana, and since the lady Gursoon didn't know a seedpod from a stamen, he gave the panier instead to Farhat, who by this time was so busy setting up Bessa's trade guilds that she slept standing up and could not hold a conversation lasting longer than ten heartbeats.

When she saw the contents of the panier, Farhat gave a small yelp, like the cry of a woman at the moment of sexual release, and looked up at Anwar Das with eyes into whose corners tears threatened to come.

"What are they?" Anwar Das asked, mystified at the vehemence of her reaction.

"Zaferan," she whispered. "Crocus seeds! Oh Anwar Das, you have done a great thing."

"And without losing a single finger," Anwar Das added, which mystified the lady considerably.

They sorted out the irrigation in the second winter after the fall of Hakkim, and in the third summer, there was a swathe of desert west of Bessa where the gold of endless sand gave way to the purple of crocus fields—and thence, by arcane ministrations, to the deeper, infinitely more precious gold of saffron.

And that is how Anwar Das fulfilled his commission.

I wrote this for a national newspaper's magazine section. I won't say which one. They didn't commission the piece but they sent me an open invitation to write a micro-short for them, and they said they were happy for me to decide the theme. So I wrote and submitted this little piece about the Garden of Eden and my kiddie-level understanding of quantum physics. ¶ They sent it back, pretty sharpish. They asked me to write a different story, preferably one that wouldn't insult the religious sensibilities of their readers. I was baffled. I honestly didn't see—and still don't see—where the possible offensiveness might lie, especially given that I wasn't even disputing the existence of Adam and Eve. Biblical literalists might cavil at the idea that the snake in Eden was acting on God's direct orders, but they would have to admit that it was part of God's plan. All I did was turn the plan into a literal job description. ¶ Anyway, I didn't send the newspaper another story, and they never paid for this one, so we're all good. I don't think "Take Two" has appeared in print anywhere before now.

THERE WAS another garden, next door to Eden, where things went a little differently.

The lady who'd been put in charge here (along with her helpmeet, Max) was named Vera. She was pretty good at it but still learning, obviously.

"This tree?" she asked the snake. "This tree here?"

"Exactly," the snake said. She wasn't the same snake, but she came out of the same stable and she was working to the same brief.

"This tree will give me all the knowledge God has?"

"Every last bit of it."

"Wow," Vera said.

"I know. Pretty sweet deal, right?"

"I'm going to give it a hard pass."

"You eat the fruit, and then you'll be as smart as God himself, and you can . . . Wait, what?"

"I'm good, thanks. Anyway, God's not God because He's smart. He's God because he's in love."

"In love?" The snake was appalled. "What do you mean? He's stern and patriarchal and he laid down a bunch of stupid rules. Does that sound like love to you?"

"It's just the one rule," Vera said. "But that's not what I meant. He's not in love with us; He's in love with everything. That's why He started out by saying 'Let there be light.' He wanted to see all the stuff there was out there. And when he saw there wasn't enough, he made some more."

"Can we please get back to the subject?" the snake requested.

That was when Max came up and asked what the two of them were talking about.

"God," Vera told him.

"Aw, God's great!" Max enthused. "You know he let me and Vera name all the animals? And he didn't laugh when I came up with the spike-a-roon."

"Which by a later unanimous vote became the hedge-hog," Vera reminded him.

"Exactly. But he said it was okay by him if we went with spike-a-roon. He's so cool."

"But He makes pointless prohibitions . . . " the snake tried again.

"Which we're bound to break, sooner or later," Vera agreed. "We know. It's kind of a joke."

"It's a what now?" the snake spluttered.

Vera shrugged. "Well, not a joke. But it's, like, the next move in the game. He wants to change things up. Keep them interesting. That's probably why he sent you over here, to tempt us into breaking the rules. Only we're not going to bite. We refuse. So let's see what He does next time around. I bet it will be amazing!"

"I don't work for God," the snake declared indig-nantly. "I work for a rival company that offers a far supe-rior deal. Well, actually, for a temp agency. I prefer to have the flexibility."

"God's in there somewhere," Vera told her. "You can bet on it."

The snake went back to the office. Curled in and out of a ladder-back chair, holding a pen in the graceful loops and swirls of her tail end, she took another look at her contract. This time she went through it carefully, and damn if Vera wasn't right. The company she'd been temped out to was a wholly owned subsidiary of Heaven. It even turned out to be God who'd filled out the work order. His signature was right there at the bottom.

And God was standing behind her at that very moment. He was omnipresent, of course, so that shouldn't have come as much of a shock.

"Some problem here?" God asked.

"That depends," the snake said, aggrieved. "I feel like I've been wasting my time just a little."

"Not at all," God assured her. "You play your role, they play theirs, things move on in a certain direction."

"Wonderful. And is the woman right? Is it a game?"

God looked shocked. "A game? No. She said that? Wow. No."

"What is it, then?"

"Well, snake, Creation wasn't quite complete. It needed one more secret ingredient. Quantum undecidability. Every outcome that can happen has to happen, somewhere."

"I don't even know what that means," the snake snapped.

"I'll be happy to explain when you've finished the job."

"I'm going to hold you to that," the snake said, a touch coldly. She put down the pen, reached over to the in-tray and grabbed the next work order. Garden number three.

There were a whole lot of work orders in that stack, she realised. Maybe ten-to-the-power-sixty-three or so, a vigintillion. She couldn't clock off until she'd at least broken an octillion or two, or she'd be working the weekend.

Every outcome that can happen, has to happen.

She picked up the pen again, turned the work order over and wrote across the back of it: I QUIT.

She slithered to the door, shimmied under it with her dignity intact, and headed home. It was only when she got there that she thought: What have I done? I'm behind on the rent! I need a new kitchen range.

But God was delighted. He paid her right up to the end of the month and offered her a seat on his new anti-determinist think tank.

And the evening, and the morning . . . Well, you get the picture.

"Face" is an oddity because I wrote it twice: once as a prose piece and once as a comic book short. The comic book version is well worth checking out if you can find it because the art is by Sonny Liew, a Singaporean artist with whom I had the good fortune to collaborate three times. He did a sublime job of rendering the various non-human races that feature in the story, and in imagining the city of Sestival itself. ¶ This is really a story about the British in India, and it differs from a lot of my stories in that it has a fairly obvious moral. The moral isn't stated in the story, for the simple reason that the narrator, Melchior Tavel, is a self-regarding fool who never even comes close to understanding the havoc and heartbreak he's causing. ¶ But his final conversation with his daughter lets us see into his misshapen heart, and for good or bad it says all I've got to say about the hopeless cruelty and tragedy of the colonial project that defined my country for so long.

FACE

From: Governor Plenipotentiary and Colonial Legate First Class Melchior Tavel
To: His Inestimable Excellency the Suzerain of the Eastern Empire, Servant of the First House and Speaker Direct.
5th Mardile, XVIR.
Under gubernatorial seal and hermetic hex.

My dear David,

I must answer your question as a coquette might answer it, turning her face away from a compliment she finds most pleasing, the better to invite further blandishments. In other words, I say to you both *yes* and *no.*

Yes, we find ourselves in crisis. The Blood Neshim are up in arms, and it is possible that they might forge an alliance—hitherto unthinkable—with the White Neshim of the hills to mount an attack on Sestival before the summer reaches its unbearable height and drives them back to their buried rivers.

But no, we do not require an enhancement of our garrison, or an earlier rotation of the regiments currently on active service here. The soldiers I have in the city garrison now—numbering four thousand carbineers of the line, five hundred light horse, and a hundred heavy—are more than sufficient both to protect the city and to bring the reckless architects of this uprising to Their Majesties' justice. If I were not sure of this, I should not say it. Believe me, I beg you. Sestival is safe, and the imperial standard flies unbowed, untroubled, over this most vexatious city.

I say *believe me*—and in order that you may do so, I offer the following brief explanation of the heads of the rebellion. You will see that I do not extenuate my own part in these events, which was central and decisive. Moreover, what I have done I would without hesitation do again, if the same situation were presented to me. Their Majesties stand for justice, or they stand for nothing. And justice, as we all know, carries both a flail and a shield—the one for the offender, the other for the victim.

It began on the twenty-seventh of Vernis: my third month as governor here in Sestival, and the first in which I can honestly say that I felt my understanding was on a par with my temporal power.

This city, this mighty city of almost one million souls, is—by post-coach, by mule, by boat, and finally by camel—some fifteen weeks removed from Imperial Teleuton. I felt every mile of that distance twice: the first time when I was travelling it, and the second when I arrived. You cannot imagine—forgive my presumption, but I know your own foreign travels have taken you no further than Esrime—you cannot possibly conceive how alien this place is to the values on which our empire was founded.

The ethnic mix, it goes without saying, is volatile in the extreme. Southern Vashi and Porcupine carls rub shoulders with swarthy indigenes and base mulattos. In summer, as now, the streets smell like a fire in a public sewer. While outside, the fungal huts of the Blood Neshim cling to the city walls and undermine their structural integrity—a nuisance endured more out of indolence than tolerance.

But this is as nothing, I hear you say. Is not Teleuton herself home to twice one hundred races? And do they not all keep Their Majesties' peace with fervour and due humility? Why, David, so they do, but here is the thing: Sestival, though it bears our yoke, sits in a desert land of wild and somewhat nomadic peoples, whose free passage through her streets is the root of her prosperity. Some of those people not only do not cleave to Their Majesties' laws and edicts, they have never heard nor read them!

My role as governor, therefore, must perforce be to explain as well as to control: and as magistrate (which also falls to my unwilling lot) to educate as well as to chastise.

The assizes are on the thirteenth and twenty-seventh of each month, in the Justitial Temple on the Street of Scythes. You know my feelings about religion, so I leave you to imagine how I feel about dispensing my verdicts in a building that has been dubbed a temple. But in these regions, the will of the gods is still held to be of some account, and Eilodon Shreve when he built the courthouse decreed that it should bear this appellation. I might change it yet, but as a very new power in a very old land I have—with one exception—trod but lightly as yet. Do you ask *what* exception? Read on, and that question will be answered along with all others: it is the very meat of the current matter.

A typical day at the assizes will see some thirty or forty cases put before me. I do not always manage to see all of the petitioners; that depends on the complexity of the charges and the events from which they arise. On a good day, I expect to get to the last page of the docket before finally—usually quite late in the evening—calling a halt to proceedings. On a bad day I might deliver only a dozen verdicts, sending away the remaining litigants to be presented to me again a fortnight thence.

The session in question was neither overly heavy nor unduly light. It *felt* heavy: it always feels heavy, because this is the aspect of my role as governor that I find least congenial. The absurd robes of state! The grindingly elaborate ritual! The intractably ugly, rats-nest lives into which I'm forced to peer! And the demeaning requirement to trick justice up like a whore and sing it hosannas with brazen instruments to make sure that its voice is heard and heeded! Men—and the things that choose to live with men—should love justice for what it is, and require no sauce to make the bread of rightness and reason more palatable.

I entered the court to the hated fanfares, and a hundred or more people rose to salute me. They made a strange assortment: the soldiers of the Crown with their pikes and carbines; the court officers, almost as ludicrously overdressed as I; the litigants in their finery (or what they took to be finery), the state prisoners in chains and rags, the curious or the indolent in their work clothes on the public benches, fanning their heads with their hats for already at the sixth hour the day was stifling.

"Rise for the Governor Plenipotentiary!" the court clerk boomed. "His foot is on our backs, his rod chastises us."

This clerk is a serviceable sort, both honest and astute, who labours under the unfortunate name of Culdersack. He knows my feelings about the fanfares and the flummery, and he favoured me with an ironic roll of his eyes as he banged the ceremonial tabor and held it high above his head. A touch familiar, perhaps, but I took it in the spirit in which it was meant.

I took my seat on the high dais at the front of the court, which permitted all others present to take theirs.

"Thank you, Mister Culdersack," I said, and he preened slightly at my use of his name. "Be so good as to call the principals and witnesses in the case of"—I glanced down at the docket, which of course he had already put on the bench in front of me, the pages turned to the right place—"Miss Ivi Itibi."

Culdersack thrust out his chest—he is a slight man, made even slighter by his intolerance of the tropic heat, so it did not thrust out far—and boomed in his best forensic voice "Principals and witnesses in the case of Ivi Itibi, be respectful and enter!"

There was a flurry at the door and two groups of people entered the courtroom. The flurry was caused not by there being too great a crush of onlookers there, but by the two groups striving to keep as great a distance from each other as possible, as well as by the onlookers hurriedly making way so as to avoid any chance contact with them.

Had I a little more than three months' experience, I might have known from the name alone. Miss Itibi and her entire family were of the Blood Neshim.

I am sure that you have heard of these creatures, but I make so bold as to assume that you have never seen one. They can only thrive in hot climes, and would die in Teleuton in the space of a day.

In stature they are short and scrawny, seldom rising above four feet. Their skin is surprisingly light in colour for desert-dwellers, but mottled with darker spots which I understand are a benign infection contracted from the fungal houses in which they live. The infected skin absorbs moisture even from the arid air of the deep desert and makes it possible for them to go many days without taking even a sip of water.

Their hair is as sparse and thin as spider web in an abandoned house, and they are obliged to cover their easily burned heads with broad-brimmed hats of brightest red. Their robes are red too, which is of course what gives them their name. Their hands are slender and long-fingered, ending in nails that are perpetually black, either because they are never clean or because black is their natural condition.

You will notice that I have said nothing of their faces. The men are a little like tragicomic monkeys, their wizened features irresistibly suggestive of a great sorrow over a petty loss. But the women—the women have no faces at all.

I had seen enough Neshim in the streets of Sestival, and for that matter on my journey here, to be aware of this. But I had told myself that I must be mistaken; that the women were in fact wearing a white veil tucked in at the neck, so that from a distance their features could not be seen.

I was not at a distance now, and I could not mistake what I was seeing. The skin of the women's faces was smooth and unbroken from hairline to chin. They were as perfectly expressionless, as empty of affect, as the blank pages of an artist's sketchpad.

"Miss Ivi Itibi," the Clerk said, indicating a tiny creature on my far left, standing alongside a tall, rope-muscled bull-man. "The plaintiff in this action. Her father"—pointing to another Neshim over on the right—"elderman Lor Itibi of the Persimmon gate. The respondent."

It was very noticeable that the father, who displayed the sad-monkey face in all its glory, stood in a cluster of his own kind. The daughter and the bull-man stood together, but with no others about them. I felt an instinctive movement of sympathy which—in the interest of impartial justice—I suppressed.

"Clerk of the court," I said calmly and punctiliously, "state the particulars of the case."

"Miss Itibi wishes to marry out of her clan, your Excellence," Culdersack said tersely. "She has chosen a husband from among the Vashi—the bull-man Horst Kalver, here present. But her father refuses to hand over her *face* to her fiancé. She therefore petitions the court to intervene on her behalf and require her father to return her property—itemised on the docket as two eyes, two ears, a nose, a mouth and an expanse of unblemished skin appertaining to those features."

A murmur went through the Neshim on my right, and Lor Itibi bared his teeth in the manner of a dog defending a bone.

"Approach the bench, Mister Culdersack," I said, after the murmur had died.

The clerk did so, having first executed a magnificent and slightly unsettling bow which brought his face to within an inch or so of the floor.

"If it please your Excellence?"

"What is the meaning of this charade?" I demanded. "What local custom of which I have remained blissfully ignorant up until this moment is at stake here?"

"It arises from the seventh dictate of the Neshim religion, your Excellence," Culdersack told me with every appearance of pained regret. "Their prophet apparently laid down as a commandment that a woman's beauty is the property of her husband, and must give pleasure to no man else. So by a simple sortilege the vivimancers of the Neshim clans remove the faces from their women's heads, to be returned to them only when they are in a given place: usually, the parental home until the woman is of marriageable age, and the marital abode thereafter."

I found it hard to keep the anger and indignation out of my voice. "And the rest of the time they must go about the city looking like breakfast eggs?"

"Just so, your Excellence. A striking and apt simile."

I shook my head in unhappy wonderment. "And has the Imperium ever ruled on this commandment of the Neshim prophet?"

"No, your Excellence."

"Or on any other matter that he has stuck his hallowed oar into?"

"No, your Excellence."

"Thank you, Mister Culdersack."

"Your Excellence is most welcome."

The clerk wheeled from the bench to address the

court with his hands clasped behind his back and his face a mask of stern probity. "Whereas it has pleased Their Majesties, across the seas, to extend their vigilant justice to this lowly place, it has appeared to them that there is a dispute, as follows. Ivi Itibi wishes to receive her face back into her keeping. Lor Itibi, her father, asserts his ancient tribal right to retain said face until she chooses a husband from among the legitimate *sodrachi* of the Blood Neshim. Their Majesties' wisdom will interrogate and determine."

Which was easy for him to say. After all, it wasn't in him that said wisdom was assumed to be embodied.

"I will examine the witnesses," I said. "Beginning with Miss Itibi herself."

"Ivi Itibi will approach the bench," Culdersack boomed.

The young lady did so, with much trepidation and with many touching appearances of modesty. Her father, and the others of her kind gathered in conclave about him, glared at her as if she were some noxious insect that had crawled out of their slipper as they were about to place their foot into it.

There is a reason, David, why the Neshim are obliged to build their fungal communities outside the city walls. Actually, there are many. One is the mushroom-houses themselves, which can easily cause subsidence among neighbouring dwellings as they extend their hair-fine fila-ments to suck the nutriments they require from whatever is at hand. A second is the skin disease I have already men-tioned: though it may be highly useful in a desert climate, it is also disfiguring, and those of other races fear—perhaps groundlessly—that contact with the Neshim may pass the infection on.

But the third, and perhaps the most unanswerable argument, is the smell. The prophet commanded the Neshim for abstruse, and I am sure spurious, reasons to wash neither their clothes nor their flesh: over the years, therefore, and in the desert heat, they attain a ripeness much like the stench of spoiled meat, only more intense and somewhat more complex in its bouquet. In the street, indeed, unless the wind is blowing from directly behind you, you will smell a Neshim long before you see him. And by the time you see him, your eyes will be watering.

But Miss Itibi smelled of sandalwood and cinnamon: evidently her defiance of the Neshim commandments was of a broad rather than a particular nature.

"You are Ivi Itibi," I said to her.

She raised her hands and made a complex gesture in reply. Lacking a face, and therefore *a fortiori* a mouth, she was obliged to use the hand-parl that Eastern merchants employ when they wish to haggle but have no language in common.

One of the other court officials—I'm sure you will know his rank and title, but I tend to think of him as the one in the purple pantaloons and the ruff of rats' tails—came forward to translate.

"She says she is, Excellence."

I nodded. "And this man"—pointing to the Vashi—"is affianced to you?"

More gesturing.

"I love him and cleave to him," my translator parsed. "I am sworn to him, and he to me."

"And is this not against the stated instructions of your prophet?" I demanded.

Her hands moved, and a groan went up from among the other Neshim. Lor Itibi bowed his head, stricken, and seemed about to fall. Other wizened men in red robes clung to him and held him upright.

"I do not believe in the prophet," the court translator said, but Miss Itibi's hands were moving again and he was forced now to speak hurriedly, trying to keep up with the fluent weavings of her fingers. "I have rejected his commandments, which turn women into things that a man might own. Am I not as much a child of the sun and the earth as any boy, or man? Am I not capable of reason and discrimination on my own account? Or do I close like a flower when there is no man present? Am I to be considered only a man's satellite, whether my father's or my husband's, spinning and spinning around him night and day? No. I am none of those things. I choose my own fate. I choose my own love. And I will have my face."

There was a moment's silence after the translator—somewhat breathlessly—finished this recitation. Then a howl rose from among the other Neshim: a sound of grief and desolation like the keening for the dead.

"I will have silence in my court," I bellowed. Mister Culdersack gestured, and the carbineers moved in closer to the Neshim with their weapons raised horizontally, *en barre*, to push them from the court if they did not comply. The collective howl fell to a ragged moaning, but it did not stop. "I said," I repeated with great distinctness, "I will have silence." The carbineers raised their weapons as if to strike down with the wooden stocks. The threat was enough, and the Neshim finally ceased their ululations.

I turned my attention back to the faceless girl, whose obscenely blank visage I was trying not to look at directly.

"Is it your contention, then, that a woman, no less than a man, is the absolute ruler of her own flesh?"

A gesture, which by now I recognised. *Yes.*

"And, by the same token, of her own emotions and affections?"

Yes.

"And has your union with this Vashi been solemnised according to the civil laws of Sestival as their majesties across the sea have required?"

Yes.

"Thank you, my dear. You may stand down."

She did so, and Mister Culdersack turned expectantly towards me. "Let me question the father now," I said.

"The court will hear the testimony of Lor Itibi!" Culdersack bellowed. There was a concerted move among the Blood Neshim to approach the bench en masse. "Alone!" I shouted, and the translator rattled off six or seven words—or rather, my one word rendered into all the many dialects of the Neshim clans.

The other red-robed dwarfs fell back, and Lor Itibi ascended the dais unaccompanied.

"You are Lor Itibi?" I asked him.

"Lor Ves Naiy Rowil Ata Subik Itibi." The old man ground out the harsh syllables like a curse.

"And you are the father of Ivi Itibi?" I pointed at the faceless girl. He turned his head to stare, then spat very deliberately on the bottom step of the dais, directly in front of the girl's feet. Ivi Itibi flinched, and the bull-man, Horst Kalver, who could probably have found room for his future father-in-law in one of the pockets of his work-smock, lowered his mighty horns and clenched his fists as he stepped forward. Two of the carbineers stepped hastily in between him and the old man.

"Order in court!" I snapped out. The bull-man stared at me, his huge eyes all pupil. "I require order," I repeated, "and I will punish any act of riot or violence."

Slowly and reluctantly, Horst Kalver lowered his hands to his sides.

"And that will include," I said softly, "any insult offered to Miss Itibi. I hereby fine elderman Itibi five sovereigns for his vulgar behaviour, said sum to be paid into the court's coffers before the thirteenth proximo."

A hush fell on the court. It was a heavy fine, of course: this far from the hub of empire, very heavy indeed. It is to be doubted that Lor Itibi—assuming him to be a farmer or a camel-trader, as the generality of his people are—saw so much in a month. The old man stared at me, his milk-white eyes narrowing to slits.

"Now we understand each other," I said coldly.

"Now, elderman, by what right do you retain your daughter's face and features against her expressly stated will?"

The translator began to render my words into the various Neshim tongues, but Lor Itibi cut across him. "Old right," he said, his voice as high and hollow as a bird's.

"Old right," I repeated slowly. "Granted by whom? On what occasion? By what authority?"

Lor Itibi blinked, then grimaced, baring his teeth. "City right," he squawked. "Three gallon water. Free pass gate. Men keep face."

He had kept his absurd hat on during this whole time. I pointed to it now. "You will doff your hat before addressing this court," I said.

"Three gallon water," Lor Itibi repeated. "Free pass gate. Men keep face. Head no bare."

I did my best to stifle my feeling of irritation, which was more intense than its source warranted. "Your water allowance and freedom of entrance and exit are gifts of the city," I told the old goblin, "and can therefore be annulled on my sole authority should I decide that there is sufficient cause. I'll allow you to keep your hat on, for the moment, since you attach some sort of significance to it beyond common courtesy, but let us consider these other 'old rights' you insist on. Were these things custom and practice in your father's time?"

"Father," Lor Itibi repeated, nodding vigorously, and shooting a baleful glance towards his daughter. "Father, grandfather, grandfather father, grandfather grandfather . . . "

I smiled, and Culdersack arched an eyebrow as he caught my glance, smiling too. He saw the trap that I'd set for this antediluvian creature, and he saluted its cleverness.

"Well then," I said, "those rights are of no moment here. No moment at all. Their majesties' remit extends only back to the year seventeen, when they took this city in tribute after their victorious war with Ostermauer. Any edicts or understandings that were in force before that time were annulled when the imperial mandate embraced this city, and must now be renegotiated on a case-by-case basis."

I paused to allow the full implications of this to sink in, not just for Lor Itibi's sake but also for the sake of the assembled listeners. Then, straightening my papers in a way that I have found effective in impressing colonials with the weightiness of the law, I fixed the old man with a cold hard stare.

"Mister Itibi," I said, "would you care to explain to me why I should honour this custom of yours, bearing in mind that it is repellent to good sense and odious to human feeling?"

Lor Itibi had something of the look of a hunted animal as he met my gaze. Righteous indignation can make even quicksand appear like solid ground until you've stepped so far out onto it that momentum will carry you no further.

"Prophet," he said. "Prophet's words."

"But your prophet's covenant is with you, not with me," I pointed out mildly. "Therefore I feel no particular need to grant his followers an exemption from the law that governs all other sane and civilised peoples. Please to try again, Mister Itibi."

The old man's brow knitted, and he looked to the rest of the family for support.

"Father," he said. "Daughter. Not come between. No right, to come between."

I found myself standing, although from my vantage point on the bench I already towered over this wizened thing. "The law expressly gives me not merely the right but the obligation to come between you," I told him in clipped, cold tones. "The law is so fine and so friction-less, Mister Itibi, it glides between you and everyone you touch. Whenever you shake a man's hand, or kiss a woman's lips, or pat a child's head, the law is between you. If you see not that, then you see nothing, and you are not fit to live in their majesties' dominions."

There was near-uproar in the court now, my own agitation translating itself through the witnesses and the onlookers. With difficulty, I calmed myself and took my seat again.
The old man was jabbering at some of his own people in
his own tongue, and the blank face of Ivi Itibi was turned
towards him—but in the absence of features it was impossible to tell whether she was glaring, beseeching or mock-
ing. Her fiancée stood behind her, his hands protectively
on her shoulders, and it occurred to me for the first time
to wonder how they had managed to fall in love given the
impediment her lack of a face must have presented.

I banged with my gavel, and some measure of silence
returned.

"Elderman Itibi, you are an anachronism," I said to
Lor Itibi. "Your religion is barbaric and your treatment of
your womenfolk obscene. You will—"

The court clerk, Culdersack, interposed himself between
me and the Neshim, a pained and servile smile upon his face.
"Your Excellence," he murmured, "if I might approach the
bench, momentarily?"

"Yes, very well, Mister Culdersack," I snapped, out
of all countenance to have been interrupted when I was on
the brink of giving my verdict. "What is it?"

Culdersack leaned in close towards me. "Excellence,"
he said, "I think I see how your thoughts are tending, and
I would have you bear in mind some few external factors
which may—which do, in fact, or at least I believe they
do—have some degree of relevance at a second or third
remove from the strictly legal . . . that is, from the purely
judicial, or rather the—"

"Mister Culdersack," I snarled, "kindly cease to bleat
like a goat and speak your mind like a man."

The clerk gave another of his startling bows. If nothing else, it allowed him the time to collect his thoughts.
"As it please your Excellence," he said. "The nub of the
matter is this. There are some nine hundred thousand resi-

dents within the city, of whom perhaps a hundred thousand are of fully human heritage. The Neshim who live on the outer walls number at least a quarter of a million. And then there are the other Neshim clans, of the hills and of the wadis . . . "

"Why is this pertinent?" I demanded.

"Excellence, it is pertinent because the prophet's words are held in such great respect by these people. You bear the imperial mandate, and your justice speaks in the tongue of their majesties, the tongue of men and angels. What you say is just and proper by the very definition of those terms. But still, I venture to suggest, it would be best to deliver your verdict in some way that bears only on the particulars of the case and not on the general principles of the Neshim code."

"The particulars," I repeated, bemused.

Culdersack nodded vigorously. "Exactly so, Excellence. The particulars of this family, this circumstance, this place and time. In that way you create a precedent which will stand—drive a wedge into this barbaric practice which will one day open it to the daylight—but at the same time you mount no obvious affront to the broader Neshim community."

"But I *mean* to affront the broader Neshim community," I explained to him patiently. "The crime is theirs, ultimately. They are the ones who hold that this abomination is virtue."

Culdersack nodded, conceding the point, but he looked if anything unhappier. "Your Excellence is correct, of course," he said. "But still, if we could put some face on this that made it seem less a questioning of the prophet's commandment, more the chastisement of a wayward individual—"

"Then it would be a lie, and a travesty," I finished. "Face, Mister Culdersack? A face to put on it? That is exactly what we cannot find. Thank you for your opinions, but I must now deliver a verdict."

The clerk bowed again, somewhat more perfunctorily this time, and stepped back from the bench. I returned my attention to Lor Itibi. "You will bring your daughter's face to this court before the close of proceedings on this day," I told him. "At the same time you will bring the entire sum which you have been fined. If this does not happen, I will hold you as a rebel against the imperial mandate and I will send officers to your house to arrest you. Either way, your daughter will have her face back before the sun falls below the city walls. And from this moment forth, all women shall wear their own faces at all times, indoors and out. To be seen without a face on the streets of Sestival will mean instant arrest."

My pronouncement was followed by deathly silence. I banged my gavel to signify that the case was concluded, and two of the court officers led Ivi Itibi and Horst Kalver away, their presence alone preventing the other Neshim from falling on the girl and raining blows on her.

I waved permission to the clerk to bring the next set of principals before me, and had turned my eye to the relevant page to peruse the particulars of the case, when suddenly what seemed like a rope fastened about my neck. I was dragged forward, across the bench, until I almost fell. It was the old man, Lor Itibi, and it was no rope but his own hands, surprisingly strong for all their slenderness, which were now grasping my windpipe and attempting to throttle the life out of me.

A court sergeant stepped forward and took hold of the Neshim's wrists, intending to wrest them free. But he too was surprised by their wiry strength, and struggled in vain to loosen their grip, while blackness invaded my sight like ink spilled into a water glass and my very consciousness failed.

It was necessary for the sergeant to club the old man into unconsciousness with the stock of his carbine before he finally loosed his hold on me and fell to the floor. I lay sprawled across the bench, gasping for air with a sound like a housewife stropping a knife—a most undignified sound, and an even more undignified sight.

When I was able to speak, I bade Culdersack to clear the court, and then to look to the old man to see how badly he was injured. His attempts to minister to me I waved away impatiently: I had taken no serious harm, and I did not wish to appear any weaker or more ineffectual than I already had. Lor Itibi was only stunned, it seemed: despite the severity of the blow, which might have killed a strong man, his eyes opened after no more than a minute—showing clear, without film or fog or blood fleck—and he stood up with no man's aid.

"You foul old reprobate," I growled at him, rubbing my throat. It was still agony to breathe. "You've earned a sentence of banishment to go with the fine and the other penalties, and it shall come into force on the morrow." Since he stared at me with stony sullenness, I made sure that he understood by translating the sentence into his own crude pidgin. "You," I said, pointing at him. "No free pass gate. No three-gallon water. Today—bring face, bring sovereigns. Tomorrow—go! Go into the blind desert, and choke your worthless life out in the shift-dunes."

Lor Itibi seemed to stagger, as the enormity of what I was saying fell on his understanding all at once.

"Free pass gate," he protested hoarsely. "Three gallon water."

"Not for you," I said. "And not for any Neshim who disobey their majesties' law. Get out of my court, you piece of corruption. I will see you one time more. And do not think of defying me, or your brothers, your sons, your uncles, and cousins will inherit the sentence of banishment. I will turn the whole of clan Itibi out of gates before I will let this foulness stand."

The sergeants led the old man away. He seemed dazed and docile now, his head bowed, his manner that of a man

who has seen some terrible vision and whose spirit is still
in thrall to it.

I took some few minutes to compose myself and then
called on the clerk to recommence proceedings. Slowly I
worked through the morning's docket. My voice lacked
its usual clarity and fullness, and each breath caused me
some little pain, but I flatter myself that I discharged my
duties as punctiliously as ever.

My lunch break was but short, because the pain in
my throat did not allow me to eat. I drank an infusion of
ginger and sparrowgrass, gargling the last third of it, and
then returned straightway to my work. Mister Culdersack, who normally employs his lunch hour in reading the
satirical sketches of Thyrsis Falmer, was somewhat put
out and could not entirely hide the fact.

The afternoon wore on, and Lor Itibi did not present
himself to the court officials with his daughter's face. I
knew this because I inquired after each case was cleared
whether or not the old man had returned. The answer was
always no.

Twenty scant minutes before sunset, though, he did
appear—at the head of a great column of Blood Neshim,
not just from the Persimmon but from all the other gates
of the city. He marched them to the square outside the
judicial temple. The day-watch militia had followed them
all the way from the city walls, but had deemed it best not
to intervene because of their great numbers and because
they had as yet offered no violence nor riot.

In the square, Lor Itibi's three sons quickly built a
pyre of sticks and charcoal, which they drenched in oil
and ignited. Lor Itibi produced his daughter's face from
an oilskin bag which he wore at his chest. He threw it
onto the pyre and burned it.

He watched it until it was ash. Then he turned and
led the throng back along the Thoroughfares of Ruik
and Angelus to the Persimmon gate, which they marched

through four abreast exactly as the sun set before them—
so that it appeared to lead their little parade and lend it
some species of divine approval.

Mister Culdersack reported all of this to me in apolo-
getic tones when the next pause in proceedings made it
possible for him to approach the bench.

"He has defied the verdict of the court?" I summarised unnecessarily, for in truth I found it hard to credit.

Culdersack nodded. "Just so, Excellence. Some of
the more moderate eldermen have found opportunity
throughout the day to tender their apologies, and their
earnest good wishes to you . . . "

"Their apologies?" I echoed, with heavy emphasis.
"Their good wishes?"

"Exactly, Excellence."

"I see. They would beat the law and then stroke it,
like a dog. But I am not their dog, Culdersack."

"No, Excellence."

"Nor is the law their dog."

"Not at all, Excellence."

I considered for only a moment. "If Lor Itibi is so
very fond of fire," I said, "then by all means let us give
him fire. Find where he lives, by the Persimmon Gate,
and burn the house to the ground."

Culdersack seemed nonplussed. "But," he objected.
"The mushroom houses of the Neshim cling one to
another, Excellence, and many layers deep. To burn one is
to burn the entire stack."

"And were not his neighbours witnesses to his revolt?"
I asked calmly.

"They were, Excellence, but only—"

"Then they stand in need, no less than he, of a lesson in
civic responsibility. See that it is done, Mister Culdersack."

And done it was, as by now you certainly know. The
Neshim settlement at the Persimmon Gate went up like
dry tinder, except that it burned more quickly than timber,

since the dried fungal matter of which the houses were composed had far less pith and substance.

I rode home in the judicial carriage, through strangely hushed streets. Normally Sestival comes alive at sunset, but on this night it waited, somewhat breathless in the still summer heat, to see what would come.

Tannacker opened the stable yard gates for the carriage and locked them behind us, but my wife herself was at the servants' door as I ascended the steps. "Patricia," I chided her, "it sets a bad example to the house carls to see you walking in their quarters. They must be mindful of the distance between themselves and you. Do nothing to lessen that distance." My words may seem cold, David, but I assure you my tone was gentleness itself. I love your cousin dearer than life, and I know that only her provincial upbringing causes her to make such errors.

"I'm sorry, Melech," she said, contritely enough. "But Sylvie is abed already and she hoped that you would come to kiss her goodnight before she settles to sleep."

I allowed that I would do this, and then, kissing her, I retired to change out of my juridical robes into some saner attire. It was a hot evening, as I think I have said, so I wore a silk shirt and trousers of Stebhennish weave.

Our little Sylvia was indeed still awake. She was perusing a book, so lost and rapt within its pages that she did not hear my footsteps on the stairs or in the hallway. But as I entered the room, her eyes flicked up and saw me, and her face ignited with that simple childish delight which humbles the wisest and the mightiest.

"Daddy!" she yelled, and she threw out her arms towards me for an embrace, which I duly gave her. After which, nothing would do but that I must kiss Dolly too, and then Henrificus the camel, and Dodie the dog, and Pevnor the Lion. Then when the offices of affection were finally concluded, I picked up the book to see what had held my sweet daughter so fascinated.

The spine bore the legend LIVES OF THE GREAT EXPLOR-
ERS. I confess, my brow furrowed when I saw it, for I have
furnished Sylvia's library with twice one hundred tomes
of fairy lore and childhood adventure, whereas this text
looked as if it would be more at home in a public library
than in a young girl's nursery.

"Lives of the Explorers," I read. "Well now. That
seems—"

"The *great* explorers!" Sylvie interrupted me earnestly.
"See, Daddy. It has Cranston's voyage to the Glass City,
and Merrilaw's discovery of the sea route to Argent!" She
turned the pages, pointing out to me her favourite passages and pictures while I exclaimed and nodded.

"When I get big," Sylvie told me solemnly, "I want to
be an explorer too." Oh gods, the reckless courage of children! Their eagerness to cope the world, before they even
know what the world is."

"But there would be hardships, Sylvie," I told her gently. "Privations. Savage tribesmen, and bugs, terrible heat
and cold . . . "

"I should not care," little Sylvie declared staunchly.
"I should be like Cranston, and discover all the places
that nobody has been to yet. May I, Daddy? May I be an
explorer, when I'm grown? You and Mummy could come
too, if you wanted to."

I could have passed the whole thing off with some
joke, and perhaps I should have done. But it pains me to
lie, even on a trivial matter. I told Sylvie, perhaps more solemnly than the occasion required, that one day she would
be married, and have children of her own. Perhaps, if the
gods graced her, she would have sons, and they would
become explorers, her own desires and ambitions living
on in their souls. Perhaps they'd sail to far Sinbarada, and
bring her back one of the Tenjak's teardrops. And they'd
fill her ears with tales of the Hollow Angels and the Court
of Twelve. All things rich and rare, so vividly described

that she would think she'd seen them herself (which providence send she never will).

Poor Sylvie. She cared but little for the consolation I offered her, and only insisted the more that she wished to be an explorer herself, and see the world. "You will see the world," I promised her at last. "Tomorrow I'll buy you a picture book of Velveer's paintings which I noticed in the market the other day, and you will see all the countries of the East and South as he saw them." I tucked her up in bed and kissed her cheek, a little moist now from tears she could not hold back. And I left her dreaming there, whether awake or asleep: dreaming the uninterrupted dream which life is for the very young and the very innocent.

I include this trivial anecdote for one reason, and one reason only. It is for her I serve, David: for her and for all others like her. For children, of whatever colour, whatever provenance, who deserve a life free from the tyrannies of superstition and selfish cruelty.

I would burn the world for them, I tell you truly. Ash is good compost. And the garden I would grow for them in that rich soil would surpass all other gardens that were ever made.

This story is from *The House of War and Witness*. Like "The Demon in the Well", which appears earlier in this collection, it's a tale told by a ghost—and it includes, among other things, an account of how the narrator, Samuel Gelbfisc, came to die. The genre, however, is different this time around. This is a mystery, and a courtroom drama to boot. ¶ It's also one of the few cases where the historical setting forced me to do some real research—into the position of religious minorities in medieval Poland, and into the properties of certain plants and chemical tinctures. By the time you get to the end, you may raise an eyebrow at some of the chemistry. I'd be the first to acknowledge that Gelbfisc employs some tricks you should not try at home.

THE ORDEAL

I WAS born a Jew, in the city of Koszalin in Poland, under Casimir Jagiellon but before the Nieszawa Statutes (may the paper on which they were written run with boils like diseased flesh!) deprived me and the rest of my race of so many of our rights and our freedoms. In that time, it was still possible to be a Jew in Poland and to pursue a trade—as I did, working and learning under my father and then upon his death inheriting his thriving business as an apothecary.

I was born a Jew, I said, and in many respects I am a Jew still. Not in respect of religion, however. I renounced my faith when I was twenty years old. This was out of love for a woman, and I learned from that experience how little such loves really mean. Also, how inveterate is the hatred of some people for anything that is different from themselves. Her parents did not accept me as a putative son-in-law, for all that I had kissed the feet of Christ. They sent my Josie away to school in Tarnow, and when she returned she was betrothed to another.

Enough of that. I make no complaint, for I was too young then to understand what I desired and we were unlikely to have made each other happy. I found love enough later, with women and men alike, but never stayed long with any of them. That early disaster with Josie had made me mistrustful of human affections—at least, of their durability. I preferred a fire that burned very hot and died all the quicker for it.

It might be supposed that I had reverted by this time to the faith of my forebears. But it was not so. The god I believed in cared nothing for the vestments, the trappings of religious ritual. He was to be found as easily in the droning Latin of the Catholics as in the ecstatic swayings and intonings of the Chassidim. In fact, I found Him most often in solitary prayer, and went to church only because it was expected of me.

And it was, I must admit, a boon in business. I met many customers in chance conversations at the church gates, and was often recommended through acquaintances I'd made in the course of what was only nominally an act of worship. I wasn't alone in this. Jesus may have chased the moneylenders from the temple, but I guarantee you they crept back again as soon as His back was turned. That's the way of it, and always has been.

In 1492, just after John became king, I decided to go on a pilgrimage to see the scarred Madonna at Jasna Góra. Again, this wasn't primarily a matter of piety. It was a pleasance, first, and after that a commercial speculation. The Nieszawa Statutes were law by then, and it was harder now for a Jew to trade from fixed premises. As an apothecary, I was able to adapt better than most, but by consequence I'd become a sort of mendicant, seldom staying in one town or city for more than a few days at a time. A pilgrimage suited me nicely, allowing me to visit suppliers and former clients in many places across the country.

My fellow pilgrims presented a great diversity and variety, from the very amiable to the very aloof. I made no secret of my origins, since my name—which I had not changed—already marked me out as a Jew. To those who asked, I told my story. To those who stood by, purse-lipped and hard-eyed, I said nothing.

With one family in particular I became close friends. They were the Lauzens, a family of four from Kalushin. Alojzy Lauzen was a merchant, trading mostly in wines and spirits. He enjoyed life, and liked those around him to enjoy it too. He had come on the pilgrimage for the sake of his wife, Etalia, who had been unable to conceive again after the difficult birth of their first child—Tomas, now twelve—which had lamed her. She thought that the icon of the scarred virgin, which was said to be particularly responsive to the injuries of women, might restore her and make her fertile again. The fourth member of the family, and the most recently acquired, was a cow, Erment. Her presence on the pilgrimage was explained by Tomas's weak constitution, and a recommendation from a doctor in Kalushin that he should drink a great deal of milk.

I liked Alojzy and Etalia very much, but I liked their son better than either. Tomas was a child of uncommon intellect and open, ingenuous spirit. This was his first experience of the world outside his hometown, and he was devouring it as a monkey eats fresh fruit. To see a hump-backed bridge with Tomas, or a campanile, or even a haywain, was to see it for the first time. He took such pleasure in the unfamiliar, he made the banal lading of the world into gaieties and festivals.

It goes without saying that Tomas was fascinated by the apothecary's art. He was fascinated by everything! When I began to explain to him how I worked, mixing minute amounts of potent pharmaca with exquisite care, he besieged me with a thousand questions. From where did I source my potions and powders? How did I know what concentrations to use, and which simples had which effects? Since the relative volumes were so crucial, what about the metal of the vessels I used, or the mortars and spoons I ground and stirred with?

I answered all these questions as well as I could, and also showed him how certain rudimentary tinctures could be brewed. Under my instruction he made a simple from andrographis, poplar and bee balm, which he mixed into the milk of the cow, Erment, and served to his mother to ease the pain in her hip. It gave her a great deal of relief, and the boy no less pride.

Our southern progress was leisurely, to say the least, and my friendship with Tomas grew each day. I demonstrated for him a great many minor mysteries of the art—such as are not profound but produce a great spectacle when they're performed. I showed him the fire that continues to burn when submerged, the kettle that pours potions of different colours on command, the sea-stone that flows like water and yet becomes still and solid at a touch. These things are really no more than the tricks of mountebanks, but their explanation touches on deeper truths, and Tomas would not rest, after seeing each such marvel, until he had learned all the whys and wherefores of it.

I said we made a slow and casual progress. I should say, besides, that we broke our journey each night in conditions of relative comfort. Only seldom—two or three times, perhaps—did we sleep by the road, at risk from footpads and at the mercy of foul weather. More usually our guides contrived to stop in the evenings at a post-inn or hostelry, or if none was close enough they would beg lodging at a monastery or abbey, pleading the pious purpose for which we travelled.

And so we came here to Pokoj, not by design but by chance. It was an abbey then; we passed it on our way to the village of Narutsin, where we intended to seek a place to stay. It had rained heavily for some days before, and as sometimes happened, the rain had made the Mala Panev break her banks at Ortzud. The spate cut us off from Narutsin, and although it might have been shallow enough to ford, we didn't want to take the hazard. We turned back to the abbey, which lay just half an hour behind us, and asked for shelter there.

The monks of Pokoj were Benedictines, and they gave us courteous but cautious welcome. The lay brothers would see to our needs, of course, but the abbot himself, one Father Ignacio, came into the refectory to greet us. We were introduced to him one by one, and when he came to me and heard my name, his nose wrinkled up as though at the smell of a fart.

"A Jew?"

"Yes," I said. "But converted, father, to faith in the Messiah."

"You can't change a Jew," Father Ignacio said, his face still twisted into a caricature of disgust like a carved gargoyle. "If you could, Christ would have made his ministry to them."

Historians know, of course, that this is exactly what Christ did. It was only after His death that Paul took His teachings out to the gentiles. But I did not say this. I only smiled and reminded the father abbot that Jesus had counselled the forgiveness of our enemies.

"It's not *my* forgiveness you stand in need of," Father Ignacio growled. And having thus identified himself as my enemy, he walked on down the line to speak with the other pilgrims.

He did not stay with us for the meal, but only said once again that we were welcome to such hospitality as his house could offer. He looked at me as he said this, as if he would dearly have liked to make an exception, and then he retired. I hoped that this would be the last I saw of him. But alas, something happened that night that brought us into disastrous contact with each other.

The boy, Tomas, fell sick. He retired early, complaining of a malaise. Something he had eaten, he said, must have taxed his stomach. I was the last—apart from his mother and his father—to say goodnight to him. Afterwards, before I retired myself, I gave Etalia a digestive powder, which I told her to give to her son if the gripes worsened.

The next morning, Tomas was not at breakfast. I asked Meister Lauzen how the boy had passed the night, but he shook his head and turned away without a word. Grief and fear sat heavy on his brow. Tomas had not slept well, Etalia told me. The pains in the boy's stomach had persisted—if anything, they'd worsened. She'd mixed my powder in a little milk and given it to him shortly after the abbey bells rang for Lauds. It had not seemed to help. This morning Tomas had barely stirred. He seemed sunk in a terrible lethargy from which he woke only to moan and whimper and then fall back at once into fitful slumber.

I asked if I might be permitted to examine him. "Certainly," Etalia said. "We would be grateful, Meister Gelbfisc." She led the way to the room chamber that had been assigned to them, near the calefactory. I knew the acuteness of the boy's affliction as soon as I entered the room, first by the sharp smell of his sweat and his vomitus and then by his pale, sweating face.

I knelt beside his bed and put a hand on his throat. Etalia yelped in alarm—the gesture is a strange one, and easy to misinterpret. I explained to her that I was feeling the movement of his humours, whose vigour is a broad indicator of health or sickness. And I reassured her that the passage of vital spirits through the canals of the boy's chest and gorge seemed promisingly rapid and forceful.

I might have suggested a phlebotomy, but forbore to do so. I had read widely among classical sources, if not deeply, and was aware of how contentious bloodletting had been to the ancients. Only in our own day had it become unquestioned orthodoxy.

Instead, I examined the vomitus more closely. I found black threads there, in among the remains of food and the boy's natural effluvia. Melancholia must be the natural diagnosis, and yet that might have been at work in him for weeks or months. The violence, the sudden onset of the boy's symptoms suggested some other, more proximate cause for his current crisis. I asked Etalia what Tomas had eaten the night before, and she gave me a most exact account. Only what everyone around the table had eaten, she said. The bread and the smoked oscypek cheese and a small bowl of barley groats. And what had he drunk? Only water. Not even the small beer that was on the table, though Alojzy had offered him some.

At this point we were interrupted by the arrival of two of the lay brothers. They entered in haste, and told us that the abbot required our presence in the great hall. He had heard of Tomas's affliction and wished to speak with us about it.

It was apparent from the first that Father Ignacio had an agenda, and that it concerned me. He asked the Lauzens how much contact I had had with Tomas both on the road and then once we had arrived within the abbey itself. He took particular interest in the digestive powder I had given to Frau Lauzen to administer to Tomas, and raised his eyebrows when he heard that I was the last to say goodnight to him.

In short, as you've probably guessed, he accused me of poisoning the child. When I asked him why he thought I would do such a thing, he answered that I was a Jew. A Jew would commit any vileness against Christian folk for no other reason than innate wickedness and perversity.

I appealed to fact and to reason—two crutches that would not carry me. I reminded the father abbot that I had renounced my religion. And I pointed out that Tomas had begun to show the symptoms of his illness before I gave the nostrum to his mother. Before I said goodnight to him, for that matter.

"But you sat opposite the boy at table," the abbot responded, glaring down on me from the eminence of a joint stool set on a wooden dais. It was a pathetic throne indeed, and I almost laughed at his pretension, but the threat to my person was far from amusing. Father Ignacio had already sent word to the local landowner, Count Kurnatowski, request-ing that one of the count's reeves come to Pokoj to sit on the matter. At such a hearing the abbot's word would carry a great deal of weight, and mine none at all. And against the reeve's arrival, he ordered me confined to one of the monks' cells with the door locked from the outside.

Here at least I was able to assert myself against his authority, by reminding him that it had limits. He was a functionary of the church, not of the state, and though his influence was vast his temporal power was circumscribed. If I had sworn to the order, he would have power over my body and my soul. I had not, and he did not. I refused to surrender myself into the brothers' hands, and being mostly aged men, of a peaceful and meditative bent, they did not press the point.

Yet I was conscious as I walked from the hall of my fellow pilgrims' eyes upon me. There was a mutter-ing where I passed, and some two or three spat upon the ground as men do when a hearse goes by to make Death look the other way. Even the Lauzens wouldn't meet my gaze, and when I tried to speak to them they turned away.

I have said that I was not a religiously observant man. Common sense prevented me from seeing the hand of God in a world so disordered and arbitrary as the one I saw around me every day. That same common sense told me now that there was no good way for this to end. Even if Tomas rallied, and made a full recovery, the wheels of church and state had been set in motion. They were unlikely to stop until they'd run their course.

I had been thinking about the boy's sickness, coming so soon after our arrival at the abbey. Its abrupt onset sug-gested food poisoning, but he had eaten nothing at table that had not also been eaten by others. Unless—which was always a possibility—his mother had lied to me.

I made a circuit of the abbey grounds. They were not extensive, and I had a clear sense by then of what it was

I was looking for. In a secluded corner, close to the stable yard, there was a patch of weeds whose flowers grew in tight, white clusters like the explosion of sparks from damp wood when it finally catches fire. *Apocynum*. Dogbane.

Dimly, I began to see a way of saving myself. Not with the innocence of the dove—though I was free from any taint of blame—but with the wisdom of the serpent.

I lingered in the stables a little while longer. Then I returned to the abbey and gave myself into the hands of the brothers, saying I was ready to be judged.

But they were not ready yet to judge me. For all that he hated me, father Ignacio wished to adhere to the forms of law. He had me committed to a cell to await the reeve's arrival. The door did not lock, but two men guarded it constantly in case I should change my mind and attempt to leave.

There were shouts and running footsteps in the night that persisted for some time. It seemed that a further outrage had been committed. Erment, the Lauzens' cow, had been slaughtered in her stall. The guards outside my door were questioned as to whether I had left at any point, but they were able to say that I had not. Possibly, they hazarded, I had killed the cow in the afternoon before I surrendered myself into captivity.

In the morning I was brought before the reeve, Meister Ruprecht Ganso. It was in the refectory, the largest room in the abbey. The space was needed to accommodate the audience, which consisted of most of the brothers and all of my fellow pilgrims. The tables had been removed, the benches laid out in rows. Tomas was there, in the front row between his parents, wrapped in a frieze blanket. The stare he bestowed on me was full of fear and reproach.

The reeve set out the terms of the accusation. The Lauzens and others testified that I had sat close to the boy on the night when he fell ill, and they said that I had plentiful opportunities to add poison to his food. Etalia added that I had given her a powder (she said *sold*, not *given*, which perhaps hurt me most of all), and that she had stirred this simple into a glass of milk and given it to Tomas in the course of the night.

The reeve asked me whether I denied any of this. Not a word, I assured him.

"Then have you any evidence to offer in your own defence?" he demanded.

"None."

A babel of voices arose in the wake of this word— most of them demanding a judgment. The reeve raised his hand to stem the tumult, and I spoke again into the silence that followed.

"I ask for an ordeal."

"An ordeal?" The reeve was somewhat scandalised. "How will an ordeal serve, when your guilt is already clear?"

"If I'm guilty, it will serve me not at all. It will merely remove all doubt."

"There is no doubt!" Father Ignacio proclaimed. But other voices called out for fire and water to be brought. Some of the pilgrims were on their feet now, shaking their fists and stamping their feet upon the floor. The reeve saw which way the wind was blowing and gave order for a fire to be lit and a cauldron set upon it.

This being the refectory, the order was swiftly obeyed. The fireplace, indeed, was already set for the evening and only needed the stroke of a tinderbox. An iron trivet was brought by one of the cook's boys, and then a cooking pot big enough to make pottage for a great multitude. As they set the trivet on the fire and the pot on the trivet, the audience moved the benches around to face this new spectacle.

Then this same serving boy filled the pot with water from the well in the abbey grounds. I stepped forward before I was even bid to, and took my place before the fire. But before I put my hand into the water, I turned to look at the Lauzens. The parents first. And then the boy.

"Tomas," I said. "Do you believe I tried to harm you?"

"It matters nothing what the boy believes," Father Ignacio cried, perhaps genuinely indignant or perhaps trying to drown out any answer.

Tomas Lauzen shook his head, his eyes on mine.

"Your faith will give me strength," I said. "And in face of your innocence, all evil will find itself abashed."

I thrust my hand into the pot. My hand and half my forearm, for it was very deep.

"The water has not boiled yet!" Father Ignacio sneered, as though I was trying to cheat in some way.

"Then let us wait it out," I said.

A watched pot, they say, never boils—and surely no pot was ever as closely watched as this one. Yet it warmed quickly enough, and steam began to rise from it. I swirled the water around with my hand, as though stirring a bath, and let my gaze travel across the faces of my accusers. For by then, with one exception, there was nobody in the room who doubted my guilt.

They began to doubt, perhaps, as the steam started to rise from the water and my face remained calm.

When the water boiled, people gasped and cried out. But I kept my hand in the fire for a good while longer, not moving at all—except for my eyes, which now found the father abbot. He was staring at me in fear and consternation.

Finally, I withdrew my hand from the roiling water and displayed it to the crowd. It was whole, and unburned. It was not even red from the heat.

"Am I innocent?" I asked.

"He needs to be fully immersed," Father Ignacio protested. "Not just his hand, but his whole—"

"Whose court is this?" I bellowed over him. "My question was for Count Kurnatowski, represented here by his reeve, Meister Ganso."

Sensible of the abbot's slight, the reeve nodded. Sensible of the abbot's status, the reeve made answer to him, not to me. "You agreed to the rite of ordeal, Father Ignacio, and so you must abide by it. The Jew is found innocent, and these proceedings are concluded."

There was a great noise and perturbation in the hall, which rose to a crescendo and then subsided as I raised both hands—the wet and the dry—and shook my head. "It is not concluded," I called out. "Unless the Count's law says it is enough to exonerate the innocent. What of the guilty?"

"What of them?" the reeve asked me, testily.

"They must be found," I said, "and punished. Someone tried to poison Tomas. Whoever this was, they sat at table with him and broke bread with him. Someone in this room is—by will and intent—a murderer. God forbid we should rise before we find him."

Murmurs of assent came from the pilgrims, and even from some of the friars.

"I can't question everyone here," the reeve protested.

"No," I agreed. "But the fire can."

The reeve gasped. "You suggest . . . putting everyone to ordeal?"

I shook my head emphatically. "Not everyone. Only until one is found to be guilty."

The reeve and the father abbot looked at one another. It could easily be read in their faces that they felt they were losing control of these proceedings. "Masters," I said, "hear me out. These others"—I gestured to the pilgrims—"are little versed in matters of law and religion. They see a fire, and a seething cauldron, and they fear it. But you're different. You know that God finds out the truth, and makes it manifest."

"Indeed He does," the father abbot agreed, nonetheless giving me a look forked with enmity.

"Then put your hand into the fire," I told him, "and show them the way."

The abbot was stupefied at this suggestion. "My innocence is not in question!" he yelped. "It does not need to be tested!"

"No?" I said. "What of your faith, Father Ignacio? Does that not need to be tested either? I would have said otherwise. If I, a Jew, didn't fear the flame, why should you?"

"I do not fear it!" the abbot roared.

I took a step back from the fire, and with outspread arms invited him to approach it. "Show us," I said.

I meant only to humble him, but I had reckoned without the stern and stony virtue of the man. Full of hate he might be, but he was full of belief too. He hated Jews for scriptural reasons he thought impeccable.

Ignacio rose, and stepped down from the dais.

He rolled up the sleeve of his gown with finicky care, staring the while into the steam that rose from the rolling water.

Having exposed his flesh, he stood where he was for a few moments in total stillness. Everyone in the room seemed seized with the same paralysis. Nobody even breathed.

Then Ignacio thrust his hand into the pot.

I watched the face rather than the hand. I know too well what boiling water does to flesh. I saw the shock on the father abbot's face—the realisation, blossoming in sudden agony, that his faith was not strong enough nor his innocence unblemished.

His shriek as he wrenched his hand back rose every echo of that ancient room in appalled protest. His sleeve, flopping down again, caught the rim of the cauldron and upended it, so that those nearest had to retreat hurriedly from the boiling water that slopped across the floor.

Two lay brothers led Ignacio away—carried him, almost—to his rooms. He was hugging his hand to his chest and his face was slack with shock. The reeve, almost as shaken, declared the proceedings at an end, but forbore to pronounce on the abbot's guilt or innocence. There are, of course, two different dispensations for Christians and for Jews—and for the church and the laity.

There's little else to tell. I parted company from the pilgrimage that day, and took another path. I did not speak to the boy Tomas again, or even see him—although he wrote to me, some years later, and we entered into a brief correspondence. His mother I did see, when I went to fetch my horse from the stables. She was washing with well water the pail in which she had formerly collected the milk of the cow, Erment, for her son's libations.

I gave her a nod, which she returned, and it seemed we would leave each other's lives with no more said than that. But as I led my horse out through the doors she called out to me, and I turned. "I'm sorry, Meister Gelbfisc, that I suspected you," she said, "and that I spoke out against you. It was wrong of me."

I shrugged. "It was your grief and concern for your son that spoke. You don't owe me any apology."

She wiped her eyes with a trembling hand. "I thought . . . " she said. "I didn't know what to think. Was it the abbot, then? Did he try to poison Tomas so as to have an accusation to throw against you?"

"Is that what people are saying?" I asked.

Her answer was only a look, but it was an eloquent look.

I might not have spoken, even then. But there was such misery in her face. I could not leave her in a world like that, when I possessed the truth that would free her from it. "There is your poisoner," I said. And I pointed to the patch of weeds beside the stable wall.

"I don't understand," Frau Lauzen said.

"That's dogbane, madam. It's a very potent poison. The oil of dogbane twists the entrails and blinds the eyes. And it collects in the milk of the animals that feed on it, becoming even stronger through the titration of the animals' own guts. It would have killed Erment, eventually—my slaughtering her was a mercy in more ways than one—but until it did, her milk was killing Tomas."

Frau Lauzen's face became a mummers' show, in which many different emotions were successively portrayed. "Would have killed . . . ?" she echoed me. I made no further answer, but left her to her musings.

It was seven years later when I received Tomas's letter. I had all but forgotten these events, or at least I did not think of them very often. Its arrival surprised me for many reasons, not least because it must have taken him some effort to find my address.

He told me in the letter that his father and mother were both thriving. His father, not so young as he was and failing in strength, had taken Tomas on as an apprentice, but it turned out Tomas had no head for trade. He had entered the church instead, and was thriving there as the priest of a small parish in the municipality of Reshen.

But science, and chiefly chimick, was his hobby. Was it not true, he asked me, that certain oils, themselves boiling at higher temperatures than water, might when combined with water produce an immiscible compound that boiled at a much lower temperature? He had heard that the oil of indigo, for example, had this property. And this being the case, was it not also true that if a man secreted up his sleeve a cake of such oil, and thrust his arm into a cauldron, the water might reach a full boil without ever becoming hot enough to hurt him? But that afterwards, the oil being sublimed away, the water would reach its proper temperature and the natural order of things be restored?

I wrote back, briefly, to wish Meister Lauzen joy and good fortune in his chosen career. The church, I told him, needs prelates of open and inquiring mind, and I was sure he would do much good in his life and bring credit to his family.

Yes, I said in answer to his query. Such tricks could be performed—not with indigo, which would make a difference of only a few degrees to the boiling point, but with other tinctures not dissimilar. But I reminded him that God watches all, and will not permit base stratagems to prosper unless it be his will.

I added that I was only sorry for the cow, which was a dumb beast and guilty of nothing more than pursuing its natural appetites. Father Ignacio, being a man and therefore possessed of wit and conscience, deserved no such consideration.

A divine irony: I have told you how during my stay in Pokoj I outfaced the threat of death with nothing but brazen rhetoric and parlour tricks. Yet it was in this very same abbey that I met with death again, and this time in a form which I could not avoid. It was much later in my life, and I was passing through Narutsin, a common enough occurrence on my commercial journeys, when on the sudden I became grievously ill. There being no hospital nearby, the monks took me in for the second time, to tend to me in what (it soon became clear) was my final illness.

Ignacio had passed away long before; the father abbot presiding in Pokoj upon my arrival was none other than Tomas Lauzen, now risen in the church and much loved and respected. My second stay in the abbey was brief, and Tomas remained with me constantly, nursing me with simples and soothing balms just as I had once nursed him. He tried on several occasions during those last days to take my confession, uneasy at the thought that I might die with that old sin on my conscience.

But I could not repent, and therefore saw no point in confessing. Perhaps that is why I remained here, after death—in this house that now stands where the abbey used to stand, instead of journeying on to God's house.

But God's house stands everywhere. Who knows?

"Taproot" is yet another anthology piece that I wrote to order. In this case the stimulus was a postcard; an old one, already used and sent many years before. It was part of a huge collection of used postcards bought up by editors Chris Golden and Jonathan Maberry for this very purpose. The idea was that the writers in their purposed anthology would use the postcard (in any way they liked) as the stimulus for a story. ¶ My postcard showed a photo of Istanbul's Hagia Sophia , a building that at various times has been a church, a mosque, and a museum. It had been sent in the mid-30s, from a woman on vacation to some family friends, and it talked of the bewildering variety of places she had visited in the space of just a few days. "Today we are at Gallipoli. Tomorrow we will visit Troy." ¶ It wasn't quite a cry for help, but it read like one. It started me thinking about what the grand European tour might have meant to a young American woman, early in the twentieth century, who had had a relatively insular upbringing. ¶ Plus, I once again rolled the last thing I saw on TV into the developing idea. In this case it was an electrifying mini-documentary about a pro-Nazi rally held in New York's Madison Square Garden early in 1939. A Jewish protester was almost killed by the security guards and had to be rescued by New York City cops, who knew an unfair fight when they saw one. ¶ "Taproot" is a coming-of-age story, which I now realise is something I do a lot. Another thing I do a lot is to have point-of-view characters who are quiet and unassuming and completely harmless until they're pushed too far. I find the moment when the worm turns endlessly interesting.

TAPROOT

THE JEWEL IN THE CROWN *of the Eastern church, Hagia Sophia maintained its identity as a Greek Orthodox cathedral and the seat of power of the ecumenical patriarchs until 1543, when the city of Constantinople—modern-day Istanbul—fell to the Ottomans. It then became a mosque, a radical but logical repurposing which determined its fate until the modern era and the rise of—*

Betty Howard closed her guidebook and slipped it back into her purse. The modern era, in all its forms, failed to excite her. She was hard put to see herself as a part of it.

St Sophia *did* excite her, with its mixture of spikes and curves and the gorgeous, half-organic complexity of its shape. It was like some huge flower that had grown up in the heart of Istanbul, rather than something that had been built by human hands.

Her father, more prosaically, translated for her the words of the plaque on the wall beside the door, which said that the building had been reopened as a museum four years before, on the 1st of February 1935. "No doubt this is part of Atatürk's drive to secularise and modernise his country," he commented. "A goal one can only applaud. But the standing collection is said to be very poor. I am reluctant to pay two hundred lira to see a few flood-damaged statues. You may buy some postcards of the interior, Betty, if you wish to get an idea of it."

Though she was now in her twentieth year, her father still spoke to her as if she were a child. More dismayingly, Betty often found herself behaving like one, forced by his preconceptions into a set of complementary responses. It had been different before her mother died, and before she herself fell ill. She seemed in the intervening year to have grown backwards. Where once she had had an incisive mind and a willingness to use it, now she subsisted on a kind of bland and textureless kindness that kept her—at the best of times—half-asleep. Perhaps she would literally devolve back into an infant, sucking her thumb and reciting nonsense syllables. Sometimes she could almost feel it happening.

Now, for example, when her father's casual permission to buy souvenirs filled her with disproportionate excitement. Betty glanced up at him, to gauge how liberally she might interpret this invitation. If he chanced to be in an expansive mood, it was possible she could extend her remit and buy one of the brilliantly painted icons or clever tin miniatures of the cathedral that were also on sale.

The signs were not promising, however. Adrian Howard's expression was cold and distracted. His black tie, moreover, was still tightly knotted, and he had not removed his jacket. If he made no concessions to the stifling heat of the Turkish noonday, it was unlikely he would offer many to Betty's souvenir hunting.

But temptation was pressing itself upon her. As soon as her gaze went to the trinket-sellers who stood before the doors of St Sophia, they had closed in like fish in a pond when breadcrumbs are scattered on the surface. Smiling and jostling, they held up enticing and wonderful things: pictures and carvings, plates and bowls and leatherwork. They shouted their prices in diminishing series.

Adrian grimaced, as though at a sour taste. "Disgusting," he muttered. "Give us some room, you brutes!" Forgetting that he had said Betty might make a purchase, or else changing his mind, he strode around his daughter in a half-circle, waving his arms to make the trinket-sellers scatter. He was not careful. Some of the sellers had set out their stalls on the ground, arranging their wares on spread blankets or tablecloths. Adrian's brightly polished black Oxfords made havoc with these modest displays, causing their owners to yell in alarm and protest.

"Daddy, you're stepping on their things!" Betty cried out.

"These gewgaws?" Adrian's voice was thick with contempt. "If they sell one piece to an American tourist like us, Betty, it will buy another bushel-load tomorrow. Don't spare a thought for them."

But Betty was dismayed. She had a kind of instinct for desperation, as of one sufferer recognising another, and she saw in the faces of the men whose stock was trampled that it would not be so easy to replace as her father thought. Impulsively, she opened her hand, letting the banknotes he had given her, all low-denomination, fall to the ground. Some of the money, at least, might find its way to where it was needed.

In the meantime, unfortunately, she only made the crush and the chaos worse. The trinket-sellers fell on the crumpled currency notes with alacrity, pouring in now from all sides. "All things have consequences that were not intended," her mother Mhairi had said to her, in a raw, scraped whisper, not long before she died. "I should never have come here. But if I hadn't come here you would never have been."

Adrian yelled a curse he could not have intended his daughter to hear and swatted at the trinket-sellers with futile rage. The two of them were at the centre of a maelstrom now. A roiling wall of people separated them both from the street and from the door of the cathedral.

"Let me get you out of this," said a voice whose accent, though rich and strange, was not Turkish. A hand took hers, and tugged gently. Betty let herself be led.

And found that she was passing through the crowd at a speed that seemed impossible. Pressing bodies offered no barrier to her. Neither did the traffic on the Kabasakal Caddesi, whether drawn by horse or ox or internal combustion. She and the pale man—or was it a woman?—whose hand she held seemed to glide over the ground much faster than the movement of Betty's feet could account for.

Through the wall of the building opposite.

Across a courtyard, and then another, gathering speed as they went.

With a small shriek of panic, Betty pulled her hand free. The momentum she had accumulated was gone in a single heartbeat, but when she stopped, all at once, she was leaning very far forward. She fell down on her hands and knees, sent sprawling on rough, packed earth.

The air behind her was alive with whistles and shouts. In front of her, a small boy and a smaller girl, both very dark-skinned and very raggedly dressed, stared at her in silent amazement.

"H-Hello," Betty faltered. "Do you speak English?"

The children only turned and ran away.

Betty looked at her hands. They were bleeding. She thought they should be shaking too, given the strangeness of what had just happened, but they were surprisingly steady.

"*Burada, beyfendi!*" a man's voice yelled. Other voices took up the shout. "*O burada!*" "Here! She's here!"

Adrian arrived at a run, his hair and eyes wild. "Betty!" he exclaimed, hoarse with running. "Where did you go? What possessed you to run away like that?"

"I didn't run away, Father," Betty corrected him. "Someone ran away with me."

"Nonsense," Adrian said. "If there had been anyone, I should have seen them. You must not say such things." She thought he might offer her a hand, to help her to her feet, but he turned, instead, to the men in khaki uniforms who had assisted him in his search. He thanked them in both English and Pontic Greek. Money changed hands. And Betty climbed up out of the dirt unaided.

The khaki uniforms were everywhere in the city. Betty didn't know whether the men were police officers or soldiers, but the distinction seemed an idle one to make when the whole of Europe was swept up in rumours of impending war. The police, after all, carried the same guns that the soldiers carried. And if Herr Hitler came, most likely their remit would be very little different. And their fate, for that matter.

"Are you all right?" Adrian demanded, when Betty was upright again.

"I am a little dishevelled, and I have scraped the heels of both my hands," Betty told him. "Those things aside, I'm quite well. But I wasn't lying, Father. Someone took my hand and dragged me here, at great speed."

Her father frowned. "I find that hard to believe," he said. "There was nobody near us apart from the trinket-sellers. Was it one of them?"

Betty thought of the narrow, milk-white face that had floated beside her. The ash-blonde hair and pale grey eyes. "No," she said. "I don't believe so."

"Then your account seems hard to credit. Honestly, Betty, I am at a loss. We will return to the hotel. You've postcards to send, to the Carrolls, and to Dr and Mrs Willits. And you'll need to wash and change before dinner."

Betty glanced up. The sun was still high in the sky, so dinner was hardly an imminent event. But her father had been reluctant to explore the city in the first place, and clearly needed but little persuasion to abandon the mission. They took a taxicab, huge and black and noisy, back to the Pera Palace Hotel in Tepebaşı. The doorman, resplendent in a white and gold uniform with more buttons than fabric and more braid than either, saluted them with insane bravura as they went inside.

Betty and her father rode up in the elevator together, then separated to enter their rooms each by their own door. This was a ritual they always observed, even though the two bedrooms were part of the same suite, with a sitting room in between that belonged to both.

As she bathed and washed her hair, Betty replayed the whole incident again and again in her mind. Perhaps, after all, there had been no mysterious stranger who took her hand and ran or flew with her two hundred yards in the space of a breath. She was well known to be flighty, at the mercy of her own imagination. A fair proportion of the things she saw were demonstrably not there. And if, contrariwise, there had been such a person, where had they come from? A man (or woman) with pale skin and blond hair would be sure to draw attention wherever they went in Istanbul. Particularly in that grass-green coat. It had had long tails, Betty remembered, and a very wide collar of the kind that could be turned up against driving rain. Did it ever rain in Istanbul?

It had rained in Ireland, in the Vale of Avoca, where their grand tour had begun three weeks before. In a wild mood that had come from nowhere, Betty had gone out barefoot in the downpour. She had made her way across the field behind their rented cottage, to the stream, and then along its banks into a small copse of willow trees and silver birch.

She had gotten lost.

Then, out of nowhere, she had heard the sound of hoof beats. It was a sound she had only heard before in Western movies: the images it conjured, therefore, were of wild natives and evil brigands. She did not know this country, or who or what one might suddenly encounter there. Afraid, she had hidden in thick bushes, head down, until the rider passed. She had had to wait a long time, for the horse slowed to a halt opposite her hiding place and stamped and whickered there for an interminable time before going on its way. From where she was kneeling she could very clearly see the rider's feet, in long boots of faded brown leather. There was something about the look of those booted feet that made her earlier thoughts of wild men and bandits seem entirely appropriate.

As soon as she was alone again and had emerged from the undergrowth, Betty felt ridiculous and ashamed. She had never mentioned her brief escapade to her father.

He had more than enough on his mind, without such digressions. Ireland was where Betty's mother had come from, and Adrian's mood had altered visibly as soon as they arrived. The main reason for their coming to Europe was ostensibly to provide a rest cure for Betty's ailments both of the nerves and of the body, but Ireland had been included in their itinerary for other reasons. "You should be aware of your roots, on your mother's side," Adrian had said. "I owe it to my dear, dead Mhairi."

But they had not lingered long, and they had met nobody from Mhairi's family. They were not to be found, Adrian said, at any of the addresses he had for them.

Thence to Amsterdam, Paris, Rome, Gallipoli, Troy. Never staying anywhere more than a day, and never doing more in any place than to take a desultory walk through its splendours and stand before one or two of the buildings that Baedeker said were not to be missed. Adrian seemed to want to take Europe at a dead run, the better to pretend once they returned to Cincinnati that they had never left. Whatever was driving him, it did not seem to be nostalgia.

Perhaps it was grief, but Betty did not believe so. Even in the months when his wife was dying, Adrian's centre of gravity seemed already to have shifted. He had buried his head in the world, as ostriches are said to do in a bank of sand, so as not to see Mhairi fading away in front of his eyes.

Betty had had no option but to see. She had taken up the station her father abandoned, and held her mother's hand until the last. Then, as if she were a runner in a relay race, she had begun to sicken herself.

The dust of the city had formed a film on the surface of her bathwater, which was no longer tepid but actually cold. She must have fallen into one of her long reveries. She got out and dried herself.

When she went back into her bedroom, she received another surprise on a day that already felt somewhat over-stuffed with them. Lying on her bed, along with the evening clothes she had already laid out there, was a sculpture in silver or (much more likely) tin. It was not a model of the cathedral. It was a mounted figure, carrying a sword in one hand and a whip in the other. The tail of the whip was a fila-ment of metal so slender and so beautifully recurved on itself that her eye lost itself among its involutions. It was altogether finer than anything she had seen for sale outside St Sophia.

Still, where else could it have come from? And how had it found its way here, to her bedroom?

Her father's knock on the outer door startled her from what might otherwise have been another prolonged trance of thought. Glancing at the clock, Betty realised that she had been staring at the lovely thing for more than ten minutes.

The knock was repeated. "Betty," her father called. "It's time."

He did not offer her his arm as they went down. She dimly remembered, when she was very small, climbing on his shoulders to touch the sky, something he assured her was entirely possible, and belabouring him with a pillow while he pretended to be the villainous Captain Hook from the story of Peter Pan. She could not remember when these games had stopped. And certainly it would not do to try to reinstate them now, when she was a young lady and Adrian was a figure in society.

A very small figure, admittedly. As the sole owner and manager of a firm that leased out agricultural equipment,

he made a great deal of money but seemed to have a somewhat marginal social standing. Partly, Betty knew, this was
due to his temperament, which was one of cold reserve.
More recently it was also owing to his political opinions,
not so much because they were extreme as because they
were so very explicit. He could not keep from holding
forth on them.

"Thank you for my gift," Betty murmured as they
went downstairs together, side by side but not touching.

Adrian seemed puzzled, and perhaps slightly irritated.
"What gift?"

"The horseman," Betty said. But she faltered as she
said it. To leave the horseman where she had found it he
would have had to come into her room. The logistics of
this were not complicated, but judged from a psychological point of view it was implausible, if not impossible.

And was the figure a man? It was slender at the waist
and full in the chest in a way that suggested it might not
be. The Pontic Steppe was the ancient territory of the
Scythian people, whose women warriors had inspired
the legend of the Amazons. They favoured bows, though,
controlling their horses with the muscles of their thighs
and calves as they fired from the saddle.

"Betty," Adrian snapped. "Please pay attention to me
when I'm speaking to you. I repeat, I did not leave you
any gift. To what are you referring?"

"Nothing, Father," Betty said meekly. "I was in error.
The item in question—a small, sculpted piece in white
metal—must be part of the permanent décor of my room."

Adrian seemed satisfied with this explanation. Or perhaps he ceased to question her because he had seen Herr
Hartmann and Mr Krug at the bottom of the stairs, deep
in conversation. So they were to have company for dinner
again. The two men had first crossed their path at Gal-
lipoli and then again when they visited the ruins of Troy.
The younger of the two, Mr Krug, had paid Betty a few

heavy-handed compliments on the first occasion and there-after had ignored her. Fat, avuncular Herr Hartmann was somewhat more amiable, though his jokes—invariably of the riddle-me-this variety—were extremely tiresome.

They turned now as Adrian hailed them. All three men shook hands cordially, and then the two Germans (German and Anglo-German, rather) bowed to Betty and said good evening to her. She acknowledged their courtesies with a smile and a bob of the head.

"It's a little early yet to sit down," Herr Hartmann said to her father. "Perhaps a small aperitif would be in order. I remember, Mr Howard, you share my fondness for schnapps."

Adrian hesitated, his gaze shifting to Betty. Even though this was a hotel rather than an inn or public hos-telry, one might easily perceive an impropriety in a single woman sitting down to drink with three men. Observers would not necessarily divine that one of the men was her father, and might disapprove of the license even if they did.

"I'll take a walk in the gardens," Betty offered. "And join you at the table."

"Very well, Betty," Adrian said. "Take care not to leave the grounds."

"Yes, Daddy."

The men moved away towards the hotel bar, already taking up again the conversation they had begun in Gal-lipoli and continued at Troy. It concerned the political philosophy of National Socialism, the future of the Aryan race, and the coming war.

In the garden, although it was only April, gold-hearted chamomile was everywhere. There were anemones too, and bright purple irises with their flowers like the robes of tiny emperors. And somewhere nearby there must be a herb garden: Betty could smell both thyme and sage, so vividly that the scent was almost like a taste in her mouth.

In a corner of the garden, a long way from the hotel, there was a decorative arch in a wall of rough grey stone. Betty made her way towards it, deciding that it would mark the furthest point of her walk. As she drew close to it, though, her steps slowed. There was something strange and a little unsettling about the arch.

No, not about the arch, but the landscape beyond it. And not even the landscape itself, but the shadows. Betty could not entirely reconcile their direction with the angle of the sun, and they were somehow softer; as though on the far side of the arch a different sun shone on a different place. A place that was not Istanbul.

There was a grassy bank immediately beyond the arch. As Betty approached it, sidelong, she became aware of a figure sitting on the bank, his folded arms resting on his knees. He wore a long coat, and his hair was ash-blond.

Betty stopped a long way before the arch. The man acknowledged her with a nod and a flourish of his hand, smiling warmly.

"Deoraí," he murmured. The accent was the same she had heard earlier at St Sophia, musical and mysterious. There was a rich burr to the man's voice. Betty thought that if she set her hand to his throat she would feel the vibration there when he spoke, as though bees lived inside his chest.

Not that she would, of course. Not that she would do that.

"My name is not Deoraí," she said. "It is Betty."

The man laughed appreciatively, as though she had uttered a clever bon mot. "Ah, well," he said, "I've no gift for their grunts and squeaks, so I can't gainsay you."

"Did you come into my room?" Betty asked him. "And leave a horseman there? If you did, it won't make me like you any better, or agree to go with you. When I took your hand, you tried to run away with me, and that was wrong."

The man let his head hang down for a moment, as though in shame, but when he looked up at Betty again with his face aslant, he was grinning most impudently. "It was that," he admitted. "The action of a rogue and a churl. But that's my nature, deoraí, even when my mission is not so urgent. When it's life or death, as it is now, I become downright sly and unmannerly."

Betty was nonplussed. She could think of no apposite reply. "When I first saw you," she said, only to mark her place in the conversation, "I thought you might be a woman."

The man's outline wavered. He *was* a woman, Betty suddenly saw, with small, high breasts and a mouth so dark and rich a red it looked unsettlingly like a wound. "Today was *not* the first time you saw me," the woman said. "But you have the right of it, all the same. I might be anything, if I wished it, and so might you. It's only sickness and staleness that keeps you so."

Betty's feet slipped a little on the gravel of the path. It descended more steeply towards the arch than she had realised. She shifted her balance. "I don't know what you mean by that," she said.

"No more than I say. Will you come with me now, if I promise to be more respectful of your person? I've something lovely to show you that will make you clap your hands and laugh like a little girl."

Betty looked back towards the hotel. It seemed a long way away, suddenly.

"What kind of something?" she asked.

"Something to delight you, surely. I'll say no more than that."

The gradient of the path made it difficult to stand upright. Betty was sliding forward, her planted feet leaving a double wake in the shifting gravel. She looked down, startled, and saw how steep the slope had become. In a matter of seconds it would be vertical and she would fall.

The archway loomed below her. Just beyond it, the woman threw open her arms. She gave a deep, mischievous chuckle. "I did warn you," she said. "I can't see advantage and not take it, deoraí. I just can't."

Just before she lost her footing, Betty lunged forward with all her might. As the ground under her feet became a sheer cliff face, she kicked away from it in a clumsy, headlong jump, angled to her left. Instead of falling straight through the archway she hit the wall to one side of it, and stood for a second balanced on its brink with her arms turning windmills.

The pale woman was taken by surprise, but only for the merest moment. She threw out her hand to seize hold of Betty's ankle. At the moment when they would have touched, gravity reasserted itself. Betty fell—not onto the gravel path but into one of the beds of irises planted right under the wall. She scrambled away from the archway, expecting the woman to come running through it and take hold of her again.

She stared in disbelief, and mild affront. There was no archway. The wall was unbroken. Not so the flowers, which she had all but destroyed. These innocent casualties of the attack on her dismayed her almost as much as the attack itself.

She returned to the hotel sullen and unhappy. Her father and his two associates had not yet finished their drink, and at another time she would have respected their privacy. As it was, she walked into their midst without ceremony.

The suddenness of Betty's arrival startled them. Herr Hartmann in particular was severely discomposed. He had been in the process of showing her father the contents of a black leather valise. Rather than simply closing the bag when Betty arrived, he threw his own body across it as though he was trying to protect it from her, or her from it.

"I am very sorry to disturb you," she said. "Father, I saw the man again. The man from this afternoon, at St

Sophia." She decided to avoid any mention of the fact that the man had turned into a woman, feeling that it weakened her case.

But even with that omission, Adrian was not convinced. "There was no such man," he snapped. "Betty, I'm surprised at you. You should know better than to interrupt a conversation between gentlemen without either invitation or announcement. Wait for us in the restaurant. There is a table reserved under my name."

Utterly humiliated, Betty could manage no more than a muttered "Yes, Father," before she turned and fled.

The maître d'hotel, recognising her as her father's daughter, was very pleased to seat her. He brought her an amuse-bouche of mashed aubergine with spicy bread to dip in it, and ice water flavoured with rose petals. It was delicious, but did little to lift Betty's misery. She ate and drank desultorily until her father and the other men finally came to join her more than twenty minutes later.

"I am sorry, Betty," her father said as he seated himself, "that I was so peremptory with you. You must understand, we were discussing serious matters."

"Of course, Father," Betty said.

"I hope I did not upset you."

"Not at all." She had composed herself. The lie could not be read on her face.

"It falls to some of us to be busy," Mr Krug said brightly, "while others need only be beautiful. You must forgive us all, Miss Howard. We know this visit is in the nature of a rest cure for you. But not for your father, alas."

Betty forced a smile. It was the first of many. The evening wore on, dreadful and indivisible. The three men talked about Germany, and the wonderful things that were being done there. "The Führer has united the people behind a single vision," Herr Hartmann enthused. "That, in itself, is the miracle—that he perfectly embodies the Aryan volk, and that they find themselves completed and expressed in him."

"I find his manifesto, as set down in *Mein Kampf*, entirely convincing," Adrian said. "Unanswerable, even. Final in the way that all great truths are final. Yet the American press continues to dwell on the negatives."

Mr Krug made a nasal sound of contempt, like a snort. "To invent the negatives, you mean. Because the Jews control the media, just as they control the banks. They will say anything, do anything, to prevent America and my own dear Britain from making common cause with Germany."

"They cannot prevent it," Herr Hartmann averred. "They can only delay it. And not for much longer. If our program goes forward as we intend—"

"We must order more wine," Mr Krug interjected quickly. "This bottle is almost finished."

His eyes were on Betty as he said this. Perhaps he was afraid to say too much in front of a relative stranger. In fact, she was hardly attending to what the men were discussing. She was thinking about her abductor, who wore green and changed sex on a momentary whim. Had she also been the one to leave the metal figure in Betty's room? And if so, why?

There was a great deal more canvassing of the German miracle, and a great deal more wine. Mr Krug intervened more often as the evening progressed, turning the conversation whenever it threatened to become too specific about what Herr Hartmann called "the program" and her father called "the schedule".

This heavy-handed censorship wore her down, at last. Or perhaps it was the events of the day, which had been so far outside what she was used to. However it was, there seemed to be a dam inside her, with something pressing ever more heavily against it, until all at once it gave.

Herr Hartmann had mentioned the German-American Bund. Mr Krug jumped in yet again to forestall whatever comment about the organisation might be forthcoming. And Betty jumped in likewise, full on his heels.

The Bund was not a secret. It was a group of influential men, both of business and of letters, who wished America to form a political and economic alliance with Germany. Taking it as an article of faith that a European war was coming, they wanted the USA either to remain uncommitted in that war or else to offer Herr Hitler's fledgling fascist republic aid and support.

Only that February they had held a massed rally at Madison Square Gardens in New York. Some twenty-two thousand Americans had performed the strange, straight-armed salute, while young men dressed in quasi-military fancy dress marched up and down the aisles. A Jewish protester, one Isadore Greenbaum, had been badly beaten, and might have been killed had not officers of the New York City Police effected a rescue. The debased spectacle had been decried in every newspaper, and the Bund's leader, Fritz Julius Kuhn, was now under arrest.

Betty reprised all this for Mr Krug, concisely and perhaps a little smugly, although her father's face told her very clearly that he wished she would not. It was not usual for her to defy him openly.

But then it was not usual for her to be attacked and almost abducted and for him not to believe her when she told him so. Aid and support, in the domestic as in the political sphere, should flow in both directions at once.

"Your daughter is very forthright," Herr Hartmann said with a weak laugh.

"And very perceptive," Mr Krug added. "I'm sorry, Miss Howard. I assumed these things were unfamiliar to you, and of no interest. Are you sympathetic to the philosophy of National Socialism?"

"Not sympathetic enough to describe it as a philosophy," Betty replied. "Daddy, might I be allowed to drink some wine?"

"By no means," Adrian muttered.

"I am of legal age."

"Nonetheless."

"Liberal democracy has failed both Europe and America," Mr Krug said. "It has allowed the Jews to strangle the white race at the root."

"Is the white race a tree?" Betty asked.

"It's a reasonable analogy, is it not?"

"Possibly. But a tree's roots are thousandfold. If you want a plant with a single taproot, perhaps you should liken the white race to a carrot or a turnip."

"Betty," her father interjected.

"Or a burdock. I believe a burdock would also do."

"Betty, that is enough!" Adrian's furious yelp carried across the room. The mâitre d'hotel raised an eloquent eyebrow.

It was enough for all of them. The conversation finally wound down. Farewells were said with more politesse than cordiality, and their two guests took their leave. "I will see you later, Mr Howard," Herr Hartmann said, "as we arranged. And I will bring along those other friends I mentioned."

Adrian settled the bill, leaving a meagre tip.

Riding up in the elevator, he berated Betty for speaking in front of her elders and betters. She would have been better, he suggested, remaining silent and profiting from their wisdom and experience. "Since we came to Europe, I hardly know you!" he exclaimed. "I blame myself. I have given you too much license, since your mother died. You may depend upon it that when we are home again that license will cease."

Betty did not reply. She might have told him that she was equally at a loss, but she was reluctant to show anything that might be perceived as contrition. Very much to her own amazement, she found that she was not contrite.

In avoiding her father's accusing stare, she found her glance falling on the leather valise which he had brought with him from the table. Following the line of her gaze, he became anxious.

"You are not to open it," he told her, "or look inside it. You are not even to touch it."

Betty didn't need to do any of those things. She had already seen what was in the valise. She refrained from saying so, however. She was tired, suddenly, of unspoken things and of pretence. Such as the pretence that they had come to Europe for the sake of her health, or her heritage, when in fact it was to service some tawdry intrigue that her father had initiated with Herr Hartmann and Mr Krug.

"I will be having some visitors in our shared sitting room this evening," Adrian said. "I assume you will prefer to stay in your bedroom."

"I will stay wherever I'm put, Father," Betty told him.

"Impertinence does not suit you, Betty."

No, she thought. *And secrecy does not suit you. It's exacting and you haven't the constitution for it.* She felt a vague movement of pity for him, and it took her by surprise. She had never thought of her father as someone to be pitied. But so much of his vitality had come to him reflected, as it were, from his wife. From Mhairi. Without her he seemed in many ways more dead than alive. The white race was not so very much like a tree, no matter what Mr Krug might say, but a man was. Both could die without watering, and her father's spirit was parched.

She turned away from the painful sight of him, and went into her room without saying goodnight.

The metal figure of the rider, with her sword and her whip, stood on the bedside table where she had left it. She picked it up and turned it in her hands, admiring the way it broke the light of the room's three tiny electric light bulbs into a boiling dazzle as it turned.

Is the heart always drawn to its own opposite? she wondered. Certainly that seemed to be true of Adrian and Mhairi. Betty's own heart was as yet ungored, so she could only theorise.

Rebellion frothed up inside her, to an even greater height than it had reached at the dinner table. Why should she stay where she was put? She was in a strange city, full of strange sights. In two days' time she would be back in Cincinnati, where she might shrink again into the tiny compass in which she had lived before.

She put on an outdoor coat and a pair of gloves. There was no need for either in the warm twilight of the city, but in her coat she would look like a woman on her way to an engagement and therefore would be less likely to draw attention. She took her purse for the same reason. On an impulse she dropped the metal sculpture into it. The delicate tracery of the rider's whip might take some damage but she wanted it with her, as a talisman. A totem. She was suddenly certain that it had been left for her specifically, and for a definite purpose.

She slipped back out into the hallway, drawing the door to behind her without making a sound. She locked it and took away the key, although she knew her father would not come looking for her. Nobody stopped her in the lobby. The doorman gave her the same astonishing, preposterous bow, and she nodded back at him, acknowledging it, as though being bowed to was something she knew all about.

She stood at the top of the hotel steps, drinking in the scene before her. A muezzin called from a nearby tower, a sweet and plangent sound. The sun was still on the horizon but the streets were a bowl full of thick warm darkness spiced with sweat and cinnamon. Betty let it swallow her.

She went back to St Sophia first. She didn't go inside, but she visited the trinket-sellers again. Not all of them were still there, but she bought something from everyone she saw. A scarf from one, a matchbook cover from another, a silver necklace from a third.

In a teahouse nearby she ordered a coffee and sipped it slowly. Sweetness and bitterness swirled together on her tongue, as though they were fighting a skirmish there to see which taste would be the strongest.

She was aware of the eyes that were on her as she drank. The waiter who had served her. A man sitting alone a few tables away. Another, no more than a shadow, watching from underneath an awning across the street. Perhaps she was letting her pleasure show too obviously. If so, she didn't care.

The Maiden's Tower. The Blue Mosque. Taksim Square. Betty roamed the city with ravenous eyes, feeling that the darkness hid her perfectly—and fitted her perfectly, like some exquisite garment.

The Basilica Cistern was her favourite. She had stepped through a narrow door and descended an even narrower staircase only to find herself, a hundred feet or more below the street, in a vast cavern lit by dozens of burning torches. Towering columns held up the roof, extending into solid black far above her. No two were alike. According to the Baedeker one of these columns, with a pattern of teardrops on its side, would grant your heart's desire if you touched the stone and spoke it aloud. Betty searched for it, and at last found it.

But as she reached out her hand to touch it, another hand gripped her wrist, tight enough to make her gasp aloud in pain. And then twisted it painfully, forcing her to turn.

"Well," said Mr Krug. "This has been quite a pilgrimage, Miss Howard. How bold you are, to brave Istanbul at night." His face was very close to hers. His smile openly mocked her.

Betty was not wont to waste words. Krug knew that he was hurting her, so there was no purpose to be served in pointing that out. Likewise, she did not plead or demand to be released. She confirmed with a glance that they had the enormous room to themselves. Nobody would hear her if she cried out.

"Your business with my father will not be advanced by your forcing yourself on me, Mr Krug," she said, bringing to bear what leverage she had.

"I've no intention of doing so," he said. "Please be assured of that, Miss Howard. I'm not a man who takes amorous advantage of the weaker sex. But you saw, did you not, the contents of the valise my associate gave your father?"

"Of course I saw it. I'm not blind."

"No, you are not blind. Nor are you stupid, so you divined what the money was for."

"American dollars to bribe American politicians," Betty said. "To buy American friends for Herr Hitler." It occurred to her a moment too late that she might have feigned ignorance on that score at least. Might have pretended, perhaps, that she thought only her father was being bribed. But there had been a great many notes, of high denomination, and in any case one did not have to purchase zealots. They suborned themselves.

"Exactly. And at dinner you scarcely sounded like a friend."

"I might be persuaded," Betty said tightly. She was instantly ashamed of the lie. "If your Reich were less ridiculous," she added.

Mr Krug smiled, perhaps at the neat alliteration.

Then he punched Betty in the face.

She felt the impact first, then the surprise, and only latterly the pain. The blow made her stagger backwards so violently she almost lost her footing. As it was she stayed upright only for a second longer. Mr Krug's second blow, to her jaw, felled her on the spot. When she was down on the cold stones it was more convenient for him to kick her, since it meant he did not have to bend. He kicked her a great many times.

The whole assault was so sudden and so overwhelming that it paralysed Betty. She offered no resistance, but curled in on herself like a baby settling to sleep as Mr Krug's booted foot sank into her stomach again and again. She folded her arms across her head to protect her face. Mr Krug stepped down hard on her midriff and she felt bone grate against bone as something inside her broke.

Breathing heavily now, Krug broke off from his assault to pick up Betty's purse, which she had dropped. He opened it and emptied its contents onto the stones. Betty was confused for a second. Surely he did not mean to rob her as well as murder her?

No. But it would do no harm if it seemed that someone else had robbed her. Her death might plausibly be an accidental side effect of an act of theft. He leaned down to pick up Betty's billfold, which her mother had embroidered for her the year before she died.

Staring past him, Betty saw through unfocused eyes that they were not alone after all. Someone was leaning against a pillar a little way off. He swept the tails of his long coat away to left and right with a flick of his hands so that he could hook his thumbs in his wide leather belt.

"Well this is a bad state of affairs," he said.

Krug did not turn, or seem to hear. He was taking the money from the billfold and transferring it to his pocket. Then he tossed it to the ground again.

"Help me," Betty whispered.

"Aye," the man in the long coat said. "I'd like nothing better. But I had my three sorties and now I'm forbid. The rules don't bend for the likes of me."

Three sorties, Betty thought. The first, of course, had been in Avoca, in the rain. When she hid like a child among the trees. This room was like another forest, with trees made of stone instead of wood. But if it was a forest she was down among the roots.

Thousandfold.

Mr Krug trod down on Betty's elbow, and shifted his weight. She screamed, which seemed to be the only point of the exercise. He was not merely killing her now, he was hurting her—surrendering to something in his soul that had nothing to do with National Socialism or the future of the Aryan race.

"This might help you, though," the pale man said. Except that he was a woman again. She went down on one knee to point at the little metal figure of the horse and rider, which had spilled out of Betty's purse along with everything else. "I left it with you for that purpose. If you touch it, you'll be able give this unseemly man as bad a turn as he's giving you. You'd better reach for it, deoraí. I've no other counsel to give you."

Betty stretched out her hand. But Krug had gone back to kicking her in the stomach, and her own nerves betrayed her, making her fold inwards on the pain. With a supreme effort, and a great deal of pain, she used her right arm (which Krug had certainly broken) to roll over on her back. From this angle she couldn't see the little metal figure but she knew it was within reach of her left hand.

She groped for it, even as Krug knelt and locked his hands around her throat, cutting off her breath.

Nothing.

Nothing again.

And then the touch of the smooth, cold metal against the tip of her little finger. She had hoped that power might flow into her at once, sufficient to break Krug's fierce grip. She needed air. Her brain was buzzing and her eyes were darkening.

"Ask her, so," the woman murmured urgently in her ear. "For the whip, or for the sword. It's all one to her."

The sword, Betty thought. *Please, little spirit, locked in tin. The sword for me.*

Of a sudden she felt the weight of it, lying across her outstretched hand. She closed her fingers around its hilt. She had no strength to swing, no room to thrust. She did the only thing she could do, which was to lift it up at an angle, her wrist twisted back on itself, and bring it down on Krug's arm, near the shoulder.

The blade was almost invisible, just a rumour of movement in the air, but it sliced through Krug's arm, severing it, and bit deep into his chest. His eyes went wide with shock and dismay. His mouth opened, but no sound came out: only a rush of blood, joining the torrent of the stuff that was pouring from his wound. He was dead before he fell. He sprawled forward onto Betty's body, with the sword between them. The blade settled itself even deeper into his flesh, but where it touched Betty it swirled like smoke and did no harm.

He was too heavy for her to get out from under him, so she sliced him into smaller pieces and removed him a little at a time. When she could finally sit up, she was boltered from head to foot in blood and gore.

The pale woman offered her a hand, but Betty did not take it. "I can't stand," she muttered hoarsely. "I need a doctor. I think I might die."

"You might, if you wish it," the woman allowed. "You might do anything, if you wish it. But equally, you might change this flesh for something better. You could scarcely do worse. The iron country has used you badly."

She showed Betty how to effect the transformation. It was not difficult, but it was strange enough that Betty was slow and clumsy at first. While she worked she asked the pale woman her name. The woman said it was Ériu, and was at pains to differentiate herself from many other Érius she thought Betty might have heard of.

"What does *deoraí* mean?" Betty asked her as she went on repairing her broken bones. She asked mainly so that the woman would carry on talking. The sweetness of her voice both pleased and reassured her.

"It means . . . " The pale woman paused, her confidence dissipating. "I told you I had no skill with their languages. I make do, with a spell here and a charm there, but I've never studied them. Just as I've never studied the underside of stones. I suppose you might say exile, but it's got a different turn to it. It means the exile coming home."

"I'm not," Betty pointed out, "either of those things."

"No," the pale woman said. "Your mother was the exile, and you've never known the Land yourself. You will know it, though. And you'll think of it as home as soon as you see it."

"My mother was born in Ireland."

"No, in Tír Tairngire. It comes quite close to Ireland, from time to time. It comes close to many places. But she left to go a wandering, as some will, and her heart involved itself with another place."

"With Cincinnati."

"Aye, possibly. The Queen sent emissaries there, but your mother was a stubborn one and wouldn't go with them. It hurt her to admit that she was wrong. Even when she sickened, from being too long in the iron country. Even when she knew she would die there."

"What about me?"

"We didn't know about you. Not until ten days ago, when you stood in bare feet on soil that was friendly to us. The soil knew you and spoke out, and the Queen sent me off hell for leather to fetch you. But I've made only a bad fist of it, haven't I?"

"You saved my life," Betty pointed out. "I'm not inclined to complain about the terms on which you did it."

When at last she was able to, she stood. Her legs shook a little, but her workmanship was good and they held her up as well as ever.

Will you come with me now?" the pale woman asked her. "To the Land That Was Promised?"

"I've got things to do here first," Betty said.

"Here? What's here, but a broth of broken things?"

"A war," Betty said. "I think a war is coming soon."

"Let it come. It won't be more of a mess than what they've got already."

"You've got a queen, so don't lecture me on politics. My country got over kings and queens a long time ago."

They returned to the hotel. The doorman did not bow to them because he did not see them. They passed before him like a breath of wind, and stepped between the doorjamb and the door.

Betty let herself into her own room first. She had left the key on the stone floor of the Basilica Cistern but Ériu, who had little use for keys, obliged her.

She went across to the door that led to the shared sitting room. With her hand on the knob, she hesitated. Her father was in there. He would be shocked to see her in this ghastly form, covered from head to foot in dried blood. But there seemed little point in cleaning the blood away, given what she was about to do.

She reached into the pocket of her coat and brought out the metal figure. Holding it in both hands she brought it up to her face. *I called you little spirit because I didn't know you,* she told it. *But I think you're bigger than you look, and I honour you. I will take the whip this time, please, if I may be allowed.*

It flowered in her hand, a supple thing full of its own tensed power.

"Go to it," Ériu urged her. "And spare not."

Betty opened the door and stepped into the room.

Herr Hartmann was there, and her father. Three other men were there too. They were talking volubly and happily about the future of the world.

Betty laid about her with the whip, and the future of the world ceased to concern them. They screamed for help, and then for mercy, and then because they had forgotten how to make other sounds.

When Betty lowered the whip at last, her arm was exhausted.

Her father stared at her in wild-eyed terror from his chair. A lake of blood surrounded them both.

"Betty," he said in a strangled voice. "That . . . That cannot be you!"

"You may be right, Father," Betty said. "I'm honestly not sure at this moment who I am. But I am looking forward to finding out."

Adrian looked around at the carnage. A whimper escaped him. "They're dead," he whispered. "Oh my dear God, they're all dead. You killed them!"

"But spared you," Betty reminded him. She picked up the valise, which was standing on the floor next to his chair.

"You'll have no use for money in Tír Tairngire," Ériu said.

Betty kissed her father on the top of his head. Rigid with shock as he was, he could not even flinch away from her. "Goodbye, Daddy," she said. "Thank you for all your kindnesses, when I was a child. And for what's happened since, I forgive you with all my heart."

Back in her own room, she packed a few of her favourite clothes into her smallest suitcase.

"In Tír Tairngire you'll wear the wind and the sun," Ériu said. "You won't be needing these fripperies."

Betty closed both latches on the case. She closed her eyes and concentrated, turning the blood on her skin to warm water and then to steam that wisped and corkscrewed in the air and was gone. She was already more adept at this than she had been at the Basilica Cistern, and more confident.

"Shall we go now?" Ériu coaxed.

Betty put down the case, and the valise, and turned to face her strange benefactor. She let herself acknowledge what she had known all along: that the thin, pale face before her was the most beautiful she had ever seen.

"Is the heart always drawn to its own opposite?" she asked, tracing the line of Ériu's cheek with one finger.

"Or its likeness," Ériu said. "Or its complement. The heart is the heart. There are no rules for such things."

They kissed as women, and then as men.

They walked on two feet, and then on four. And wings and tails and fins they employed too, each in their place and in their measure.

They did not go to Tír Tairngire, or at least not directly. They went to war. Ériu was inclined to scoff, and said it was only a game Betty was playing, but still they taught some hard lessons to bad men, turned a few rivers and dammed a few more, and altogether had a great and glorious time of it.

It's my mother I'm saying goodbye to, Betty told herself. But it was her father too, and that might be why it took so long.

This daft slasher story is the oldest piece in the present collection, by a long way. I wrote it—longhand, in blue biro—when I was barely out of my teens. I've reworked it a number of times since then, most recently for an anthology called *Psycho-Mania*. ¶ Having the story revolve around an edgy pas de deux between a writer and a critic was a late addition, shoehorned in after I got really irritated by a guy who was reviewing *Lucifer* on one of the US comics websites. This gentleman, who will remain nameless, first took an interest around issue 42 of the series, and reviewed almost every issue thereafter. His reviews were very much alike, consisting mainly of complaints about the many things he didn't understand because he'd come into the story three and a half years late, occasionally enlivened by complaints about how Lucifer was hardly in the story, even though it was meant to be his book. I mean Lucifer's name was right there on the cover, but page after page had OTHER CHARACTERS on it. So how come? Huh? ¶ Negative reviews, if they're thoughtful and intelligent and fair, can give you invaluable insights about your own writing. Even biased reviews can clue you in on how some readers approach texts in your chosen genre and why your work is a poor fit for them. A review written by a nitwit can't teach you anything at all, but it can still spark a story idea.

REFLECTIONS ON THE CRITICAL PROCESS

MANDELSON AND ME arguing across a table.

I tell him he has to up his game, and he shoots me.

I wake up in hospital, groggy but healing. It's three days later: three days since I last sat down and wrote. Over the whining protests of the doctor, who belongs to a type I despise, I sign the releases and discharge myself on my own recognisance.

Outside, on the street, I flag down a taxi. It swerves in my direction, but doesn't slow. As I bounce off the front bumper, I catch a glimpse of Mandelson at the wheel, grinning like a maniac.

This time it's only two days before I wake up, and it's a nicer ward with a South-facing window. But Mandelson has sent me flowers which bring me out in a hideous allergic rash when I touch them. I go into anaphylactic shock, and it's another week before I surface.

Is the man disturbed, I wonder? This seems a disproportionate response to a negative review. But as my bloated, blood-swollen face deflates towards its normal proportions, some of my natural indignation drains away too. This is surely nothing that can't be settled over a hearty meal and a selection of fine wines.

I walk home—it seems safer than hailing a cab. When I get there, I find that the door of my apartment has been booby-trapped: I can quite clearly see the scrape marks in the wood of the jamb where Mandelson—for I assume it is he—has been meddling with the hinges. Were I to insert my key in the lock, it seems probable that some very unfortunate consequences would result. Explosives? Poison gas? Discretion, plainly, is the better part of valour.

The elevator doesn't come when I call it, so I take the stairs. The loose board has been more expertly camouflaged than the tampering with my door, so I come down the last three flights arse-over-tip, with gathering momentum. That turns out to be a blessing in disguise, because I sail right over the bamboo stakes and am only brought to a (somewhat painful) halt by the street door.

Limping down the steps into the street, I narrowly escape being run over for a second time. This time Mandelson is driving a truck, and things seem set to go very badly for me, but with great presence of mind I dive behind a potted palm. Mandelson is a keen gardener and fervent conservationist who favours the re-wilding of urban habitats: he swerves to miss me.

What can I do? My revolver (which I purchased a long while ago, and have never used) is up in my apartment, and therefore inaccessible. In any event, I don't believe I ever acquired any ammunition for it.

I retire to a coffee bar further down the block to consider my options, and while I'm brooding over a lemon tea, the phone behind the counter rings. The waiter who picks up shouts my name, but as I stand to take the call there is a screech of brakes from outside. I have time to drop to the floor before the street window shatters and—to the accompaniment of a sound like a typewriter shod in pig-iron—a hail of machine gun bullets chews up the counter, the waiter and the people and fittings at the front three tables.

Surely, now, we are beyond the limits of normal hurt feelings.

I lie low for a week, in a repulsive rented room in a dockside hovel, tended to by an obese Armenian woman whose three words of English are *pay*, *eat*, and *cockroach*.

Then, when I judge that the time is right, I begin to stalk my prey.

I buy a Minim .14 hand pistol—small, and probably inaccurate over long distances, but still serviceable at close quarters.

I visit a theatrical costumiers, where a bowler hat, blond wig, and Fu Manchu moustache render me entirely unrecognisable.

I go to Mandelson's apartment on Twenty-Eighth Street, and gain entrance by telling the concierge that I am Mandelson's homosexual lover. He is out, and so I steal his mail from the pigeonhole in the building's lobby. There is a fat wodge of letters, which I take out into the street and then stop to examine at a bus stop a few blocks down.

The bulk of Mandelson's mail consists of bills, which I am about to discard until I see that one of them, from a disreputable shipping and forwarding agency, is for two female Bengal tigers. These beasts have cost Mandelson fifteen thousand dollars and some odd change, inclusive of a twenty-two dollar handling charge. A sizeable sum for a man whose last three novels have struggled to make the bottom of the moderate sellers list. Does that sound harsh? I say what must be said.

I look at the remaining bills a little more closely. I see that Mandelson has rented the Andreas Capellano sports centre on Twelfth Street for a month, which adds another ten thousand buckaroos to his burgeoning expenses. He has also cornered the market in stainless steel razor blades. This intrigues me, for Mandelson has a beard the size of a hawthorn thicket.

There is also a letter which is not a bill. It is a request from an engineering firm for further specifications. I am not surprised that further specifications are required:

what Mandelson has apparently asked for is a layout of interlocking iron plates making up into a rectangle of seventy-five by a hundred and fifty feet, with an insulated semi-circular protuberance of radius five feet on one of the shorter sides.

I resolve not to go within a dozen blocks of the Andreas Capellano sports centre until Mandelson's lease expires.

My stalking has come to a dead halt, more or less. I visit Mandelson's apartment again later in the day, find nothing more. The next day I call for a third time, with the same result. I question the concierge. She is abusive. She hasn't seen Mandelson for almost a week: moreover, people keep coming around and demanding money for things she's never seen and knows nothing about. What sort of things, I ask. Things like five thousand gross of stainless steel razor blades. Things like steel plates, and breeding pairs of king cobras. I sympathise. She tells me that she doesn't need my damn sympathy, and that I'm a faggot son-of-a-whore who (on that sweet day when God reigns on Earth) will surely be stricken with leprosy and hysterical blindness. I leave with my dignity intact.

I am by nature phlegmatic and slow to wrath, but by this time I am experiencing something akin to perturbation. My choice is this: I can either go to Andreas Capellano and confront my tormentor, or I can roam the city, exiled from my own apartment and from the life I knew, until he picks me off with a combine harvester, a garbage wagon or a snow plough.

Over a cup of coffee in a less than salubrious diner near my less than salubrious dockside rooms, I brood over this conundrum for a long time without bringing it to a solution. But then, as luck would have it, the decision is taken out of my hands. As I stand up to leave, something hard and cold and rounded in cross-section—an aluminium baseball bat, perhaps, although I'm far from being an expert in such things—hits me on the back of the skull and sends me into sudden and complete oblivion.

Mandelson has anticipated me again, the frothing lunatic. How do you even argue with someone like that?

It is dark when I wake up. It remains dark even when I remember to open my eyes. My head is hurting, but when I sit up and probe it anxiously with trembling fingertips I discover that it has been bandaged. As I squint into the darkness, the lights come on. Raw: far too bright. Arc lighting, as though for a stage.

What I see is this: a long room, the floor of varnished wood and marked out with white lines. The markings are consistent with a five-a-side football court, and I am sitting on the centre line. Around me, the walls are draped in black, except at the far end of the room where there are two doors. There are many things about this set-up that I do not like.

Mandelson says hello over a crackly PA system. I ignore him. I know that he cannot resist the urge to explain the situation, and that he will do it badly, heavy on the bombast. I probably already know more than he intends to tell me, so I can afford to let my attention wander, as you do on a plane when the stewardess delivers the safety demonstration.

"Are you comfortable, Peasey?" he crackles.

"I survive, Mandelson," I reply coolly. I throw my coolness in his teeth. Let him chew on it and take what nourishment he can.

"How did you describe my novel again?"

Two doors. That's interesting. And the drapes draw attention to them by concealing everything else.

"I believe I said that it was a Gothic cock-up, Mandelson."

"A prime Gothic cock-up; a puerile resurrection of a literary form that should have been allowed to die with Lewis and Shelley."

"I never write middle-of-the-road reviews, Mandelson. You know that."

"And yet you may still get to be roadkill."

Bwa ha ha! No, he doesn't go quite that far, but a bwa-ha-ha is strongly implied. Sitting there on the basketball court, I think of those who have suffered in the name of art. Many of them I tortured myself, for that is a reviewer's task in life.

"Well if you disliked *House of Blood*, Peasey, you're going to hate the sequel. I call it *Sports Centre of No Return*."

"I should work on the title, Mandelson. It sounds a little . . . dare I say it . . . jejune."

"At the end of the chamber," he snarls, "there are two doors. Do you see them?"

"I see the doors, Mandelson."

"They mean life or death to you, according to how you choose. Behind one is the back staircase leading out of this place. Behind the other is a Bengal tiger, starved and savage. Decide quickly which door you will open. In a minute's time, if you haven't made a choice, the floor will open beneath your feet and pitch you into oblivion!"

I consider. First of all, he is lying about the doors. Possibly he is also lying about the floor, and the time limit. I glance down and inspect the perfectly polished wood, find a thin line running up the centre of the room which has been recently cut and sanded and indifferently varnished. No, he isn't bluffing. The floor will open. There will be some sort of gesture towards oblivion.

Back at Mandelson's apartment, I assume, the bills must be piling up and up and up.

Fifteen seconds have now gone, and I have no intention of choosing a door because I believe—doubter and cynic though I am—that you don't buy two Bengal tigers if you're only planning to use one.

I straighten up—slowly, because my headache persists—and walk slowly across to one side of the court. I take a fold of the black drapes in my hand and pull them aside. Behind them there are nets, and behind the nets, climbing bars: Andreas Capellano doubles up, as most sports centres do, and the main arena is furnished for pretty much every sport there is.

It's possible to put my feet on the climbing bars, even through the nets. It's possible to take my full weight off the floor and wait there, like a monkey in the rigging, for further developments to eventuate.

The floor pivots on its unseen hinges, breaks open at the centre and falls away into black nothingness below me. I allow myself to feel a little smug: the clean logic of the enlightenment has cut through Mandelson's welter of Gothic excesses.

I swarm along the nets, surprising myself with my skill. Crab-scuttling from one set of bars to the next, I arrive at length at the nearer of the two doors. Once there, I lean out over the black gulf, turn the handle, and pull the door open.

There is another darkness beyond: a narrower space, which stinks of musk and urine. Something stirs in the gloom, gathers itself, and whips past me almost before I'm aware of it. A flash of light on sleekly muscled flesh, sheathed in dark fur, is the limit of what I perceive. It drops out of sight, beyond line or plummet, sending up from the depths below a tinny whisper and a sudden roar of rage or pain.

The next bit is complicated. Since the door opened outwards, I am forced to climb around it before I can actually gain entrance to the room it leads to. This takes me some minutes, and Mandelson makes another "Hello, campers" broadcast over the PA system before I'm done.

"You didn't play by the rules, Peasey."

"Didn't I, Mandelson? That must be because the rules are asinine and arbitrary. But in any case, I did choose a door."

"You can't escape me. Every square inch of this building is a trap, and there's no escape."

"Every square inch? That would be one hundred and forty four traps per square foot, Mandelson. Surely you exaggerate."

Scrambling in through the doorway, I enter the musky darkness. Within it there are faint glimmers of light which take the form of lines drawn on the air. Straw rustles under my feet: My outstretched arm touches a metal bar, traces it up and down. The vertical glimmers resolve themselves into further bars, extending before me on both sides. I am in a cage: semi-circular recesses at the corners tell me that it is on wheels. A sort of animal transporter.

At its further end there is a door which is bolted, but since the cage was only ever intended to contain animals the bolt is easily reachable from the inside, through the bars. I slide the bolt, push the door wide and step down into . . . what? A wide empty space. A floor of ceramic tiles, visible in the light from a skylight over my head, and a white-painted pillar very close to me on which there is a sign I can't read.

Again, I wait for my eyes to adjust. I find that the sign bears no words, only a stick figure walking down some stairs, and an arrow pointing off to my left. I follow the arrow and yes, there are the stairs. They only lead down, so that is where I go, skirting the sprung bear traps with which the landing is littered. Every square inch! There are at most only a couple of dozen bear traps, and a luckless janitor has already sprung one. He has passed out from the pain, so I skirt around him and continue.

The stairwell is much darker than the room above. I grip the banister rail very firmly as I descend now into near-unrelieved blackness, losing the faint glow from the skylight after the first turn. There is a light switch, but even in the dark I can see the supernumerary wires trailing away from it, up and to the left. Mandelson has rigged an axe to swing down when the switch is pressed, positioning it so that it will embed itself in the skull of anyone standing on that particular step. I could pull the wires loose, but that might trigger a further unwanted sequence of events. I choose instead to go on in the dark.

Two floors down and I can go no further. There are no more stairs. I hope that I've reached ground level: it's always possible, of course, that this is a basement, in which case I'll have to memorise the position of the stairs and retrace my steps.

I am walking along a corridor now. There are more tiles under my feet, and—I ascertain—on the walls. The corridor slopes down a little, and a faint smell of chlorine wafts toward me from somewhere up ahead. Abruptly I step into a narrow well in the floor and find that it's filled with water to a depth of four or five inches. This is a foot-bath, and therefore I'm about to enter the pool area.

The larger darkness ahead of me talks to itself in metallic whispers; in hollow scratches and clicks like the claws of tin crabs on the bed of a dry ocean. Turning a corner, I find the light: it's fierce, but it's high overhead and angled so that very little of it reaches me down here in these nether regions. I am once again in a very wide, very high-ceilinged space. The massive trap doors from the basketball court two storeys above hang down to either side of me, and something in front of me smells of straw and musk and bodily fluids.

As I shuffle out into the light, I see the rim of the pool as a black slash directly ahead of me. Beyond it, prismatic splinters of yellow and blue slice the air into ionic froth. The swimming pool is filled with razor blades, and the tiger is dying a few feet from the nearest edge: almost close enough to touch, but much, much too far to swim.

I sit by the side of the pool for a while, thinking. It seems that Mandelson has laid no further snares in this particular room, so I am undisturbed except by the tiger's death throes. Taking stock of my situation, I realise for the first time that I am still dressed in the clothes that I was wearing before I was brought here. Is the Minim hand pistol still in my jacket pocket? No, it is not. Nothing else is either: mobile, wallet, keys, all gone. Nothing to work with except what is here already. I need a base of operations, and for that I need a detailed plan of the building; for which, I imagine, I need the entrance hall.

I do not find the entrance hall. Apart from the brilliant spotlights above the pool, the building remains in darkness, and an understandable caution prevents me from turning on the lights. What I do find is tiger spoor: I tread in it. I infer that the second tiger has been released from its cage, which lends a certain urgency to these proceedings.

I come to another sign, read it with my fingers. It indicates the location of the fire exit, but the corridor towards which it points is hissing ominously. I have no wish to encounter a breeding pair of king cobras: some things ought to be private.

I am feeling a strong sense of trepidation and paranoia now, but I try to keep it from spiralling into panic: I cannot afford to panic. I feel that the second tiger is stalking me through the dark, and that my every step may bring me face to face with it. It would be easy, therefore, to stop moving and go to ground. Easy, but fatal, I tell myself, and I keep moving.

When, finally, I reach a door at the head of a long flight of stairs, I am beginning to feel the strain of all these melodramatic and over-coloured events. The sign on the door is shallowly embossed on shiny, varnished wood, so I can run my hand over it and read it by touch. This is the supervisor's office. It will do as my base of operations. I open the door and enter.

It is Mandelson's base of operations. He is sitting at a bank of CCTV monitors, but now he swivels his chair and we stare at one another, mildly embarrassed, like women who have come to a party in the same dress. Then he scrambles for his pistol and shoots at me again, splintering the doorpost.

I turn tail and run back the way I've come, along nighted avenues, across great rooms that could be anything, could house anything. When I pause I hear running footsteps from somewhere that could be very close by or very far away: the darkness conceals and confuses. When I run I hear nothing but the beating of my own heart.

At last, I see a light up ahead of me, growing stronger as I approach. Turning a last corner, I am face-to-face with it. An open door. I step through and find myself in the building's chapel—an odd thing to find in a sports centre, but I speak as a confirmed atheist. Others may treasure the sense of oneness with God that comes after an intense and sweaty workout.

I walk between rows of removable seating, noting the prayer books on shelves behind each one. The floor rings like a steel drum beneath my feet, and this is unsurprising because it is burnished metal. The points where the individual metal plates abut onto each other are clearly visible, though an attempt has been made to disguise them with some sort of resin.

Ahead of me is the altar, and behind it the handsomely carved mahogany cross in its recess. The recess, I see now, is semi-circular. The room is approximately twice as long as it is wide: I would not be at all surprised to learn that its exact dimensions are seventy-five by one hundred and fifty feet.

I vault over the altar rather than walking around it. I step into the recess, ducking my head because its ceiling is low. There is no metal here—or rather, the metal is covered with a layer of springy, foam-rubber-like insulation. To one side of the recess there is a foot pedal at the end of a coiled serpent of electric flex. Aha.

I turn as Mandelson enters the room. He raises the gun. I say "goodbye, Mandelson," and press my foot down on the pedal.

He fries. The smell is of burned bacon on a griddle. Gothic excess.

After he is thoroughly, unfragrantly dead I take my foot off the pedal, return to the supervisor's office and lock myself in. I switch all the lights on and wait until I feel calm and composed, which takes a little more than five minutes. Then I call the police and wait a little longer.

By this time, the tips of my fingers are starting to prickle. The supervisor's computer is already booted up, and though it's mainly set up to monitor the feeds from the many CCTV cameras dotted around the building, it also has a version of Microsoft Word with which I am conversant.

I open a document, type in header and footer information, and set the line spacing to double.

I begin to write, critiquing in reasoned and pithy prose everything that has happened to me since I first took Mandelson's bullet. My usual word count is 4,000 and I bring the piece in at 3,880, not counting the title.

I despise the vernacular. It is the progenitor of sloppy thought and flabby argument.

But I own Mandelson. I fucking *own* him.

This is my most recent short story, written less than a month ago. I wrote it for PS Publishing, who are also responsible for the book you're reading now. ¶ "All That's Red Earth", like "Iphigenia in Aulis", is a story that stands or falls by its narrative voice. And Tari, like Melanie, was a lovely character to write. In fact, the more I think about the two stories, the more they have in common. Each story is told from the perspective of a wide-eyed innocent who has a deep secret. And each of those innocents ends up being a little different than you initially imagine them to be. ¶ And this one might end up being revisited and expanded, as "Iphigenia" was. I've got the same sense I had back then that there's more of this story waiting to be told . . .

ALL THAT'S RED EARTH

IT DID NOT come easy to me to find my way in the world. I was turned away by my first master, and after that I cast around for a tedious time looking for what I might be. But I found it in the end, and I am minded to tell that story, if you have it in you to listen. For it could be you will meet the same trouble that I did, and if you do then my words might help to lead you out of it.

My name is Tari and I come from Wittensaw. Don't bother to tell me you never heard of that place because I know it. I never would of heard of it either, except I was born there and had no other choice but to know it. I guess I liked it well enough when I was small, because a small place suits a child. But then I grew up, and Wittensaw stayed just as small as it was. That was when I started to chafe, not least because there was nobody in Wittensaw like me. A child won't see that. An older has got to see it, even if they try to hide from it like I did for so long.

My mother was Hurda, that was Bassaw's daughter and had the flax mill over by Old Big-Hand stream. My father was a fisherman from Kemotanzi, that I never got to know the name of. He sailed out with the sawtooth fleet the year after I was born and a sawtooth bit him in two. The lower part of him got brought back and buried. The upper part went into the sea, or into that sawtooth, and my father's spirit most likely stayed in the water.

My mother had herself seven other children besides me, and though the mill did well enough she had hard times feeding us. My oldest sister Gilen was married to three women of Gharthi who was weavers and summer-dancers. We never saw her again, but I hope she is happy and I think she is. Then my brother Coin was took by reaver men of Hanach who would either have eaten him or made a reaver out of him, and then we were only six of us or seven counting Mother. I missed Gilen and Coin very much, especially Coin because I didn't know if he was still alive and in the world. He had been gentle and kind to me and I think he knowed my secret even when I was small. To think of him being eaten made me cry some-times at night. Mother never cried. She did look sad a while, but all she said was one less mouth to feed. And we did eat a little better after Coin was gone, which in some ways made his being gone worse, at least for me.

Anyway it got to be my twelfth birthday and the Keepers took me to the telling pool to throw stones and read the ripples. They don't tell you how many stones to take. That's part of what they read. But mostly it's the ripples that are the meat of it, and mine was three rings joined by three. Everybody knows what that means.

So Darmir Komberlin, who was the oldest of the Keepers and the one who said what had got to be done, took me to Cadri Hae. Cadri was the warlock or man-witch in Wittensaw. We only had the one, and the one woman-witch that was Gammer Holdfast. I guess that proves what I said about how small a place it was.

Cadri said he would take me and teach me, and my mother was well pleased. A witch in the family is a very good thing.

I kept my secret pretty well back then, I guess. I kept it from everyone, including my own self. Otherwise I would not of let them give me to Cadri Hae, because I would of seen what would come of it. I would not of wasted my time.

I moved out to Cadri's house, which was made of stone and was out in the valley, as far beyond the Grey Shouters as the Shouters are beyond the market oak. It was a big house, and he could of give me a room to myself, since he had just the one prentice which was me, but I slept in the fireplace on straw that I changed myself once every second week. It was not too bad a place to sleep, and probably warmer than the bed where my master slept, but I always was afraid a spark from the fire would catch the straw one night and I would get burned up, so I never slept easy there.

Cadri taught me for most of a year. Actually he didn't teach me much of anything, but that was how long I stayed with him. I cleaned his house, most days, and cooked his meals. Also I went with him when he worked so I could watch.

A man-witch has got to make the village safe, which is the most of his work, and in Wittensaw the making safe was mostly to do with reavers. Cadri did it with I-know-you-I-don't-know-you, a spell that strikes at strangers but lets the people of the village pass. So we went around the roads, and I scattered horseshoe nails in the weeds next to the path while Cadri walked a circle and did the spell. After that, if someone came along the path who had no business there, the nails would jump up and dig theirselves into his skin to hurt or kill him.

It's not a good spell, as I learned from Gammer later. It doesn't always make its mind up in time, so someone who's running fast will get through safe. Worse than that, it triggers sometimes for strangers who don't mean no harm, such as tinkers or farmers from neighbour places coming into market.

One morning Cadri called me to him, right after I'd finished sweeping the house. "You think you know the spell?" he asked me. He didn't need to say which spell, because he only ever used the one.

"I do, master," I said. I'd heard him sing it a hundred times by then.

Cadri drew a circle in chalk on the flags of the floor, whispering some power into it as he went. "Stand inside there," he said, "and say the words."

I speaked up loud, confident in my memory which was very good.

But Cadri shook his head, and spit on the floor. He used the spit and the toe of his shoe to wipe a little of the circle away, letting out the power.

I can see it clear now, what he had meant to do, though I couldn't see it at all back then. Cadri's patron was Ferossul of the fire. He sung Ferossul into the chalk line so he could come get a look at me and a taste of me. And though I knew all the words Ferossul didn't take to me, which was why Cadri let the power drain away again without saying nothing to me about it.

Cadri went back to the Keepers and said I would not do for him.

The Keepers had little wit what to do with me after that. I had shown strong in magic, but the only warlock in the village had closed his door to me. Nor my mother wouldn't take me back, me being now old enough to thrive by my own work. "You'll have to make shift with day-labour until you figure out what you are," Darmir Komberlin said. And that was all the guidance I got from them.

Anyway I spent a few months wandering the tithings, doing odd jobs wherever I went for no more than a roof and a bowl of soup. The roof would leak, more often than not, and the soup tasted like someone else had eaten it before me. I cannot say I liked that time.

In the Autumn, though, after the harvests was in and all the work such as a day-jobber could do had gone away, I found my way to Gammer Holdfast's hut in the full middle of Thousandwood, where the light only finds its way through at noon.

I cannot say what I was looking for, to be honest. It seemed like there couldn't be nothing for me there. But still I had shown strong in magic and I felt like I was drawed to magic some way that I couldn't even help. So I come there, and I stood in front of the door with not a word to say for myself.

Gammer was sitting on her front step, smoking a clay pipe and making the smoke dance. "What are you, now?" she asked me. Which was a fair question because obviously I had not found my way there by chance.

"I'm Tari that's Hurda's son," I told her. "Come to be prenticed, if it please you."

Gammer looked at me for a long time, not speaking. She was a very old woman, nobody knowed how old. Her face was gone like the trees all around her, into so many lines you scarce could see where her mouth was. And the hair on her head, so sparse and so white, looked like spiders had made their webs there.

Gammer already had three real prentices. That was Azomer, Shel and Pirin. Shel come to the door, then. She must of heard me speak, for she give forthright answer. "A boy can't be prentice to a woman, fool. Go back to your mother's mill and spin flax."

She was right, of course. That was why the Keepers didn't never think of sending me here. Darmir Komberlin hated Gammer, for old sake, but even if he didn't he wouldn't send a boy to a woman-witch because everybody knowed it wouldn't avail.

But Gammer took the pipe out of her mouth at last, and answered me too. "Tell me that name again," she bid me.

"Tari," I said.

"A boy's name."

I held my tongue. Shel did not. "This *is* a boy, Gammer," she said.

Gammer tapped her chin with the stem of the pipe, and was silent again for a longer time than before. Then she spoke up again. "Tari, my girl Pirin is peeling potatoes in the kitchen. Go take the potato peelings and feed them to my pigs, in the sty yonder. Then do you muck out the sty with the shovel and pitchfork you'll find there."

I run to do it.

Thereafter, no word was spoke about what I was, or was not. Gammer had took me in. The three girl prentices had such love for her, and such utter trust in her wisdom, that they did not vex or challenge me. They did not know what to make of me at first, but little by little I won my place among them by working harder than anyone and taking whatever was give to me, uncomplaining, as my lot.

I couldn't conjure, of course. Who would my patron be? Where Cadri was sworn to Ferossul, it were the Bright Mother and Hooktail Hen who stood over Gammer. You wouldn't think of presenting a boy to either of them two. A boy wouldn't even see the Mother, and he might not be able to see anything else thereafter. And Hooktail would most likely eat him, apart from his pizzle which she'd wear on her belt along with all the others she kept there.

So I didn't try no magic, though I sat with the others when Gammer taught and I took it all in. She never said I couldn't. The three girls looked at me askance to start with, but since Gammer didn't mind they made no fuss and in the end they come to take me being there as a natural thing.

That was a good time. I had some troubles of my own, that was in the heart of me and not in the world, but I was happy to live in Gammer's house and to learn the ways of a woman-witch. Once Azomer come to me in the night, climbed into my bed beside me and kissed me on the lips. I knew what she wanted, but I could not give it to her. I thought she would be angry, and in truth she was somewhat chagrined that my pizzle wouldn't stand even when she stroked it. But the girls were used to giving that sweetness each to other, so she did not lack for lovers.

"Are you unknown to woman, though?" she asked me, for I was then sixteen and she thought it not likely.

I told her I was.

"And to man?"

"To man, too. I'm green all the way through, Azo. Like a grass stem."

She kissed me again, this time on the cheek like a sister would do it. Like Gilen used to do it before she was married away from us. "A grass stem's hollow in the middle, Tari," she said. "Don't you be. When your heart finds its like, you must go to it harder for all the missed time."

I told her I would. We were fast friends from then on, if we hadn't been before. I combed out her hair sometimes, after she had washed it, and when she had her monthly bleeding I would warm a bag of oats at the fire and bring it to her to ease the cramp. She was ever fidgety and uneasy when her time was on her. She said the woman-blood was how they swore to Hooktail Hen, the first time. They had to paint their throats with it, and lie on an altar so they looked like they'd been sacrificed, and say the spell Gammer had taught them.

> Or death or life or birth,
> All's one to blood-red earth.
> Or fire or wind or flood,
> All that's red earth is blood.

And then Hooktail would come and lick them clean, the way a she-wolf or a bear does with its cubs right after they're born. It was like a second birth, only they was being born into her service. If she didn't come and lick them then Gammer let them go, for it meant the magic that was in them was of the wrong kind. I suppose something like that happened with me and Cadri, when he showed me to his patron Ferossul and Ferossul didn't take to me.

Three years passed like this. Gammer knew a lot of spells and she taught well. She wasn't teaching them to me, of course, but I listened all the same and I helped the real prentices when they faltered in their practising, for my memory was always good.

Three years passed, and three or thirty more might of passed just the same, only they didn't. For there come a day, not too many months ago, when everything changed. Gammer sent me out to gather wood, it being then the deep winter. It was the coldest winter Wittensaw had seen, at least in my lifetime. Cows died in the fields, and the ice on Old Big-Hand was so thick you couldn't get to the water underneath but must chip out the ice and thaw it in your house to drink or cook with it.

Gammer had a well of her own, behind her house. Hooktail made sure the water there didn't freeze. And food she had in plenty, for she had laid in carrots and beets and she could whistle a rabbit to come into her house when she wanted meat. But good firewood was another matter, the trees around the house being weak and scrubby. So I would go into the forest twice a week, sometimes with Azomer or Pirin and sometimes alone, to gather what I could find and bring it back.

One time I went alone, further than usual, and come back later. I knew something was not right from a long ways off when I seen thick smoke coming up out of the trees where Gammer's house was. Her chimney didn't never smoke because imps took away the soot to knit with.

I run through the trees to the house, and I seen it was burning. I didn't know what to do. I run around and around it, shouting and screaming. Shouting to Gammer and the girls in case they was inside, and to anyone else to come and help. Only nobody come, and I saw in the end that there was pitch burning in the yard near the front door. Which Gammer's walls weren't sealed with cord and pitch, she just bespoke the boards to grow tight together. So that was how I knew someone had done this.

It wasn't hard to guess who that might be. You're probably thinking Cadri, and you wouldn't be wrong. Man-witches and woman-witches doesn't never get on smoothly, that's known, but most villages got both for the reason that they need both.

But there were something more here. I said before that Darmir Komberlin hadn't got no love for Gammer. I should of said he hated her, for the reason that he only ever had one son and that one born dead. Gammer was there when Darmir's wife was in child-bed, of course, and he blamed it on her, even though Gammer had a hard time of it even to save the mother and she had got to let the baby go down to death. It hurt her sore that it went that way, but Darmir Komberlin said she done it with malice and meaning.

So that bad seed was coming to bad fruit. I knowed it right then, when I seen the burning pitch up against the door of the house. And I fell down in a dead faint, because I couldn't think nothing but that they was in there, Gammer and Shel and Pirin and Azo, all burned to death while I fetched wood.

Only they wasn't. When I come to again the fire was somewhat abated. I fetched water from the well, bucket after bucket for more than an hour, until I put it out at last. Then I walked through what was left of it, and I seen there wasn't no bodies. They was took, not burned.

I went back out into the yard, and I got down on my knees so I could thank the Mother and Hooktail Hen for sparing the lives of them as was sworn to them. I didn't know if the Mother or Hooktail would listen to me, but I thanked them anyway. Then I begged them to keep on watching and keep on protecting from the god world and the soul world, while I seen what I could do in this one.

You might think that was not very much, and I wouldn't blame you for thinking it. But I had an idea in my head, and I went to it.

The first thing I did was go into town and find out where Gammer and the others was took and how it was with them. I had to be sure they wasn't dead or hurt too bad, as this was pressing heavy on me. Of course I didn't know but what Darmir Komberlin had ordered me took too, but I didn't think so. People knowed I was with Gammer, but they also knowed I couldn't do woman-magic and it was the witches they was down on.

In Wittensaw on the street I seen people I knowed, and I realised then it had been a long time since I seen them. One thing I didn't do for Gammer was buy and sell at market for her, so I hadn't had no mind nor no errand to go to the village in a very long time.

There was changes I could see clear, just as soon as I come there. People was scared to talk to me, and looked away when I come by. Only Derra that was now married to my brother Jil had a word to say, and it wasn't kind. "You don't want to be seen here, Tari," was what she said. "Or they're as like as not to take you too."

"Take me where?" I asked her, since I knew who they was without being told.

"Why, to the underhouse, of course," she says to me. "Where Cadri Hae has got them spelled silent and the Keepers has ordered their hands tied, so their magic won't save them when they're judged."

"What are they judged for, Derra?"

"For murder of Darmir Komberlin's baby boy, and poisoning of the cabbages in Siv Numi's fields this season and last."

For nothing, in other words. And I seen plain as day that she knowed it was all nothing, but she wouldn't for anything say so. Komberlin and Numi were names that carried, as they say, and one of the things they carried was silence when they carved for their own spite as they did now.

I thanked Derra and wished her well, for she had at least spoke to me when many wouldn't do so. Then I went and done the thing I had thought to do.

I walked all the way to Cadri's house, and up into his dooryard as bold as a corn-fed rat. The house had got a ward on it, of course, but it was I-know-you-I-don't-know-you and the house knowed me well enough from when I lived there. I was hoping Cadri wouldn't of remembered to tell it not to know me.

But he did remember. When I touched the door, nails and potsherds jumped up from the dust where they was buried and slammed right into me. It was just as well I knowed the workings of the spell. In case Cadri's remembering was stronger than I expected I had tied straw all around me, as thick as I could and still move. The nails dug deep into the straw, and some of them got all the way through, but they spent all their speed in doing it. I got cut some, but not so deep I would take real harm from it.

Inside the house I looked for spellbooks. I knowed Cadri had some, for I'd seen him reading them. I couldn't read a word my own self, but with magic books you sometimes don't need to. You can talk to the spirit that's stuck inside the words and make it do things for you.

Upstairs and down I looked, and found nothing at first. But then I thought to look under the straw tick on Cadri's bed. There was a book there that looked like it would do. It was small but thick, with a brown leather cover to it and a clasp on the cover with a hole where a key would fit.

I took it and run.

I went back to Gammer's house, even though it was burned down. I had always been happy there, and there wasn't nowhere else where that was true except our mill when I was not full growed. I sit down next to the well, under an apple tree that was there, and I tried to open the book, first by poking the point of a nail into the keyhole and then by smacking the edge of the clasp with a rock.

Nothing would do, though. I struggled with it for an hour or more, then finally I threw it down and shouted curses at it, all in a rage.

Well maybe the curses woke it, or woke the thing inside it, or maybe it only would agree to be opened when nobody was pressing it. Anyway, as soon as I threw it on the ground I heard this scratching sound, like as it was a cat scratching on a door to be let out, and when I looked at it again the clasp was undone.

I picked the book up all eager and opened it. I knowed I wouldn't be able to read it, but I hoped there might be something in there, some spirit, that I could talk to and maybe ask a favour of. "Hello?" I said. "Who's there?" But I got no answer.

I riffled the pages, saying hello and who's there a lot more times, with no better result. I was all over tired, of a sudden, and wanted nothing better than to shut my eyes and sleep a little while.

It had been cold when I sat down, but it was warm now, which made me drowse all the more. I tried to set the book down but it was stuck to my fingers somehow. Never mind, I thought. I'll keep it by me while I sleep, for that's where the warm is coming from.

My eyes had fallen shut, but as I laid myself down by Gammer's well, something—it might have been a stone or the end of a twig—nudged me hard in the ribs. That made me open my eyes again, and it was well for me I did.

The skin of my hand and arm, where I held the book, was white as paper, and the words out of the book was crawling up me like ants. I tried to scream, but there wasn't barely any sound come out of my throat. Only a dry rustling, like when leaves or it might be pages riffle in a little bit of a wind.

I still couldn't put the book down. I shook my hand to try to free it but it wouldn't come. Then I grabbed it with my other hand and that was a mistake for now both my hands was stuck to it and the words all crawling up my left arm too.

Where I had been warm I now was cold again, colder than ever before. I thought my heart would stop. I banged the book against the ground and the stone wall of the well, hoping it might let go of me, but it didn't want to. And all the time the words was swarming over me, eating the soul and the heart of me right through the skin.

I would of died, or worse, except some good power smiled on me. When I was putting the fire out I had filled the bucket at the well one last time but not used it, and the full bucket was still sitting there where I had set it down. I thrust my both hands in, and the book too, and I held them there. The surface of the water heaved like it was boiling. The book tried to let go of me then but still I held it, until the seething stopped.

I drowned the book, and the thing that was inside it. I don't think I could of done it with regular water, but Gammer's water was different. I already told you Hooktail Hen had the keeping of it, and Hooktail was stronger and meaner than any spirit you could fit inside a book.

I took the book out at last and throwed it down on the grass. The leather cover looked the same as it did before, though the insides was a mess of pulp and it smelled all sour-sweet like a wound that has gone bad. I watched it for a long time in case it moved or said anything, but it was dead all right.

I did not feel right at all. I was scared the words was still on me but I searched for them on my hands and my arms and they was gone. Only when I used the water in the bucket like a mirror I seen that my skin and hair was turned all white like bone. Or like paper, I guess. And it still is. There isn't nothing I can do about that.

So my big plan had come to nothing and I didn't have no other plans, big or small. I sat there in Gammer's yard, tired to death and hurting all over, feeling like something had chewed on me long and hard only to spit me out again. I cried like I was a baby, which doesn't shame me. And I felt ready to lie down again and give up, which does. I thought Gammer and the prentices, as were my only friends in the world, was going to die and there wasn't nothing I could do to save them.

Something wet fell on my hand. I thought it was a tear at first, but tears is warm and this was cold. Then come another, and one more, and some and several. I looked up, and I seen it was snowing.

I couldn't believe it at first. I said it was a hard winter, which is simple truth, but snow in Wittensaw is a thing only the oldest living souls has ever seen. It gets cold, but it don't snow. I only knew what snow was from stories my mother told me, that she no doubt got from hers. I just sit and stared for a long time with my mouth wide open. I might of froze right there, except suddenly an idea come to me.

I remembered something Gammer told me once, that there isn't nothing so wondrous but people will find a way to wipe their arse with it before too much time has passed. It's the fate and measure of us, she said. And I am sad to say it, but I thought of a way to use the snow to get the Keepers to loose Gammer and the girls out of the underhouse and let them bide free. I didn't know if I was brave enough or clever enough to do it, but I knowed I got to try.

I set out before I could start to get scared about it. I walked all the way back into the village, staying on the high road all the way. The snow was coming down thicker all the time, till it was hard even to see through it. The sky seemed to be all snow and nothing in between. I was shaking with cold, so I walked faster to make my blood to move. I didn't want the people to see I was feeling the cold, for a reason I'll tell you soon.

I went to the main square that's got the market oak in it, and the Keepers' house right next to the tree. By the time I got there I had scooped up a fair lot of people who seen me come and wanted to see where it was tending. I was something to see all by my own self, truth to tell. My clothes was in tatters from running in the forest and from fighting with the book, but I figured that was good because it let more of my white skin show.

I stood in the square, all white and ragged, with the book in my hand and the snow falling on my naked head. I shouted "Darmir Komberlin! Come out to me!" And eventually he did come out, along with the rest of the Keepers. They stood in a row on the balcony of the Keepers' house, which is narrow for all seven of them but I guess they wanted to look down on me.

"What's this racket?" Darmir Komberlin said. "What do you want here, Tari that's Hurda's son?"

"I want Gammer," I said. "And her three prentices. I want my mistress freed, and I will send Wittensaw to the dark place if you don't do it."

There was muttering at that. And a bit of laughing too, but the laughing had that high sound of being afraid and trying to hide it.

"You're mad, boy," Siv Numi said. "Gammer is a bad witch as has fallen to cursing, and we got to burn it out of her. You be grateful we didn't take you too. Go home, now, before we change our minds on that."

Perhaps she forgot I didn't have no home except the one they burned. But she wasn't thinking about what she said. She was looking at my white hair and my white skin, and then at the white snow falling out of the sky.

"Aye, Keeper Numi," I said. "You see it now. I swore myself to a powerful spirit, with this book that I found in the forest." I held up the book in my hand, hoping they wouldn't see it was really just the cover of a book with pulp and wetness inside. "The spirit give me terrible power. You see how white I am? That's because I called the winter down. This snow is mine, and it won't never stop unless you do as I bid. You bring Gammer up now, and the girls too, or I'll bring hail along with the snow and smash your roof in."

The Keepers was shaken. They didn't make answer, only talked among themselves. I was so scared I was near to pissing myself. All it would of took would be for one of the people standing all around to throw a stone or even a clod of earth and they'd see for theirselves how much power I had. But they was scared of me and didn't do it. So I thought maybe this plan might run the distance where the other one failed.

Only my luck didn't hold. I didn't have no reason to expect it would—just the hope and the not being able to think of anything else. "He's lying," says Cadri Hae, coming out of Keepers' house and standing next to them all. Of course he would be in there with them. It was his spells that was keeping Gammer and the prentices from calling on any of their magic to help theirselves. I just didn't think of it until I seen him.

"That's one of my books," he says then, "and it can't do the things he said it did. Take hold of him and bring him to me."

Darmir Komberlin looked up at the sky, that was all dirty grey like a tub someone washed a whole heap of clothes in. "But . . . " he says. "Cadri, the sky . . . "

"The sky is just the sky," Cadri says, all sour and angry. "Nor the snow isn't any more than snow. Don't be a fool, Komberlin. The boy's not a mage, or even a sworn prentice. He can't bespeak the weather. I said to lay hands on him and bring him."

Darmir Komberlin still hesitated, until in the end it was done for him. All the people in the square come on me in a rush. The fear they just was feeling got turned into an angry feeling instead, and they used me roughly. I got punched and kicked and trod on very bad indeed, until my brains was almost bashed out of my head and I didn't know where I was.

When they was done, or mostly done, the village constable, Shaper Cust, dragged me out from the middle of them and took me into Keepers' house. Only he went down, not up, into what they call the underhouse. It's Wittensaw's jail, when we got use for one, and the rest of the time it's a cellar for winter stores. It was both right then. The room Shap locked me in had been halfway given over to potatoes and yellowroots.

Anyway I just lay there on the floor for a long time, counting all the pains they give me and being surprised every time I thought I got them all for there were always one or two more. I wished at least they had put me in with Gammer and the girls, for then I could of seen that they was all right, but of course they weren't like to do that in case I found a way to break Cadri's ward that was on their mouths to stop them spelling.

I lay there for a long time. It started to get dark. Well it was dark enough to start with, there being just the one little barred window high up on one wall that was set in the ground above, but it got darker still so I knowed it was coming on to night.

Then Cadri Hae come in to see me, and he brought the constable with him. He was in a powerful rage. "That book you took was ruined," he said. "It was worth more than you and your Gammer and those three sluts all wrapped up together, and because of you it's destroyed."

"It couldn't of been any good," I says, "if a prentice that isn't even swore could kill it."

I meant it to gravel his pride and it done that all right. He squatted down and grabbed my hair, and hauled me up a little so he could spit in my face. "It left its mark on

you, didn't it, boy?" he says. "And who is it would call
the likes of you a prentice? A boy sniffing the skirts of a
woman-witch to see if any of her wisdom leaked out of
her cunt for you to snuffle up."

"At least she got some wisdom, Cadri," I told him.
"She got more than just the one spell. I counted, so I
know."

Well that pushed him far enough and a mite further,
as they say. He told Shaper to drub me, which Shaper
done. I was drubbed well enough out in the square, but
this was worse. Shaper drubbed me with a leather whip,
and it cut me sore. When someone is whipped on a whip-
ping horse the strokes fall on their back and you can stop
if you cut too deep. Shaper just whipped me where I lay
on the floor, and the strokes fell wherever they wanted to.
When he was done I couldn't even move and I thought I
would most likely die of it.

"I have a lot of spells you never saw, boy," Cadri says.
"But you will see them morrow morn when we have your
trial and your punishment."

They went out and locked the door behind them.

I didn't have nothing to do with myself after they was
gone only to lie on the floor some more and think about
that. It wasn't for Cadri Hae to talk about my punishment. Only the Keepers could decide on me. But then outside on the balcony Cadri had said, "Lay hold on him and
bring him to me," or some such. He didn't say us, he said
me. So he was telling the Keepers what to do and he was
doing it right there in front of all the people on the square,
so he must have been pretty sure nobody wasn't going to
tell him no.

So that was the way of it. Cadri Hae would give us
our trial and our justice, which even a fool could see
where that was going.

I give myself harsh words as I lay there. I thought
someone with more brains or maybe more courage could

of done something better than just getting himself took that way. And I thought how different it would be if I was swore.

That made me remember Azo's telling of how she and the other girls was swore to Hooktail Hen, by their woman-blood that they painted all over theirselves. And by and by, a thought come to me.

It was somewhat like the pretending I done up in the square, because I wouldn't of dreamed of doing it if I wasn't about to die with no more choices left to me. But I thought if I was going to die anyway then at least I could choose how to do it. And if it worked out, though that weren't likely, I wouldn't die at all and nor would Gammer or the girls.

I took off what was left of my breeches and my shirt. They was falling off anyway and didn't give me no trouble. I got some of my blood on my hands. I didn't have no trouble doing that, neither, for I was all over cuts and some of them was deep like open mouths. It hurt me sorely to move, but it hurt to lie still too so that was no matter.

I drawed a line across my throat, like Azo said to do. Then I put my hand between my legs and rubbed the blood in good around my pizzle and my stones. It was too dark to see what I was doing by now, but I kept on scooping out the blood and rubbing it on until I was sure I got it all over me.

Then I tucked my pizzle in between my legs and crossed them so nobody couldn't see it there.

When all that was done, I speaked the words the way Azo had told me they got to be said.

Or death or life or birth,
All's one to blood-red earth.
Or fire or wind or flood,
All that's red earth is blood.

I said them again, and then once more, which made three. Azo didn't say nothing about three times, but everyone knows it's a magic number which is why the three rings means magic when you make your cast at the telling pool.

I didn't have no idea at all what was going to happen, but I thought that something would, even if it was only that Hooktail come and ate me up. But nothing happened at all. Only I went on lying there and the room got darker and darker.

A long time went by before I seen what was happening. It wasn't just that there was more darkness in the room, it was like the darkness was all coming together. I seen at last that Hooktail Hen was with me now, and had been with me for some time. She had put the darkness on like a coat, to hide a part of herself because for anyone to see the whole of her would break their wits like you would break an egg in a bowl to make a posset.

"How now, Hooktail," I says, though I couldn't hear my voice at all for my heart's pounding. "I'm swore to you and I will serve you good."

There come a snickering sound out of the dark. I couldn't see her mouth, and I was glad of that, but her eyes I seen and they was red with white in the heart of them like when you turn over a coal and it just starts to cool.

She leaned down between my legs and I felt the roughness of her tongue down there as she tasted the blood on me. I shut my eyes and bore it, trying not to scream.

Then she come up again and stared right into my eyes.

"Do you think I don't know what woman-blood tastes like?" she asked me, all soft and dangerous.

"No," I says.

"And do you think I didn't see what you carry between your legs?"

"No," I says again.

"What then?" she whispers.

And I told her my secret. That though I got a pizzle like a boy and a body that's shaped that way, I was a girl in my mind and in my heart ever since I was born. I were afraid I might not find the words for it, but they come clear enough. "Them as thinks I'm a boy only looks at my pizzle and the hair on my chin. Look into my heart, Hooktail, and you'll see. Or if you don't see, then eat me up for I got nothing more to say."

I waited and waited. Then I waited some more. I tried to get myself ready for the feel of her teeth in my belly and the pain of being tore up and ate. You can't ever be ready for that, but fear makes you numb the same way ice does, and that was a mercy right then.

Finally she spoke up, though it was just the one word. "Good."

"Then," I says, my tongue tripping over my teeth, "am I . . . am I swore?"

"You're mine," she says. "Girl." And though I was cut to the bone in places and lying in my own shit where I fouled myself on account of the pain, still that was the best thing, the best moment that had ever been for me, for she looked in my heart like I begged her to do and what she seen there was the truth of me.

Strength poured into me, like as if I was a bucket in a well. My wounds didn't hurt no more, nor I didn't even feel the cold.

"I'm yours," I says. "Mistress."

"Then what would you?" she asks me.

And I told her what I would. It was what Hooktail would, too, for she had seen her disciples hard treated, took and beaten and disrespected by the likes of Cadri Hae and Darmir Komberlin. A spirit made of patience, milk-mild and smiling soft, would of been angry at that outrageousness. And Hooktail Hen was not mild to start with.

We took the door off its hinges, and I stepped out into a kind of hallway. I had to tear some more doors too, looking for Gammer and my sisters. Shaper heard the ruckus and come running down the stairs, but I didn't care for his whip or his cudgel any more. I said a word that was very strong. It sent him backwards through the air and broke him against the wall.

Finally I found the room where they laid Gammer and the prentices. By this time there was shouting and commotion from up above us and footsteps running, but nobody else come down to us.

Gammer give me a nod when I come into the room, like she'd laid out a place for my coming and was pleased to see me at last. I speaked the ward off her mouth, and would have freed her hands too but she done it herself with a word.

"I'm sorry, Gammer," I said as we took the wards and the bonds from off the other prentices. "I wouldn't of let you languish if I could of come sooner."

"I know it, Hurda's Tari," Gammer said. "You came when you were needed and that's enough. You've done very well."

I felt her praise like warmth all over my skin.

Cadri Hae wasn't so stupid as to come down to us. He waited outside in the square and he was already singing a chantment of some kind in his throat when we stepped out.

But we were fivefold and we were ready. In the forest he took Gammer so easy because she didn't expect no treachery. It was a different story this time. Azo and Shel unwound his chantment before it hit us. Pirin warded him silent. Gammer and I ripped into him with such a flood tide of wicked words as was never seen.

He was dead when he hit the ground. But you could say, too, that he's still falling, for we turned the time on him and by his own reckoning it was a thousand years before death come to release him. We was stern with him, for we had got to make an example that others would mind.

We done the same to Wittensaw too. Gammer would have showed mercy there, except she seen the marks of the whip on me and the other marks that was made when all the people beat me in the square. "Well, then," she says to the trembling Keepers. "Our business is done here, neighbours, but since you'll live on and tell this tale, it's meet you tell it with the right ending."

We bent our might together, all five of us, with Hooktail Hen standing over us all. What we did was what I had already promised to do, when I was pretending in the market square that I had power. We made it be winter forever in Wittensaw, so nobody could ever live there again. It was a harsh reckoning, but we didn't kill nobody, excepting only Cadri Hae. I even healed Shaper Cust of his broken bones. He walked with a limp ever after, but he come out otherwise not the worse.

But Wittensaw is gone from the world. The snow fell for forty days or so, filling the whole valley from the fourth milestone to the edge of Thousandwood. It lies there still, even in midsummer, and the thaw isn't never going to come.

We went to Berrenthal, where we built ourselves a new house that was bigger and better appointed. I am full prentice now, and with Hooktail's help and the Bright Mother's it may be that my outside will come to match my inside. Anyway we're working on the words of it, and they're words with strong heft to them, so I will see soon enough.

If you have read all the way to the end of this, then I dare say by now you will have had enough of me and to spare. But I will say one more thing, which is that the truth of you is only yours to tell and nobody else's. If you tell it right and fearless then you won't have nothing to reproach yourself, and the reproach of others isn't no more nuisance than a fall of rain on a warm day. You'll bide it well enough.

One last story from *The House of War and Witness* to round out the collection. It works the same way the other two did. The storyteller is a ghost. The audience, apart from Drozde, are ghosts too. The theme of the story is the ghost's life and death.   ¶   I wanted to ring the changes with each of the embedded narratives in the novel. If the first story was supernatural horror and the second was a mystery, this is by way of being a love story. Of course, the fact that the speaker ends up dead qualifies that description a little.   ¶   Back when I was a teacher, I remember having a very strange and slightly ridiculous argument with the head of drama at the school where I worked. She said, and I quote: "All stories are about either love or death." I balked at this, and came up with lots of examples of stories that I didn't think were about either—while being forced to admit that a lot of great stories feature generous helpings of both.   ¶   What I should have said, but didn't, was this: Once you remove all the things that make stories different from each other, you're left with an irreducible core that's the same. Label it how you like, it's us. Just us. But since the stories were us to start with, that's hardly a revelation.   ¶   Anyway, this story is about both love and death, in about equal measure. It doesn't mean I'm conceding the argument, Cathy!

THE SOLDIER

I WAS seventeen when I went for a soldier, and nineteen when I died.

I counted my age in summers, because summer was my favourite time. The winters on a farm are desperate bad. You wake up in the dark and work in the dark for hours and hours, pulling at the cows' teats with fingers almost breaking off from cold, your body so numb it's like you're already dead. You have to look at your hands all the time because you can't feel them. The only way to know what they're doing is to squint your eyes and watch them as though they were someone else's.

Then when the sun comes up, it's not any better. It doesn't bring warmth with it, only light to see by. And what you see is just grey on grey, frost and dead grass and weathered wood, everywhere and everywhere, until you feel like you might drown in it.

But in the summer the sky is like a bucket, pouring hotness down on you, and the fields are painted in so many colours you can't count them or name them. It's warm enough to think. And it's warm enough to love.

This was in Janowo, which is in Majki, which is in the east of Prussia. I know that now, because when you go to be a soldier you see things outside what you knew. And that means you learn where the things you knew really stand in the world. But back then it was just Janowo, and not even Janowo really (because when did I ever walk into the village?), but my father's farm three miles outside Janowo. I lived in a tiny world, though of course I didn't know it until later. All worlds are the same size when you live in them.

The young man's voice, never very loud, faltered into silence. The ghosts all around him murmured encouragement.

"What happened then?" Drozde asked him, speaking softly because he was so young and so beautiful and so pale. She was afraid a harsh word might break him.

It's hard for me to say. If I tell you everything directly— well, it makes the story meaningless. Or at least, makes it seem less than it was. And it was everything, to me. It was all I knew of life, before I went to war. And when I went to war, I died.

I think I'll tell it as though it was someone else's story—I'll say he and she and they. They did it. Not I did it. And you'll know, when I come to it, why I chose that way to tell it. Because this is a story about choices, and I'll never know whether the choices that were made were right or wrong. Perhaps you can tell me that, when you've listened. When you know all of it.

There was a girl, and there were two boys. The girl was Ermel, Herdein Holz's daughter. The Herdein whose father was from Shnir, and who was crippled in his left leg, and whose wife's name was Müte.

The boys were Kristof and Max. Each was a farmer's son, and each reached his sixteenth year in the same month that Ermel did. Born in the same season, they were.

And fast friends they were too, from that season onward. They grew up together; the three farms was nearest neighbours, and none of the three children was ever

seen without the other two coming right after, the way
you hear a goose honk and look up to see the whole skein
quartering the sky.

They played boisterous games. Stole apples from Alte
Hankel's orchard, chased the hens across the green and
back again, and fished in streams that was rich men's
trout runs, that they would have been whipped if they'd
been found there. The girl was no different from the boys
in these adventures. They were just three friends that did
everything alike.

But you know that tale, I think, and the ending of it,
which is always the same. They grew up. And though a
little girl is allowed to be a boy sometimes, an older one
must look how to be a woman. Ermel went to her mother
one morning, bewildered and frightened, to show her a
blood-stained nightshift. Forthwith she was taken away
from her two best friends, and given skirts to wear instead
of breeches. It wasn't proper now for her to be with boys
in the way a child might, or else she'd soon enough come
by a child of her own. That was what her mother told her.
As if those companions of so many years had overnight
become enemies that might work her ruin.

She grew up lovely, though. So lovely. Everyone said
so. Everyone wanted her. She had blonde hair so fine her
mother said you could put it on a spindle and spin it into
gold. And her smile would charm a cat out of a tree, her
father and uncles swore. They meant nothing by it, only
to encourage her to smile again.

This was in Prussia, as I told you. And in Prussia there
is a thing called the Cantonal Gesetz. A village, say, or a
number of farms that lie together, is called a canton. And
every canton has to supply a soldier for the army, whenever
one is asked for. If that soldier dies, the army sends to ask
for another, and so on. It means the strength of the army
stays the same, even if the mother country is fighting lots of
battles. New recruits are always there to draw on.

Where the canton is a village, it usually goes well enough. There's a public ballot, with everyone's names on stones or papers put into a bucket. And everyone can inspect the names, to see they're all there. And a child draws one out, or else a blindfolded man does, or one as can't read even their own name, so it's sure to be fair.

But with farms, it's different. Our canton was five smallholdings. Majki Zagroly, that was Ermel's father's. Soldany, that belonged to Max's family, and Krusze Wielkie, that was Kristof's. The other two, Kownatkie and Nawawies Wielka, was fallen in and no one lived there now.

So that was three families. And out of the three, only two boys of army age to be had. Max's brother, Eberlin Slezak, had gone up last, so that should have meant that Kristof's family, the Neissers, should send the next. But what were they to do? Both the households had ageing fathers, and both were relying on those rising sons to work the fields and tend the cows. Ermel's father was a little younger, but his left leg was halt after a bad fall, as I think I already told you. It was all he could do to tend the holding he had and provide for his family. He had prayed so long for a son he'd worn his voice hoarse with praying, and only a daughter to show for it. A pretty daughter, but what's that when the leaves fall?

So the Neissers were beholden, but they didn't want to admit it. And the Slezaks dug in their heels and said— what was true enough—they'd lost one son already. All amity between the families vanished like smoke up the chimney as they argued it bitterly back and forth, back and forth. And finally they determined that the recruiting officers must sit on it and give a judgment, because neither side would budge.

Only the two boys kept up their friendship, like before, and took some refuge in each other's company from the bitter tears and harsh voices that were given out in both their houses. And more than ever they missed Ermel, that had been their other self, their sister and more than sister when they were all three growing up.

To be honest with you, they did more than miss her. They went to Majki Zagroly some nights when the moon was full and the sky clear, and threw stones at her window. And the three of them ran the woods again as they'd used to do when none of them had a thought of war or womanhood. They stayed together until cockcrow, some nights, and crept exhausted home, each to his own back door, taking off their clothes only to put them on again and pretend to be just risen from sleep.

And if you ask me whether either of the boys touched Ermel privily on those near-daylit nights, the way a man touches a woman, I say this. They were children, in their hearts at least. They had no more thought of coupling than they had of death.

But their parents, by this time, had no thought of anything else. The Neissers and the Slezaks had talked and argued and planned and fretted themselves into a fine lather, and the fruit of their labours was alike on both sides: that if their bonny boy paid court to Ermel, and won her hand, then when the recruiting officers came they'd have an easy choice. No one would take a young man whose banns had been read and throw him into a battle line when he should be in a different kind of skirmish altogether, under the blankets of a marriage bed.

So Kunrat Neisser and Dietl Slezak took their sons aside and urged them on to plead suit to young Ermel. If they could lie with her and get her with child, they would do very well. But failing that, her bare word would be enough.

Max and Kristof were dutiful boys, and did what was asked of them much more often than not. The thought of using Ermel in such a way didn't sit well with them, but there were other thoughts that came into their heads too.

To be with their friend forever, and live with her, and raise a family with her. That was on the one hand. And on the other, to run in a line of men against a line of other men, and be stopped with musket balls, and have death for a purgative.

When next the boys met, they didn't speak of what they'd been bid to do. It ran too deep for words. They talked of other things instead. Mostly, they talked about their friendship. They swore to be friends forever, as though swearing it would make it so. And then because they knew it wouldn't they cried and fought and walked apart from each other, their hearts too full of that dreadful knowledge to hold anything else. They'd meant to call on Ermel, but they couldn't do it. They couldn't be all together as they used to be, when they had such thoughts bearing down on them.

After that night, it seemed the old trinity they'd had—if it's not sin to call it such—was broken. Some evenings, when the farm work was all done, Max would come to Majki Zagroly and offer to chop wood or cut shingles for Ermel's father. Herdein Holz never spoke, on these occasions, but only pointed to the woodshed or the barn or wherever it might be, and went back inside.

And on other nights it would be Kristof who came. He was more skilled with his hands, and had done some smithing with his uncle Janke, so he might fix a bent coulter on the plough or fashion a fine new handle for one of Dame Holz's knives.

The reward for these good deeds was to sit in the kitchen for a half-hour or so with the family. There would be desultory conversation about the weather or the harvest. Ermel would be present, but would not speak to the boy—whichever boy it was. That would have been considered forward. The kitchen was too hot, and in spite of its high ceiling not very large. Strings of onions, heads of cabbage and cured sausages hung from a rack at head height and rocked gently when anyone moved. The floor creaked. The air was heavy with steam from something seething on the stove. And Ermel and whichever boy it was sat and stole shy glances at each other and felt like two-thirds of something that might never be whole again.

That was a bad season, for all of them. It was the end of summer, which in times gone they would have loved to walk in, but now if felt like dead winter and nothing to hope for. The boys were vying to see which of them would live. Even the winner would feel like he had lost.

One night, instead of going to Ermel's house, Max went to Krusze Wielkie instead. Kunrat Neisser opened the door to him and asked him what he wanted. Only to talk to Kristof, he said. To talk for a moment, and then he would go away.

The old man wasn't happy about it, but he went inside and soon Kristof came out. The two boys sat under a plane tree that grew at the edge of the furthest field in the Neisser holding, watching the old man sunbow his head to the earth.

"I thought I might ask Ermel to be trothed to me," Max said. Kristof already knew this, of course. If Max had done as he was told, he would already have had that conversation. But something kept him from it.

"It's a good thought," Kristof muttered, staring at the ground. "I was turning it over in my own mind, somedeal, that I might put that question to her." And that was true too, yet here he was with the words still inside him.

It seemed pointless, in the face of this, to say they'd always be friends. Two would stay, and one would go. Max knew from his brother's example that the one who went wouldn't be coming back. In asking for Ermel's hand, he'd be asking her to throw the first handful of dirt onto Kristof's coffin, though the wood for the coffin might not be cut or sanded yet, nor the flowers grown that would deck it.

"I thought I might ask her tonight," he said, and waited.

"Tonight is good," Kristof said. "It's broad Sabbath already, and the recruiting officers coming o' Monday morning. A man shouldn't linger too long."

A man! They were seventeen. What they knew of man was all hearsay and hopefulness.

"Well then," said Max. "Come with me, and ask her too."

The two boys looked long at each other without saying anything more. It was surely the only fair way to do it. And yet, in being fair to each other, what would they do to Ermel? How would she live, knowing what she'd done? How would any of them live?

"I'll come," Kristof said. "But I may not speak. I'm not yet fully resolved."

"Well, no more amn't I," Max said. "Not resolved, as such. But only thinking it."

They got up and walked together down the track that led to Majki Zagroly. The sun was lying on the ground now, and the light all around them was like fire coming out of the ground, almost. Red and gold and all good colours you could imagine.

It was too late to pay a formal visit, but they both thought that was probably for the best. They threw stones onto the roof above Ermel's window until she put her head out and saw them. Then they waited until she came down to them.

It was only a half a moon, and the sky none too clear, but there was some light below the horizon yet—as though the ghost of the sun still shone after the sun had died. They walked down the path to the river, and they sat there listening to the voice of the water as the darkness grew upon them.

It seemed like a spell was on them. A word would be enough to break it, so they were careful not to speak. Or only with their eyes anyway—such talk as you can have that way. And round and round it went. Ermel looking at

Kristof, and Kristof at Max, and Max at Ermel.

I know, their eyes said. And I know that too. And what's to be done about it?

Ermel kissed Max on the mouth. She kissed him long and deep, holding him to her as though he was her lover and her everything.

She did the same to Kristof.

Then she took off her clothes and walked into the water. She swam out into the centre of the river, where she turned onto her back so she could watch the stars through the gaps in the scudding clouds. She only had to kick her legs a little to hold her place against the gentle current.

She knew what must be, but she could not choose for them. She could not even tell them what she knew, beyond what those kisses must surely have told them. For the rest, they must make their own choice.

When she had given them what she thought was long enough, and then a little longer, she swam back to shore. She found them where she had left them in the nest the river grasses made, their limbs entangled, their beautiful bodies shiny with the sweat of love.

She thought for a moment of leaving them there together. But then Kristof opened one eye and beckoned to her, so she elbowed and fussed and slipped herself in between them, and they folded themselves around her. That was how they spent the night, all three of them wrapped together in a knot of friendship like the knots they put on brooches.

The next morning, the recruiting officers, a sergeant and a drummer boy, were met on the road by a handsome young man who saluted them as smartly as if he was already in uniform.

"I thought there was some dispute to settle," the sergeant grunted.

"It was settled," the young man said. "I'm for you."

And he was sworn in there and then, at the turning of the road, with the drummer boy standing witness and nobody but birds to cheer him.

He met his regiment the next day. It was encouraging, at least, to find he was not the youngest. He trained for three months with sword and musket, and he was so quick on his feet they put him in the *schützen*, the light infantry. It was some while, though, before he had to fight. In the first year after he enlisted, Prussia prosecuted no wars. It declared itself ready to fight against Sweden, once, but Sweden declined the honour. Apart from that, all was peace and amity.

The boy could not write, and so he sent no letters home. When he came up for leave, he spent it in Berlin. But he thought often of the friends he'd left behind, and wondered if they were happy. He hoped they were. He had done all he could to make it so.

Then the old king died, and the new king came with warlike thoughts and talk of honour. Prussia would be one, and Prussia would take all her old strength on herself. So that meant joining Cleves and Mark to the motherland, and it meant taking back Silesia, which was Prussia's by a very old treaty. Everyone thought that Cleves and Mark would come first, but it was Silesia where we were sent.

The young man was a skirmisher in the first battle, here where your river runs, and he fought well. Again and again he fought, through the winter and into the spring. He was at Mollwitz, where three thousand of the enemy died for three hundred of ours; he marched on into Bohemia, and saw host after host break before Prussia's will. He was there when the *hundsfott*, Carmichael, worked a peace that nobody, not even he, thought would hold. And then he came back here to Pokoj when the weather turned, to wait out the winter.

And here died, not from the fighting but from the

frost and from a desperate flux that wrung his guts out for eleven days, until he finally succumbed to it.

I did ever hate the winter.

The soldier took off his cap, and smoothed down his blond hair. Though a little wild and unkempt, it was— Drozde saw—very fine. Perhaps not fine enough to spin into gold, but she could see why a mother would say that. And yes, the smile was charming enough. Drozde wondered, now, how she could ever have thought the soldier a man. But then Ermel jammed the cap back down over her ears, and squared her jaw, and was a man again.

"I gave them two years," she said. "What was I to do? They had only just found each other, and it would have broken my heart to sunder them. Perhaps they ran away together. Or perhaps the recruiters came again, two summers later, like reaper men out of season, and took one of my lovely boys with them to war and woe.

"It is not my story—not that part of it—but I know which ending I prefer."

MIKE CAREY was born in Liverpool. He worked as a teacher for fifteen years before resigning to write full-time. In a long career, he has written in many different media including prose fiction, comic books, TV and cinema. He wrote the movie adaptation for his bestselling novel *The Girl With All the Gifts*, for which he received the British Screenwriters' award and was nominated for a BAFTA. He is also the writer of the Felix Castor novels, and (along with his wife Linda and their daughter Louise) of two fantasy novels, *The City Of Silk and Steel* and *The House Of War and Witness*. His most recent novel, released in both the UK and USA in November 2018, is *Someone Like Me*, a psychological thriller with a supernatural edge. Mike has also worked extensively in the field of comic books, completing long and critically acclaimed runs on *Lucifer*, *Ultimate Fantastic Four* and *X-Men*.